The Three Jays

The first Broughton family novel

G. M. Cooper

HeronsCroftBooks

The Three Jays

Copyright © G. M. Cooper 2023

This book is a work of fiction. Names, characters, businesses, organisations, places and events are either the product of the author's imagination or used fictitiously. Any resemblance to actual persons, living or dead, events or locales is purely coincidental.

ISBN 978-1-7384846-0-7
Published in Great Britain by HeronsCroftBooks
Second edition 2024
Printed by Amazon KDP

To Sheridan
without whose support and encouragement
this novel would not have seen the light of day

Remembering Jesse
and the men of the 55th

CONTENTS

(including maps of Bearshott Village and Northern India)

Prologue

I suppose you could say that my adventures began with my journey to London in the late summer of 'fifty-six. I was seventeen. Until then, I had lived an ordinary life with an ordinary family in an ordinary village. The first day of the rest of my life was a Tuesday, and it was wet.

Long before dawn, Joe roused me with a thump on the door. Scrambling into my clothes by the feeble light of one guttering candle, I picked up my knapsack and followed him down to the kitchen.

Bella, half asleep and new to her duties, had employed the bellows too vigorously, scorching the outside of the porridge pot whilst leaving the centre lukewarm. Spooning some of the glutinous mess into a couple of bowls, we ate in silence.

I collected the storm lantern from its hook beside the back door to light our way across to the stable. In addition to the small dwelling-house, Joe's tenancy included a yard, outbuildings, and a paddock, from where he ran his carter's business. His rig was a four-wheeled, covered affair, with a canvas head on which were painted his details (*Jos. Broughton – Carrier – Allnutt's Yard, Bearshott, Mx*).

It had rained heavily during the night; a muddy puddle stretched from door to door. In the short time it took to cross the yard, icy water had seeped into my cracked leather workboots, and the raw morning breeze had penetrated my jacket.

The mare was ill-tempered and stubborn, given to nipping. That morning, she was her usual cussed self, the leather was stiff, and my fingers were cold. It took the best part of half an hour to get her harnessed and put to the wagon.

'I do miss that Clopper,' Joe sighed.

I clambered aboard, hung the lantern on the lamp bracket, and shoved my bag under the seat. I saw Joe give it a long look, but he made no remark about it being much bulkier than usual.

There was an overhanging canvas canopy, which afforded some protection to the driver, but the box was still fairly open to the elements. Joe dragged out a couple of tar-coated capes from beneath the seat.

By the time we pulled out of the yard the sky to the east was beginning to lighten, though overcast, with no glimmer of sun. A few of the cottages on the other side of the road showed faint, flickering lights, shadows passing back and forth, but my home was in darkness.

We had several collections to make before heading into London. Our first pick-up was from Oliver's nursery, down Crane Lane. Mr Oliver owned a good-sized piece of land that ran behind the back gardens of both Greening's cottages, in the Lane, and those in Trafalgar Terrace, in the main street, where my family lived. He had many crates of produce – fruit, vegetables, and flowers – to be taken up to Covent Garden. After stowing them on racks in the back of the wagon, Joe turned the rig around and drove back to the Green, making another stop at The Bury gatehouse before heading east along the main street, past the schoolhouse where my best friend was lodging. He would soon be up and on his way to work. I had told no one what I proposed, not even him. I had no idea when I would see him again. I pledged myself to write to him, eventually, when I had news to tell.

After two or three more stops the wagon was full and Joe gave the mare the office to pick up speed. Having made our last collection, and with nothing more to do except sit in the drizzling rain whilst the horse plodded steadily along the ten miles or so to London, I shrugged the waterproof cape more firmly around my shoulders, and thought about what I intended to do there, torn between curiosity as to what I might discover, and anger at the lie I'd been living, the secret that had been kept from me, the brother I had not known of.

1: June 1841

Humfrey Kimber's mood was not improved by being obliged to wait for the boy who was supposed to be attending the gate to come and open it for him. He had, he felt, already been made to wait for an unconscionable length of time by the Greenings' housekeeper. It was now close on two o'clock, and he was hungry and thirsty, not even having been offered a cup of tea. There was a solitary public house in the village; he had called there only the day before, to record the details of the occupants. Hardly the quality of establishment he liked to patronise, but one which, he trusted, could supply him with some lunch. Catering in the main to the local labourers and mill workers, and not being on a post-road, there was no ostler to take charge of his gig. There was not even a handy urchin to whom he could flip a coin to look after it. Kimber was obliged to hitch the pony's reins to a post outside and trust all would be in order when he returned. Ordering a beef and mustard sandwich and half a pint of beer, he sat himself at a window table, where he could keep an eye on his carriage.

As he munched, Kimber leafed through his paperwork. Although the Registrar had said that the survey could take as many days as needed, he had made it plain that he expected the completed forms to be submitted no later than the tenth, which meant that Kimber must not only finish the survey today, but would be obliged to forgo his usual Wednesday evening bridge party, spending the time instead in collating the data and producing a fair copy. Now that he had a comprehensive list of the Greening family members and their staff, there remained only a handful of cottages to visit.

He had drawn himself a map of the village as an aide-mémoire. Few of the cottages were numbered, and the survey was to be presented in strict geographical order. Places such as The Bury, the public house and the handful of businesses were named, but there were many dwellings lying off the main street down little anonymous alleyways.

The public house was called The Admiral Lord Nelson. It had once been known as The Robin Hood, but when two blocks of cottages had been built on the other side of the road and named Waterloo and Trafalgar Terraces, a complimentary change of name had been proposed. Some customers wished to keep the old name, but the majority of the male community, arguing that it was better that their drinking place should have the name of a real hero, rather than a fictional one, carried the day. Mothers, sisters and wives, although not permitted to vote on this critical issue, were canvassed for their opinions. Almost every woman chose the one-eyed, one-armed hero of Aboukir and Trafalgar, on the irrefutable grounds that he was younger, more dashing, and dead.

Fronting The Bury's gatehouse lay a triangular stretch of common known as Wyck Green. Three roads led from it. Waleric Lane snaked its way north along the eastern boundary of the estate until it converged with the lane from Whitton, whereupon the road bore west along the northern boundary and so on to Isleworth. The road that ran due east from the Green was known variously as High Street or Main Street, sometimes the London Road. The third ran due south to the banks of the Crane, terminating at the entrance to the gunpowder mill.

As a courtesy, Kimber had first called at The Bury, the

principal residence in the village. Denied an interview with the head of the house himself, Mrs McBride had told him that she would obtain the information on his behalf, in a day or two, and he should call back on Wednesday morning. Say what he might, he was unable to persuade the housekeeper to complete the forms any sooner. He had now spent three days in this dratted backwater. No doubt he would have to waste another tomorrow, hanging around the registry office.

By half past four, Kimber had only one more household in the centre of Bearshott to visit, an end cottage in Trafalgar Terrace, on the southern side of the main street, home to the Broughton family.

Red bricks had been laid neatly herringbone-wise, forming a short path between the roadway and the cottage's doorstep, and across the front of the building, disappearing around the corner into a side passage. Summer flowers crowded the tiny garden, tall delphiniums, lupins and agapanthus jostling for space, the gently swaying bright blooms inviting the bees that buzzed amongst them. The front door boasted a knocker contrived from an old horseshoe. Kimber gave it a loud rap.

A young girl opened the door, an infant perched precariously on one hip, its thin fingers entwined in her hair. The baby looked poorly: rheumy brown eyes over-large in a clammy pinched white face, mucus running from its nose. Not long for this world, Kimber thought; this would be the only census it would appear on. The child suddenly sneezed, spraying the girl with snot. Kimber recoiled involuntarily, edging backward and raising his clipboard to cover his own mouth and nose, determined not to catch the child's cold.

'I need to speak to your father,' he said from behind this barrier.

The girl regarded him dispassionately for a few seconds. He was stick-thin, all awkward angles, with an expression that, in a woman, might be described as shrewish. Apparently deciding there would be no harm in answering, she said, 'He's gone to work.'

'Your mother, then.'

'She's away birthing my sister.'

'Any adult – grown-up, then? Anyone older than you?'

' 'S only us.'

Exasperated, Kimber, determined to finish the poll this afternoon, mentally reviewed his options: return later, when one or other parent might be at home; ask the landlord of The Admiral Lord Nelson, who would surely be familiar with the family; or press on with his questions.

'What time will your father arrive home?'

The girl shrugged, then offered, 'When it's getting dark.'

'Where does he work?'

'At Mr Oliver's.'

'The nurseryman? Down Crane Lane?'

She nodded. Damnation! It seemed unlikely that this child could provide all the details he required, but perhaps, with careful questioning, he might elicit sufficient information to satisfy the Registrar. She had, after all, already disclosed her father's occupation, which he duly entered on the form as 'gardener'. Kimber took his identity card out of his pocket (not that she would be able to decipher it) and held it up.

'Parliament has ordered that everyone must say who was sleeping in their home last Sunday night. This is my card. It tells you my name and that I am allowed to ask all the people who live in Bearshott. Do you think that you might be able to remember who was in your house on Sunday? Who lives here, and if you had any visitors?'

She surprised him by taking a step nearer – he resisted the impulse to retreat – and peering at the pasteboard rectangle. She surprised him still more by reading aloud, 'Humfrey Kimber. That's you? What's this other name, then? James Gooch, reg…regis…'

'Registrar. He is the man that the Government has ordered to collect this information from this village.'

'Not you? They didn't ask you?'

Kimber felt himself to be at an unexpected disadvantage.

The child was taking charge of the conversation.

Annoyed, he replied, 'The Government asked Mr Gooch, and Mr Gooch asked me to be the enumerator for this district.' He hurried on before she could ask anything else. 'Well, can you tell me your name, how old you are?'

'Caroline. I'm seven.'

'And the baby?'

'Josiah. He's two.'

He paused, pencil in mid-air, doubtful.

'Two? Are you sure? He's very small for two.'

She hefted the boy more securely onto her hip. 'He's been ill,' she said, adding with a sigh, 'A lot.'

There were, Caroline disclosed, three other children living in the house, of whom the eldest was ten. She was unable to say how old her parents were but thought her expectant sister was twenty or so. Taking a guess, Kimber entered Mr and Mrs Boughton's ages as forty-five and forty.

Only one further question to be asked, though he doubted the child would know the answer. Despite Bearshott's proximity to both London and Surrey, the majority of the inhabitants had claimed to have been born locally. This family would surely be the same.

'Were you all born in Middlesex?' he asked.

She seemed, as he had expected, puzzled by the question. He decided to try another tack. 'Where do your grandparents live?'

'Grandfather lives in Isleworth.'

Middlesex, then. A tick, and the end of the interview with this rather tiresome girl. With a flourish, Kimber stowed his clipboard in his document case and his propelling pencil in his top pocket and bid her good day.

Caroline paused a moment, watching him head over the road and enter The Admiral, a slight frown on her forehead. Why, she wondered, had he not asked about her other grandfather, the one who lived in Ewell? Closing the door, she said, 'Shall we go and see what Georgie is up to?'

George was in the back garden, kicking a ball against the hen-house wall.

'You know Father doesn't like you doing that. It puts the chickens off laying,' she remarked, dumping Josiah on the grass.

The garden was long and narrow. The kitchen, scullery, and earth closet doors opened onto a concrete yard, beyond which lay a grassed area. A path ran down the centre of the plot; two wooden poles supported the washing line that ran along its length. Several outbuildings, including the chicken shed, lay along one boundary. A low fence separated the allotment at the far end of the garden, where the family's soft fruits and vegetables were grown.

Caroline massaged her hip. Even though Josiah was underweight, he was heavy for her. Her dress felt damp. Lifting his frock, she removed the sodden clout. Not dirty, only wet, she saw. Dropping the cloth into a bucket of water in the scullery, she picked up a tub of goose fat and a fresh clout.

'Is it time for supper yet?'

Caroline paused from larding the grease onto the child's sore bottom. 'Not until Daniel and Will get back from school.'

'Well, I wish they'd hurry up. I'm hungry.'

'You're always hungry, Georgie. There you go, Joss, nice and clean now.'

Josiah managed a wan smile. He seemed disinclined to move from the spot where she had put him. Another prolific sneeze shook his small frame. Caroline wiped his nose with the hem of his frock.

'How about some nice milk?'

The jug of milk was kept in the cold cupboard in the kitchen. Filling two beakers, Caroline handed one to George and offered the other to Josiah. George downed his straight away and went back to kicking his ball, but Josiah only took a couple of sips before pushing the cup away.

Caroline wished her mother would come home. She did not know what else to do for the child; he did look extremely ill. She hoped that he wouldn't die, especially whilst she was looking after him. She thought her mother would be terribly upset if he did. Besides, she was quite fond of him herself; he was a rather sweet, good-natured boy. Well, there was nothing much she could do, except keep him clean. The day was warm. Josiah looked ready to drop off. She fetched her drawing book and pencils and sat beside him on the grass.

Cheery whistling heralded the homecoming of Daniel and Will. They bore down on their younger brother, shoved him out of the way, and raced up and down the garden, passing the ball between them.

George knew better than to complain of this cavalier appropriation of his game. Plumping himself down beside her, he squinted at Caroline's drawing.

'What's that?'

'Man who came to the door.'

'Looks like a spider.'

'Yes,' she reflected, 'he did, rather.'

Josiah was asleep on the ground, thumb tucked into the corner of his open mouth, his breathing uneven and rattling. There seemed to be no point in disturbing him. Caroline rose, collected up her drawing things, and announced that she was going to get their supper.

'Oh, good! Me belly feels like me throat's been cut.'

'Don't let Mother hear you talk like that, Georgie, not unless you want a good leathering.'

'Joe says it. Why can't I?'

'Joe is all grown up. You're only five.'

Their mother returned home just as Caroline was washing up the supper things. A glance at her face warned the child not to ask any questions.

'Where's Joss, Caro?'

'Asleep on the grass,' she replied guiltily, realising that she hadn't checked on him for the best part of an hour.

Elizabeth Broughton went out into the garden. Four or five hens were scratching around the boy, oblivious to his presence. She bent down and picked him up, gently laying him against her shoulder.

'Poor little mite. Whatever's to become of you?' Carrying him through to the front room, she laid him, still sleeping, in the woven Moses basket. It was meant for babies, but Josiah was so small that he could, just about, still fit in it.

Usually, she would ask her sons about their school day, but today she was too tired. Bebe's labour had been protracted, draining for those trying to help her, as well as herself.

'I'm going to lie down for a bit, Caro. Come and get me when Joss wakes up. And try to keep those boys quiet.'

Some hope, thought Caroline. Although, as the only daughter still living at home, she was expected to help her mother with household chores, her older brothers rarely took any notice of what she said, so it was as well for her mother's peace that they took themselves off to play on the Green with their friends. She wondered about Bebe's baby. Was it a boy or girl? Was it even alive? Any mention of her eldest sister usually resulted in her father stomping off to The Admiral for the evening.

The boys were still out when Edward Broughton came home, tired and grubby after a day working in the warm sunshine. Elizabeth had hot water ready for him in the scullery. Cleaned up, he ate his supper in silence. Finally, when he'd eaten, he rested his elbows on the table, raised an eyebrow at his wife, and said, 'Well?'

'Girl,' she replied. 'Going to call her Elizabeth.'

'Huh! Trying to butter us up. Well, it won't work. She's not coming here. And,' he added, 'you're not to offer to look after it, Elizabeth. She made her own bed, she can lie in it. Enough is enough.' Selecting a pipe from the rack on the mantelpiece, he tucked it into his pocket. 'I'm going over to The Admiral.'

Elizabeth watched him cross the Green, waving to his two sons as he went. She sighed. She could hardly blame him.

After all, this was not the first time. Bebe and her baby would stay in the workhouse for a few more days until she had recovered. After that…well, perhaps one of her sisters would take her in. Louisa was just up the road in Isleworth, but her husband had some standing in the town, and would undoubtedly refuse to give his embarrassing sister-in-law a home. Sarah might offer. She lived in London, where no one need know Bebe's history. Clearing the table of Edward's supper dishes, she noticed Caroline's sketchbook.

'What have you been drawing today?' Caroline opened the pad. 'Who's that?'

'The man who came this afternoon.'

'Man? What man?'

'He wanted to know about who lives here.'

'Who lives—? Oh, you mean the census man? He looks a bit scary,' Elizabeth observed.

'He wasn't scary, just silly. And he smelt, and he had shiny hair. Georgie said he was like a spider.'

'Well, he doesn't sound very nice. It's a pity he didn't come when your father or I was in. Is he coming back?'

'No, I don't think so. He went away.'

'Time for bed, now. Be careful you don't wake the boys.'

A narrow wooden door, next to the chimney breast, opened onto a steep staircase that curled around to the right, leading to a small triangular landing, off which two doors opened into the front and back bedrooms. Caroline often thought how wonderful it would be to live in a house where the stairs started in one hall and ended in another, instead of being hidden away in a dark and poky cupboard. The doors at the top had been left open, so that, at this time of the year, the evening sunshine spilling through the bedroom windows provided some dim light. In the winter, whether the doors were open or not, the staircase was dangerously dark.

She crept into the smaller back room, which was used by her parents. Josiah lay sleeping in his cot, under the window, a muslin hood shielding his eyes from the light. She thought he looked a bit better. His breathing was not so ragged, and there seemed to be a faint pink tinge to his cheeks.

Caroline and her brothers slept in the larger front room. Glancing through the window as she undressed, she could see her older brothers, kicking a ball about the Green with their friends. She crawled into bed beside the sleeping George, careful not to disturb him.

The following morning, Elizabeth walked the three or so miles into Isleworth, carrying a bag containing some food for Bebe, and clothing that Josiah had grown out of for her baby. The new workhouse had only been open a couple of years. It was a large, forbidding brick building, in the shape of a cross, three and four storeys high. A wall ran around the whole perimeter, enclosing storage and work rooms, creating courtyards that segregated the inmates and ensured that no one could enter or leave unnoticed. Inside the main entrance lay a waiting hall, with a porter's room. A throng of people were already there, begging admittance, objecting to being asked to leave, or requesting to be allowed to see one of the inmates. When she at last reached the front of the queue, Elizabeth asked to visit her daughter in the infirmary.

The porter opened the admittance and discharge register and ran a tobacco-stained forefinger down the list of names. 'She's left.'

'Left? Are you sure?'

'Discharged herself and her baby this morning.'

Outside, Elizabeth walked back to the Twickenham Road, uncertain what to do. Whyever would Bebe leave so soon? After yesterday, she needed at least another day or two of bed rest. The matron would have allowed her to stay for that short time, surely? She must have gone to Louisa's. There was nowhere else in Isleworth that she could have gone, that she was aware of.

Elizabeth's father had a large grocery and general store in the centre of the town. Louisa and her husband, Simon, who worked for him as a shop manager, lived in the two-storey apartment above. Elizabeth toiled up the wrought iron stairs that ran up the outside of the building to the first floor. She was wary of those steps; in wet or icy weather, they were very slippery. How Louisa managed to go up and down them safely whilst carrying shopping, or one of her children, she did not know.

Rattling the knocker, she waited for the door to be opened. Fortunately, Louisa's husband should still be at the shop. Although it was early closing day, he generally did not get home until about three o'clock. She would be able to have a private word with her daughter. A trim maid opened the door and ushered Elizabeth into the small breakfast parlour at the rear of the chambers, where her obviously harassed daughter sat with her children. Scraping and banging sounds could be heard coming from the front sitting room, where Louisa would usually receive visitors.

'I wish you'd let me know you were calling this morning, Mama – I'd have put you off. As you can hear, we're rather at sixes and sevens today.'

'Whatever is happening?'

'They're taking out the window.'

'What's the matter with the window?'

'Nothing. It's so that they can get the piano in.' Seeing her mother's astonished expression, Louisa added defensively, 'We thought Benji would like to learn.'

Elizabeth looked doubtfully at the four-year-old prospective child prodigy, presently sitting under the table and employed in smearing chocolate-covered hands on his mother's skirt. She produced the most encouraging remark she could think of: 'What a lovely idea. I'm sure you're right.' Privately, she was already dreading the hours she foresaw she would be required to spend listening to the ham-fisted efforts of her eldest grandson. Louisa did not respond well to criticism.

A loud bang, and some muted male mutterings, came from

the other room. Glancing at the doorway, Elizabeth could see the servant, working in the small kitchen. She rose and closed the door. Seating herself, she looked anxiously at her daughter.

'I've actually come to ask – have you seen anything of Bebe?'

'Bebe! Hardly, Mama. You know Simon and Grandpapa would never agree to her coming here. The child is due about now, I suppose?'

'Yesterday. A girl – Elizabeth, she's calling her.'

Louisa raised a scornful eyebrow. 'Trying to turn you up sweet. I doubt Papa will allow her home?'

'No, not this time. She went into the workhouse, but when I called there this morning, they told me she'd discharged herself. I can't think where she might have gone if she hasn't come to you.'

'Maybe to the man? Has she told you who the father is?'

Elizabeth shook her head. Louisa looked at her shrewdly.

'You think you know who it is.'

'Maybe – but I could be completely wrong. If I'm right, he can well afford to see her and the child established somewhere.'

'You'd better write to Sarah, see if Bebe's gone there.' Louisa eyed her mother's parcel. 'What do you have there?'

'Some of the baby clothes Josiah's grown out of.'

'Well, you won't want to be carrying them back home, Mama, and it would be a shame to see them go to waste. They should do very well for baby Farley to play in.'

With an inward sigh, Elizabeth handed over the bundle. She was very fond of her second daughter, of course, but she was a truly single-minded and acquisitive girl. Louisa, like all their children, had inherited her parents' good looks, fair colouring, and blue-grey eyes. Alone amongst the siblings, Louisa called them 'Mama' and 'Papa', which she felt to be more refined.

Louisa had high hopes. With no obvious heir, she was

optimistic that, when her elderly grandfather eventually fully retired, her husband would take over his business. She would have preferred a villa in one of the leafy lanes on the outskirts of the town to this apartment overlooking a busy street, but living over the shop had one major advantage: Simon was always on hand, should he be needed, and so appeared indispensable. She lost no opportunity to curry favour with her grandsire, to entwine him with her little family. Her daughter was named Louisa – not after herself, but for her late grandmother. Her two sons were both named after the old man: Benjamin and Farley. She saw herself as occupying the position that her mother should have held, had she not married Edward Broughton. It was a constant source of embarrassment to her that her mother, the only surviving child of the wealthy tradesman, had chosen to marry a common labourer, however handsome and charming.

2: The Bury

At about the same time that Bebe Broughton was discharging herself and her baby from the Brentford Union workhouse, Margaretta Gwynneth Tudor Greening was sitting in bed, propped up by feather pillows, a Norwich silk shawl around her plump shoulders (in case any whisper of a draught should creep into her bedchamber through the resolutely closed windows), sipping a cup of hot chocolate. Her somewhat unprepossessing infant lay in her lawn and lace-bedecked crib, sleeping soundly.

Margaretta sighed. Her labour had, as always, been mercifully easy but unedifying. She was yet to know that this would be the last time she would be brought to bed. Her husband, rather older than herself, was already on the road to becoming the respected businessman he now was when they married more than twenty-five years before. Naturally, he had been eager for a son and heir, who would eventually join the family company: 'Greening & Son' had a good ring to it. 'Greening & Sons' sounded even better. The couple had enthusiastically done their best to achieve this laudable outcome. Sadly, some early pregnancies had not gone to term. They had had to wait a full five years before a lusty son was born. This was the twelfth child she had given birth to since then, of whom only five were still living.

The child grew restless and started mewling. Margaretta

17

reached for the embroidered bell pull that hung beside her bed, but, before she could tug it, the nursemaid entered and scooped up the child.

'Probably ready for her feed, madam,' she said briskly. 'The wet nurse is here.'

Margaretta settled herself more comfortably into her pillows. This one looked as though she might survive, judging by her healthy colour and strong suck. Well, she had done her duty by the child: she had carried her for nine months, given birth, and fed her twice. Now, the wet nurse and the staff in the nursery would take full responsibility for her continued wellbeing. The girl would be brought to her once a day, providing she was well and content, when her mother might, or might not, briefly hold her youngest daughter. As far as physical and material needs went, she would want for nothing. As for her emotional needs – well, Margaretta did not consider that a child blessed with the comforts of life could possibly feel the lack of human kindness and warmth. The business of a son was to grow up a gentleman, to attend a good university, to make his mark in the world, and to make his parents proud. A daughter merely had to be ladylike and decorative, possessed of good taste without being too clever, and to marry well. Finer feelings hardly figured.

Two wet patches appeared on the front of her nightgown. Margaretta viewed them with distaste. This was the aspect of childbirth she disliked most. Her breasts were full, hard as rock and tender to touch. Soon they would be tightly bound, and would remain painfully so until her milk dried up. In the early years of her marriage, she had been persuaded by the midwife to express milk for her babies, to be fed to them by means of a glass bottle. As she grew more in command of her household, she exerted her authority and refused to have anything further to do with the messy, humiliating procedure. She was not, after all, one of those coarse, bovine wives of Matthew's labourers, but a lady, in essence if not in name, and could employ someone else to do 'that sort of thing'.

She picked up the small notebook that was on her bedside table. In it, she had recorded lists of possible names for the new addition. Not for Margaretta Greening the Williams and Johns, the Sarahs and Mary Anns, so beloved of the labouring classes at her gates. She had a more flamboyant and romantical taste in given names. Her eldest son had been baptised Tudor Matthew, for her father and her husband. Thereafter, the latter was happy to give her free rein in the choice of names for their subsequent progeny. She was determined to be singular. Daughters Phaedre Athene and Euphronia Marguerite had, eventually, followed Tudor. Twin boys had been born five years ago. The name of her first son had inspired Margaretta to call them Roman Petrus and Saxon Alaric. As alike as two peas in a pod, hardly anyone could tell them apart, certainly not their parents.

She skipped the first page, on which were listed boys' names. One had a circle around it. Had this child been male, it would have gone through life saddled with the name Plantagenet (Stuart and Norman having been considered too commonplace). Margaretta considered the female names she had noted, crossing some through and underlining others. She read these last out loud, trying the sound of them on her tongue. Finally, she came to a decision. Satisfied with her choice, she put the notebook aside, settled down for a nap, and thought no more of the matter.

Late in the afternoon, Matthew Greening entered his wife's bedroom. Having returned from the mill, he had first changed his working clothes for dinner dress. He was relieved to see that the detritus of her recent exertions had been removed.

'Well, my dear? Congratulations.' He dropped a kiss on Margaretta's brow.

'Perfectly well, thank you, but I believe I will keep to my bed for a few days.'

'Very wise, my dear. Another girl, I understand?' She nodded. 'And what shall you call her?'

'Philadelphia Eugénie.'

He blinked. Sometimes, he wished he had not given her carte-blanche in the matter of naming their offspring.

'Well, that's certainly – er, distinctive. But – isn't 'Eugénie' a little French?'

An all too familiar mulish set to her once pretty mouth forewarned him that this was not an argument he had any hope of winning.

'I *believe*,' she responded heavily, 'it is from the *Greek*.'

'Ah! Well, I daresay you have the right of it.' He pulled a folded paper from his pocket. 'I had a letter from Tudor today. He tells me he will not return home at the end of Trinity. He has been invited to spend the holidays with a friend in Sussex.'

'Friend? What friend?' she asked, mildly interested.

Matthew perused the letter. 'Here we have it: Dominic Rustbridge.' He cocked an eyebrow at his wife. 'Do we know his people?'

'Rustbridge, Rustbridge – Sussex,' she mused. Then, triumphantly, 'Distant relatives of the Norfolks, I believe. Yes, that connection will do very well. I daresay you will be wanting to go down to dinner, now? I shall have a light meal brought to me here, and then I shall rest, so I shall bid you good evening, Matthew.'

Matthew was familiar with his wife's ideas of what constituted a 'light meal'. Twenty-odd years of childbirth followed by such had turned the pretty girl he had married into a mature woman of somewhat larger proportions, though still, he had to admit, attractive in her own way. Hence the continuing pregnancies. Kissing her cheek, he wished her good evening and went off to his dinner and cigars. Margaretta picked up the magazine she had been studying before his arrival and became engrossed in the latest fashions depicted. Both their eldest and youngest children were thus dismissed from the minds of their doting parents.

3: Christmas 1841

Each Sunday, a procession left Bearshott and made its way between the thorny hedgerows of Waleric Lane to its junction with Whitton Lane, and thence on to Isleworth. On high days and holy days, and in good weather, nearly all the inhabitants of the hamlet would be present. In bad weather, only the most ardent souls assayed the weary trek.

It was customary for the churchgoers to congregate on Wyck Green at about eight o'clock in the morning, so that they might enjoy a convivial chat with their fellows as they trudged along. The men and older boys were expected to walk, but the elderly and infirm, and those with young children, hoped to hitch a ride on one of the several carts.

Mr Oliver kept his own carriage, but always stopped to offer a ride to any who did not mind riding up top with the driver. A number of the other market gardeners also offered lifts in their carts. Abel Allnutt, the carter, if his wagon were not laden ready for Monday's deliveries, would drive it into Isleworth himself, and would take up as many as two dozen worshippers. Old Mother Wilkinson, who claimed to be eighty-nine and Bearshott's oldest inhabitant, insisted on riding in her own 'carriage'. She lived with her four unmarried grandsons, ruling them with a rod of iron. Her transport was a vast wooden wheelbarrow, in which was laid a thick blanket, together with several cushions. She would sit in this contraption – holding up a parasol if the sun were shining, an umbrella if it were raining – with her button-booted feet dangling over the front, her grandsons pushing her turn and turn about, for all the world like some exotic sultana.

Matthew Greening naturally had his own carriage. Equally naturally, only his family ever had the chance to ride in it. His household staff and estate workers were also provided with a wagon for the journey. Despite there being plenty of space, none of his workers at the mill, nor his tenants in Crane Lane, were ever offered a place in the vehicle.

The villagers had a particular interest in attending this Christmas Day service at the parish church of All Saints, for Joseph Broughton, of the hamlet of Bearshott, was to marry his sweetheart, Harriett Clarke, of the hamlet of Whitton. Even better, they were also entitled to a day off on the morrow. Some lucky few might even be given an extra holiday on the day after, since the Feast of St Stephen fell on Sunday, when they did not work anyway. Although they received no pay for days when they did not work, many hoped to receive a Christmas box.

Despite the bitterly cold morning, it was in an excited holiday mood that the congregation made its noisy way to church. Joe would normally walk with his father and brothers, but today, as a mark of the occasion and to keep his polished boots and Sunday best clothes clean, he sat up beside Abel Allnutt.

Joe had met Harriett the previous year, in the very church in which they were now to marry. He had inherited his father's looks and manner. Harriett was a plump little person of sixteen, her chief attraction being her beguiling smile and dimples. Each was well pleased with the other. Joe became assiduous in his church attendance. Their courtship had progressed along conventional lines: a nodding acquaintance and a brief conversation; walking home together after the service until the road divided; and, eventually, invitations to take tea with the Clarke family, or to accompany them on any jolly occasion.

Harriett was not permitted to visit Joe in Bearshott, either at his lodgings or at his parents' cottage. Consequently, all Harriett knew of his way of life she learned from Joe himself. Like many another nineteen year old, Joe exaggerated the good bits and forgot to mention the rest.

Mrs Clarke had borne at least one child each year since the birth of Harriett, her eldest, and most were still living. She was, once again, pregnant. Harriett was looking forward to running a home for two. Her mother's perpetual state had dictated that the task of rearing her siblings had largely fallen on her shoulders. She had left school at nine and had never had any permanent paid employment.

The marriage was one of three to be blessed that day at All Saints by Reverend Glossop. In recognition of Benjamin Farley's standing in the community, and his long connection with the church – he had previously served as Churchwarden and a member of the Parish Council – the vicar gifted his grandson a free wedding, the ceremony to take place late in the morning, after the Eucharist. All the parishioners from Bearshott and Whitton who were interested would be able to remain after the sacrament to witness the wedding, even if they were not invited to the celebrations.

The Christmas service was enjoyed immensely. The congregation sang the carols with gusto, particularly *God Rest You Merry, Gentleman* – a firm favourite. Many even paid attention to the entirety of the sermon. Afterward, those not staying for the wedding shuffled out of the church, receiving a handshake and Yuletide wishes from the vicar.

The Bearshott and Whitton parties reorganised themselves as the church emptied: Bearshott (for the groom) to the right of the aisle, Whitton to the left. Harriett, her father, and some of her sisters left the nave and went to wait in the porch until it should be time to make their entrance. Family members occupied the prime positions in the front pews, the Clarkes alone taking up three full rows on the bride's side. The women further back in the congregation, not being related to either one of the couple, craned their necks to see these interesting people, speculating, remarking upon their attire and the poor behaviour of the Clarke brood, and tut-tutting at the size of Mrs Clarke's swollen belly. It was generally agreed that she was too near her time to be out and about and that she should, in any case, have learnt to keep her legs closed for five minutes.

The Bearshott relatives were neither so numerous nor so rowdy. All Joe's younger brothers and sister Caroline were in attendance, and Benjamin had returned home from Ewell, to stand as groomsman. Of the older girls, only Louisa was present. Sarah had sent a pretty vase, together with a note, sending her best wishes for the couple's future happiness, and apologising for being unable to give those wishes in person. Catherine and Lucy were in service, and therefore working; they each promised to visit, whenever that should prove possible. Of Bebe, nothing had been heard.

As they waited for the vicar to finish his farewells, and to re-enter the church via the west door, Harriett removed the cloak that had covered her best dress. A confection of greenery and ribbons was placed on her head, and in her hand she held a Bible. At last, all was ready. The vicar and his party processed down the aisle, followed by the little bridal group. A ripple of stifled amusement, mixed with consternation, ran around the church as it was noted that Harriett's headdress appeared more Crown of Thorns than bridal. Joseph, waiting with his brother Benjamin as supporter, was oblivious to this design faux pas, and thought she looked splendid.

Had Joe and Harriett married during the summer months, one of their neighbours would, perhaps, have lent them the use of a barn for the celebrations. Trestle tables would have been set up, laden with the dishes the women of the village would have been busy baking in the week beforehand, and bowls of fruit. There would have been kegs of beer and jugs of lemonade and, maybe, a bowl of punch of indeterminate recipe. After the feast, the tables would have been pushed back to make room for country dancing, accompanied by anyone who could play an instrument. The occasion would have been seen as an opportunity for the whole village to make merry. A Christmas Day wedding, held in a church some distance from their village, precluded these jolly arrangements.

Mr Farley had offered the use of his dining room. Louisa had made discreet enquiries; her report on the Clarke family impelled him to extend to them an invitation only to partake of a small glass of something and a piece of wedding cake before they wended their way back to Whitton. A sit-down meal was enjoyed by the Broughton party later in the afternoon, followed by noisy games for the younger members and cards for the adults. Later, some of the party entertained the others with their singing, accompanied by Elizabeth on the piano, on which she was rather out of practice.

At the end of the day, Louisa and her family returned to their apartment whilst the rest of the party bedded down as best they might at the Farley villa. Joe and Harriett had exclusive use of his mother's childhood room. Unfortunately, he had imbibed rather too freely and fell asleep immediately. Harriett spent her wedding night squeezed into the single bed, kept awake by her new husband's stentorian snores.

Allnutt arrived with his wagon in the middle of the following morning, ready to convey the Broughtons back to Bearshott, once they had returned from the Sunday morning service. Joe made Harriett known to him; the carter was his employer. Neither bride nor groom looked their best. Joe had a hangover, and Harriett was heavy-eyed through lack of sleep. Daniel and Will found this hilarious, and sniggered to themselves until Edward gave each a clip around the ear.

As the wagon pulled out of Isleworth, Harriett noticed an unkempt woman, a baby at her breast, staring intently at them; she drew back into the shadows of an alleyway as they trundled passed.

'Did you see?' she said to Joe, tugging his arm. 'That woman.'

Joe looked where she pointed, then immediately turned away. He cast a glance over his shoulder. Busy nattering amongst themselves, none of the family had noticed his eldest sister. Although he knew that his mother had been anxiously waiting for any news of her, he decided on the spur of the moment not to stop. After all, if Bebe had wanted to, she could have approached, rather than hiding in the shadows.

'It's no one,' he replied.

Arrived at Bearshott, the party broke up. It was understood that the newlyweds would attend Trafalgar Terrace later, to enjoy a belated Christmas dinner. The invitation had been extended to include the widowed Abel Allnutt, but he had cried off, pleading a prior engagement; he was promised to his particular cronies in The Admiral Lord Nelson, to indulge in some serious drinking, and in Ringing the Bull. Since he was a dab hand at this game, and the loser bought the ale, he looked forward to getting pleasantly squiffy, with little call on his purse.

Harriett was eager to see her new home. She had never visited Bearshott; all she knew of it she had learned from others. The yard itself was a sea of frozen mud slicked with ice crystals. To one side lay wooden outbuildings – a large barn, storerooms, and stabling. A flight of open stairs ran up between the two latter, accessing the lofts that lay over them. She paid scant attention to any of these details. She was only interested in the tidy cottage that lay on the opposite side of the yard.

Joe handed Harriett down from the cart, adjuring her to mind where she put her feet, since the ice hid deep puddles, and gathered her traps from under the front seat. Mr Allnutt tipped his hat to the bride, shook Joe's hand, and wished the pair much future happiness. Harriett was somewhat disconcerted to see him stride off across the yard and enter the house. She was even more surprised when Joe began to carry her luggage up the wooden staircase, calling down to her to 'hurry up, slow coach!' and to always be sure to hold on to the rail, as the steps became very slippery in wet weather. Dismayed, Harriett gingerly followed him. Telling her to wait on the landing, he opened one of the doors at the top and disappeared inside with her bags.

'Right, Mrs Broughton!' scooping her up in his arms. 'Welcome to your new home!'

Joe carried Harriett across the threshold of the loft apartment that lay over the stables and set her back on her feet. 'What do you think? Cosy, isn't it?'

Harriett looked about her in dismay. Instead of the neat little house she had understood they would be living in, her home was to be this one large, dark attic room above the stables. It was his mother to whom Joe owed the spotless condition of the lodging, and the pot of poinsettia that stood on the table. But no amount of cleaning could eradicate the warm smell of horse that emanated from below.

'You do like it, don't you?' Joe asked anxiously. 'You can soon do it up – you know, prettify it a bit, can't you?'

Swallowing her disappointment, she smiled up at him. 'Of course I can. But – there are already some pretty things here.'

For Elizabeth had made some colourful cushions, Catherine and Lucy had sent table linen, and Louisa had given them the bedspread (purchased, with staff discount, from Farley's Emporium) that now adorned the new double bed that Joe and Edward had made to replace the narrow one that Joe had been using.

Daniel and Will had contributed a map of the village 'so that their new sister shouldn't get lost', including information about the principal residents (mostly derogatory), whilst Caroline had made a card, a picture of a woodland path on the front, which stood somewhat lopsidedly on the table. Inside, both she and George had signed their names, whilst Josiah had pressed his painted handprint.

'That's the ticket!' Joe exclaimed, relieved. 'I have to go and see to Clopper now. You have a poke about up here – see where everything is.'

Left alone, Harriett looked about the wretched room in despair. The floorboards were an imperfect fit. A cloud of dust rose up between the gaps as Joe worked below, and she could hear him whistling and talking to the horse as he groomed and watered the animal. Harriett sat on the edge of the bed and wept.

By the time Joe returned, Harriett had composed herself, and had made a thorough investigation of the loft. In addition to the new bed, there was a table and two chairs, a cupboard that held an assortment of crockery, another that contained some of her husband's clothing, a chest of drawers, a rug, a wash-stand with its bowl and ewer, and a small brazier. A screen had been placed across one corner of the room, behind which was a commode. It seemed that all their lives were to be spent in this one room.

'Neat, isn't it?' Joe said cheerfully. 'You'll soon get used to things.'

'I'm sure I shall,' she answered bravely, 'but – where do we cook?'

'Oh, we go over to the house for our meals. There's a fine stove there.'

'Mr Allnutt has a housekeeper, then?'

'Well – not exactly,' Joe said carefully. 'Mrs Dennis used to come and do for him, but her husband died in the autumn, and she's gone to live with her daughter. We thought – *I* thought – that you could do the cooking and cleaning over there. After all, there's not much to do in here, is there?'

'You want me to do *charring*?' his bride said indignantly.

'He'll pay you a proper wage,' he wheedled. 'We'll be able to do this up a bit, maybe even move into one of the cottages, eventually.'

'How do you know I can cook?' she demanded.

'All women can cook – everyone knows that.'

'All *men* know that!' she snapped. 'Oh, dear, Joe, we're

having our first quarrel, and we've only been married a day!'

'Well, things are bound to be a bit strange, just at first,' he replied awkwardly. Then, after a pause, 'Nothing more for us to do until it's time to go over for dinner...Mrs Broughton, how do you feel about trying out this bed?'

During the first week of the New Year, as they were finishing their supper early one evening, there was a knock on the kitchen door. Harriett left Joe to answer it, Mr Allnutt being out; she still knew hardly anybody in Bearshott, so their caller would not be wanting to speak to her. Piling the crockery onto a tray, she took it off to the scullery. As she was drying up, Joe stuck his head around the door.

'We need your signature, Harriett.'

She followed him back into the kitchen, where sat a rotund, bewhiskered individual, dressed in a greatcoat, his beaver hat before him on the table, beside a sheaf of printed papers.

'This is Mr Wimble, Harriett. He's an agent for the Provident. He's going to come every Monday, to collect the insurance money. If I'm not in, you'll have to pay him.'

'What insurance money?'

'It's life assurance, my dear, just in case anything should happen to you or your husband.'

'What sort of 'anything'?' she puzzled.

'Well...death, my dear.'

'Joe!' Harriett cried, aghast, grabbing his hand. 'You're not going to die, are you?'

'No, goose! It's just in case, like Mr Wimble says. Supposing I had an accident driving the cart, say. They'd pay you some money, to keep you going, as it were. Or, if it were you, so that I'd be able to pay for our children to be looked after.'

'We don't have any children,' she objected.

'No, I know we don't *now*, but who's to say we won't by this time next year. I should need to pay someone to look after it, shouldn't I?'

'My mother could do that – or yours,' she replied desperately. The thought of the perpetually fecund Mrs Clarke having anything to do with the rearing of his future offspring made Joe quail.

'It doesn't mean something *is* going to happen. It's – it's a safety net.'

'Well,' she said dubiously, 'it looks like bad luck to me.'

It occurred to Joe, not for the first time, that his beloved often displayed a stubborn disinclination to take his advice unless some other person could be found to back him up. 'Grandfather suggested it.'

'Oh, well, if Grandpa Farley thinks it's a good idea, that's different.' Harriett, being in awe of that venerable gentleman, placed great faith in Benjamin's business acumen. 'But how much will it cost?'

'One and sevenpence-halfpenny a week, for ten years. If your husband died before the end of the policy, you would receive twelve pounds. Or, if it were you who sadly died, Mr Broughton would receive twenty-two.'

Harriett's eyes widened. She had never even held one whole sovereign.

'So, if nobody died, we'd get paid after ten years?'

'Er, no, my dear. Allow me to explain…' Wimble did his best, but it was doubtful if Harriett fully grasped the concepts of mutual assurance, fixed terms, bonuses, actuarial tables, policyholders and premiums.

Finally persuaded, Harriett laboriously – and some-what illegibly – wrote her name on the documents.

'Well done, Mrs Broughton. You shan't be sorry. So soon as you've been accepted, and made your first payment, you'll both be covered.'

After Wimble had left, Joe poured them both a mug of beer. 'There, Harriett – we've made our first decision as man and wife.'

'I still think one and sevenpence-halfpenny is a lot every

week for something we probably won't ever need,' she grumbled.

Joe gave up and changed the subject.

'I'm taking a load down to Epsom tomorrow,' he told her. 'I shall be gone overnight, back sometime Wednesday afternoon.'

This would be the first time Harriett had been left alone. She had, of course, known that there would be deliveries to be made that would occasion Joe being away from home, but had airily assumed – on no evidence at all – that such journeys would be few and far between.

'But what shall I do whilst you're gone?'

'Well, there's this house to clean – Mr Allnutt's going to pay you to do that. Then you can always go over the road and visit my folks.'

She pouted and wound her arms around his neck. 'I shan't like being on my own,' she warned.

Inwardly, Joe sighed. He could see married life called for a lot of tact. 'I'll bring you back a present,' he promised.

His wife immediately cheered up and speculated on just what sort of present might be obtained in Epsom.

Joe returned, as anticipated, on Wednesday afternoon, and drove into the yard. Harriett came out onto the landing at the head of the stairs to greet him, pleased at his return and eager to see what he had brought her. He dragged a large box from under the front seat and carried it up. 'You'd better open it inside,' he warned, setting it down on the floor.

Folding back the lid, Harriett peered into the box. Squealing with delight, she lifted out the puppy.

'I thought he could keep you company whilst I'm working.'

'Joe, he's lovely,' she cooed. 'Oh, you dear little doggie! What shall we call him?'

'Whatever you like.'

She thought for a moment. 'I know – Epsom. Where you got him for me.'

Joe, fervently hoping that Harriett would never again refer

to the puppy as the 'dear little doggie', wished that she had thought of a more dog-sounding name, whilst, at the same time, being mildly pleased at her inventiveness. He forbore to tell her that the animal had actually come from Ewell, where he had stopped the previous night with his Uncle James and family.

4: Four Years Later

It was never established how, when and where the two women became acquainted, but it was generally accepted that it must have been Bebe who sought out Harriett, either from malice or curiosity. The Broughtons had not heard from her since she left the workhouse in the summer of 1841 – she could have been in Twickenham or Timbuktu, for all they knew. Since they never spoke of her, and the village gossips refrained from talking about her in Harriett's presence, Harriett was only aware of an older sister who, like Sarah, Catherine, and Lucy, lived elsewhere. She knew nothing of her salacious history.

Whatever the circumstances of their first meeting were, the two women soon became firm friends. Harriett was somewhat in awe of the smartly dressed older woman – she did not recognize in her the tramp she had glimpsed on the day of her wedding. Bebe soon let Harriett into the secret of her identity. Making Harriett promise not to divulge her presence in the district, Bebe explained that she had 'married above her' and her family had disapproved. Even the gullible Harriett thought this a strange response to a good marriage. She could not understand why the Broughtons would spurn such a sophisticated, worldly daughter. Bebe embellished her tale with stories of a previous wife incarcerated in Bedlam, incompetent lawyers, worthless contracts, and broken promises. Harriett listened wide-eyed, confused but credulous. It seemed that her exotic new friend, left a widow, had been cheated out of her rightful inheritance and possessions, and was now obliged to live in rented rooms in Hounslow, scraping a living as best she might, until such time as 'the Courts' should find in her favour. The fantastical tale was like something out of a sensational penny dreadful. There was no mention in Bebe's history of a daughter, nor of the two sons who had come before.

Harriett asked where her unusual name had come from. For once, Bebe's account was truthful. Although she had been christened Elizabeth after her mother, she said, her parents had decided to use the pet name Betsy, to avoid any confusion. Later, her sister Sarah had started to call her Bebe, after her initials – Betsy Broughton – and the name had stuck.

Harriett was finding life at Allnutt's Yard dull. As the business expanded, Joe was away more and more often, leaving her with only the dog for company. When deliveries could be made in a day, even this companionship was denied her, since Joe would take Epsom up beside him. When Joe was absent, the animal lay across the threshold, ears a-prick. Epsom was a one-man dog, and that man was Joe. As a pup, Harriett had adored its big eyes and feet, the way it would play ball and fetch sticks, and the compliments it attracted when she took it for walks. But out of puppyhood, Epsom had grown large and strong. She was not fond of walking and resented the long walks that Joe said the dog needed, whatever the weather. She dared not let him off his leash, although she could barely hold on to it, for he rarely came to her call, and she was worried that she would lose him. Joe, on the other hand, only had to whistle and Epsom would come running.

Harriett took to shutting the dog in the stable when Joe was away, letting him have the run of the yard and the field behind to do his business. When Joe arrived home unexpectedly early one day, and found Epsom locked away, he admonished her severely. Thereafter, he generally took the dog with him, laying under the box seat, or, if Abel was not making the journey, sitting up beside him, from which position of advantage he greatly enjoyed challenging any other dog they passed. The episode drove a further wedge into the couple's already fragile relationship.

When Joe was at home, Abel and he would sit at the kitchen table talking endlessly about work – how to come by new contracts, whether to purchase another cart, planning new routes. When they were together in their little loft, Joe, tired after a long day loading and unloading heavy goods, liked to relax with a book. Harriett, who could barely sign her name, was bored to tears.

She was not fond of housework. She would only do the minimum that she thought she could get away with, eventually leading Mr Allnutt to remonstrate with Joe that he was paying his wife a proper wage and expected her to do a proper job to earn it. When Joe took this up with Harriett, she tossed her head, said she had better things to do than char for a smelly old man, and subsided into silence. Harriett was not given to arguing. She would show her displeasure by refusing to speak and could show Joe the cold shoulder for days on end.

At the time of her wedding, Harriett had looked forward to being free of caring for her younger brothers and sisters. But in her loneliness, she began to long for children of her own. In the first years of her marriage, she had often crossed Wyck Green to the house in Trafalgar Terrace, where she liked to play with George and Josiah. Caroline, she found intimidating. Whenever she tried to start a conversation with her, the girl would look at her with her big blue eyes, as though trying to decide whether she was worth talking to. Eventually, both boys went to school, and Elizabeth could no longer pretend that she needed her help.

As each successive month passed with no sign that she was pregnant, she grew more and more frustrated and ill-tempered. The more depressed and sullen she became, the less Joe was interested in doing his duty as a husband. Harriett was tempted to return to Whitton, but there was no certainty that she would be welcomed back. Mrs Clarke had two more mouths to feed since the wedding – Thomas and Isabel – and one of the other older girls was now doing the work that Harriett used to do for her. Into Bebe's eager ears, Harriett poured her tale of woe. Bebe had neither forgotten nor forgiven Joe for turning away on his wedding day.

'What you need,' she told Harriett, 'is something jolly to be doing. And now you don't have to look after the dog, you could come and stay with me sometimes, if you'd like? When Joe and Mr Allnutt are both away, and you don't have to cook their suppers.'

'Ooh! Could I? Really?'

'Of course you can. We'll have a fine old time.'

And so it was, one Tuesday morning in the spring of 1844, Harriett had set off on the road to Hounslow, carrying a small portmanteau containing a change of clothes and her night things. Bebe had promised to meet her on the outskirts of the town, to show her the way to her lodgings. These turned out to be a couple of first-floor rooms overlooking a busy thoroughfare. After Allnutt's Yard, Harriett found them rather noisy, however Bebe pointed out that they could enjoy themselves going out and about, without having a long walk home afterwards along dark country lanes. Besides, from the apartment's windows, they could observe what was occurring in the street below, and quickly join in any activity that appealed to them.

That first day was spent roaming about the town, so that Harriett should become familiar with its layout, and not get lost should she ever be out on her own. Harriett was round-eyed at the many intriguing shops, the interesting sights, and the smartly dressed people – so superior to the unsophisticated hamlets of Bearshott and Whitton.

In the evening, Bebe took her guest to the Nags Head, an

inn on the High Street, where they sat at a table beneath one of the front windows. There were few other women in the bar room, the clientele being mostly men of the labouring sort, or slightly better – perhaps commercial travellers, or tradesmen. It was obvious to Harriett that her new friend was a frequent customer, by the number of greetings that were called out to her; several men approached their table. Bebe introduced her 'cousin from out of town', though permitted none to take a seat. They stayed for about an hour before Bebe suggested they move on to see 'what was to do elsewhere'. 'Elsewhere' turned out to be the Red Lion, another coaching inn on the same road. Again, Bebe and her 'cousin' met with many friendly greetings and offers of drinks, none of which were accepted.

'That will do for this evening,' Bebe said to her companion. 'It doesn't do to look too keen.'

Harriett was not quite sure what this meant but was not sorry to be returning to her sister-in-law's lodging. She had had a long walk in from Bearshott and had spent most of the day since her arrival out and about.

'That's so pretty,' she said later, admiring Bebe's lace-trimmed nightgown. 'I wish I had something half so nice.' Her own was plain, made of serviceable, hard-wearing cotton, with not so much as a ruffle to adorn it.

'Well, we might be able to do something about that, one day,' Bebe laughed, getting into bed. 'I hope you don't snore. I'm a light sleeper.'

'No, I don't. At least – if I do, Joe's never said.'

'Good. Blow out the candle, would you?'

Allnutt's Yard was so busy that Joe and Abel – and Epsom – were usually away all week, sometimes together, but often on separate deliveries. Harriett would spend Mondays doing Abel's housework whilst waiting for Mr Wimble to call for the insurance premiums. As soon as he had left, she would collect her bag and set off for Hounslow. Elizabeth would watch her from the other side of Wyck Green, and wonder. She understood that Harriett must feel lonely whenever Joe was away. She saw little of her, now that all the children were at school. She supposed that Harriett was spending time with her family in Whitton.

Harriett could not help but feel a twinge of jealousy whenever she saw Bebe's wardrobe. Each week, there seemed to be another piece of clothing, or gewgaw, to admire and exclaim over. Whenever they went out for the evening, there was one ornament that Bebe always wore – a stickpin brooch, adorned with a little silver cat with red eyes. She fastened it at her throat, on a lapel, or on the brim of her bonnet, but mostly she pinned it on the left shoulder of her dress or cloak. When Harriett asked her why she favoured it so, Bebe said that she wore it in remembrance of her late husband; it was the last present he had given her.

'It's only a bit of trumpery, not worth anything much, but it's sentimental, you know? Harriett, you should buy yourself some little thing – Joe would like to see you in something pretty.'

Harriett was not the least bit interested in whether Joe might like to see her in something pretty, but she would be glad not to appear so dowdy in front of Bebe's friends. So far, Bebe had not asked for any money toward their outings in Hounslow – Harriett assumed that she was in receipt of some sort of income from her dead husband's estate, until such time as 'the lawyers sort things out'. She would bring most of the housekeeping money Joe had left her, and her wage from Mr Allnutt, but even she could see that the sum amounted to nowhere near their expenditure.

'Mr Wimble,' she began one Monday morning, 'Mr Broughton and I have been discussing matters, and we have decided that we cannot afford to continue with these payments.'

'My dear lady, it would be most unwise to cancel these policies. You will have paid in all this time for nothing. I think

I should have a word with your husband.'

'No, there's no need. He has told me to tell you that we no longer want them.'

'But his life insurance policy goes back further than your marriage. I really cannot sanction cancelling it without speaking to him directly.'

'What about the one for me, then? Can I just cancel that?'

'I suppose so, if you insist. But it might be a case of 'penny wise, pound foolish', you know.'

'As you can see, we don't have any children, and that was what Joe was chiefly worried about, so we don't need it, after all. Please may I just cancel that one, then?'

Wimble, annoyed at the loss of some commission, gave in. He made an entry in the Broughton's paying-in book and updated his own records. Harriett had another sixpence to contribute to the Hounslow pot.

The letter arrived by the second post. Harriett could just about decipher Joe's name on the envelope. In the top left-hand corner of the envelope was a design that she thought was familiar. Fetching the insurance documents, she compared it with the larger one on the policy. It was the same. It must be Mr Wimble, writing about the cancelled payments. Harriett screwed the letter into a spill and used it to light the kitchen stove.

Although cancelling one of the insurances enabled Harriett to pay a little more towards their food and drink, it was still a drop in the ocean in comparison with the sums Bebe was laying out.

'I wish I could give you more,' she said, 'but unless Joe earns more money somehow – or dies…Not that I want him to, of course.'

Bebe had already heard all about the life insurance policies. She did not want Joe to die either. She wanted a far more subtle revenge on him and the rest of her family.

'Well, there are ways you could make a bit whilst you're

here, you know. Enough to buy armfuls of pretty frocks and trinkets.'

'But how?' Harriett wrinkled her brow. 'I don't understand.'

'I'll show you. Soon. Now, put your bonnet on and let's go. We're meeting Charlie at the Nags Head at nine.'

Charlie was already seated at their preferred table when they arrived, a pint of ale in front of him, and in company with another man, who he introduced as Victor 'in town just for the night, on his way up north, and looking for some jollity.'

Victor was liberal with his money, standing the merry group saucers of whelks washed down with glasses of gin and brandy. Once he saw that Charlie was fairly attached to the prettier woman, he set his sights on gaining the younger girl's interest. Harriett, not having received so much male attention for many months, was immensely flattered.

Bebe, keeping a weather eye on Harriett, eventually nudged Charlie, who thereupon announced that it was getting late and time to break up the party. By now somewhat foxed, Victor, insisting that the night was still young, tottered off to the bar. Bebe ushered Harriett out into the street, leaving Charlie to deal with their evening's companion. Harriett did not know whether to be glad or sorry. She had enjoyed Victor's company but was becoming uncomfortable at his increasing familiarity.

The evening set a pattern for those that followed. The two women would meet Charlie at one of the many public houses in Hounslow where he would introduce them to a fresh male acquaintance. One evening, Charlie suggested to Harriett that she should treat herself to a new frock; Bebe 'could show her where the best might be got'. To be able to dress in the same style as her sister-in-law was Harriett's dearest wish, but the cost was far beyond her purse. Charlie told her that he had had some luck on the horses and was greatly in funds. He could well spare some of his winnings – he would give her five pounds so that she could kit herself out. Harriett, heart ruling head, could find no fault with this plan. Charlie was a good friend, and Bebe was encouraging her to accept his gift.

'Bebe can hold the purse for you, for safety. And perhaps you'd better leave your new clothes with her as well. You won't want to be carrying them back and forth from Bearshott, will you?'

The next day was spent browsing the clothes shops along the High Street. Eventually, Harriett selected a dress in a printed cotton – neither so grand nor so expensive as the satins that Bebe liked to wear, but far prettier and more fashionable than even her one Sunday best frock.

'There's some money left,' Bebe told Harriett. 'Why don't you go back for that bonnet you liked? It's just the style to go with your new dress.'

Over the following weeks, the pair made several more such expeditions. A mention of Charlie's name always seemed to guarantee them a discount on their purchases. Harriett, lost in the pleasure of acquiring a new wardrobe, failed to keep track of her spending. The purse seemed to be like the pot in Grimms' tale *Sweet Porridge* – never empty. There were always more coins jingling about inside.

'I'm afraid the gees weren't so good to me today,' Charlie said one evening as the three sat in the Red Lion. 'I'm afraid I shall have to ask you to repay me, Harriett.'

'Repay?' Harriett was mystified.

'The money you've been borrowing from me. How much does it amount to, Bebe?'

'Thirty-seven pounds, nine and eightpence three farthings.'

'But – but – I thought that was a present!'

Bebe laughed. 'Silly goose. What man would give you such a sum for nothing, apart from a husband or lover? And even he would expect something in return, I'm sure.'

'Well?' Charlie put in. 'When can I expect payment?' The carefree, good-natured, and generous Charlie she had become accustomed to had disappeared. The one now frowning at Harriett across the table was a different person entirely.

'But – I can't!' wailed Harriett.

'Then you must find some other way to repay your debt.' Charlie downed his drink. 'I'm off. Bebe – sort this out. I'll meet you here tomorrow – you can tell me then what you've decided.'

'Bebe, there's no way I can pay him back,' wept Harriett.

'You'll just have to tell Joe – get him to give you the money.'

'Joe hasn't got that sort of money, either.'

'Grandfather Farley, then? He'd give anything to avoid another scandal.'

'Scandal?' Harriett sniffed, momentarily diverted.

'I wasn't really married to a rich man – nor to anyone else, you little fool. I disobliged my family by giving birth to a bastard. Everybody in Bearshott knows the sorry tale. I'm surprised no one's told you. I was in pretty dire straits before Charlie came along, I can tell you. But he's a hard man, I should warn you. Don't think he'll let you off – he'll want every last farthing. And don't think you can just disappear back to Bearshott, either. He'd just send some of his pals to make a stink.'

'What shall I do, then?' An idea occurred. 'If I got a job, somewhere – a proper job, I mean – couldn't I pay him back a bit each month?'

'Well, he *might* let you do that—'

'Ask him for me, Bebe, he'll listen to you!' Harriett cried hopefully.

'—but then there'd be all the interest.'

'Interest? What's that?'

Bebe, reflecting that Joe had landed himself with a proper simpleton, explained that Charlie would want a monthly fee, on top of the original debt. 'He usually charges one thousand percent. You couldn't pay that back in a month of Sundays.

You'd better just pay him what you owe him now, as quickly as possible.'

'But how?' Harriett sobbed.

'You could work for him, as I do. If he thinks you're good enough, of course.'

'Work? Doing what?' Charlie did not seem like Harriett's idea of a businessman. He came and went at odd times and kept very irregular hours.

'Well, the men he introduces us to in the evenings. Some of them want a bit more than just a cheery drink.'

'I don't know what you mean,' Harriett sniffled.

'Oh, Harriett, I think you know perfectly well what I mean,' said Bebe shrewdly.

The following day, they joined Charlie in the Nags Head, where he was dining on a pork pie and pickled eggs, washed down with a glass of Madeira.

'Well?' he addressed Bebe, ignoring Harriett.

'She'll do.'

Charlie was immediately all smiles. 'Well, sit down, the pair of you. Order whatever you like – on me.'

In the mid-afternoon, they made their way back to Bebe's lodgings, Harriett swaying slightly under the unaccustomed effect of several glasses of brandy. Charlie slipped a guinea into Bebe's hand and bid her go and lose herself for an hour or two.

When she returned two hours later, she found Harriett alone, sitting on the bed, swathed in the bedspread, her eyes puffy from crying.

'He – he said – he had to make sure I wouldn't embarrass him,' she hiccoughed pathetically.

'Charlie prides himself on having the best girls in town,' Bebe observed. 'What else did he say?'

'He said to ask you about keeping clean and such. And he said I need my own lodgings.'

'Well, we can't both work out of here, can we? Bed's not

big enough for four. Well, not usually.' She paused. 'Cheer up. Didn't he tell you, you can keep some of your earnings every time? You'll soon be able to buy some more clothes, or save enough to leave Joe, if that's what you want. Besides, what other job do you know of that lets you take a week's holiday every month?'

'He gave me this.' Harriett opened a fist. The little stickpin with the red-eyed silver cat twinkled in the light coming through the window.

'All Charlie's girls get one. Just make sure you wear it where it can be seen whenever you go out on the pull.'

Harriett was terrified.

'I think I'm going to have a baby!' The prospect of an event that she had so longed for now filled her with dread.

'Well, that's all right. Joe will never suspect—'

'Yes, he will! We haven't – you know – for months!' cried Harriett.

'Oh. Well, in that case, you'll have to get him to – 'you know' – pretty sharpish. You can fiddle the dates later,' said the ever-practical Bebe.

'S – syphilis?' Joe stammered, aghast. 'But – but how? I mean—'

'You must have lain with a woman who had the disease,' replied the doctor.

'But I haven't—' Joe stopped. Maybe he had, unknowingly. The doctor had seen it all before, too often. A young man, frequently working away from home, looking for companionship during the long, lonely evenings. Now, he could see, his patient had recalled at least one foolhardy liaison.

'You should refrain from marital relations with your wife until we get on top of this.'

'Oh, I shall,' Joe responded grimly. 'I'm not sure of all the symptoms – what to look for, or to expect?'

'Well, there's the hard lump on the privates – the chancre – and mouth sores, to start with. Then there might be a rash on your body. Your wife might miscarry, or your children might be born with the disease. It could, eventually, lead to madness, or even death, if left untreated.'

'And the treatment?'

'Not very pleasant, I'm afraid, Mr Broughton. Mercury. I advise that you start a course immediately. You should also send your wife to see me. But don't tell her what for. I shall tell her she needs treatment for something quite different. We don't like to alarm the ladies with evidence of their husbands' – er – misdemeanours. Just make sure she comes.'

Driving home, Joe thought back. He had not lain with Harriett since she lost the child. About three months before that, he remembered her being unusually attentive: asking how his day had been, cooking his favourite supper, enticing him into bed…Harriett was the only woman he had ever had sex with. She had not caught the disease from him. He had caught it from her. Some other man had given her both the pox and a child.

'I'll be leaving Epsom with you this week.'

Dismayed, but striving not to show it, Harriett looked up from her breakfast. 'Oh? Why's that?'

'I shall be staying a couple of nights in Guildford – got a big job down there. Their dogs don't get on with Epsom – they bark at each other all the time. So, they've asked me not to take him.'

'Don't they have a barn or something, where you can shut him away?'

'No,' Joe said shortly, eyes narrowed. 'They don't.'

'Well, how about your mother, then? Perhaps she'd—'

'Why on earth should she? He's your dog. Aren't you going to visit your folks in Whitton, same as usual? I'm sure the children would love to see him.'

'But he's so big,' objected Harriett. 'He might knock the

little ones over.'

'I'm sure there are enough 'big ones' to make sure he doesn't.'

Harriett shrugged a plump shoulder. There seemed to be nothing more to say.

'I'll be driving through Whitton. Shall I take you up?'

'Oh – no, thank you. I need to wait for Mr Wimble to call. And I have to tidy up for Mr Allnutt.'

Abel had already left with the smaller cart, bound for the London markets. Another idea occurred.

'Mr Allnutt will be coming back tonight, won't he? Perhaps he could—' She caught the black look Joe was giving her. 'No, of course he couldn't.'

As Joe harnessed Clopper to the big wagon, the subject of the discussion jumped up onto the box seat, tail wagging furiously, ready to go.

'Sorry, boy. Not today.' Joe said, scratching behind the animal's ears. He knotted the rope they used as a lead to its collar and tied the other end to a ring set into the wall. Throwing one last glance over his shoulder at his faithless wife, standing in the kitchen doorway with her arms folded, he drove out of the yard and set off around the Green and up Waleric Lane.

The howls echoed around the Green.

'The neighbours will be complaining again,' said Elizabeth.

'It's good of Abel, letting us put him in the stable.'

'Poor Epsom.'

'Poor Joe. What a thing to come home to. Abel reckons he should be back in another couple of hours.'

'Will you tell him, Edward? I don't think I can.'

Joe drove into the yard just as the sun was setting. The wheels of the big wagon were caked in mud; it had been pouring on the journey home. His father was waiting for him, slouched under the eaves out of the rain.

'What's the matter with Epsom?' Joe said as he clambered down. 'Is he hurt?'

'It's not Epsom that's hurt, son,' Edward put a hand on his shoulder. 'It's Harriett. It's bad, Joe, real bad.'

Joe took a deep breath and looked his father squarely in the eye. 'Tell me.'

Edward told him.

Abel had crossed the yard once he was sure that Joe had been given the news. Unlatching the stable door, he said, 'I'll see to the horse, lad. You take care of your dog.'

Joe bent down and whistled. Epsom appeared in the doorway, hackles rising. Joe held out a hand. A growl started deep in the animal's chest.

'Hey, boy! Come on, Epsom, it's me,' Joe gentled.

Epsom's lips rolled back, revealing slavering fangs. Keeping his eyes fixed on Joe, he stalked stiff-legged out of the stable. Joe took a step toward him. Snarling, the dog bounded toward his master, swerving past him at the last moment and running off into the night.

'Well, I'll be blowed,' Abel said, scratching his head. 'Did you ever see such a thing? Must've turned his brain.'

Joe stood staring after the dog, a set look on his face. 'I'll look for him in the morning. Don't want him hurting anybody.'

'Better take a gun, then,' Edward said. 'I'll come with you.' He paused. 'Perhaps you want to see where—?'

Joe nodded.

5: An Examination

'S HOCKING DEATH OF YOUNG WIFE', 'INQUEST OPENS TODAY' screamed the headlines in the Monday morning edition of *The Hounslow & District Enquirer*. Normally, such an initial report would be buried somewhere on the inside pages, but the body had been open to view for several days, and those who had found her and transported her to the mortuary had freely discussed the ghastly experience with anyone who would stand them a pint. Consequently, the paper's artist had been given his head and had produced a pen and ink drawing, rendering Harriett in life, the howling dog, a gruesome depiction of the state of the corpse, and the horror of the labourers at the sight. The imaginative compilation occupied pride of place on the front page.

The inquest was held in Hounslow Town Hall. The room was filled to capacity. The local rumour mill had been running at full tilt. The strange circumstance of Harriett's death, her connection to one of Isleworth's respected families, and her unhappy marriage were the facts that had been poured over, dissected, and reassembled over many a cosy hearth. The inhabitants of Hounslow, Isleworth, Bearshott and Whitton had not enjoyed themselves so much for years. Whilst most were prepared to hear the evidence before making up their minds, some had come down decidedly on the side of one or other of the two apparent possible causes of the death. It had been an unfortunate accident, or she had been deliberately run over. On the face of it, the former was the more likely, but rather dull. The mere possibility of the latter ensured that there was standing room only in the courtroom.

Nineteen upstanding citizens had already been sworn in and taken to view the body of the deceased, as affirmed by the foreman. Many members of the jury appeared distinctly unwell, a detail that was noted with pleasure by the observers, mentally licking their lips at the prospect of being both repulsed and excited by the gory particulars.

The first witness to be called was the doctor who had examined the pathetic remains.

'The deceased was a well-nourished young woman of about twenty years, low in stature, and somewhat inclined to corpulence. She had recently lost a child. Her body bore the signs of first-stage syphilis.'

This was an unexpected development. The spectators whispered, wriggled in their seats, and leaned forward, agog, full of morbid curiosity. Obviously, the husband had been playing away from home. The coroner frowned. He would have preferred this diagnosis to have remained private, out of deference to Harriett's family.

'The deceased had suffered catastrophic injuries. The body had almost been severed at the waist, the trunk and the pelvic area being only connected by a strip of skin and the remnants of her dress. The belly was eviscerated. The liver showed signs of the disease associated with heavy drinking. The face was engorged, with the tongue and eyes protruding. The remnants of a string, or rope, remained knotted around the deceased's left wrist.'

'And to what do you attribute these injuries, doctor?'

'I conclude that the deceased was run over at least once by the wheel, or wheels, of a heavy wagon.'

' 'At least'?'

'There are signs that could indicate that a wagon passed

over the body in two directions.'

'Coming and going – back and forth, do you mean?'

'I do, sir.'

These horrific, though fascinating, revelations far exceeded the assembly's expectations. Surely not an accident, then?

'Who identified the victim, doctor?'

'Mrs Clarke was able to identify her daughter, and a number of other persons came to view the body. Some recognised the dog and knew to whom it belonged.'

'How long had the deceased been dead, do you estimate?'

'The remains were quite cold, and rigor had passed. The back of the body was dry, as was the ground beneath it. I believe the rain started in the early hours of the morning on the day she was found. I conclude that the fatal injuries were sustained sometime on the Monday.'

The next witness to be called was the labourer who had come across the body on the previous Tuesday evening. He deposed that his attention had been drawn to the body by the howling of the dog that was attached to her by a long rope. There was a large pool of blood at the side of the road, together with 'some other stuff'. She was not lying in the road, where he would have seen her when he passed by earlier in the day, but off to one side, in a ditch. The rope lead, he said, had caught around a bush. But for that, he thought the dog would have pulled the corpse into the woodland at the side of the road. He had, upon viewing the unhappy sight, been violently unwell, but when he had recovered somewhat, he had cut the rope and secured the dog to a tree, away from the body. He had then sought assistance from a cottager further along the road back toward Bearshott.

'You say that you would have seen the body if it had been lying in the road. How is it that you did not see the pool of blood in the morning?'

'It was in a large puddle, sir, you could only see it if you were close. In the morning, I was walking on the other side of the road – toward Whitton.'

The persons next brought forward were those who, it was believed, were the last to see Harriett alive, including Elizabeth Broughton.

'I saw my daughter-in-law at about eleven o'clock last Monday,' she said. 'She was walking on the other side of Wyck Green, toward Waleric Lane. I did not speak to her, nor did I see her after.'

'She had the dog with her?'

'Yes, sir.'

'What did you think of that? Was that usual?'

'Well – no sir. It was a large animal, and she was quite small. She found it difficult to hold on to him. She would complain that he could pull her over.'

'I see. And is it the case that the dog was her property?'

'Yes. Her husband gave it to her when they married.'

'And yet she was not accustomed to keeping it with her?'

'No, sir. Joe – my son – normally took it with him on his deliveries. It being too large for Harriett to manage easily. And she was not fond of walking.'

'Where did you believe she was bound?'

'Whitton, sir, to visit her mother, as she did most weeks. Or so she said.'

Dismissing Elizabeth but telling her not to leave the court in case there should be more questions for her later, two more witnesses reported seeing Harriett on the road to Isleworth.

Mrs Clarke, dabbing a cloth to eyes puffy with crying, took the stand.

'Now, Mrs Clarke, we do not wish to distress you further, but can you just answer a few questions?'

Mrs Clarke nodded vigorously.

'Yes, Your Honour. I want to know who did this to my poor girl.'

'Well, Mrs Clarke, that remains to be seen. It may well have been just an unfortunate accident.'

'In that case, your lordship, why didn't the one what did it stop and say so?' she demanded. 'No, I know full well who's behind all this—'

'Now, now, Mrs Clarke. I appreciate that you're upset, but you mustn't be making wild accusations, you know. Could you just tell the court this: was your daughter in the habit of visiting you whilst her husband was working away?'

'No, sir, she was not. At least, she did from time to time, but not regular, if you know what I mean.'

'How regularly?'

'Maybe every couple of months or so. The last time she stayed with us, was when she lost the child. And that was about six or seven weeks back.'

'Thank you, Mrs Clarke. You may stand down.'

'But what about the life insurance?'

'Life insurance, Mrs Clarke?' the coroner queried, slightly at a loss. 'Whose life insurance?'

'Harriett's. He – her husband – made her sign some papers. He was to get a lot of money if my girl died.'

This was too good to be true. Yet another motive! Excited chattering broke out in the courtroom. One person in the gathering knew better. It being a Monday, and being as usual in the district, Wimble had decided to attend the inquest on the body of one of his clients. He might have lost some commission, but, on the other hand, the cancellation of the policy had saved the company twenty-two pounds.

'And then there was the dog.'

'The dog? We've heard evidence about the dog, madam.'

'Not about when Joe came back home and it nearly bit him, you haven't. And that dog was as fond of him as anything, so why did it go for him and run off? And why did Joe shoot it?'

The coroner felt the proceedings were rather getting out of his control; the evidence was not being presented in the correct order. Since the dog could hardly give evidence, even if it were alive, he would ignore Mrs Clarke's last remarks. But the question of life insurance was another matter. He decided to break for lunch.

Those of the Broughton family who were attending the inquest lunched in one of the town's better inns.

'All that nonsense about the insurance – don't worry about that,' said Wimble, who was enjoying a glass of ale and a snack in the same public house and encountered Joe at the bar. 'You only have to tell them that Mrs B cancelled that policy months ago, and I wrote to let you know of it.'

'She did?' Joe was puzzled. Wimble's eyes narrowed. He excused himself and downed his drink. He decided he had spent enough time in Hounslow and would head for home.

The afternoon session opened with the husband's evidence.

'You are Joseph Broughton, of Allnutt's Yard, Bearshott?'

'I am.'

'And what is your occupation?'

'Carrier.' Although most of those present were already aware of this, a frisson of anticipation ran around the courtroom.

'And you identified the body of your wife on Saturday last?'

'I did,' Joe whispered, ashen-faced.

'Please tell the court about the last time you saw your wife.'

'It was at breakfast last Monday, sir, before I left on a job.'

'And what were you driving that day?'

'The wagon.'

'This is a large vehicle?'

'Yes, sir, the biggest we've got.'

'Where were you going? What was your route?'

'I drove up toward Isleworth, for a couple of pick-ups, then back down along the road through Whitton and over the Crane, then through Twickenham and on to Chertsey, Woking and Guildford.'

'A long trip.'

'Yes, sir. I was away for four nights.'

'And you saw no one you knew on your way? You didn't see your wife on the Isleworth road?'

'No, sir. But I saw some of her family in Whitton and stopped to have a word.'

To the court in general, this was somewhat disappointing. The theory that had been developing did not look so promising, after all.

'Where did you understand your wife to be going that day?'

'Whitton, to see her mother.'

'And yet we have heard that Mrs Broughton was not expected, nor, indeed, had she visited her family for some weeks.'

'I don't know anything about that, sir. She always said that's where she was going whilst I was away.'

'Hmm. Now, about this question of the insurance on your wife's life—'

'There wasn't any, sir. We had cancelled it some weeks ago. We had a letter from the Provident confirming this. Which I didn't keep.' Even more disappointing. The commonly held theory that the husband had done away with an inconvenient wife dwindled away.

'Have you anything further you can tell us about this sad occurrence?'

'Well, sir,' Joe began, 'I heard the doctor say that Harriett might have been run over by a wagon turning around so it got her twice. But I don't see how – that road is too narrow to turn a big rig around, you'd have to drive about half a mile up the road to where it widens out.'

The coroner was annoyed. Someone should have checked the location. He decided to go on the offensive, to search for any weakness in the husband's evidence.

'You are familiar with the location of the incident, then? You know precisely where it occurred? How is that?'

'My father showed me on Saturday morning, when we were out looking for Epsom.' Someone in the gallery stifled a giggle.

'Epsom?' the coroner frowned.

'The dog, sir. That's what Harriett called it.'

'Why?' the coroner puzzled, diverted from his line of questioning.

'She thought that was where the dog came from, that I had bought it for her whilst I was out on a delivery to Epsom.'

'And where did it come from?'

'Ewell.' More giggles from the gallery.

'So, your wife thought you had gone to Epsom, when in fact you had gone to Ewell?'

'I went to Epsom *and* Ewell.'

'I see.' The coroner looked over the top of his glasses. 'Did you often mislead your wife about where you were going?'

'I didn't – I just didn't tell her I was going to Ewell as well. To visit my uncle.'

The coroner raised an eyebrow. 'A family party? Might not your wife have cared to accompany you on that visit?'

'No – yes – I don't know,' Joe stammered.

'Hmm,' the coroner regarded Joe sourly from the bench, then returned to his original questions. 'So, in your opinion, how do you account for your wife's injuries?'

'I should say she was pulled into the road by the dog, just as a wagon was passing, and fell under the wheels.'

'And the wagoner didn't stop because—?'

'If he was driving a heavy load, he likely wouldn't have felt more than a slight bump. Probably knew nothing about it.'

'But surely she would have screamed. He would have heard that, would he not?'

'I don't know – perhaps Epsom was barking, and he took no notice. Perhaps he was deaf.' Rather more stifled laughter.

'Silence in court!' The coroner glowered at the gallery. 'About the dog. It seems that his behaviour after was out of character. How do you account for that?'

'I suppose his mind was turned, sir. I had to shoot him, in

case he attacked anyone, which was a great pity. He was a good dog.' Since this sentiment was more sorrowful than he had as yet expressed regarding his wife's death, in the minds of the onlookers, Joe went from bereaved husband to possible murder suspect to hard-hearted villain.

'If you have nothing further to say, you may stand down. Is there anyone further to be heard in this matter?'

The coroner's officer passed him a slip of paper. The coroner raised an eyebrow.

'Really? She's not on the list. Oh, well, let her take the stand.'

'Call Elizabeth Broughton.'

Edward and Elizabeth looked at one another in consternation. She felt that she had already said all there was to say about that dreadful day – what else could the court want to ask her? She made to get up from her seat when her eldest daughter entered the courtroom.

Bebe, smartly dressed, made her leisurely way to the witness stand, a half-smile on her lips. Looking around the room, she saw a number of men who she knew very well indeed, including some on the jury, though they all avoided catching her eye. She was confident that, whatever she said, there would be no disputation about her evidence. She confirmed her name and direction, and, when asked what occupation she followed, she said she was 'living on her own means' and also did a little dressmaking for 'the better sort of clientele'. She also received a small allowance from her grandfather, Mr Benjamin Farley of Isleworth. Since Benjamin was not in court, there was no one to confirm or deny this surprising assertion.

'And what evidence do you have to give, madam, that might assist the court? I understand you did not see Mrs Broughton on the day of her death.'

'No, sir. But she was on her way to see me, as she often did when my brother was from home. She told him she was visiting Whitton because she knew that he would not permit her to visit me if he knew of it. We were sisters by marriage, you understand, and very fond. Neither of us was welcomed by the rest of the family.' Bebe dabbed her eyes with the wisp of a handkerchief. The affecting sight underlined the husband's lack of emotion. The Broughtons present squirmed and protested amongst themselves. 'Poor Harriett. She found in me a kindred spirit, as it were, sir.'

The coroner grunted. 'But what have you to say to the point?'

'Well, two things came to my mind. Firstly, the life insurance—'

'Yes, yes, we've already heard about that,' the coroner said testily.

'Sir, Harriett told me she had cancelled the policy, but that Joe did not know of it. The insurance company wrote to him about it, but she burnt the letter before he saw it. She insisted that Joe thought the insurance premiums were still being paid. He was still leaving her the money to pay them.'

'Why would she cancel the policy without her husband's agreement?'

'She thought it a waste of money, sir. She would rather have the sixpence a week it cost in her pocket.' She paused and looked around the court. 'Secondly, she always wore some particular jewellery about her – a silver stickpin, with a cat mounted on it, that I had given her as a gift, and her wedding ring. Nobody has mentioned these items, I wondered if she was wearing them when she was found – no one has reported finding them.'

'Thank you, Miss Broughton. Call Mr Joseph Broughton back to the stand.'

Bebe smirked at Joe as they passed one other. Revenge was sweet, even if it had taken an unexpected direction.

'What do you have to say about this life insurance, Mr Broughton? You gave evidence to the effect that you had received notification from the insurance company. Yet apparently your wife destroyed this letter before you saw it.'

'That's the first I've heard of it – I thought it had gone astray in the post. I saw the insurance agent later, and he told me of it. And also, of course, there's the paying-in book, which shows that the policy was cancelled.'

There seemed to be nothing further to say on this head.

'Has any of your wife's jewellery been returned to you?'

'No, sir, nor have I received her reticule.'

The labourer who had discovered the corpse was recalled and confirmed that he had not removed any items – indeed, the sight of the body was so unpleasant he had not gone near it, let alone touched it. One man who had attended the scene had made a search of the undergrowth nearby for any of the deceased's belongings, but, he believed, had not found anything.

No witness could be found who had any knowledge of the missing items.

'It seems that there are two logical explanations for the death of this unfortunate woman. One, that she fell beneath the wheels of a passing wagon, either because she tripped or because her dog pulled her into its path. Two, that she was deliberately run over, and that she was then robbed of her valuables, either by the same person or somebody unidentified who came upon her lifeless body later,' stated the coroner. Although the husband was the obvious suspect if the act was deliberate, and might well be arrested, he had to be scrupulous. 'Any statements that have been made concerning the matter of the life insurance may be disregarded.'

The jury retired to a side room, where jugs of ale had been provided to help them with their deliberations. Some of the men were uneasy. The fact that Harriett wore such a pin could mean only one thing, and might have some material bearing on the case. But how to put this to the court without admitting their own indiscretions? Finally, they agreed on the wording of a note to be passed to the coroner.

'I have received a note from the jury, with some further

information, which may possibly be relevant,' commenced the coroner, 'to the effect that the wearing of such a brooch as described by Miss Broughton is well known in the Hounslow area to indicate that the wearer is a common prostitute. Call Miss Elizabeth Broughton to return to the stand.'

But Miss Elizabeth Broughton had already slipped away.

Other motives for murder, if such it was, presented themselves: perhaps a disgruntled customer, her pimp, or even the victim of blackmail.

The crowded court eagerly anticipated the verdict. The whole proceedings had been most satisfactory. It was better than any theatrical melodrama.

The jury returned an open verdict.

'WOMAN'S HORRIFIC DEATH'. 'DRAMATIC REVELATIONS'. 'MOTHER ACCUSES YOUNG HUSBAND'. 'JURY VERDICT'. So squawked the special edition of *The Hounslow & District Enquirer*, rushed out that evening. All the day's sensational disclosures were reported, enlarged, and dissected, and illustrated with sketches of the distraught mother, the young husband, and a general view of the courtroom, together with pen portraits of the principal witnesses, with comments on the demeanour of each. Joe did not fare well at the hands of the reporter. It was remarked that he had shown more sorrow at the death of his dog than at the death of his spouse. Harriett's reputation was torn to shreds. The editor rubbed his hands with glee. This was a story that would run and run. He had high hopes that it would be picked up by some of the London press.

Over the next few days, several new eyewitnesses to the tragic scene came forward and sold their 'exclusive' stories to the paper. One or two of the accounts were so vivid that the witness might almost have been there.

An expert on the behaviour of dogs contributed his thoughts on the matter. He felt it highly unlikely that a loyal pet would so turn on its master unless it had reason to be afraid of said master. It was noted that the animal had not attempted to attack the labourer who had found the corpse, suggesting that it was in perfect control of its wits. An exposé of the town's seedy lowlife was poured over at many a breakfast table, the husbands with trepidation, their wives safe in the delicious knowledge that their own households were sacrosanct, whereas they had always had their suspicions about their dearest friends'.

The overall tone of the coverage that emerged was the implication that, by means as yet undiscovered, the husband had murdered the wife, and that in due course so it would be shown. One correspondent was moved to assert that some person 'in authority' was protecting Joseph Broughton, preventing justice from being done, and this had been achieved by 'nobbling members of the jury'. The editor was moved to print his letter. The only person of any influence connected with the family was the grandfather.

Benjamin Farley composed a short and pithy letter, pointing out that he had been confined to his home since before the unhappy accident, suffering from gout, and so it could be shown. He did not know any of the members of the jury. Furthermore, anyone who had bought the jury had wasted their money, since the desired verdict was, presumably, one of accidental death, and not the open verdict they had returned. He further intimated that, should anyone repeat such a slander in his hearing, he was most willing and able to seek redress at law. Since many members of the jury were also up in arms at the assertion that they could be bribed, the editor was obliged to print a disclaimer, stating that the suggestion came from a private individual, and was not supported by *The Enquirer*.

Although no one could ever show that Joe was other than where he said he was, the sly innuendos and outright accusations levelled at him persisted, becoming more and more overt. One theory that gained credence was that the conveniently absent Charlie – if he even existed – had nothing to do with the matter, and that it was, in fact, Joe who had sent his unhappy wife out to work the streets of Hounslow.

Elizabeth and Edward were in despair, but Benjamin was made of sterner stuff and advised his grandson to bide his time in silence. Encouraged by Joe's failure to object to this biased coverage, *The Enquirer* embarked on a campaign, calling for the authorities to bring him to book.

The London papers did, indeed, show some interest in the story, much to the satisfaction of *The Enquirer*'s editor. Having made their own inquiries at the Provident's London office, however, the city's hacks decided there was nothing newsworthy, other than the grisly details. They had spoken to Wimble about the only issue that could be proven one way or another. He confirmed the cancellation, the subsequent sending of a letter, and the weekly completion of the paying-in book showing that only one policy was in force. His observations regarding Joe's reaction to the news that his wife had cancelled the other policy he kept to himself. His would not be the voice that might send a man to the gallows.

In due course, with the assistance of his grandfather's man-at-law, Joseph Broughton sued both the editor and *The Hounslow & District Enquirer* for defamation and the publication of a libel.

Between arriving home late on Friday afternoon and the inquest on the following Monday, Joe had been constantly in the company of various relatives and friends, all concerned for his well-being. The question of life insurance had not crossed his mind. After the revelations in court, it became imperative that the all-important paying-in book be found.

Joe searched fruitlessly through all the boxes, drawers, and cupboards in the loft that he and Harriett called home. Next, he rummaged through Abel's kitchen, and then his other rooms, reasoning that, since Harriett always did Abel's cleaning on a Monday whilst she awaited Mr Wimble, she might have kept the book there. He did not think it could have been in Hounslow; she had produced it last Monday and had been on her way to the town when she died. It should have been either on the body or back in Bearshott somewhere. He searched the stables and barns, although he knew his wife avoided both if she could.

Finally, having drawn a blank, he made another, more intensive, search of the loft, pulling out furniture, upending the bed, and lifting the rugs. Under one of these, he at last found what he was looking for. Beneath a loose floorboard was secreted a box containing, not only the paying-in book, but a fat canvas purse full of coins – Harriett's share of the money she had earned for Charlie. He put the purse back in the hidey-hole, and screwed the board down. He gave his mother the book, together with the money that should have been paid over on the day of the inquest, and the next week's premium. He wrote to the Provident, directing their agent to call, in future, at the house in Trafalgar Terrace for payment. Acknowledging this new arrangement, the insurance company informed Joe that Mr Southern had now taken the area over from Mr Wimble.

6: The Three Jays

'Hey, you! Get out of our tree!' Caro shouted, picking up a windfall and lobbing it at the intruder. The rotting apple made a satisfying squelchy sound as it struck him fair and square on his left ear. Jumping down, he made a dash for the front hedge. Before pushing through, he turned, pulled some fruit out of his pockets and, waving them at us, poked out his tongue.

'Who's that?' I asked.

Georgie shrugged, but Caro said, 'I think he's just moved into one of the cottages around the corner.'

We threw ourselves down in our favourite spot, shaded from the August sun beneath the largest, knobbliest tree. We often climbed up into its branches, but it was too sultry for such exertions. We contented ourselves with making whistles out of grass stems. Our little orchard lay in the wedge-shaped piece of land on the corner of the main street with Crane Lane.

'Father should fill that gap in,' Caro remarked, her back against the tree trunk.

In truth, Father didn't much mind the children that came scrumping. The orchard was very productive. There was always plenty of fruit for our own table, and for Mother's jams and chutneys. She often put baskets of apples and pears at our front gate, so that people could help themselves to our spare harvest.

'Keep still, Georgie,' commanded Caro, pulling a small sketchbook and pencil from her apron pocket.

'Oh, not again,' said Georgie, rolling his eyes.

'Don't be silly, George,' she said severely.

'He can't help it,' said I, putting in my fourpenny worth. 'He was born that way.'

Caro, from the advantage of her thirteen years, merely raised an eyebrow and tutted at me, but Georgie grenaded me with his half-eaten apple. Honour satisfied, he stretched out full-length in the long grass, chin propped up in both hands, a butter wouldn't melt smile on his face. With a few deft strokes, Caro committed his likeness to paper, before blacking out some of his teeth.

'Oi!' laughed Georgie, taking the drawing. 'I'm going to keep this to show everybody what a horrid girl you were when you're rich and famous.'

Those days lazing and larking in the orchard with Caro and Georgie were some of the happiest of my life. He was just about my best friend, then, and Caro always held a special place in my heart. She often had the care of me when I was sick, read us bedtime stories, drew funny pictures, and protected us from the boisterous attentions of Daniel and Will.

'What shall we do today?' asked Georgie, of no one in particular.

'It's too hot for anything much. I suppose we could go out to the Green, see if there's anybody there to play with. Or we could go down to the river.'

'The river, the river!' I cried.

'You'll have to walk all the way,' Caro warned. 'You're too heavy for me to carry you now.'

'I will, promise.'

Caro raised a sceptical eyebrow. 'Let's go and tell Mother where we're going, then.'

Mother was sitting outside the kitchen door, hemming yards of material. She looked up from the dress she was making for Philadelphia Greening and smiled.

'I'm going to take the boys down to the river,' Caro told her. 'They can paddle in the shallows for a bit.'

'Take some water, then. And Joss – try not to leave your shirt behind this time!'

I threw my arms around her neck, face uplifted, waiting for the kiss I knew would come.

We walked hand in hand around the corner and into Crane Lane. The boy who had invaded our orchard earlier came out of the end cottage. He was a rather stocky lad, of about Georgie's height. I expected him to dive inside when he saw us, but instead he leant nonchalantly against the doorframe, arms folded, and watched us as we passed.

'Ignore him,' Caro ordered, head high.

I was sure I could feel his eyes boring into my back, but I managed to obey Caro until we reached a curve in the lane that would take us out of his view, where I sneaked a look back over my shoulder. He was still there. He grinned at me and made a gesture that I took to be a friendly wave, though I suspect it was something quite different.

Beyond Greening's cottages lay the entrance to Oliver's Nurseries.

'Let's go and say hello to Father,' Caro suggested. He was Mr Oliver's head gardener. It being the summer, he worked through the long hours of daylight, so we often didn't see much of him, other than on Sundays.

Mr Oliver was working in his office, but he came to the door when he saw us. He never seemed to mind when we dropped by. Calling out a greeting, he pointed out where Father was working, gave us a cheery wave, and returned to his paperwork. There was a rack full of seed packets outside his office door.

'You'd be good at that, Caro,' Georgie said, pointing to the illustrations on the packets. 'You should ask him if you could do some.' Caro made a noncommittal noise in her throat. Even at eight, I knew that her dearest wish was to paint 'proper' pictures.

Father was in one of the greenhouses, tending tomato plants. The sun beat down on the glass; it was stiflingly hot.

'Where are you all off to?'

'We're going down to the river, for a paddle.'

'I wish I could come with you,' he said, wiping his brow with the back of his hand. 'Be careful not to fall in. And try to remember to bring all your clothing back with you this time, Josiah!' He tousled my hair. I grinned up at him.

'I'll try to remember,' I told him, 'as long as I don't get dis...dis...What's that word, Caro?'

'Distracted?'

'That's it – as long as I don't get *distracted*.'

Father laughed. 'No, please don't.'

We hung about a while until the heat in the greenhouse became too much. Uncomfortably sticky, we left Father to his work and wandered on down Crane Lane to the river's edge, where a wide, flat, pebbly shelf stretched from the water's edge across to a small ait. The main course of the Crane lay on its far side, its currents too strong for us, but the shallows were ideal for paddling, unless the river were in spate. We discarded most of our clothes, took off our shoes and stockings, and thankfully waded in.

After some time spent horsing around in the shimmering backwater, we clambered onto the little island to sit beneath its trees and watch the traffic on the river.

Crane Lane bent westward, skirting the bank, ending at the entrance to the gunpowder mill about a hundred yards off to our right. We liked to watch the mill's punts carrying their cargoes downstream to the Thames, waving to the men on board, most of whom were well-known to us, as they lived in and around Bearshott.

Dozing in the shade, we were startled by loud shouts. There were often accidents, mostly minor, though we had heard stories of fatal explosions at other mills along the waterway. Our peace disturbed, we dressed ourselves and trailed back home.

Caro, Georgie, and I went to school in Bearshott. Mr Greening had funded a smart hall, and installed Mr and Miss Rowlatt to teach the children of the village. Caro and Georgie had first gone to school in Isleworth, but as soon as the new school was ready, they had transferred. Caro was a particularly apt pupil. Mr Rowlatt made her a monitor, to help his sister with the younger children.

On our first day back in the autumn, we were joined by several new pupils, including the boy from the Crane Lane cottages. We had seen him around the village from time to time during the summer, but always cut him dead, convinced he was still taking fruit from our orchard, although, despite laying many elaborate ambushes, Georgie and I had never caught him.

His name was Jonathan Tickle; he was the same age as me but looked older. He was so behind with his reading and writing that he was made to sit with the youngest pupils. More than once, he was obliged to wear the dunce's cap, which Georgie and I found excessively diverting, and took great delight in making rude remarks about him.

As it chanced, there was already a boy with the same first name in that class; Miss Rowlatt began to call him John T. Soon most of the school began calling him Jonty, but Georgie and I, much to my later regret, persisted in referring to him as 'Thickie Tickle'.

Jonty kept himself much to himself. He rarely spoke except when addressed directly by the Rowlatts. He sometimes came to school with a black eye, or a limp, or a fat lip. Georgie and I speculated that, although we hadn't managed to do so, someone, somewhere, had caught him stealing. We eagerly looked forward to the day when he would get his full just deserts and would suffer the age-old punishment doled out to thieves. Much to our disappointment, though luckily for Jonty, he always appeared with both hands still firmly attached to his wrists.

By and by, we learned more of his history. He lived alone with his father, his mother, brother, and sisters having died the previous year, of the consumption. The curiously ill-named Mr Tickle worked at the powder mill, and was a drunkard, frequently lashing out at his only surviving child who, one would have thought, he would rather have taken greater care of.

And so we would have continued, at daggers drawn, I dare say, were it not for the day that Father brought Jonathan Tickle into our home. By this time, there were only we three younger children still living in Trafalgar Terrace; Daniel had a clerical position in Twickenham, and Will had half-heartedly gone to work for Grandfather Farley, as a shop boy, with a view to being 'trained up'. It was a Saturday in April, just before tea-time, when Father ushered Jonty into our cottage.

'Eliza,' he began, 'can we find space for this young man, do you suppose? He's been a bit in the wars, as you can see.'

Mother could, indeed, see, as Jonty was carrying his left arm in a sling. For one brief, glorious, moment, I thought that the bandage might be hiding a handless stump.

'I'm afraid he's broken his wrist,' Father continued, dashing my ghoulish hopes. 'He – er – fell out of a tree.' This was better. Father had obviously caught him in our orchard.

'Oh, dear, poor you.' Mother put a gentle hand on Jonty's shoulder. 'I expect it's quite painful? Do come and sit down.'

Jonty perched himself on the extreme edge of a chair, determined not to be comfortable.

'Mr Greening's farrier was passing – he managed to set the broken bone, said it's a clean break that should mend quite easily.'

'Well, that's a relief,' Mother smiled at the boy. 'Come and say hello. Although I expect you all know each other from school? This is Caro, this is George, and here is Joss. What should we call you?'

Jonty was silent, glowering at the three of us. He did not want to be in our home, and we certainly didn't want him in it.

'Jonty. They call him Jonty,' Caro said finally.

We eventually discovered, by diligent eavesdropping and subtle investigation, that Jonty had not fallen out of a tree – ours or anyone else's – but had, in fact, been on the receiving end of a more than usually brutal assault by his father who was, once again, drunk.

To this, Mr Greening took exception – not because of Tickle's treatment of his son, but because he was intoxicated whilst working at the gunpowder mill, which could have had catastrophic consequences. Tickle was left to sleep it off in his own home. Father, aided by Martin Oliver, persuaded Mr Greening to keep him on, though in a less dangerous role, provided he sign the pledge. To do him credit, Michael Tickle did his best to remain, if not entirely sober, at least not rip-roaringly drunk. In this, he was greatly helped by Mr and Miss Rowlatt, who were leading lights of the local Temperance Movement.

It was decided that Jonty should stay with us for some days, whilst his father 'regained his composure'. None of us was pleased at this turn of events. Mother and Father tried to involve our guest in the conversation, but he was stubbornly monosyllabic and, needless to say, we three made no effort to befriend him or to involve him in our games.

The following day being Sunday, we made our way to Isleworth for morning service. Jonty scuffed and muttered his way to Isleworth, trying even Mother's good temper. After church, we went to visit William's grave, which lay in that quiet corner of the churchyard used exclusively for child burials, before going on to Grandfather's for dinner. The little headstone read *William Broughton 1824–1824*. It was after this William that Will had been named. Mother sometimes placed flowers on the grave, and also another nearby, which had only a rotting, illegible, wooden marker, that, she said, was the burial spot of another infant relative.

Grandfather did not seem to me in the least perturbed by the unexpected addition to his table. The person who was most put out was Louisa. She and her family had recently moved out of their apartment above the store and taken up residence in Grandfather's villa, since (so she said) he had been growing increasingly frail and forgetful, and she was concerned for his safety. He looked pretty stout to me, though he did ask me a couple of times over dinner how my mother did, even though Mother was sitting right next to him. Louisa had taken upon herself the management of his household. The simple task of adjusting the dinner table to accommodate one extra person threw her into a monumental tizzy, which was not ameliorated when Jonty's inability to handle his cutlery correctly became apparent, no allowance being made for the fact that he was temporarily disabled.

Louisa's bad-tempered display was the first time I had felt any sympathy for Jonty. I did not care for her, nor for her snotty children. She had a way of looking at one as though at some lesser species. Even Mother came in for this treatment at times, presumably because she had 'married beneath her'. Goodness knows where this attitude had come from. She had been raised in the same lowly cottage as the rest of us and, had Mother not married Father, would not even have been born.

'Let me help you,' I offered. 'It must be difficult with only one hand.' I glanced at Jonty as I took his knife and fork and was surprised to see unshed tears on his lashes. I cut his dinner up for him, handed him back his cutlery, and said, 'There, you should be able to manage with just a fork, now.' He was still not very handy, but at least there was no further danger of him sending his dinner skidding across the table.

On the way back to Bearshott later that day, I walked beside Jonty, feeling somewhat awkward; we had been at loggerheads for so long. Caro was walking with Mother and

Father. I could almost hear the sigh that Georgie hadn't, in fact, uttered, as he fell in on Jonty's other side. For a long while, none of us spoke.

Georgie picked up a stick and swished it through the grasses growing in the verge. After a while, he suddenly said, 'So, eaten many good apples lately?' I glanced at him, horrified, but he was wearing his angelic look. For a split second, Jonty's brows drew together, but then he grinned.

'Lots!' he said, and began whistling through his teeth.

Jonty stayed with us until the following Wednesday. Caro moved out of the front bedroom and slept on a truckle bed in the other; she said our chattering kept her awake, and she needed her sleep, even if we didn't.

It was only after I had been inside Jonty's home in Crane Lane that I truly appreciated how lucky our family was. Greening's cottages were hovels. The old thatch was filthy and sagging, full of sprouting weeds, housing any number of small creatures. The chimneys had not been swept for years. Many panes of glass were broken or missing entirely and the window and door frames were rotten. Jonty's father had stuffed rags in some of the many cracks and papered over the windows, but icy drafts eddied around the Tickle cottage, picking up the dirt from the earth floor. A layer of grime covered everything. Occasionally, one of the women from the other cottages would take pity on Mr Tickle, damping the floor to lay the dust and sweeping it out, and flicking a duster around, but he was so belligerent when in his cups that such charitable overtures were few and far between.

Michael Tickle was illiterate. He could not sign his own name, but had to make his mark with a cross, and even that wavered all over the place. There was nothing to read in Jonty's home, no one to help him with his reading and writing. He was amazed at the number of books we had. Grandfather Farley usually gave Mother one for her birthday. Of late, he had taken to slipping her volumes from his bookroom, telling her that he would not be reading them again, and she may as well have them. (They would often be restored to his library. Whenever Louisa visited Bearshott, she would examine our bookshelf and, picking out any that she recognised, would say, 'Oh, I wondered where that had gone! I'll take it back for you, shall I?' Forewarned of her visit, on one occasion Mother took care to hide the copy of *The Adventures of Roderick Ransom*, a favourite of Georgie's). Mother was particularly fond of Dickens and Austen. Caro used to read aloud to Georgie and me, from Mother's old copy of *Grimm's Fairy Tales*. When we were little, we often had nightmares about the stories, but as we grew older, we found the goriest ones were those we preferred. We were allowed to look at any book that interested us. All our family excelled at reading. Such opportunities had never come Jonty's way; it was no surprise that he had never learnt the trick.

As our friendship grew, Jonty would call at our cottage on the way to school, and would often return with us in the afternoon, whilst his father was still at the mill. It became usual for him to be given a place at our table, to have Mother comb his hair before we set off in the morning – as she did for Georgie and me – and to listen to his news. She ordered some primers from Grandfather's shop and started to help him with his reading. In time he had improved enough to sit with us, away from the young children, whom he towered above.

He also towered above me. I was small for my age, a result, Mother said, of my being such a sickly infant. I did grow over the years, but not above middling height, unlike the other Broughton boys. I am not much like them. They are all fair-haired giants, whereas I am somewhat swarthy of complexion, with dark curly hair. It is only when we smile that most people can catch the resemblance; we have all inherited Father's mischievous grin.

Jonty also loved to look at the numerous pictures that were pinned to our walls. Some were framed prints, purchased on trips to Isleworth or Hounslow, but most were Caro's drawings. At school, she had a habit of doodling in the margins of her books, earning a clip around the ear from her teachers in Isleworth, but Miss Rowlatt recognised her talent, and hit upon an idea whereby this might be developed.

She had a cousin who happened to be an up-and-coming portraitist. He had his studio in Camden Town, and, she thought, could be willing to take Caro on as a pupil. She made discreet enquiries with the artist before laying her plan before Father and Mother. At the outset, they were wary of committing their youngest daughter to the care of a stranger, who might be leading the hedonistic lifestyle of the artistic set. The Rowlatts assured them that this was far from the case, Arthur Haddington being an upright and sober fellow member of the Temperance Movement.

After an exchange of assurances, and an invitation to visit Camden Town, it was finally agreed that Caro would take this opportunity. In return for preparing his colours for him and some occasional modelling, and general domestic duties, Haddington would accept her as a pupil. If she proved to be as talented as Miss Rowlatt believed, he undertook to help her to gain commissions on her own account, so that she might, eventually, earn a living with her paints and brushes.

Caro was over the moon. It was a sad day when we waved her goodbye. Both Mother and Caro were in tears, and I have my suspicions about Father. Joe had undertaken to convey her to Camden and to see that she and her belongings were safely installed. When he returned, he came over to our cottage and described, in careful detail, Caro's room, Mr Haddington's studio and workshop, and such of the remainder of the house as he had been permitted to see. Reassured, Mother looked forward to receiving the first of, she trusted, many interesting letters.

Over the next two weeks, Mother checked our post box (made by Father to Caro's design and mounted on the wall next to the front door) several times each day, until, at last, the eagerly-awaited letter arrived. She read it aloud to us –

Father, Georgie and me, and Joe, who had come across for supper.

Caro was ecstatic about everything. Mr Haddington was a very gentlemanly man (heavily underlined). He had allowed her to open the door to several important clients, though not to be present as he took their likenesses. Her domestic duties were light, since a maid-of-all-work came each day. Mr Haddington referred to his studio as his atelier. She was learning all about pigments, and how to mix them to his satisfaction, and he was teaching her about perspective. Her little room was cosy, hardly suffering from drafts at all, and she had a lamp, so was able to read a little, if she liked, before going to sleep. She would be home for Christmas, as Mr Haddington was invited to stay with one of his Academician friends for the festivities, if Joe could collect her? Father and Mother were satisfied.

That summer, Georgie, Jonty, and I were together just about every day. With no Caro to supervise us, our games became more adventurous. We would often go out as soon as breakfast and our chores were done, and not return until the sun was beginning to set. We particularly enjoyed going to Hounslow Heath, where its wild landscape provided ample scope for our escapades. We took our slingshots, flew kites, made 'dens', and put the wind up any girls or smaller boys that dared to invade our territory.

In one of our early games, we were a gang of highwaymen – Caro having been reading *Rookwood* to us before she left – taking it in turns to be the notorious Dick Turpin. But the other children we played with grew bored of only being allowed to be coachmen, victims, and tavern keepers, and drifted away to play their own games. For a while, we three wandered over the Heath, sometimes joining in other children's games, but mostly just mooching about, taking potshots with our catapults. We missed having a theme for our play, yet no replacement for the highwaymen game occurred to us.

We were saved by Napoleon and Mr Rowlatt. Not our Mr Rowlatt, but his father, who had served in Wellington's army. He came to Bearshott, at his children's invitation, to talk about his experiences in the Napoleonic Wars. The largest room in our little school was used for the event and, as entrance was free, was packed as full as it would hold. Smaller children were confined to their elders' laps, and many people had to squeeze themselves in around the edges of the room. All the Bearshott Broughtons were in attendance that Saturday evening. Even Mr Tickle came, together with Jonty.

The raised platform built across one end of the room normally accommodated the teacher's desk and a blackboard and easel. The desk had been cleared of its usual paraphernalia. On it lay some large rolls of paper – which turned out to be maps – and a number of intriguing artefacts, whose mysteries were yet to be explained. Some more papers, threaded through with string, hung over the blackboard.

Captain Rowlatt was a skilful speaker, able to describe, in vivid and exciting detail, the major battles he had himself fought in, including that at Waterloo, whilst never emphasising his own part (we learned, later, that his captaincy was due to a field commission, and he had twice been mentioned in dispatches). Like Nelson, he had only one arm; one of the exhibits was his own jacket, with its shredded right sleeve covered in old brown bloodstains, together with the ball that had splintered his arm bones. He was able to describe the parts various armies had played – he did not think all our allies were of much use – and who had led them. His charts included plans of the various battlefields and the dispositions of each army.

The veteran's lecture was further enlivened with many interesting anecdotes: Napoleon liked to tuck his hand inside his tunic because, it was said, he suffered from chronic indigestion; Wellington was known as 'Old Hooky'; every soldier who fought at Waterloo, Ligny or Quatre Bas in 1815 was awarded a special campaign medal, the first to be sent to the next of kin of those men who had been killed in action (Captain Rowlatt's own medal, with his name impressed around the edge, was on the table) and received two years' extra pay and service; Wellington's horse, Copenhagen, was given a full military funeral when it died.

The Captain also spoke a little about Nelson's victory at Trafalgar, which had taken place ten years before Waterloo. He did not know as much about naval strategy as he did about soldiering, but was able to impart such interesting snippets as that Nelson's famous signal should have read *England confides that every man should do his duty*, but, there being no flag for 'confides', 'expects' was flown instead. Napoleon had adopted the message, and had broadcast a French version to encourage his own men. And when Nelson died, his body was put in a barrel of brandy for the journey home. At the close of his lecture, the old soldier invited his audience to come and look at the objects displayed on the table; he would try to answer any questions that were asked of him.

Georgie and I went to bed that night, our heads full of heroic deeds; it was a long time before we settled down to sleep. We could hardly wait for Monday when we would next be allowed to go off to the Heath. Over dinner the following day, we told Grandfather about the Captain's talk, but we must have confused him somehow, for he only said that he had once danced with the Emperor's wife, and that Wellington had put him in charge of a troop of cavalry.

Mondays were generally wash-days, when most housewives were glad to have their children gone from under their feet. The day bid fair – the sun was shining, and a light breeze stirred the trees. The laundresses had no fear of rain spoiling their sheets, shirts, and shifts, and we looked forward to a day spent under cloudless skies.

Georgie and I collected Jonty and made our way, along with many of the other Bearshott children, to the Heath. As we went along, we described, to those who had not had the good fortune to be present on Saturday evening, the glorious actions we had heard about. We felt we were experts and knew all there was to know about the battles. That day was the first of many that summer when we played the Waterloo game.

There were often children from the southern outskirts of Hounslow and Isleworth playing on the Heath, and occasionally from Whitton and Twickenham. Naturally, they were all seen as interlopers to 'our' part of the Heath. We allowed them to join in our wargames, but the Twickers had to play Frenchmen, whilst the others were the Prussian army. Being unsure of exactly what role this had played, sometimes the Prussians fought on the English side, and sometimes on the French, wherever it was needed to even up the numbers. If we were short, some girls were allowed to be soldiers (although they had to be the ones who 'died' first), but generally they were 'camp followers'. Now, Captain Rowlatt had not mentioned these in his lecture, so where the idea came from, goodness knows. Luckily, we had no real idea what such women might be doing, so in our games they sharpened swords, reloaded guns, mopped brows, and did a lot of bandaging. The Waterloo game usually ended with 'Hoogoomon'. We battled to close the gates against overwhelming enemy numbers, before winning through and being knighted by the Iron Duke himself.

Sometimes, when we three were playing by ourselves, we would act out Nelson's death aboard the *Victory*. Jonty, one or other arm stuffed inside his shirt, died a glorious, noisy, and blood-curdling death, whilst Georgie and I heroically dealt with the dastardly French sniper. After, we would stow Nelson in his brandy barrel, and pretend to drink the barrel dry. Georgie's interpretation of the effects of too much drink was most realistic and, at first, very funny to watch. But he and I soon realised that it reminded Jonty of his father, and the game was quietly abandoned.

That summer passed pleasantly enough, the last real summer of childhood. Jonty and I were nine. He was destined to leave school before the next summer, although I would continue my education for another two or three years. Georgie was twelve and would soon be looking for work. He had started to keep company with boys of his own age, rather than with us.

A week or so before we were to return to school for the autumn term, it seemed as though every child within a five mile radius had come onto the Heath. The entire day was spent playing the Waterloo game – for the last time, as it happened. The following days were wet and windy, and none of us were allowed out onto the muddy common. It was also the last time that Georgie played with we younger children.

The mammoth game ended, as usual, with our version of the siege of Hougoumont farm. Jonty had fashioned a sword for himself, out of two pieces of wood bound together, and was waving it about his head, to the serious danger of all those nearby. Leaping onto a small hillock, he suddenly yelled, 'Up the Jays!'

'The Jays?'

'Sure. You, me and Georgie,' he panted, taking another vigorous swipe at some poor Twickers.

'Er…Georgie is with a G, not a J,' I pointed out.

'Oh,' said Jonty, crestfallen.

'Never mind,' I grinned, slapping him on the back. 'It's a good name. The Jays it is.'

7. Igloo

The Bury sits four-square between Bearshott and Hounslow Heath. Any rider, or vehicle, wishing to go from the village to the Heath must travel up Waleric Lane, take the turn to Isleworth, and so on to the southern outskirts of Hounslow town, a distance of over seven miles. The shortest route, were the owner to permit its use, would be along the tree-lined avenue that extended between the eastern lodge, opposite Wyck Green, across the front of the main house, and straight on to The Bury's western boundary – a distance not much above two miles. Those on foot were obliged to follow the longer route via Crane Lane, as far as its entrance to Greening's powder mill, then take the footpath that ran across the back of the works yard, and so onward to the Heath.

Matthew Greening was very jealous of his rights and had made moves to have access to this footpath, which ran across his land, denied to the village, claiming that its proximity to the mill rendered it dangerous to users. However, reference to old maps proved beyond doubt that this was an ancient right of way, in existence long before the powder mill had been constructed, and his application came to nought. He considered fencing the footpath along its entire length, but not only would that prove costly, it would also inhibit his workers' access to the willow, alder and dogwood that grew there, which were necessary in the manufacture of his gunpowder. He contented himself with having several large signs erected, embellished with skull-and-crossbones, exhorting walkers to keep to the path BY ORDER, and commanding his workers to ensure that nobody strayed off the narrow way by so much as a step onto the yard. In this, he was also frustrated, for the majority of users were the families of the men working at the mill, and a blind eye was turned to any infringements.

One mizzly day during the short Easter school break, Joss and Jonty were kicking their heels in the Tickle cottage, trying to decide how to spend the day. Had they thought of it sooner, Joss said, they could have gone up to Covent Garden with Joe. Georgie had gone off somewhere with his friends, and most of their other playmates were being kept indoors, because of the weather.

'I could show you another way to the Heath,' Jonty offered. 'It's a bit muddy, I expect, but you won't mind that. It's shorter than the footpath.'

Joss's brow wrinkled. He could not think where such a path might be and said so. Jonty grinned.

'I found it when I was looking for apples, ages ago. After I got chased away from the best ones in the village.'

Joss laughed at the memory. 'Georgie was a fine shot, wasn't he? Alright, show us.'

The boys crossed the lane outside the cottage. On the other side, a narrow ditch – fairly dry, despite the rain – lay between the roadway and a high bank topped with hawthorn. Checking that no one was coming along the lane, Jonty stepped across the ditch, clambered up the bank and pushed his way through the prickly hedge.

'It's harder when the leaves are out,' he called down to Joss, unhooking his jacket from a thorn. 'It's a lot thicker, then.'

Joss scrambled up behind him and found himself at the edge of a small woodland. To their right, open land undulated toward Bearshottbury and its formal gardens, presently shrouded beneath a blanket of ground mist. A colony of wild rabbits, disturbed by their arrival, scuttered off to their warrens. Joss and Jonty plunged into the wilderness and were soon hidden from the view of anyone who might happen to be looking out of one of The Bury's many windows.

Joss looked about him. 'Well, I can't see any apples,' he remarked.

'I didn't say I *found* any. C'mon, this way,' Jonty said, plunging deeper into the undergrowth. 'This wood goes right across to the Heath. You have to watch out for the bailiff, though. He sometimes comes into the woods to patrol along the footpath.'

The woodland had largely been left to fend for itself. No hand had been set to cut back shrubbery, root out saplings, or tidy away fallen tree trunks, only the stretch behind the powder mill being coppiced. Matthew Greening viewed it only as a pleasant backdrop to the nearer landscape. Never venturing there himself, he was uninterested in its management, content to let nature have its way. The resulting tangle was paradise to two small boys bent on adventure – especially when they were where they had no right to be. The 'shortcut to the Heath' was quite forgotten in the excitement of exploration.

The wood was full of climbable trees and logs, pools of standing water, and small clearings. A dried-up streambed, a long-ago tributary of the Crane, snaked its way in a big loop, heading back toward the powder mill. Joss and Jonty scuffed through the woodland litter, sending showers of dead leaves into the air. The rain had become lethargic, unable to decide between producing a good downpour or just drizzling away the afternoon. Only the most determined raindrops were able to penetrate the thick canopy, and the boys were immune beneath its protection.

'We must tell Georgie about this!'

'Of course – but no one else. We don't want the whole of

Bearshott turning up,' warned Jonty.

Pushing further into the dense brushwood, careless of snaggings, they came upon a near-circular glade, in the centre of which stood what appeared to be a pile of rubble. On closer inspection, they found it to be a round, domed, stone hut. Its floor, set at a lower level than the surrounding ground, was thickly carpeted with the woodland detritus that had blown in through the open doorway.

'Wow!' breathed Joss, entranced. 'Did you know this was here?'

'No. Never been this far in before,' replied Jonty. 'What do you suppose it is?'

'Dunno. It looks very old. I bet cavemen lived in it.'

'Can't've done – it's not a cave. Romans, maybe? I wonder if there are any skeletons in there? Or armour?'

Having equipped themselves with a couple of stout sticks from amongst the rubbish lying about outside, Jonty was the first to step into the little building, but found himself falling, the floor level lying much lower than they had supposed.

'You alright?' called Joss anxiously, peering into the gloomy interior.

'Fine, just a bit winded. All these leaves are like a carpet,' said Jonty, getting to his feet. His head was now on a level with the bottom of the doorway. 'Let me see if I can get out again.' Running his hands over the stonework looking for possible handholds, he was surprised to find a short iron ladder bolted to the wall. Grabbing it firmly, he gave it a good shake. 'There's a ladder here,' he called up. 'Seems to be alright.' Mounting the four rungs, he observed, 'It's cold in there.' He eyed the doorway speculatively. 'If we hung something across the door, and cleared out all the leaves, this would make a great den, wouldn't it?'

They climbed down into the hut. A thorough examination of the floor disclosed, to their unacknowledged relief, no bones, nor, to their loud disappointment, any swords, daggers, or helmets, Roman or otherwise. They began to scoop up armfuls of leaves and toss them out of the hut.

'This won't do,' panted Joss. 'They'll only blow back in. We need to make a door, first.'

'Yeah. And we need something to put the leaves in, or it's going to take forever to get them all out.'

Reluctantly, having decided that they would not be able to continue with their renovations until they had provided themselves with some bags, or shovels, and something with which to block the doorway, they abandoned the hut for the time being.

Looking over his shoulder as they left, Joss remarked, 'You know what it really reminds me of? An igloo.'

Jonty stopped and studied the building. 'You're right. It's cold enough inside to be made of ice.'

They wandered deeper into the wood. Men's voices warned them that they were nearing the mill yard. The disputed footpath lay before them, and beyond it the assorted buildings that constituted the works.

'Look!' said Joss, pointing. 'There's your dad.' They stood on the path for a while, watching the activity in the yard, until they heard the sound of a dog barking somewhere in the woods behind them.

'That's the bailiff's dog!' warned Jonty. It was not many minutes before the bailiff appeared, armed with a cudgel, with a ferocious hound of uncertain origins straining on its leash.

'What're you two boys doing here?'

'Just looking.'

'Make sure that's all you do. Be off with you. And keep to the path – it's dangerous down there.'

That evening, Joss told Georgie about the igloo. The worsening weather continued for several days, so that nearly a week passed before the boys could return to the site. In the meantime, they had acquired some old sacks and a length of rope. Georgie, at thirteen, had largely outgrown most of Joss and Jonty's games, but their description of the little stone hut intrigued him, and he was eager to see this marvel for himself.

It took them some time to locate the clearing since neither Joss nor Jonty had an accurate recollection of the route they had taken, resulting in a somewhat heated debate that threatened to bring the expedition to a summary end. Happily, harmony was restored when they stumbled across the dried-up streambed and agreed that the igloo lay nearby.

Walking right around the building and subjecting it to a critical study, Georgie finally gave it as his opinion that it was not so old as the younger boys had hoped, though he could not suggest when it might have been constructed until the interior had been cleared out. They set to with a will, and after about an hour had succeeded in emptying out the debris. The circular inside was brick-lined and measured about three yards across. The floor sloped into the middle, where there was a drain. Poking into it with a stick, Georgie said that, despite all the rubbish that had lain over it, it did not appear to be blocked. Three heads hovered above the drain, although it was far too dark to see into it.

'Well, that'll be handy,' pronounced Jonty. Joss and Georgie gave him querying looks. 'We shan't have to go outside to piss!'

Joss shivered. 'We'll have to build a fire if we want this as a den. And we'll need candles.'

'And something to sit on,' Jonty added.

They stood about for a while, discussing the articles that would turn the cold space into a cosy den. Agreeing that they had done all they could for the time being, one of the sacks was secured across the entrance to stop any more leaves from blowing in.

During the remainder of the Easter holidays, and after school, Joss and Jonty trailed back and forth, until the igloo was furnished with a small brazier (scrounged from Mr Broughton), a broken chair (recovered from the ditch in Crane Lane), two crates and an old lamp (found in a shed in Allnutt's Yard), and some cushions (donated by Mrs Broughton). Since the clearing was some way from the footpath, the bailiff never came anywhere near, and the boys were able to enjoy their hideaway without fear of discovery. Georgie, his curiosity satisfied, was content to leave his juniors in sole possession.

Philadelphia knelt on the nursery window-seat, her chin cupped in one hand, her favourite doll tucked under her arm, looking out over the formal gardens and open lawns to the woodland beyond. She was particularly watching for the two small figures she had sometimes seen at the woodland's edge; she wondered where they went when they disappeared from view. She had never heard anyone else mention them, nor had she ever noticed Papa's bailiff walking that way. Perhaps they could only be seen from up here on the third floor.

Her lessons over for the day, her governess had retired to her own quarters. She had had her tea and Nurse had left her to play by herself until bath time, after which, if Mama had no company, she would be taken down to the drawing-room to kiss that opulent lady goodnight. Papa would not be present. He would still be at his mill, or perhaps away on some business. Philadelphia felt no affection for these two remote people. It was only on Sunday mornings that she spent any time with them, when they all went to church, and even then she did not share their pew.

Her only companions, if they could be called such, were to be found amongst the servants whose job it was to feed, wash and dress her, educate her, and produce her for her parents' inspection when required, but otherwise to keep her out of their sight and hearing. She felt little affection for her governess – a strict disciplinarian – or her nurse, neither of whom were given to bestowing a gentle word or a hug. The only servant who showed her any kindness was the nurserymaid, a girl of about fifteen, who had recently joined the household and was homesick for the jolly, noisy family she had left behind in Feltham.

Returning to the nursery after a visit to the water-closet

along the corridor, Philadelphia noticed that the door leading from the nursery wing to the servants' staircase had been left ajar. She had never penetrated those mysterious depths, nor had she ever been outside the house unaccompanied. She had no idea where her boots and coat were to be found – they were always produced by one of the servants, ready for her to put on whenever she went out – but as she was doubtful that she could put them on without assistance, she wasted no time in searching for these articles. Holding her doll tightly, she peered around the door. Hearing no sounds from below, she crept forward and began to descend the stairs. At the bottom, she found herself in a wide, flagged passageway. To her right, a room – thankfully empty – which appeared to be an office of some sort (she could see a desk with papers on it through the open door), lay across the end of the corridor. To her left, a number of doors seemed to lead off the passage into other rooms. At the far end, servants were crossing to and fro around a large table covered with crockery. The clattering of pots and pans, and the sound of talking, warned her that there were plenty of people about, any one of whom might come into the corridor at any moment. In front of her, the door to the kitchen yard stood invitingly open to the spring sunshine. Hearing a raised voice that seemed to be getting nearer, Philadelphia took a deep breath and dived through.

She had never been in the kitchen yard before, but she could see that it met the carriageway that ran in front of the house, beyond which were the gardens and grounds she could see from the nursery window. Creeping forward along the side of the house, she peered around the corner. No carriage stood in front of the main door, no gardener was tending the flowers, there were no scythemen on the lawns, and there was no sign of the lodgekeeper at the Bearshott entrance away to her left. Throwing caution to the winds, Philadelphia took a firmer hold on her toy and sprinted as fast as she could across the drive, through the formal garden and on to the grass beyond. The land was uneven; a dip enabled her to sit and catch her breath, out of sight of anyone on the ground floor.

She gained the edge of the wood without incident. Too scared to go far by herself, she only ventured deep enough to be hidden from the house. Looking about her, she noticed a faint track leading further into the wood and could see that it came from the direction of the village.

Nervously, she slowly followed the path as it snaked its way around trees and bushes. If she became frightened, she could turn around and follow it back to the beginning, but it just might lead her to the two children she had glimpsed from time to time. After twenty minutes, Philadelphia came out into a small clearing, in the centre of which was a small building. The ground all about had been trampled down.

'Hello?' she called. There was no answer. She tried again. Receiving no reply, she cautiously approached the building and stood in front of the sack that was tied across what seemed to be a doorway, trying to pluck up the courage to look inside. Gingerly, she lifted one corner and twitched the canvas aside. After the bright May sunshine, it was very dark inside. It took a moment or two for her eyes to adjust to the gloom and to realise that two pairs of eyes were regarding her from below. Convulsively, her hand tightened on the sacking. She stepped back, and the sack came away from the door. 'Oh!'

'Careful!' warned a voice. 'Girls! Useless!' Then, suspiciously, 'Are you on your own?'

Philadelphia would have liked to put her thumb in her mouth, as she did whenever she was worried or tired. Hugging her doll close instead, she nodded. There came much muttering from below.

Joss and Jonty climbed out of the stone hut. 'Well, who are you, anyway?' demanded Jonty, arms folded across his chest.

'She's the Greening girl,' observed Joss, who had recognised the dress sewn by his mother.

'That's torn it. She'll go and blab to her father.'

'No, I won't!' she said indignantly.

'That's a load of my eye and Betty Martin! 'Course you will. Girls can never keep secrets.'

'I can.'

'Well, why are you here?'

She thought she might cry. These boys were rough and rude, particularly the big one. She was regretting her little adventure and would have liked to be back in her nursery with all her toys. The thumb crept into the side of her mouth. 'I saw you,' she mumbled around the digit and through her doll's hair. Joss and Jonty looked at each other in consternation.

'That's torn it,' said Joss gloomily. 'Might as well pack up.' Jonty aimed a kick at a lump of wood, shying it into the undergrowth.

Removing the thumb, Philadelphia offered, 'No one else saw.'

Jonty frowned at her. 'How can you be sure?'

'They would've made a fuss.'

'Hmph. Why are you here, then?' he demanded again. Replacing the thumb, Philadelphia shrugged. 'You must know why you're here! Honestly!'

'I wanted to see where you went.' She hesitated. 'And – to see if I could play with you.'

'We don't play with little girls,' Jonty announced.

Philadelphia was getting cross. She had risked a beating by stealing away from the house; she had never before been outside unaccompanied by one of the servants; she had had a long and tiring walk through a huge and creepy forest, which was probably full of unseen but fearsome creatures; and finally, the very children she had hoped would become exciting new friends turned out to be two scruffy bullies who didn't want her around.

She stamped her foot (not so effectively as when she did so on the wooden floorboards of the nursery) and said, 'Then I shall tell my Papa all about you. And he will tell his bailiff.

And he will come, *with his dog*, and lock you up! And you will die in prison, or go to Australia, and it will serve you right!' With that, she burst into tears.

'There!' said Jonty, disgusted. 'Told you so! Can't keep a secret and cry when they don't get their own way.'

'Yes, maybe, but what are we going to do about her?'

Hiccoughing, Philadelphia, her tears gradually drying, watched the two as they debated her fate. Eventually, they seemed to have come to a decision.

'What if we let you join our gang? As a sort of mascot?'

'What gang?' she sniffed.

'Well, us. And Georgie, sometimes.'

'Who's Georgie?' she asked, mystified.

'He's – well, never mind who he is, he just comes sometimes.'

'What's a mascot?' she asked suspiciously.

'It's like – a – a symbol,' Jonty said.

'A *special* symbol,' Joss added hurriedly, with a sideways warning glance at Jonty.

'What would I have to do?'

'Nothing. Just swear to keep the igloo secret.'

'What igloo? I don't know what you mean.' Philadelphia could feel the tears coming again.

Impatiently, Jonty gestured at the stone building. 'That,' he said, 'is the igloo.'

Philadelphia frowned. 'No, it's not. It's an icehouse.'

'Icehouse? What's an icehouse?'

'Somewhere where ice is kept, of course.'

'What ice? There's no ice in there,' said Jonty. 'Sounds like nonsense to me.'

'It's not nonsense. You collect the ice when it's cold and put it in there and it keeps cold all the time until you want to use it.'

'Hah! So you say. So why isn't it full of ice now?'

'Papa doesn't use it. I think it might be broken.'

Joss, feeling that they were wandering away from the issue at hand, intervened. 'Never mind all that. It's an igloo to us. Now, what about this mascot thing? You would have to swear to keep the igloo – icehouse – and us, secret. On pain of death.'

'Alright.'

'Repeat after me: I swear—'

'I swear.'

'On pain of death—'

'Or transportation,' interjected Jonty.

'On pain of death or transportation.'

'To keep the secrets of the igloo.'

'To keep the secrets of the igloo.'

'So help me God.'

'So help me God.'

'Signed…What is your name, anyhow?'

'Philadelphia Eugénie Greening.'

'Phila what?'

'Poor little cow,' said Jonty, sympathetically.

'I am *not* a – what you said. And it's not my fault. I didn't choose it.'

'We'll have to find another name for you, or half our time will be spent just saying your name whenever we want to talk to you. What do your friends call you?'

Not being blessed with any friends, Philadelphia offered, 'The servants call me Miss Philadelphia.'

'Well I'll be blowed – that's even longer! And I'm not calling you 'miss' – sounds like school. We'll have to think of something else.'

Seeing the corners of Philadelphia's mouth beginning to turn down, Joss added hastily, 'Of course. A *special* name. Like a secret code for the igloo. How about…' thinking hard, 'Philly?'

'But that sounds like a horse. I don't want to sound like a horse. Or any other animal,' she added hurriedly. Mentally chopping her name up into smaller segments, it was finally agreed that she would be known simply as Phia.

Phia very nearly threw a spanner in the works by suggesting that the boys ought to have secret igloo names too. Agreeing on one name had been tiresome enough; the boys did not want to waste any more time on the topic and said so most forcefully. The bottom lip began to quiver again.

'But we already have a secret name!' Joss said. 'The Three Jays!'

'Why am I a Jay? I thought I was to be Phia?'

'Not you, silly,' said Jonty, exasperated. 'It's us and Georgie.'

'But you said Georgie doesn't come here,' she objected.

'Never mind that. It doesn't matter whether he's here or not. *And*,' he added, forestalling any such suggestion, 'we won't be the Four Jays, because none of your names begins with a J!'

'Neither does Georgie's,' Phia muttered.

Joss hastily intervened, before the argument could develop further, suggesting that the newest member of their secret society might like to see inside their headquarters. Whilst Jonty rearranged the sacking across the doorway, Joss guided Phia down the little iron ladder. The gloomy depths of the stone hut were unlike anywhere she had ever been, and privately she found them rather disappointing. However, determined to claim these two fascinating beings as friends, she admired the various pieces of broken furniture, agreed that Elizabeth's cushions made them most comfortable, and said, with truth, that the small fire certainly warmed the place up, so that one would never suspect the building's original purpose.

Expanding on the notion of forming a secret club, Jonty said that all the best societies had some sort of signal that only members knew, and that they should do the same. Debating the suggestion, it was finally agreed that crossed fingers on the right hand laid upon the left wrist would serve as a greeting when in other company, and crossed fingers on the left hand would serve as a warning of some unspecified, but deliciously frightful, danger.

As they sat around the brazier, Phia told them how she had managed to slip away from The Bury without being seen (as far as she knew). Even Jonty was secretly impressed by the pluck she had shown, disguising his admiration by suggesting that, another time, she might like to smuggle some cake, as well as herself, out of the house. Phia promised to try, although, she said, she was rarely left alone with any food. Talk of food reminded Jonty of his dinner. Peering past the sacking, he observed that the light was failing, and it was perhaps time they should all be getting home.

Together, they walked back through the woods, pointing out various landmarks that Phia should take note of so that she shouldn't get lost on her way to the hut. She left them at the edge of the wilderness and made her way back across the broad sweep of open ground.

'Do you think she'll be caught?'

'Probably,' Jonty replied gloomily. 'Perhaps we'd better not come here for a few days.'

A man weeding in the formal garden looked at Philadelphia curiously as she passed but made no remark. The kitchen door was ajar. Pausing, she could hear the bustle of servants preparing dinner. Peeping cautiously around the door, she saw that there was no one in the corridor; the path to the stairs was clear. Taking a deep breath, she ran across the passage and up the stairs. She did not notice the housekeeper watching her from her office.

Georgie rarely thought about the Three Jays. He had been mildly interested when Joss first told him of the igloo and, having examined it for himself, he was content to let his juniors have their fun without him, merely giving half an ear whenever they had some new tale of their secret den to relate. However, when they had told him of Philadelphia Greening's visit, he warned them against encouraging her, for not only would she be in trouble herself if it were discovered, but he was also pretty sure that it would not be just Joss and Jonty who would have to answer to her father. Having done his duty by them in issuing this warning, Georgie thought no more about it.

Joss and Jonty avoided going onto Greening land for several days, but as time passed with no dire retribution exacted, they concluded that either Philadelphia had not been caught, or, if she had, she had kept their secret, and that it was safe to return to the stone hut. The trips to the igloo were resumed.

Philadelphia would watch for them from her nursery window. If there were no one about, neither the household servants nor the men working in the gardens, she would sneak out of the house to join them.

Philadelphia's initial success had emboldened her. No one appeared to have noticed her absence. She plucked up the courage to open the stair door, creeping down to peer carefully into the passageway, noting the servants' routine, and working out when the way across to the exit would most likely be clear.

Mindful of Jonty's exhortation, she tried to hide her tea-time cake in her pinny pocket, but the maid noticed and began tut-tutting about the crumbs which, she said darkly, would have to be emptied out by Somebody before the garment could be washed, and she hoped that Miss was not going to make a habit of it. Philadelphia assured her that she only wanted to save the cake for later, not being terribly hungry just now, and put it back on her plate. The maid sniffed, advising her to eat up as she had other things to do and, besides, Madam would not care to know that her daughter had lost her appetite. Philadelphia meekly ate the cake. Since she, like her mother, had a sweet tooth, she was rather glad not to have to share.

8: Summer 1851

Georgie had discovered girls. More specifically, the person of Miss Minerva Shelley, who lived on the opposite side of Wyck Green, and who occupied his waking thoughts and, damply, some of his sleeping ones. They had known one another all their lives. Where once Georgie and his particular pals, Brandon White and Tom Fletcher, had adjourned to the Green after lessons, there to kick a ball about, or rag the younger boys, he now steered them to the patch of grass that fronted the Shelley gate, where they would lounge about, hoping, for his part, to catch a glimpse of this goddess. That she took no special interest in him, either on the Green or at school, diminished his feelings not a jot.

One day at supper, the Broughtons were enjoying a family meal together, talking over the doings of the day.

'How about you, Georgie?' said Elizabeth. 'What have you done today?'

Her son looked up from his plate. 'I wish you would not call me that,' he said.

Elizabeth's brow wrinkled in puzzlement. 'Call you what, dear?'

'Georgie,' he replied. Elizabeth and Edward exchanged glances.

'What would you like to be called, Geo—dear?'

'Call me George.'

'Oh!' Elizabeth said. 'Alright.'

Edward smiled to himself and picked up his newspaper, whilst Joss looked at George astounded, his spoon halfway to his mouth.

'Put it in your mouth, Joss, before you drop it on the tablecloth,' Edward advised.

Later, Joss and Jonty discussed this episode at length.

'I know what it is,' Jonty pronounced eventually. 'He thinks he's grown up.'

Joss mulled this over, before agreeing that it seemed the most likely explanation for George's peculiar behaviour. They took to saying, 'Here comes call-me-George' whenever he came into view, though not loudly enough for him to hear.

They began to keep a close eye on George's comings and goings, to see if this opinion (to them, entirely unwarranted) manifested itself in any other way. It was not long before they noticed how much time he and his friends spent on the common, not kicking a ball around as they used to, but hanging about apparently doing nothing.

It was some while before they linked this inactivity to the Shelley home. Sensing some further mystery, they asked Mr Broughton if they might borrow his telescope and took to spying on George in earnest. Crouching behind the front garden wall, the telescope trained on the further side of Wyck Green, they imagined themselves detectives.

George's strange behaviour whenever Minerva Shelley appeared, magnified by the spyglass, soon put them in possession of the facts of the case. Jonty in particular thought this hilarious.

'My eye! Call-me-George fancies Skinny Minnie!' he hooted. 'Who'd've thought?'

Edward, returning from an evening spent playing cribbage, observed, 'Mr Shelley was in The Admiral this evening. He complained about you boys hanging about in front of his house. I hope you haven't been making a nuisance of yourself, George.'

'No – no, father. It just happens to be a comfortable spot, that's all. We'll go somewhere else.'

'Good,' grunted Edward.

To George, the reprimand was like a cold shower. The fledgling crush suffered a body blow. It was not long before he began to wonder what on earth he had seen in Minerva Shelley. For her part, she was rather sorry that Brandon White would no longer be lounging in front of her home.

Towards the end of the summer term, Philadelphia informed the boys that she would not be able to come to the igloo during the holidays, as her brothers and sisters would be coming home: Tudor was taking a short vacation from his work at the Foreign Office, Phaedre and Euphronia were returning from their finishing school in Bath, and the twins were coming home from their boarding school. Many treats and outings were being planned.

Jonty also expected to be unable to visit the stone hut often; his father had secured work for him at the mill. He had wanted his son to leave school and start to earn a living, but the Rowlatts had persuaded him to let Jonty return to school in the autumn, for at least one more year. Joss was to help out at Oliver's nursery. They agreed that they would not expect to see Phia again until September, when all her visitors had left.

The day before her sisters were due to arrive, Philadelphia made one final trip to the igloo. She was so excited by the prospect of the delights in store that she was quite happy to say goodbye to her friends for two or three months.

Laoise McBride watched the little figure scamper across the parkland and disappear into the woods. Her lip curled. It was not her responsibility to care for the child. No doubt the governess was taking a nap and the nurserymaid was flirting with the boot boy. As for the parents – if they had no interest in the wellbeing of their daughter, why should anybody else? They did not realise how lucky they were. Some people struggled to feed and clothe their families, and had to watch helplessly as one by one their children died. Angrily, she crammed her sister-in-law's letter back into its envelope.

Philadelphia thought herself in heaven. The arrival of her siblings heralded a change in her lonely routine, passing from solitary days spent in either the schoolroom or the nursery to being the pet of her sisters. She was in awe of her eldest brother, Tudor, with his magnificent whiskers and air of superiority. He was old enough to be her father. She had hardly ever met him, but even he had a kind word or two and carelessly flicked her cheek with a tobacco-stained finger.

Only the boisterous twins threatened to spoil her enjoyment. At fifteen, they had no time for baby sisters – nor, indeed, older ones – and largely ignored her. But when no other amusement offered, they took to invading the nursery, tossing Philadelphia's toys about, exclaiming over those that they remembered from years ago, and knocking jigsaws, the Noah's Ark, and game pieces all over the floor. When the governess happened to look in as they were emptying the baby house whilst Philadelphia sat on her bed, thumb in mouth, tearful but uncomplaining, she reported their behaviour to their mother, stating that she could no longer work in a house where she was expected to supervise the tidying up of the nursery in addition to her usual duties. Margaretta Greening, afraid of losing the relatively inexpensive services of the woman, forbade Roman and Saxon the nursery.

In search of other means of expending their surplus energy, the twins began to explore The Bury itself. They roamed the house, generally making a nuisance of themselves. They investigated the cellars, kitchens and scullery, and were chased out of the butler's private sanctum. They hid some of the cutlery laid out ready for an evening dinner party, and ate several Maids of Honour which had been baked especially for afternoon visitors, thereby sending the cook into hysterics, which brought Mrs McBride onto the scene. The threat of another complaint sent them to the top of the house. They spent a happy hour, rummaging amongst dusty boxes of unwanted articles and old furniture in the attic, which came to an abrupt end when they barged into a room used as a dormitory for the servants and surprised a housemaid in a state of undress. Following the resulting uproar they were banished from the house altogether, and took themselves off to examine the various outbuildings.

After a failed attempt to cajole the stable lad into saddling up Tudor's spirited mare, and finding nothing to interest them in the milk parlour or laundry, they decided to take a look at the powder mill, and headed across the sun-drenched open ground in front of the house toward the woodland.

Matthew Greening watched with disfavour as the labourer wheeled a load of wood across the yard to one of the cylinder houses. Against his better judgement, he had yielded to the pleas of the Rowlatts and had kept him on, despite his history of drunkenness. True, Tickle had, to all appearances, remained sober; nevertheless, he had instructed the foreman to only give him tasks that kept him away from the more dangerous areas of the works. He was aware of at least three dozen fatalities in the district's gunpowder mills in the last fifty years and was determined to take no chance that might add to that number. And now, here was Tickle's loutish son as well, scuffling across the yard. He would instruct the foreman to keep a close eye on the pair of them. At the least hint of trouble, they would be given their marching orders. His reflections were interrupted by his sons, emerging from the woods.

'Hey, Pa!' called Roman, looking about. 'What's to do here today?'

Matthew's chest swelled with pride. How different were these two lads to those who worked at the mill: intelligent, refined, smart (though perhaps rather dishevelled today).

Superior in every way. He hoped that one – or, better, both – might be interested in the business after Cambridge. Tudor's decision to enter the Foreign Service had been a disappointment. 'Come!' he beamed. 'Let me show you around.'

The site occupied the best part of one and a half miles along the north bank of the Crane, where several punts plied up and down, moving supplies from one part of the works to another. Matthew explained that the manufacture of black powder required three ingredients: saltpetre (imported from India), charcoal, and sulphur. He waved toward the woodland they had just left.

'We grow willow and alder all along the back of the works, to make our charcoal. The wood is taken to the cylinder houses to be burnt,' indicating three brick buildings, 'which takes about eight hours or so. Then it's left to cool overnight before being removed and put in the storehouse.'

The three wandered through the works, Greening expounding on the various processes as they went. He related how the grough saltpetre, being impure, had to be refined, first by dissolving in water and boiling, then being left to cool and form crystals, then boiled and recrystallised twice more before the saltpetre – now called sal prunella – was refined. The crystals were then boiled once again, in the melting houses, and the resulting liquid was poured into copper moulds and left to cool, forming nitre cakes. The third ingredient, crystals of sulphur (he explained) had also to be heated and melted twice. He pointed out the composition mills, where the prepared nitre, charcoal and sulphur were separately ground into fine powders, ready to be combined in the mixing houses.

Warming to his theme, and delighted with the interest shown by his sons, Greening described the uses of the numerous buildings: the water-driven incorporating and glazing mills, with their tanned hide floors; the magazines, corning and dusting houses. They looked in on such ancillary buildings as the cooperage and the millwright's, the site manager's and foreman's offices, the packing shed, and the sluice, where the workers could have a wash.

Michael Tickle wiped his handkerchief around his face. Chopping wood was hot, thirsty work, even in the shade of the wood. Greening's presence in the yard made him nervous, as it always did. But today he felt jumpier than usual, probably because of the presence of the Greening twins and the way the three had stood looking at him, seemingly discussing himself and, maybe, Jonty. He was glad to see them move off. He fervently hoped that the Rowlatts were right; more schooling would enable his son to get better work than this. He could do with a drink.

Jonty was even hotter. He had been given the task of stripping the bark from the wood that his father collected and cutting it into three-foot lengths. The afternoon sun beat down. His penny halfpenny would be hard-earned today. After stacking the timber in the woodshed, he looked about him, expecting to see his father trundling another load across the yard. With no sign of him, Jonty sat himself down on the woodpile. Before long, tired from the heat and the hard work, he began to nod off.

'Oi, lad! We're not paying you to sit about!'

Jonty jerked awake and jumped to his feet. 'Sorry, sir.'

Looking at the pale, sweaty face, the foreman took pity on the boy. Tickle was nowhere to be seen, the afternoon was drawing to a close, and he doubted much more work could be got out of the lad. Besides, if he was tired, he would be more likely to have an accident with the sharp saw he had been using. 'Alright, son, get yourself off home.'

Rather than heading up Crane Lane, Jonty went up onto the footpath at the back of the works. Searching through the coppice, he found a barrow half-filled with cut timber, but no sign of his father. It was pleasant in the shade. Jonty had not visited the igloo for some time, and he decided to cut through the woods and pay it a visit.

He had not gone far before he heard talking off to his left and realised that the two Greening boys were also taking a short cut through the woods. Crouching down behind a fallen log, he tried to see the pair, meaning to wait until they had passed before doubling back to the footpath. Deeper voices behind him warned him that Mr Greening, his bailiff and, more worryingly, the bailiff's dog, were also in the woods, cutting off his retreat. He decided to make a run for it.

'Hey! You! What are you doing there? This is private land and you're trespassing!' bellowed the bailiff. 'Shall I let the dog loose, Mr Greening?'

Greening had recognised the fleeing figure. 'No. I know who that is. I'll deal with him. And his father.' Hearing the shouts, Roman and Saxon ran up, wanting to know what all the hullabaloo was about. 'It's one of the village boys, making a nuisance of himself.'

Disappointed to hear that the dog was not going to be let off its lead in pursuit of the miscreant, Roman said, 'We'll see him off for you, Pa!' and the pair hared off after Jonty.

Even though it was Greening land, Jonty was far more familiar with the layout of the woodland than were the twins. For a while, he was able to keep heading in the right direction without them gaining on him, until, already tired from a long day spent sawing timber under a hot sun, Jonty felt he could not go much further, and made for the shelter of the igloo. Exhausted, he tumbled through the doorway, banging his forearm on the ladder as he went, and cowered in the well of the little building.

He could hear the twins calling out to one another, sometimes sounding very near, at others fading into the distance. Although they knew of the icehouse, having come across it years before, they had not appreciated its possibilities as had Joss and Jonty. Fortunately for the latter, it did not occur to them to search it.

Eventually, the sounds of the chase disappeared, and Jonty

felt it would be safe to climb out of the igloo and go home. As he put one foot on the bottom rung of the ladder, he heard a snuffling from the doorway above. Had Joss been with him, he would have put on a show of bravado and gone on up to confront whatever it was. By himself, tired and a little scared, he was too nervous and crouched back down.

It was beginning to get dark. The day had been hot and sultry. The evening, contrariwise, was growing cold and damp. Jonty tried to mount the ladder once more, but found his arm hurt too much to grip the ironwork.

As Edward and Joss were walking down Crane Lane the next morning, on their way to Oliver's Nurseries for the day's work, they met Michael Tickle coming up the road.

'Did Jonathan stay with you last night?'

'No, Micky.'

'He didn't come home after work. I've just been to the mill. The foreman said he told him to get off home about six o'clock or so. No one seems to have seen him since.'

'Did you see him yesterday, Joss?' Joss shook his head. 'You're sure? You don't know where he might have gone?'

'No, Father.'

After checking his cottage, in case Jonty had returned home in the meantime, Michael accompanied the Broughtons to the nursery, to make enquiries there. With no new information, and with no idea of where Jonty might be, Martin Oliver suggested that two more of his workers should help make a thorough search of the route from the mill yards to the village. Joss, loudly complaining that he should be allowed to help in the search for his friend, was sent home.

Joss tracked George down to the little school, where he was helping the Rowlatts paint the walls of the classrooms. Now fifteen, he was due to leave for Isleworth in a few days, where his grandfather's connections had secured him a job on the canal as a lengthsman. Joss explained that Jonty had disappeared, somewhere on the way home from the gunpowder mill. He had not been seen since the previous afternoon, and Father, Mr Tickle and a couple of other men were making a search along Crane Lane. George looked at him narrowly.

'He'll have cut across the woods, won't he?'

'That's what I thought,' said Joss eagerly. 'Could you come and look with me?'

'We ought to tell Father.'

'But if we do that, he'll tell Mr Greening, and Jonty will be in terrible trouble. Couldn't we just go and look by ourselves first?'

'Well, if we're caught in there, we'll have to tell,' insisted George.

They made their way through the tangled undergrowth, carefully searching about as they went, until they came to the glade where the silent icehouse stood. Fearfully, Joss pulled back the sacking curtain and peered in.

'He's here!' he called over his shoulder, and made to go down the ladder.

'Wait!' George commanded, worried that no sound had come from Jonty. 'I'll go first.'

Jonty was lying on the floor of the igloo. George felt his cheek and was relieved to find it warm. Gently, he patted the pale face and called his name. With a sob, Jonty awoke and looked wildly about.

'It's alright, Jonty. It's only me – George.'

'My arm hurts,' Jonty whispered. 'I couldn't get out.'

'No, I know, old man. Don't worry, we'll have you home soon.'

Jonty was large for his age, nearly as big as George. It was difficult for George to manoeuvre him up the vertical ladder out of the icehouse, even without having to take care not to knock the injured arm, which he could see, by its strange angle, was broken. Joss did what he could from above, grabbing Joss by his clothing whilst George steadied him from below and pushed him upward. The necessarily rough

103

treatment had its effect. Once out of the igloo, Jonty was violently sick.

'Thank you,' he mumbled. 'They were chasing me. I was so tired…and then I fell…'

'Don't try to talk now. Tell us all about it later.' George looked at Joss. 'We can't get him home by ourselves. You stay with him while I go and get help.'

Miserably, Joss nodded.

9: *Aftermath*

The repercussions of Jonty's adventure were swift and painful. Edward wielded the rattan cane across Joss's backside half-heartedly. It had languished in a cupboard for years, hardly ever used, but Matthew Greening and the Rowlatts were adamant that the trespass merited some significant punishment. Jonty avoided this particular fate, even Greening conceding that a night spent alone in the cold with a broken arm, followed by the trial of having the limb reset, was corporal punishment enough. The Rowlatts had to work hard to persuade the mill owner not to sack Michael Tickle, which would have led to the pair being evicted from their tied cottage. However, Jonty was barred from ever again working at the mill. George came in for the lion's share of the criticism. He was blamed for not disclosing the younger boys' incursions onto Greening land, thereby tacitly condoning their actions.

Matthew Greening had the gap in the hedgerow where the boys had pushed through replanted, and all his hedges fronting Crane Lane and Waleric Lane were threaded through with barbed wire to discourage future invasions. The bailiff emptied the igloo and built a bonfire. The twins, hearing of this, pawed and exclaimed over the poor possessions and took great pleasure in putting a match to the pile.

Philadelphia escaped unscathed, her parents remaining in

blissful ignorance of her involvement with Jonty and Joss. Mrs McBride kept her own counsel.

The atmosphere in the Broughton cottage, usually so warm and placid, grew icy. Joss, only able to sit with care, was sulking because he was banned from visiting Jonty. George was in a sullen mood, after the scolding he had received – apparently he 'should've known better' (as though he would ever peach on his brother!). He was due to start work on the canal the following week, but he decided to go to Isleworth early, to escape any further recriminations.

It had been arranged that George would share Will's room in the Farley villa for the time being. Louisa, Simon, and their children were now firmly ensconced there, Grandfather Farley now only nominally the head of the house. Louisa prided herself on her benevolence in providing board and lodgings to her much younger brothers. With a large family to provide for, she looked forward to receiving the additional rent from George. Although he was to give up half his room, she did not think it necessary to make any downward adjustment to the sum Will was paying for the room, meals, and laundry, which was deducted from his shop wages.

On Saturday afternoon, George made the rounds of all his friends in the village, to say his farewells. Elizabeth had laid on a high tea as a treat. Joe came across from Allnutt's. He and Edward promised to take George over to The Admiral later, to give him a proper, grown-up, send-off. Joss and Jonty had pooled their resources some weeks before and bought him a metal fob in the shape of a shield, onto which they had, somewhat inexpertly, scratched his name, followed by 'Up the Jays'. George promised Joss that he would attach it to his key chain just as soon as he had one. Elizabeth presented him with a copy of Melville's *White Jacket*. He received this with particular pleasure, being very fond of tales of the sea (he was hoping to save enough money from his wages to buy the author's new book, due to be published in the autumn, which was, apparently, an exciting tale about whale hunters). The festivities led to a thaw in relations; by the end of the meal, harmony had been restored.

The following morning, the inhabitants of Bearshott gathered on Wyck Green, ready to walk together in the bright morning sunshine to attend the service at All Saints. Joe drew up in Abel Allnutt's smaller cart. Joss declined the offer of a lift, as he felt that walking would be less painful to his sore posterior than sitting in a jolting wagon. Jonty, still feeling rather under the weather, gratefully accepted the ride.

As the chattering, plodding cavalcade neared Isleworth, Matthew Greening's carriages came up behind. During their excavations in The Bury's attics earlier in the week, the twins had come across a battered old post horn, which Roman now blew up as if he were a postboy on a stagecoach. Joe edged the cart into the side of the road, whilst the walkers retreated to the verges. The Greening party swept past, ignoring the villagers. As they passed the wagon, Roman and Saxon called out to Jonty, asking if he had fallen down any good holes lately. Philadelphia felt sick with shame and embarrassment. She risked a glance at Jonty as their carriage overtook the cart. He was staring straight ahead, looking pale but (she thought) noble and heroic with his arm in a sling. She wished she could say something to him. She hoped that he would see the crossed fingers resting on her left wrist. Perhaps she might be able to catch his eye in church. The Greening family box pew was opposite that occupied by the Broughtons, where sometimes Jonty and his father were offered seats.

After church the Broughtons made their way to Benjamin Farley's house for their usual Sunday lunch. Will took George up to the room they were to share, where he unpacked his belongings, setting his small library up on a shelf, *White Jacket* joining *Mr Midshipman Easy*, *Roderick Ransom* and *Two Years Before the Mast*.

Louisa was very much the gracious hostess, seating herself at one end of Benjamin Farley's long dining table. She was determinedly elbowing her way up the social ladder, modelling herself on the wives of her grandfather's wealthier acquaintances. Of the Forrester children, only the three eldest were present; usually only fourteen-year-old Benji was allowed to eat with the adults. Louisa would have liked to send Joss up to the nursery to eat his dinner with the younger children, but the first time she had proposed this arrangement she had met with such looks of astonishment and disapproval from her parents that she had never suggested it again.

Benjamin Farley was seated at the opposite end of the table, to all appearances the head of the house, although in practice the servants took all their instruction from Louisa. He always dined with the family when the Broughtons were present, generally having a tray in his room on other days. According to Louisa, he preferred to be quiet and to take his own time over his meals. His former friends were gradually ceasing to call, having been denied him too often, being informed that he was taking a nap, or a little unwell, or just about to go out. When they did succeed in seeing him, as often as not Louisa would be present, apparently busying herself with some fancy needlework, but obviously listening to their conversation, sometimes even going so far as to join in.

The Broughton party left after tea, riding back to Bearshott in Allnutt's cart. Elizabeth produced a cushion for Joss, which he accepted gratefully. Will and George repaired to their room, where Will explained that, though he rarely spent the evening with his sister and her husband, he often visited his grandfather for an hour or two and gave him a game of chess. He did not care for shop work and was unsure what he was being 'trained up' for, since it was plain that the Forresters intended that Simon would take over the business when his grandfather finally relinquished the reins.

'Simon bosses me about in the shop, and Louisa bosses me about at home,' Will complained. 'Simon's a pompous prat, and Louisa thinks she's Lady Muck. I'm thinking of giving it all the go-by.'

'Really?' George's brow wrinkled. 'What would you do instead? Won't Grandfather be upset if you leave?'

'I don't think Grandfather would notice. And if he did, I doubt he would care. Between you and me,' Will lowered his voice, 'I think he's going dolally.'

George thought back over recent family Sunday dinners. If Will was right, that would explain some of the more cryptic observations made by his grandfather. 'They wouldn't have him put away, would they?'

'I don't think they could. You need the signatures of two doctors, and he's too highly thought of in the town. I shouldn't think they would find two who would agree. Besides, Louisa's not next of kin, Mother is, and she would never allow it. He doesn't come out of his room much now anyway. I expect they'd get a nurse in.'

George digested this sad piece of information, then recalled his question. 'So, what would you do instead?'

'I was thinking,' said Will carefully, 'that I might join the police.'

George was taken aback, Will never before having expressed any interest in such a career.

'Where? London?'

'I'm thinking of trying Surrey. They've only just started,' answered Will, 'and Benjamin has promised me I can lodge with him if I can get a position in Epsom.'

'When?' George asked, hoping that his brother did not mean to leave immediately.

'Soon, I hope. I've applied, and I'm waiting to hear.' Will noticed George's crestfallen expression. 'Don't worry – you'll be fine. And I was thinking – do you fancy having a look at this Great Exhibition they're all talking about?'

Louisa, Simon, and their three older children had attended the Exhibition when it had opened in May – not on the opening days, which would have cost them one pound each, but during the second week, when the admission fee had dropped to five shillings, which was still dear enough to ensure that they would not be rubbing shoulders with the hoi polloi. Since when Louisa had been at pains to ensure that all her acquaintances knew that her family had been one of the first to visit the attraction, describing at length (though not necessarily with any great accuracy) the many interesting marvels, positioning the catalogue where visitors could not help but notice it, and extolling the educational benefits accrued to any child fortunate enough to be taken to see it.

So, when Will asked Simon if he might have a day's holiday in order to accompany George to the show, that they might be similarly educated, it was difficult for him to refuse the request on any other grounds than that he was needed at the shop. Fortunately, Grandfather Farley had been present and, in a rare moment of lucidity, said that the shop could go along perfectly well without Will for one day, and gave his permission. Simon had nothing left to do but agree, only stipulating that the day should be Thursday when the shop was closed in the afternoon anyway, and that Will would forfeit the half day's pay. Benjamin then further astounded the company by opening his wallet and taking out a guinea which, he told Will, was to cover the brothers' expenses.

Will wrote a short note to Joe, asking that if he happened to be making deliveries to London on Thursday, would he mind taking himself and George up beside him? Joe's reply was received by the second post. Provided the boys could get themselves to Bearshott by half past five on Thursday morning, he would be glad of their company, and could take them as far as Covent Garden. Will dashed off another note to Caro, in Camden Town, telling her of their plans, in the hope that she might be able to join them.

Louisa remarked, somewhat tartly, that it was highly improbable that the boys would wake up early enough to get themselves to Bearshott by that hour of the morning. For the second time in as many days, Benjamin surprised everyone by suggesting that they could very well go the evening before; their parents doubtless would be very glad to see them.

Louisa, determined to have the last word, said that she would instruct the cook that there would be two less for supper on Wednesday. She was sure they would not wish to waste time eating, and that Mama would also be very glad to feed them.

The journey into London was a jolly affair. Will belied his years by being just as excited as his younger brother at the prospect of the day's outing, and the pair chafed at the time wasted at every delay. Joe set them down near Covent Garden, as promised, directing them to Piccadilly which, he said, would take them to the southern side of Hyde Park and the exhibition ground. They strode along this busy thoroughfare, with its magnificent houses and shops, past the Gloucester Hotel and Coffee House from where, only a couple of years before, they would have had to take the mail coach home. Elizabeth had given them three shillings towards their expedition, warning them to keep two back for their rail fares home. As he set them down, Joe produced half-a-crown from his jacket pocket, bidding them to have some refreshment on him. With all this largesse at their disposal, the boys were confident of enjoying the day to the full.

No reply to Will's note had been received from Caroline. They had made such haste along Piccadilly that they arrived at the showground early; it still wanted twenty minutes to nine. Will had written that they expected to get there between nine and half past. They had no choice but to wait outside the entrance in case she came.

It had been some months since they had last seen their sister. When Caro did, eventually, arrive – just as they were thinking of giving her up – she looked so unlike her old self that they nearly overlooked her. George blinked a little but saw nothing amiss in his old playmate. Will thought privately that her dress was rather flamboyant, and that Mother would not approve. He also noticed that she seemed inclined to think herself, with her town polish, very sophisticated, and her brothers mere yokels. He firmly quashed such pretension by taking charge of the little party, paying their shilling entrance fees, and laying out a further shilling to purchase a catalogue.

They first marvelled at the glittering exhibition hall itself, the Great Shalimar, which towered above them like a giant greenhouse. Its complex iron and glass design had earned it the sobriquet of the 'Crystal Palace'. There were already thousands of visitors in attendance; the Broughtons foresaw that their progress around the many exhibits would be slow. It now being above four hours since Will and George had set out from Bearshott, they thought first to refresh themselves at one of the many booths offering coffee and pastries, after which they referred to the catalogue, intending to plan their route around the twenty acre site. It was obvious that, with all the crowds and queues, they would not be able to see everything in only one visit. However, the thick volume, with its long lists of exhibitors, was of little help, and when it was later realised that Will had accidentally left the cumbersome directory on the table where they had been sitting, it was agreed that they would not try to retrieve it but that they would wander around the two floors and look at any display that caught their eye. Caro was particularly keen to see the international stands with their exotic products and colourful costumes, and the Koh-i-Noor diamond (Will and George, craning their necks to see over the crowds gathered around this fabulous item were disappointed. They had thought it would be much larger). Will was interested in all things scientific, especially the working models. George was interested in everything, but most fascinated by the flushing public toilets, expending several pennies throughout the course of the day in using them, whether he needed to or not.

At four-thirty, Caro announced that it was time for her to leave. Arthur was coming to meet her, and they were to go to a soirée in the evening.

'A what?'

'A soirée, George. It's French for evening party.'

'It's *pretentious* for evening party, George. And when,' Will demanded of Caro severely, 'did Mr Haddington become Arthur?'

Caro tossed her curls and looked mutinous.

'Well, I hope you enjoy it, Caro,' George intervened hastily.

Walking back from the entrance, whence they had escorted Caro, and seen her walk off on the arm of the artist, Will remarked, 'Caro's getting just like Louisa, full of herself,' adding to himself, 'or, worse, like Bebe.'

The brothers spent another hour or two at the show, investigating such curiosities as had been of no interest to Caro, before leaving and heading for home, buying themselves a couple of meat pies to sustain them on the trek to Chiswick, where they were to take the train to Isleworth.

'This is your length.' Nicholas pointed to a building on the far bank. 'From that cottage, up around the bend in the river, as far as the black and white boathouse on the other bank. Both sides of the river, o'course.'

'How do I get across?'

'Use the church ferry – they'll take you across for free. We'll go there now. I'll introduce you to the ferrymen, so they know to expect you.'

The pair headed back towards All Saints, the old man explaining his new duties to George as they went. 'You're to make sure the banks aren't overgrown, keep the towpaths clear, and repair any weak spots with puddle clay.'

'Puddle clay?'

'There're piles of clay and grit in the yard. You just mix them together with a drop of water and slam it into any places in the banks that have started to collapse or are leaking. We'll take a bucketful out with us this morning and I'll show you how it's done. You need to be here by six-thirty in the summer, an hour later in the winter, whatever the weather. D'you think you can do that?'

'Yes, sir,' George nodded. He looked at the wizened,

weather-beaten face of the old lengthsman. 'Have you been doing this work long, sir?'

'Ooh, must be about forty year or so. I was just such a nipper as you when I started.'

George was startled. That would make Nicholas about fifty-five – younger than his father – though he looked much older, with his wrinkled, ruddy, chapped cheeks and white whiskers. Well, he thought to himself, if that's what forty years of working on the canals does for you, I shan't be here long.

10: Caro

Caro came back home early in the New Year, bringing with her far more luggage than she took when she left for Camden Town four years before. As well as cases full of clothes and sundries, there was all the paraphernalia of an artist's trade.

Will and George had, of course, described their visit to the Great Exhibition the previous summer, but I could see nothing amiss in Caro's appearance – she was wearing a dress of sober cloth, similar to those worn by all the women of the village – apart from her eyes, which were red rimmed and swollen.

As far as I know, Caro told no one the reason why she had come back to us so precipitately. When Mother once tentatively mentioned Arthur Haddington, Caro burst into tears and fled the room. We each drew our own conclusions, and he was never mentioned again. Even his cousins, the Rowlatts, claimed to be none the wiser.

I had been in solitary possession of the front bedroom ever since George had gone to Isleworth, except when Jonty came to stay. Now, I was to share with Caro once again. We had a cupboard and a chest of drawers between us. My few changes of clothing occupied less than half the latter. Caro squeezed her dresses, coats, and cloaks into the cupboard, several hatboxes were piled into a corner, and the top of the chest was covered with a fancy cloth and littered with brushes, combs, mirrors, and perfume bottles.

Initially, all the art kit had been dumped in Father's shed. With the help of Will, George, Jonty and me, he constructed another, for Caro's use as a studio. Caro had spent the first couple of weeks back with us listlessly mooning about or sitting with an open book on her lap whose pages were seldom turned, but when this room was finished, she set to and sorted through all her equipment, laying it out as she wanted, and explaining its various mysteries to Jonty and me.

The huge folder, that looked like the covers of a book, threaded with cord down one long edge to make a hinge, and fastened closed with two more lengths of the same on the other edge was, she told us, her portfolio. Between these covers were kept safe and flat numerous drawings and watercolours.

The strange wooden object that vaguely resembled a chair was a donkey easel, we learnt. The painter would sit astride (very unladylike, Caro remarked) with a canvas mounted on what looked like the chairback. There were, she told us, large studio easels, which the artist would stand in front of, but she could not afford to purchase one for herself and, anyway, the works she produced were not that big. The donkey easel she had acquired second hand.

'Funny name for a magazine,' remarked Jonty, leafing through a booklet he had picked out of an assortment of papers. '*The Germ.*'

Caro looked up from the colours she was arranging on a shelf.

'Oh, that was published a couple of years ago, but it didn't sell very well. I've only kept it because it has an illustration by Holman Hunt.' Jonty looked questioning. 'He's a well-known painter. I met him last summer when I was visiting Benjamin.'

This seemed to me very strange. 'Benjamin knows a painter?'

'No, no,' Caro seemed embarrassed. 'We – a friend and I – had gone to Ewell for the day, and Mr Hunt was sitting in a field painting. He – my friend – knew him, so we went over and spoke to him.'

With her equipment now easily to hand, Caro's spirits seemed to revive. She began to work on small projects. George recalled the day, years ago, when we three had been in the orchard, and she had made a comical sketch of him. He still had it, tucked away, waiting for her to become famous. That was the day we first met Jonty, I reminded them.

Later, when Caro came up to our room where I lay still awake, I said, 'Caro, do you think you could do a drawing of the three of us – Georgie, Jonty, and me?'

She smiled. 'The Three Jays, you mean? Of course, I will.'

Just before Easter a letter arrived for Caro, redirected from her old address in Camden Town. She turned it over in her hands, a puzzled expression on her face.

'That looks important,' Mother remarked eventually when Caro had made no move to open it.

Caro looked up. 'It's from the Royal Academy,' she said, showing us the cipher on the envelope. 'But I don't know why they would be writing to me.'

'Only one way to find out,' Father said.

Caro took a deep breath, then ripped the envelope open. 'Oh,' she said, reading the letter, a look of blank astonishment on her face. 'They've accepted one of my paintings for the Summer Exhibition. But I didn't—' She stopped, crumpling the letter in her hand.

'But that's good news, isn't it?' asked Mother.

'I suppose so.' Caro sat down and, laying the letter on the table, she flattened it out and carefully read it through.

'What's the Royal Academy, and why are they having an exhibition?' I asked at last.

'It's a sort of club, Joss – all the most famous artists belong to it. Every year they hold an exhibition, where anyone can submit a painting, whether they're famous or not, and a committee looks at them all and chooses the best ones for the exhibition,' Caro explained. 'And it seems that they have picked one of my paintings.'

'Then yours must have been one of the best?'

'I suppose so,' Caro said again.

'What was your painting of, dear? Shall we be able to go and see it?'

'Yes, Mother, of course. It's a public exhibition.' She looked at the letter again. 'It opens on May the third.'

Caro did not want to go to Varnishing Day when she would have met other exhibitors, nor did she seem to want anyone else to know of her success. We – Father, Mother, Caro, Joe and I – attended the following weekend. Although we had all visited London at various times, only Caro was familiar with that area. We followed where she led.

Trafalgar Square heaved with pedestrians. Nannies pushed perambulators and shepherded their smartly dressed charges whilst barefoot, grubby urchins in rags dabbled their fingers in the fountains. Hawkers were crying their wares as beggars held out their cupped hands, pleading for alms. Bewhiskered soldiers, aloof and important in their regimentals, strolled about, ignoring the many shoppers laden with interesting parcels. Tourists consulted their guidebooks and exclaimed over the sights. Vehicles of every description jammed the roadway. The Southampton to Waterloo stage swept past, a blast on the horn demanding passageway. Numerous carts lumbered along, laden with all manner of goods, cabbies deftly inching their hackney carriages through the traffic. A Pickfords wagoner was involved in an altercation with the driver of a Fortnum and Mason's cart.

We, in our turn, exclaimed at the bustling spectacle, like any country bumpkins. We were amazed by Nelson's Column. It was hard to believe that originally it had been designed to be even taller. Caro informed us that the statue of a gentleman on horseback depicted King Charles the First. Father (no monarchist) remarked that his statue was, quite rightly, somewhat lower than that of the great admiral.

The wide façade of the National Gallery occupied one side of the Square. Mounting the short flight of steps, we went in via the Royal Academy's entrance and, after studying the list of exhibits displayed in the vestibule, made our way to the West Room. And there, nicely positioned at eye level, was Caro's painting, entitled *The Gun Powder Mill, Bearshott*. The picture was a study in oils; a panoramic view of the powder mill, as seen from the opposite bank of the Crane.

'Oh, Caro,' breathed Mother, 'that's *wonderful*. But when did you paint it?'

'Last summer,' replied Caro, looking a little conscious. 'I was in Surrey for a day or two and made some sketches and notes whilst I was there, then painted it back in the studio.'

Father studied the painting. 'Your mother's right, Caro. It really is wonderful.' Looking at her along his shoulder, he added, 'We're very proud of you, Caro.'

She gave him a rather watery smile. 'Thank you, Father.'

'What are you looking for, Joss?' asked Joe, breaking a rather awkward silence. 'I don't think you're supposed to get close enough to wipe your nose on it.'

'Jonty's dad,' I replied. I had examined all the little figures in the picture, trying to spot anyone I knew.

'They aren't anybody in particular, Joss, they're too far away. Except this one,' Caro pointed to a tubby man in a suit, standing in the middle of the scene. 'He's supposed to be Mr Greening.'

Having admired Caro's work to the full, we wandered around, looking at the other exhibits. Caro was delighted to find that pieces by two artists she particularly admired were hung in the same room as her own. She pointed out Holman Hunt's picture entitled *The Hireling Shepherd*.

'I think this is the one I saw him painting last year.'

Mother did not admire Millais' offering. 'It's very lifelike, of course,' she pronounced, somewhat erroneously, ' but isn't it rather – morbid?'

'It's Ophelia, Mother, it's supposed to be tragic. And poetic.'

'Ophelia who?' I demanded.

'Ophelia nobody, Joss. She's a character in Hamlet. You know – Shakespeare. She drowns herself.'

Joe and I looked at one another and simultaneously groaned, 'Oh, Shakespeare!'

Arthur Haddington's painting was in the East Room. Joe spotted it first.

'I say, Caro, that looks just like you!' he exclaimed. Haddington's canvas was huge, dominating the room. Labelled *Galatea*, it depicted a life-sized nude statue in a classical setting. Although the figure was realistically painted as though made of white marble, to those who knew her the likeness was plain to see. Furthermore, the kneeling male figure clasping it around the knees and looking adoringly up was unmistakably meant for Haddington himself.

Caro flushed a deep red and seemed about to take to her heels. Joe grabbed her hand and, drawing it through his arm, forced her to walk calmly beside him out of the building.

'Well,' said Mother brightly, 'I think a nice cup of tea is called for.'

'I think something stronger is called for,' said Father.

Joe took us to the Welsh Harp, in Covent Garden, a short walk from the Square. I had never seen anyone down a sherry so fast as Caro did.

In the middle of June, another letter arrived from the Royal Academy. Someone had bought her painting and Caro was to receive ten guineas by money order, less fees. She did not appear very pleased at the news. For some days she looked thunderous if anyone mentioned the matter, until Jonty announced unwittingly that 'someone' had told him that the picture was now displayed in Mr Greening's library.

Caro began to receive commissions for her work, some as a direct result of the exhibition itself, some from friends of the Greenings, and others from people she had known in London. In the autumn, it came about that the leaseholder of the little shop Mother owned in Isleworth did not want to renew. Mother turned the premises over to her talented daughter, to set up a studio and gallery to display her work. Caro moved into the Farley villa with Louisa and George – Will had become a police constable, and was now living in Dorking. I had the front bedroom to myself once more.

11: Consequences

Abel Allnutt had decided it was time for him to retire. His seventy-five-year-old bones complained at every early morning, heavy load, and rainy day. His recently widowed sister having suggested that they share her home in Hertford, and with no children or other family ties in Bearshott, he had agreed. Telling Joe of his plans, to forewarn him that at best he would have a new employer, at worst that he would be laid off, he was surprised and pleased when told that Joe would be interested in purchasing the business himself. The money received from the now defunct *Hounslow and District Enquirer* years before, in settlement of his defamation claim, had been prudently invested upon Benjamin Farley's advice, and there were now more than sufficient funds to buy Abel out.

It was ten years since Harriett's death, and Joe was still living in the loft they had shared. He had recently begun walking out with Elspet Rowlatt. Undoubtedly, the owner of a tidy house and business would be a better prospect than a labourer living in one room above a stable. The transaction was concluded and Abel was seen off with, in addition to everyone's good wishes, a muffler knitted by Elizabeth, a useful box decorated with marquetry made by Edward, and a watercolour of Wyck Green showing the frontage of Allnutt's Yard contributed by Caro.

After a week of washing down, repairing, and polishing,

Joe moved into the house vacated by the old man and took Joss on, training him to handle the smaller cart, whilst he himself drove the larger wagon.

Although he had been barred from working at the mill, nothing had been said about Jonty being employed elsewhere on the estate. The bailiff disliked the mill owner, despised the twins, and felt rather sorry for the boy. Jonty was strong, big for his age. The bailiff took him on as a labourer, taking care to set him to tasks away from the main house or the mill yard. Though Matthew Greening remained in ignorance, it had not been long before his housekeeper had noticed.

'That boy's arm seems to have mended well, doesn't it?' she remarked casually to Philadelphia one day when they happened to pass one another on the nursery landing. 'I often see him, digging away, over along the Isleworth lane. He's a very strong lad, isn't he? Quite handsome, too.' She moved on, satisfied by the girl's eager expression that she had said enough.

Philadelphia had had little opportunity to speak with either Joss or Jonty since the latter's fall. No one suspected that she, too, had played in the igloo. She was never allowed to go into the village by herself, or to mix with any of the village children. Only on Sundays at church, when they sometimes exchanged their secret sign, was she reassured that her friends had not forgotten her.

Her governess was still in the habit of leaving her alone in the afternoons, setting her some scholarly tract to study. It being summer, Philadelphia requested permission to take her books out of doors, so that she might benefit from the fresh air as she read. For a week, Philadelphia sat out in the gardens in the afternoons, always in view of the house, but never in the same place twice. Finally, when she felt sure that her family and the servants had lost interest in her comings and goings, she headed for the fields bordering Waleric Lane.

Michael Tickle peered around the trunk of the tree and,

seeing himself unobserved, settled his back against it, pulled his flask from his jacket pocket and took a swig. Michael was not enjoying life. He hated his job. Greening and the foreman were suspicious of him, only allowing him to carry out the most menial – and lowest paid – tasks. The other men and women working at the mill seemed to look at him sidewise. He hated the poky, dank, draughty cottage he lived in, hated having to rely on the charity of his neighbours to keep it clean, do his laundry, and put hot food on the table. No way was he going to do any household chores himself – that was woman's work. He was angry with his wife for dying and leaving him to bring up the boy alone. He would have fared better if Jonathan had gone the way of the other children. But most of all, he resented the Broughtons.

Jonathan spent more time with them than at home. If he wanted advice, it was Edward he turned to, not to his father. It was easier when the boy was younger, when a good thrashing kept him in line. Now he was taller and stronger than his father, and Michael was secretly afraid that Jonathan would retaliate in kind if he were to deliver any such punishment now. Edward called him 'Micky', as if they were mates, but he was rarely invited to the Broughton cottage, or even to spend the evening at The Admiral. Everyone knew the history of that family, and yet they acted as though they owned the place. Worst of all, Elspet Rowlatt was being courted by Joe Broughton.

Michael had spent years trying to please the Rowlatts, signing the effing pledge, attending their interminable rallies, allowing Jonathan to stay on at school. And what was the point of all that additional 'education'? With all his extra learning, he was still only a labourer like his father, a job he could equally well have started a year or two ago, and could have been paying for his keep.

He could not believe that Elspet would be so mercenary. True, Joe now had a snug house and his own business to offer, but surely she realised that he had done away with his wife, and that the money that bought the business had been cheated out of the newspaper, just because it had not been quite proved that he had committed murder.

He had a mind to up sticks and leave them all to it. He could easily find work in London, in a manufactory, perhaps, which might pay better and would not mean working outside in all weathers. As for Jonathan – well, the high and mighty Broughtons and their very dear friends the Rowlatts could have him. Maybe, before he left, he would tell one or two people some home truths.

On the day after her arrival in Bearshott on a visit to her in-laws, Mona Shelley's youngest daughter complained of a headache and a sore throat. The child was allowed to lay on the sofa whilst her brothers and sisters were sent out to play on the Green with the village children.

Her grandmother made up some lemonade, which Mona persuaded the child to try. She took a sip, then refused any more, saying that it hurt her throat to swallow.

Peering into her mouth, Mona could see that the child's tongue was reddened, with a pale coating. A doctor was sent for and confirmed what Mona feared. Her daughter had scarlatina.

The doctor advised feeding the child with sops, encouraging her to drink, sponging her little body with tepid water to bring her temperature down, and shaving her head and wrapping it in wet cloths. Her mother followed these instructions assiduously, but to no avail. Three days later, the child died.

The doctor put the village under quarantine. Anyone who happened to be visiting was unable to leave, including George, who had come to spend the evening with his father, and Margaretta Greening's sister, who was staying at The Bury for several weeks.

As news of the epidemic spread, families shut themselves in their cottages and kept their children under close and worried observation. Within the next two weeks, most of the households with young children were infected. All Mona's children succumbed, as did over half of those in the village. Minerva Shelley caught the disease but survived. Two of her sisters did not.

Matthew Greening had his gates locked and barred and would let no one enter his estate. He forbad anyone who had young children to go to work at the gunpowder mill until the pestilence had passed. Many of the women who laboured there were affected, leaving the mill short of workers. The foreman was obliged to reassign the depleted workforce, to cover the absentees' duties. He set Michael Tickle to help out at the incorporating mill.

Elspet Rowlatt looked sadly around the schoolroom. Her mind's eye conjured up the little faces of her pupils. There would sit cheeky Jimmy Barker, next to him shy Susan Taylor, next to her the irrepressible Mary Ann Mount. And so on. Hardly any would answer the next roll call. A clattering outside drew her attention. Through the window, she watched another hearse, bearing two small coffins, pass by, bound for the churchyard in Isleworth.

Charles had losses from his class, too. She thought that there were now only about thirty or so children left – not enough to justify two classes. Just about enough to keep the school open. At supper the previous evening her brother had said that he doubted the school board would continue to fund the salary of two teachers. Under the circumstances, he was minded to quit and seek other employment, leaving her in sole charge. The monitors had, so far, escaped the disease, and would be able to assist her with the younger ones.

Elspet knew what other employment Charles hoped for. Almost since childhood, he had dreamt of becoming a missionary; only his care of her had stopped him from applying sooner. No doubt he now believed that she would marry Joe Broughton and he could go to China with a clear conscience. It was by no means certain that Joe would propose. From the gossip she had heard, it seemed as though his first marriage had been a disaster. Would he really be willing to embark on another? And would she accept, even if he did? He was pleasant enough company – at her age, she was unlikely to find any great passion – and he now owned a comfortable house and ran an apparently thriving business, but she loved teaching. Female married teachers were frowned upon. In all likelihood the board would not allow her to stay unless she were single. If it were a choice between the school and Joe, she was not sure that she would pick him.

Michael Tickle put on leather slippers and entered the gunpowder mill for his shift which, due to the shortage of workers, had been increased to nine hours instead of the customary six. This work was more to his liking than gathering the wood to make charcoal. It was also much better paid – forty pounds a year, though he would only be paid that rate until the usual workers returned.

It was noisy inside the incorporating mill due to the falling water and the grinding millstones. Very different from the peace and quiet of the woods, but he was becoming used to it. The two other men working in the mill left to fetch another tubful of charge from the magazine. Alone, Michael took a nip of whisky. That was the only downside to this job. There was almost always someone else around.

Tickle watched sourly as the dry charge was laid on the stone bed and sprinkled with water from a copper watering can. He had been sent to work in the mill, certainly, but was still not entrusted to carry out many of the processes.

'You may as well go back to cutting wood for now, Tickle. There's nothing for you to do here for about three hours.'

Although it was a relief to be out in the fresh air, as he chopped wood he thought about how he might be able to swing a permanent job in the mill. He could certainly do with the extra money. He shook his flask. About half full, he reckoned.

'But that's all my eye!' exclaimed Philadelphia hotly.

'I beg your pardon?' her mother said icily. Her aunt stopped plying her needle, raised an eyebrow, and tut-tutted. 'Wherever did you learn such an expression?'

'One – one of the servants,' Philadelphia stammered.

'You are never to use it again. I find it hard to believe that a child of mine would model her speech on that of a servant. Go to your room. I do not desire to hear from you again today. You may have a tray in the nursery.'

Matthew Greening's dinner table was usually graced with business associates, friends, or family, with none of his children in attendance, but the enforced quarantine had reduced the company to immediate family only. He was not much in the habit of noticing the comings and goings of his youngest child, but even he could hardly overlook the empty seat to his right. When he enquired of his wife why this might be, the quelling look she gave him, and a sniff from his sister-in-law, seated to his left, warned of some mystery.

'She has a headache, and is taking supper in her room,' Margaretta averred. Matthew did not pursue the subject in front of his twin sons, the only other diners, but demanded an explanation from his wife later that evening, when Margaretta held forth on the iniquities of servants and the poor judgement of their daughter.

Matthew woke in the middle of the night, suffering from chronic indigestion. Lack of other adult male company had led him to partake a little too freely of the after-dinner port, he surmised. As he lay awake, he pondered Philadelphia's use of the vulgar expression. Something was niggling at the back of his mind. The expression was vaguely familiar. He tried to recall which servant he had heard using it.

It was not until the next day, as he strolled through the mill yards, that he remembered. Tickle! Not Michael, but that lout of a son of his – John, or whatever his name was. It did not for a moment cross his mind that his daughter might be on familiar terms with the boy, or even know him, but he could not countenance any possibility that she might be associating with the village children. Any such suspicion could seriously harm her future prospects.

Discussing the matter later with his wife, a solution presented itself. When the quarantine was lifted, and his sister-in-law was able to go home, she would take Philadelphia with her. Her own daughters were of a similar age. Philadelphia would benefit from the company of her cousins, sharing their lessons and, no doubt, confidences. Her aunt undertook to present her to polite society, provided Matthew committed to defray the expense.

George found himself out of employment. The foreman had taken on another man to cover his length in George's enforced absence, found him a keener worker, and offered him the job on a permanent basis. George regretted the loss of his wages – which he had not, in any case, received whilst confined in Bearshott – but not the loss of the job, which he had found tedious and uninteresting.

He had, in fact, inherited Edward's youthful wanderlust. Beyond family, he had no ties to keep him in Middlesex. The bustle of nearby London did not appeal, nor did any sort of indoor work. He wanted adventure, to have a look at the world for himself, rather than reading about it in books. His favourites had always been those about the sea. He was determined to become a sailor.

The senior hand was supervising Michael Tickle as he shoved mill cake around on the bedstone between the stopped vertical edge runners. His usual partner had had the inconvenient misfortune to slip and break his leg. He was forced to use Tickle instead but was keeping a keen eye on him. He suspected the man was drinking, though he had not caught him at it, nor could he smell it on his breath. Hardly surprising, given the strong odour given off by the gunpowder.

A lad poked his head around the door and called out, 'Mr Walker! You're wanted in the foreman's office. There's to be a meeting.'

There had been mutterings of dissatisfaction at the increased shifts and redeployment of workers, with no extra pay offered, and no wages at all for those barred from coming to work. Greening had agreed to meet some of the workers to discuss their grievances. Walker was loath to leave Tickle alone but was keen to hear what the mill owner would say, although his expectations were small.

'Alright, Billy. I'll be there in a jiffy. Tickle – you can lift the charge off whilst I'm gone. Make sure you don't spill any.' He watched as Tickle picked up the wooden scuppit and began to scoop up mill cake, carefully tipping it into an empty tub. Satisfied, he padded across the leather floor, took his slippers off at the door, and went to his meeting.

Tickle, having finished clearing the heap of mill cake from between the first pair of runners, took another empty tub and carefully did the same for the other pair. This was his opportunity to show some initiative. With the other man out of the picture, this was his best chance – maybe his only chance before the quarantine was lifted, rumoured to be soon – to demonstrate he could be trusted with more than chopping wood. With luck he might be promoted to permanent work in the gunpowder mill.

He knew what to do next, although he had never done it himself. Cover the bedstones in leather. Put down the scotches. Start up the water wheel. Turn the runners onto the leathers. Stop the water wheel. Brush up the charge that had been under the runners. Put it in the tub with the rest of the mill cake.

He went to the door and peered out. There was no sign of Walker. Taking the cap off his flask, he took a big swallow of the spirit. He looked across the room at the stationary grindstones. There was the pile of leather pieces, there the scotches, there the brush, there the silent water wheel. He might never get such another break.

Picking up four pieces of leather, he began to lay them flat on the cleared bedstone between each pair of runners. He worked quickly, eager to complete the process before Walker returned. As he was about to lay the last piece, he caught the sound of excited voices in the yard outside – no doubt the workers who had attended the meeting. Dropping the leather pad onto the bedstone, he hurried to the water wheel. There was no time now to start up the wheel, but he could show that he knew what was next to be done.

'Ah!' he said as the other walked in, 'I've done the leathers. I was just about to start up the wheel again, to get to the rest of the powder.'

Walker looked at him narrowly. 'I'll take over, now. It takes a bit of practice, letting just enough water onto the wheel. You get ready with the brush.'

Tickle was annoyed that, yet again, he was being side-lined. Perhaps a friendly approach might help. He asked conversationally, 'How did the meeting go? Any news?'

The meeting, as Walker had suspected, had not gone well for Greening's workers. There had been a lot of claptrap from the mill owner along the lines of 'all being in this together', 'all pulling our weight in this time of crisis', 'serving the community', and so on and so forth. He would not be swayed. The longer shifts were to stay until the rest of the workforce returned, there was to be no more pay for the extra hours, and the workers who were temporarily laid off would not be paid for doing nothing. There was little his workers could do to bring pressure to bear. A few muttered about finding other work, but since Greening's Gunpowder Company was the main employer in the village, and for some miles around, the chances of doing so were slim.

'No, nothing's changed,' Walker scowled. Somewhat distracted, he glanced at the bedstones, checking the leather pieces laid in front of the runners. 'He's got us over a barrel.'

Tickle went to fetch the brush from where it was propped up against the wall near the door. He heard the plash of water behind him falling on the wheel, and the creaking as it began to move. The heavy grindstones started their circuit of the bedstone, the leather pads deadening the sound.

As he picked up the brush, he noticed the two scotches lying on the floor. In his haste to get to the water wheel before Walker returned, he had forgotten to put them on the leathers, to stop the runners rolling off the end onto the cleared bedstone, where a spark might ignite any left-over composition.

He spun around, a warning on his lips.

Edward, and everyone else from miles around, heard the explosion. The workers at the nursery threw down their tools and rushed down Crane Lane towards the mill. Matthew Greening was standing outside the foreman's office when the blast went off. His bailiff was patrolling the footpath running behind the mill yard. Young Billy was strolling past the gunpowder mill.

The explosion had blown the wooden roof off the incorporating mill. The water wheel had been blown to smithereens. One pair of runners had completely come away from their framing, one heavy stone coming to rest on what remained of Walker's body.

The brick blast walls flanking the gunpowder mill had largely contained the eruption, the force of which was therefore concentrated front and rear. Michael Tickle had been blown out of the open doorway and across the yard. Billy was blown into the river. Up on the footpath, the bailiff lay groaning, mortally injured, hit by flying debris. His dog had whimpered its last. The elderly mill owner and his foreman had been knocked off their feet but, apart from some minor abrasions, were unhurt.

Billy was beginning to drift into the middle of the Crane.

Edward jumped in after him. As he reached the boy, a loosened branch fell from a tree on the riverbank, catching Edward on the head. Knocked out, he released his hold on the body and sank beneath the water.

At the inquest, held as soon as quarantine was lifted, it was reported that Walker had some money worries, and was cast down when the men had failed to persuade Matthew Greening to increase their pay. Only Walker was near the mechanism. Two workers testified that, immediately before the explosion, they had seen Michael Tickle standing in the doorway, nowhere near the seat of the blast. Everyone knew that he was not allowed to carry out any but the most basic tasks, and only then under close supervision. Ergo, it was impossible that he had had any hand in the disaster. The wooden scotches having been consumed in the ensuing fire, no one realised that they had not been laid on the leathers – an omission that Walker would never make.

A verdict of accident was delivered, although many people believed that Walker had either made a mistake or had deliberately engineered the catastrophe out of spite against Mr Greening.

Philadelphia had not seen Jonty since the village went into quarantine. Roman and Saxon – who had only come home a day or two before – were far too nosey and unpredictable to risk sneaking out to meet him. She would not be attending any of the funerals. Even if the village had not still been in isolation, it would not have been thought to be either appropriate or necessary for members of Greening's family to be present. A wreath for each one, a black-edged card of condolence signed by Matthew and his wife attached, was considered a sufficient mark of respect.

Foreseeing the possibility of some objections from Philadelphia, it was only the day before her departure, when the servants dragged a large trunk from the attic and began to lay her clothes inside, that she learned that she was to go to live with her aunt's family. She was unable to escape to meet Jonty to explain and bid him farewell. There was no servant she would trust to give him a message. She did not even glimpse him as her aunt's carriage swept her away from Bearshott.

12: Secrets

As it chanced, the doctor was already in Bearshott at the time of the accident. At the sound of the blast he abandoned his patient, jumped into his fly, and headed for the mill.

The first buildings he reached were unscathed. The only evidence of the disaster was the crowd of wailing workers milling about in the yard. Further on, the ground was strewn with debris from the incorporating mill, which was now on fire. From time to time, the crack of further explosions could be heard from within. The blast walls were blackened but had held firm, protecting the adjacent buildings, funnelling the blast forward towards the river and backward towards the footpath and woodland, where some of the trees were smouldering.

On the riverbank a partially submerged punt lay lopsided, slowly filling with water. Some men appeared to be dragging bodies from the river.

Several people who had been nearby were covered in blood, hit by flying splinters of wood, lumps of brick, and metal shards. Matthew Greening, with no obvious injury, was seated on a chair brought from the foreman's office, some of his female workers fluttering around him. His foreman, nursing a slight head wound, was directing the men operating the mill's fire pump. Once he had treated Greening for shock and his superficial abrasions, and commiserated with him, the doctor turned his attention to the other victims of the explosion. Michael Tickle, Walker, the bailiff, and Billy were beyond aid. Edward had been pulled, half-drowned and concussed, from the river. After the doctor had bandaged his head wound, Joe had brought his father home, where he had been laid on a couch in the parlour. His sodden clothing having been removed, he was helped into a nightshirt. Due to the thick bandage, his hair could not be properly dried, nor his nightcap fitted on his head. Edward was seized with a fit of shivers. Joss banked up the fire, whilst George fetched more blankets.

Edward smiled up at Elizabeth. 'Don't worry, Eliza. Just taken a bit of a chill, that's all.'

By the following morning, Edward had begun to cough up frothy sputum and was complaining of pains in the chest. One moment he would say that he was hot and would push the blankets away. The next, he would be shivering and asking for the fire to be lit. Joe rode for the doctor, urging Clopper to something approaching a gallop. (Alas! The strenuous exercise proved too much for the old horse's heart. The next morning, Joe found Clopper lying dead in his paddock.)

'An infusion of peppermint. Or fenugreek. Either would do. Or, if you cannot get hold of them, warm salt water I have found to be beneficial in soothing the throat,' the doctor advised. 'Tincture of opium will ease the pains in the chest. A purgative will cleanse the gut. Bring down his temperature with a lukewarm bath, if possible, or else wipe the body frequently with damp cloths.' Edward was racked with a fit of coughing. 'Make a mustard blister, to draw out the congestion. He would do better if he could be got to bed. I will look in again tomorrow, Mrs Broughton.'

The tin bathtub was lifted from its hook on the scullery wall and filled with tepid water. Between them, Joe and George managed to manhandle Edward into the tub, whilst

Elizabeth draped a clean nightshirt in front of the fire, before filling a warming pan with hot coals and slipping it between the sheets of their bed. It was more difficult to get Edward out of the bath than it was to help him into it. Getting him up the narrow twisting staircase to the back bedroom afterward was even harder.

By the end of a week, Edward seemed rather better, although the daily application of leeches 'to relieve the humours' (the doctor remained an adherent of the remedies of his youth) and the exhausting effects of liberal doses of castor oil, had left him rather weak. The family began to hope that the doctor's diagnosis of pneumonia had been incorrect, and that he was indeed only suffering from a bad chill and the after-effects of ingesting river water.

There having been no new cases of scarlet fever for some days, the village was taken out of quarantine. Joe and Joss resumed their deliveries, George returned to the villa in Isleworth to collect his belongings, and Jonty went back to labouring at The Bury. Without the bailiff's care in giving him work out of sight of the house, his presence soon came to the Greenings' notice. He was summoned to the mill owner's office.

Greening was deeply sorry for his loss, etcetera, etcetera, but Jonty must understand that the tied cottage was reserved for mill workers; he must vacate by the end of the week. He could, as a concession, however, remain working on the estate if the new bailiff found his work satisfactory. Dismissed, Jonty made his way out through the kitchen quarters. Seeing him in the passage, the housekeeper came out of her office.

'I was very sorry to hear the sad news of your father,' she commiserated. 'Such trying times in the village. All those poor children dying, too. Well, at least Miss Philadelphia is away and out of it. Goodness knows when we shall see her back here again.'

If she had hoped for some reaction, she was disappointed. Jonty looked at her narrowly. Mrs McBride had never deigned to notice him before, had never even spoken to him. He suspected her of mischief-making. Gruffly, he thanked her for her good wishes and went back to work.

As he toiled, he pondered his problems. His father had to be buried, and he did not know how he was going to pay for the funeral. He had to find lodgings in the village. He was sure Greening would have no hesitation in having him forcibly evicted if he were still in the cottage at the end of the week. Normally, he could rely on the Broughtons to advise and help him, but with Edward so ill, he could not possibly trouble them. Joe might have a room he could rent. But the question his mind returned to again and again was the news that Phia was gone.

Elspet Rowlatt called at the cottage that evening, bringing with her a bowl of stew for his supper. As he ate, Jonty told her of his troubles. She pledged her brother's services to help with the arrangements for his father's funeral. She understood that the mill had some insurance cover in case of accidents. Charles would take up the matter with Mr Greening, to ascertain whether Jonty – and the other bereaved families – had any claim. Jonty was welcome to move into Charles's room, when he left the village, if Joe could not take him in. Offhandedly, Jonty mentioned that Miss Greening and the twins had left The Bury, and wondered where they had all gone. Miss Rowlatt said that the twins had returned to their university (which Jonty already knew) and she understood that Philadelphia had gone to live with relations.

A chair had been placed in front of the back bedroom window so that, when he felt like it, swathed in a shawl, Edward could sit and look down his garden. The sounds of his wife moving about her kitchen and scullery drifted up through the open casement. Although he had not been dosed with any of Elizabeth's 'opening medicine', as she preferred to call it, for a day or two, he was still experiencing the laxative effects of the castor oil. Previously, his chamberpot had been emptied and cleansed by one of his sons, but they had now returned to work. Edward determined to make his way downstairs to use the privy, to spare Elizabeth this unpleasant task. It was the first time since he had been brought home from the mill that Edward had attempted to move around without assistance. Gingerly, he made his way across the bedroom, steadying himself by holding onto the furniture. Stepping out onto the dim landing, he realised that his need to evacuate gave him no time to get to the closet. He would have to make use of his pot after all.

Turning back to his bedroom, the shawl fell to the floor, landing around his feet. He began to bend to retrieve it, lost his balance, and crashed backwards down the winding staircase.

Elizabeth rushed into the parlour, to find Edward's senseless body spilling, face up, out of the stair cupboard. She could not move him by herself, even had that been advisable. Joe had gone to look at a horse to replace Clopper, Joss was away making a delivery, George was still in Isleworth, and Jonty was somewhere in The Bury grounds. Most of her neighbours had returned to work, either at the mill or elsewhere. She ran across the Green to the gatehouse and tugged the bell for all she was worth. The lodgekeeper, after sending his young son to the stables to ask one of the lads to ride for the doctor, accompanied Elizabeth back to her cottage.

Edward was still unconscious. Bruises were beginning to appear on his face. Expertly, the lodgekeeper felt down Edward's limbs and announced that none seemed to be broken. All the hurt appeared to be to the head. Together they eased Edward out of the stair cupboard, composing his limbs and placing a pillow under his head, and awaited the doctor.

'I'm afraid your husband has done himself some serious injury, Mrs Broughton. He must be moved as little as possible, but obviously cannot be left to lie here on the floor. You must have a bed made up in this room. He must be tended, night and day, but I must tell you, the outlook is very grave. He may, or may not, regain his senses. If he does, and is in pain, give him laudanum.'

White-faced, Elizabeth asked the doctor exactly what injuries Edward had sustained.

'I believe he has broken his head, Mrs Broughton, and I am afraid there is no remedy for that. You should prepare yourself for the worst. If he regains his senses, his speech may be impaired, or he may not be able to speak at all. He may be out of his wits. Keep him quiet – don't allow a lot of people to troop in and out. Keeping him comfortable is the best you can do for him, now. I'm sorry.'

'But – could he not have just broken his cheekbone? You can see, all the bruising is to his face.'

'All the bruising that you can *see* is to his face. There may be internal bruising to the brain. A heavy blow to the back of the head may manifest itself in contusions to the front.' The doctor picked up his bag and reiterated, 'Just keep him as comfortable as you can, Mrs Broughton. I will look in again tomorrow.'

Elspet Rowlatt, on her way to enquire after the invalid, was disturbed to see the doctor driving away from Trafalgar Terrace. She assumed that Edward's pneumonia had taken a turn for the worse, although Joe had told her that he seemed to be improving and the family was hopeful that it would not be long before he was up and about.

The door was opened at her knock by the lodgekeeper, on his way back to The Bury to procure some help in getting Edward off the floor and onto the couch. Elspet entered the cottage to find a stricken Elizabeth kneeling on the floor at the foot of the stairs beside her husband. A fresh bandage was wound around his head. The diffused blood around his right eye socket and down his cheek was taking on a purple-black hue. His breathing was shallow and laboured. Elizabeth raised tear-filled eyes to her visitor. There was no need for explanation; it was all too apparent what had occurred, and what the prognosis must be.

Elspet immediately saw the need to get Edward off the floor. Rather than the couch, she offered Charles's new campaign bed, recently purchased ready for his trip to China. It was not wanted for two or three weeks, by which time it was sadly clear that Edward would have no further need of it.

Elizabeth would not contemplate leaving Edward's bedside, maintaining a vigil throughout his illness, always accompanied by one or more of the boys. Louisa and Caro arrived, offering to prepare a meal and to relieve their mother for at least one night so that she could get some sleep, but, though glad of her daughters' company, Elizabeth would not abandon her post. Louisa undertook to write to her absent brothers and sisters, and to Edward's brother, James.

The day following his fall, Edward briefly awakened. His gaze slowly travelled across the faces of those assembled at his bedside. Only when he saw his wife did he show any sign of recognition. Looking intently at her, he made some unintelligible sounds which might be taken for 'hello', willing her to understand. Elizabeth was holding one of his hands in hers. Edward struggled to lift his other arm, and clumsily patted her hand. The effort seemed to exhaust him. His hand dropped down onto hers and stilled. His eyes remained fixed on his Eliza as he drifted back into a coma. He lingered for another two days without regaining consciousness.

Elizabeth gently laid Edward's hands on the coverlet, then, taking his poor battered face in hers, kissed him. Dry-eyed, she rose and went to the mantelpiece to stop the clock, and straighten his pipe rack. Louisa had brought some black crape from the shop. Quietly weeping, she went around the house, draping all the mirrors, whilst Caro closed all the curtains. As soon as the seriousness of Edward's condition had been understood, Joe had made time to go into Isleworth to order the best coffin that could be procured. He and Joss had already collected it. It was lying ready over in Allnutt's Yard. Elizabeth sent her menfolk over to The Admiral, with strict instructions not to return for at least two hours so that she and her daughters could wash and dress Edward's body. When they returned, they brought the coffin with them, and gently laid Edward in it, his hands crossed on his chest. His head bandage had been removed, but nothing could be done about disguising the livid bruising – Elizabeth was against the use of any paste or cream. The coffin was lifted onto the dining table, and the campaign bed was stripped of bedding and folded up, ready to be returned to the Rowlatts.

Joss and George walked around to the nursery, to beg some laurel for a wreath to hang on the front door of the cottage. Caro picked flowers from the garden to place in the coffin. Elizabeth went up to the room she had shared with Edward for so many years and put on her one black dress. She pulled all her other dresses from the wardrobe, emptied her tallboy, and packed everything into a suitcase. She never wore anything other than black for the rest of her life. Her only jewellery would be her wedding ring and a gold locket containing a curl of Edward's hair.

All their preparations made, the family waited for the first of the visitors who would call over the next day or two to offer their condolences. Joe took Louisa back to her home in Isleworth. There were funeral arrangements to be made, black-edged mourning cards to be ordered and sent out, and announcements to be placed in the newspapers.

The sad procession left Bearshott, bound for All Saints church. Edward's coffin, now closed, was carried in a glass panelled hearse pulled by black-plumed horses. Elizabeth rode in a carriage behind, accompanied by Caro. Louisa and her family would be meeting them at the church, together with Sarah and her husband. Benjamin, Joe, Daniel, George, and Joss walked behind the widow's carriage. They, together with Louisa's husband, were to be the pallbearers. Will, Catherine and Lucy were not able be present.

Jonty walked with the Rowlatts. He could not help remarking the difference between Edward's funeral and that of his father, whose coffin had been taken to the cemetery on the back of Joe's wagon, nor how many Bearshott residents turned out to pay their respects as the cortege passed. The only other mourners at his father's funeral had been the Rowlatts. Joss and George had been too preoccupied with Edward's illness to attend, and Michael Tickle had not made any friends in the village. Edward was laid to rest in a quiet corner of the churchyard, in a simple plot suitable for a labouring man.

Afterward, the mourners were invited to take refreshment at the Farley villa. The congregation had included several acquaintances of Benjamin Farley, Martin Oliver and one or two workers from his nursery, and a smattering of Bearshott residents, including the father of young Billy, conscious of the fact that Edward had sustained his initial injury whilst trying to pull his son's body from the river. Bebe Broughton had seated herself toward the back of the nave during the service and had thus avoided being noticed until she walked into the villa.

'What are you doing here?' Louisa demanded furiously, grabbing Bebe's arm and pulling her into the library.

'My dear Louisa, what should I be doing here? Paying my respects to my dear father, of course.'

Louisa snorted. 'You showed no respect for him when he was alive. No one wants you here.' Her eyes narrowed. 'How did you find out, anyway?'

Bebe laughed. 'If you don't want people to know things, you shouldn't put notices in the papers. You never know who might read them. Now, I think we should go out to our guests, don't you?'

'*Our* guests!' Louisa gasped. 'You have nothing to do with the matter!'

'Really? Were it not for me, our parents could never have married.'

'And how they must rue the day that you were born!' Louisa snapped. She bit her lip. She could hardly have Bebe forcibly ejected, much though she would have liked to. 'You're not to upset Mama. She is taking this very hard. And Joe—'

'Ah, yes,' Bebe purred. 'How is dear Joseph? He did rather well out of that business, didn't he? I am so looking forward to seeing him again.' She linked her arm through Louisa's. 'Come, Louisa: put your claws away. You must introduce me to – well, everyone. I'm sure I shan't recognise half of them.'

Louisa pulled away. 'What is it you really want, Bebe? If you make trouble—'

'My dear Louisa. What trouble could I possibly make? Besides, I'm not the one screeching like a Spitalfields drab.' Bebe opened the library door. She glanced back over her shoulder at her sister. 'How is dear Simon? So changed from when I knew him. I should hardly have known him, so fat has he become.' She laughed at Louisa's outraged expression. 'Come, sister. Stop pulling caps. You can't win, you know. You care too much about what people think, whilst I care not at all. By the by, I didn't see Grandfather at the church. Is he still with us?'

'He's not well,' Louisa replied stiffly. 'He keeps to his room.'

Bebe looked at her shrewdly. 'Ah, that's where you keep him, is it?'

Before Louisa could think of a suitable retort, Bebe sailed out of the room, head high, and made for the drawing room, where the mourners were gathered. Despite her protestations, she was nervous. She could hardly expect her family to greet her with open arms. Taking a deep breath, she entered the room and looked for her mother. Much would depend on how she received her.

The folding doors between the drawing room and the dining room, where the refreshments were laid, had been thrown open. The widow was seated by the fire. Bebe, followed by an apprehensive Louisa, threaded her way across the room. For a short while, she was obscured by the well-wishers paying their respects.

Sarah noticed her first. Laying a hand on her mother's shoulder, she bent and murmured in her ear. Elizabeth looked up, just as Joe, on her other side, saw Bebe – the authoress (he thought) of all the trouble between Harriett and himself – and started forward. Elizabeth grabbed Joe's hand and held him back. Louisa looked at her brother and shrugged, a resigned 'well, what could I do?' look on her face.

Ignoring her siblings, Bebe bent her head to Elizabeth's and whispered tearfully, 'I'm sorry.' Whether she were sorry for her father's death or was apologising for her own past misdeeds was unclear. Elizabeth enfolded her wayward daughter in her arms.

Most of those in the room knew who Bebe was, although she had not been seen in the town for ten years, and covertly watched the tableau. They were only young children when she had left, but Caro and George realised who she must be from her striking resemblance to their mother. Unlike their elder brothers and sisters, they did not know the reason why she was estranged from the rest of the family, only that there was some great mystery surrounding her, and that she was never mentioned.

'Who's that?' Jonty asked, his mouth full of cake, nudging Joss with his elbow.

'Dunno. Some sort of cousin, maybe?'

'Well, she don't half look like your mum.'

They wandered aimlessly around the room. Most of the company were talking nineteen to the dozen, catching up on each other's news, and paid them little attention. They went out into the garden, sat on the terrace steps, and watched the younger Forrester children, who were being kept occupied and away from the adults.

'Now, who have we here? Not more of Louisa's children, surely?' Joss and Jonty turned at the low musical voice. Bebe stood smiling down at them. She was soberly dressed, not in the black favoured by the other women present, but in dove grey. Her only ornament was a little brooch. Everything about her was quiet elegance. She might have been the cherished wife of a well-to-do businessman.

'Let me see – one of you must be Josiah.' She searched their faces. The boys were similar in colouring, but Jonty had put on weight and muscle whilst labouring at The Bury and had outstripped his shorter friend. 'Ah. They told me you were a sickly child.' Her smile robbed her words of any offence. 'Tell me, Josiah – no, Joss, is it not? – what do you do with yourself these days?'

Joss, somewhat mystified, replied, 'I work for my brother Joe.'

Bebe laughed. 'Your brother Joseph. That must be fun.' Some more guests came out onto the terrace. She opened her reticule and took out a sheet of paper. 'If you ever want a change, do come to see me. This is my direction.' She held out the paper. Baffled, Joss took it. 'We hope to see you one day soon. Goodbye.' She put out a hand to lightly touch Joss's hair, smiled farewell to Jonty, and went back indoors.

'How odd,' said Jonty. 'Sure you don't know her?'

'Nope,' Joss replied, stuffing the paper in his trouser pocket. 'She seemed quite nice, though, didn't she? Perhaps Caro knows.'

They went back inside themselves, to find that Grandfather Farley had come down from his room and was now holding court, ensconced in a large wing chair, a rug wrapped over his knees. Of Bebe there was no sign.

The mourners started to disperse, friends first, followed by those family members who had some way to travel. Joss was to walk back to Bearshott with Jonty, Joe and the Rowlatts.

He went to bid Grandfather Farley goodbye.

'So, you're Josiah, are you?' Joss had become accustomed to the strange utterances of his grandparent, but even so found it remarkable that two people had said almost the exact same words to him in the space of an hour.

'Yes, Grandfather. I'm Joss. And this,' pulling him forward, ' is my friend Jonty.'

Benjamin studied Jonty for a moment, then said, 'The boy with the broken arm. Couldn't pick up his peas.' He paused. 'They tell me your father died in that blast at the mill. Nasty business, that. Someone not doing their job properly, no doubt.' He turned back to Joss. 'He was a good man, your dad. I didn't think he was, at first...I don't know why your mother came. Not invited. Damn cheek!' Louisa, hovering nearby, hastened to intervene.

'That's enough, now. You must be getting tired, Grandpapa.' She beckoned to her grandfather's nurse. 'Nurse will help you back to your room. You can have a nice nap before dinner.'

On the walk back to the village, Joss and Jonty fell behind Joe and the Rowlatts.

'Phew! That was embarrassing. Your granddad's getting really muddled.'

'Maybe,' Joss replied thoughtfully.

When they reached Bearshott, the Rowlatts left the Broughtons at Allnutt's Yard and walked on to the schoolhouse. Sitting at Joe's kitchen table, nursing a glass of beer, Joss asked Joe who the woman was. For a moment, he regretted asking the question, Joe looked so angry. 'That was Bebe – Elizabeth. Our oldest sister.'

Joss's brow wrinkled. 'Sister? But I've never heard of her. Why does no one talk about her?'

Joe seemed to collect himself. 'Sorry, mate. You need to talk to one of the girls about it.'

Joss had to be patient. Even had she been around, Joss would not have asked anything of the waspish Louisa. Caro was staying on at the Farley villa, where her mother was also going to spend a few days. Sarah was on her way back to London, accompanied by George, who was going to make enquiries about joining the navy.

He remembered the paper Bebe had given him and took it from his pocket. *Mrs Elizabeth Caxton, 75 Cricketfield Road, Clapton* he read.

It was nearly two weeks before Elizabeth returned to the cottage in Trafalgar Terrace. Caro had come with her, to see her settled in.

Joe had engaged Isabel Clarke, Harriett's twelve-year-old sister, as a servant, hoping that having help with the heavy work would make his suit more appealing to Elspet. The room over the loft was needed for her, and Jonty was now lodging at the schoolhouse. Joss first asked Caro what she knew about Bebe.

'Only that she did something dreadful and father wouldn't let her in the house. I think she did something awful to Joe and Harriett. No one ever talks about her. I don't think you should ask mother – it might upset her, what with everything else.' And with this, Joss had to be satisfied.

It was Jonty who supplied the next piece of the puzzle. Her brother Charles having left, bound for Asia, and being in want of company, Elspet had taken to inviting Jonty to sit with her when he was not visiting Joss or The Admiral. One evening, they had been discussing the accident at the mill, which led to talk of Edward Broughton's death and funeral, and lastly to the appearance of Bebe Broughton. Elspet had heard from Joe himself that Bebe had been instrumental in Joe being suspected of having a hand in Harriett's death, though exactly how this had occurred she did not know. It was obviously all lies – after all, Joe had won his case against the newspaper that had accused him in print of killing his wife.

Joss was still not satisfied that there was not something more to the mystery. Caro having returned to her gallery in

Isleworth, the only person left to ask was Elizabeth. One evening, he was fidgeting about, trying to pluck up the courage to broach the subject.

'Mother,' he began, 'Grandfather Farley isn't very well, is he? He must be very old.'

'Nearly ninety.'

'He gets very muddled sometimes, doesn't he?'

Louisa having reported Benjamin's conversation with Joss to her mother, Elizabeth had foreseen that Joss would, eventually, raise the matter. She put her hand to the locket containing Edward's hair and sighed.

'Well, I suppose it doesn't matter, now,' she said sadly. 'I expect you want to know about Bebe?' Joss nodded.

Elizabeth went up to her bedroom, returning with the box in which she kept important documents. Unlocking it, she rifled through the contents until she found the papers she was looking for. Setting aside the box, she sat with them in her lap.

'Bebe is my oldest daughter. But I think you already know that much?' Joss nodded again. 'When she was twenty, she had a son – William. His father refused to marry Bebe or to pay to maintain the child and he abandoned them. They lived with us here, to begin with, but it was very overcrowded, even though Louisa had just married Simon, and Sarah had gone into service. Caro was only one and George wasn't even born yet. My father – Grandfather Farley – knew a clergyman in the north who helped girls like Bebe. Together, they found her lodgings and some work, and she and William moved away. But then, when he was two, he took the measles and died, and Betsy – Bebe – came back home. You remember sometimes when I take flowers to my William's grave, I put some on another? That's where Bebe's William is buried.'

Joss waited. There was obviously more to come. The story so far did not seem to have led to any estrangement.

'Then Bebe met a man who worked on the waterways. She went off with him, travelling up and down the canals, all over

England. She wrote from time to time. They had married, she said. Then one day, she came home, bringing her baby son with her. She told us she was afraid that he might topple into the water and drown. She asked us to take him for a while. Well, all the older ones had left by then, and one more baby didn't make much difference, after all.' Elizabeth paused. 'And I do love babies. Then off she went again. For two years, we heard nothing of her. And then,' Elizabeth sighed heavily, 'she turned up again, large with child. At first, we thought she and her husband...well, there was no husband, of course. And she would not – or could not – tell us who the father of the baby she was carrying was. Edward was furious. He would not allow her into the house, nor was she to think of leaving her latest baby here. You can't blame him, of course. Anyone can make a mistake once, but not three times. And then, later, there was all that unpleasantness with Harriett...'

Joss wrinkled his brow. He had no memory of any child other than Daniel, Will, Caro and George living in the cottage as he grew up. 'Did she take the other baby away with her, then?'

Elizabeth looked at him steadily, then handed him a piece of paper. 'No, dear,' she said calmly. 'She didn't. The other baby was you.'

13: *August 1856*

I looked down at the paper Mother – *Grandmother* – had given me. It was my birth certificate. 'Josiah Tomas Broughton (I read), born Devizes Union Workhouse, fifth of June 1839, father Tomas Harys, waterman, mother Elizabeth Broughton, of The Merry Maid, Devizes'. My head swum. Whatever else I had imagined, I had not expected this. Never had anyone in the family given me cause to think I was not who I thought I was. And not only in the family. Some at least of our neighbours must have known. I glared at her angrily, tears rolling down my burning cheeks.

She was utterly calm. I suppose she must always have known that this day would come, sooner or later, that one day I would have to be told about my true parentage. I could not trust myself to speak. In truth, I didn't really know what to say. I laid the certificate down, rose, and walked out of the front door, careful not to slam it. Though I was angry enough to shake the house down, I took refuge in what I imagined to be a dignified silence. Ill-tempered, I stomped around the village, resolutely ignoring anyone who passed by. I fetched up in Crane Lane, outside the deserted cottage that had once been a home, of sorts, to the Tickles. How I wished that I were ten again and that Jonty, Georgie and I could go and hide ourselves in our igloo. George. Not my brother, but my uncle.

My mind tried to adjust to the new relationships. Grandfather Farley, who had, unwittingly, let the cat out of the bag, was my great-grandfather. My brothers and sisters were my aunts and uncles (well, at least I wasn't so closely related to Louisa. I supposed that was why she looked down her nose at me, until I remembered that she looked down her nose at almost everyone). My nephews and nieces were my cousins. The only true brother I had was lying in an unmarked grave in All Saints cemetery. And the third baby? I had left home without finding out whether it was a boy or a girl, dead or alive.

I had never in my life before been in such a black mood. My head throbbed with it. I trailed on down Crane Lane, past Oliver's and on to the river. I was minded to wade across to the little ait, where we had often played as children, until I saw debris from the accident still eddying on its bank. Thwarted, I slouched off along the footpath that ran behind the mill yards.

There was still one incorporating mill operating, so gunpowder production was possible, though curtailed. The remains of the one where the explosion had occurred were being dismantled. A huge pile of bricks lay between the site and the riverbank. Wagons queued to be loaded up and to cart the rubble off. The vast edge runners and bedstones, apparently undamaged, had been retrieved and were propped up against one of the blackened blast walls. One of those stones, I had heard, had squashed one of the victims.

I sat cross-legged on the path and watched the bustle below. Men were going in and out of the ruined shell by what had obviously once been the doorway. There, Jonty's dad had been blown to bits. Somewhere along this path, the bailiff had died. And there beyond was the river where Father – grandfather – had tried to rescue the boy. If it were not for that, he would be alive and well, and I would still be in happy ignorance. I put my head down on my arms and wept.

I had heard it said that a good cry makes you feel better.

Another lie. Both my mood and my headache got, if anything, worse. I didn't want to go home, nor did I want to talk to anyone who didn't already know. I didn't want to have to explain, not even to Jonty, not today. Finally, I got up, wiped my eyes and my nose on my sleeve, and continued along the footpath. It was beginning to get dark. There were no children playing, no sound of laughter, not even the sound of hooves or a carriage crossing the Heath. It felt as though the world had shunned me. I decided to go back to Joe's, to ask him about the trouble between his sister and his wife. If there was more bad stuff to learn, I might as well know it all now.

Joe sighed. We sat at his kitchen table, cradling mugs of tea. He had sent Bella back to her loft. He did not want her to hear what he had to say about her sister.

'Harriett and I, we were very young when we married. I was nineteen, she was two or three years younger,' he began. 'I was away a lot, sometimes all week. She was too much on her own, you see, with nothing much to do. At first, she would help Mother with the little ones – you, and George. But then you went off to school, and she wasn't needed anymore. Somehow – *somehow* – she met Bebe. Well, you've got a pretty good idea of what sort of a woman she was, haven't you? They started meeting up, every week, whilst Abel and I were off doing our deliveries. And Harriett – my *wife*—' Joe paused; his mouth set in a grim line. 'Well, she started working with Bebe. With men. You know what I mean? Then, one day, she – Harriett – had a dreadful accident. She was walking along the Isleworth road. She had the dog with her – I had bought her a dog – and it seems that she got pulled under the wheels of a passing wagon. There was an inquest, of course. And Bebe turned up and made sure that everyone knew what Harriett was doing whilst I was away. Then she disappeared. And as far as I know, nobody heard from her between then and when she came to Father's funeral.'

'But why,' I asked, 'did no one ever tell me?'

'Well, you were only a nipper then, too young to understand. Besides, you had never met her, not since you were a babe. And later – well, there didn't seem to be any point. It was kindly meant, you know.'

'Yes, but later,' I persisted. 'When I was older, and could have understood?'

'I guess no one thought about it. We were all used to you being just one of the youngsters, you see. You were happy, living with Mother and Father and the rest, weren't you?'

I nodded, tears near the surface.

'But now, Joe...Well, no one is who they were anymore. It's – it's *too much*, somehow. There are too many questions still. Like, who was Tomas Harys? Where did he come from? Where is he now? And what happened to the other baby?'

'I'm afraid only Bebe can answer those questions, lad. All I know is, it was a baby girl, and she was called Elizabeth.'

I thought about the paper She had pressed into my hand. 'Mrs Elizabeth Caxton', not 'Mrs Elizabeth Harys'.

'What do I do now, Joe?'

'Take your time. Have a proper think about it all. Don't rush off at half-cock. You want to stay here tonight?'

'Please.'

In bed that night, my mind went over and over all that I had been told. Surely there were some clues that I should have picked up on. But I could think of none. Not any word or look that would have given me a hint. Not even from Louisa. Eventually I drifted off to sleep, waking with a start some hours later. Louisa! Her children – the Forresters – were a mixture of her and Simon. Of course! Any time I looked at my reflection, I should have known, or suspected. The Broughton children – the *real* Broughton children – were all fair-skinned, blond, and blue-eyed giants. I have brown eyes and dark hair, a sallow complexion, and am at least half a head shorter than even the girls.

The best part of a week passed. I had avoided going back

154

home, bunking down with Joe. I was glad to be taking his smaller cart out by myself; it gave me plenty of time to think. I told Jonty. He was sympathetic, said all the 'right' things, but I sensed he was distracted. Thinking of his father, no doubt. It was not until the Sunday that I saw any of my family, other than Joe, again.

The most immediate problem I faced was what to call everyone. Joe assured me that nobody would be expecting to be addressed as 'aunt' or 'uncle', even if they knew of the disclosure which, he was pretty sure, they didn't. The first names I had always used would be fine. It would attract far more comment if I called them anything else. The trickiest problem was – well, obvious. My head told me I should say Grandmother, but my heart refused to accept anything other than Mother.

I had driven the small cart to church. Mother, Joe, Elspet Rowlatt and Jonty were my passengers. Minding the road, avoiding the churchgoers walking to Isleworth, and keeping control of the horse gave me sufficient excuse not to talk. After the service we repaired, as usual, to the Farley villa.

Grandfather Farley was sitting in his wing chair by the hearth, his nurse hovering nearby. He never left the house, these days. He was gently helped to take his place at the head of his table for lunch. He moved his food around on his plate, occasionally taking a mouthful which he would chew and then spit out. His nurse was ready with a cloth, to wipe his mouth, and pick up the mess. Louisa and Simon kept up a flow of conversation at the other end of the table, determined that no one should notice this behaviour. By the time the tea-tray was brought in, later in the afternoon, I realised that Grandfather had not spoken a word during the whole of our visit.

I went up to him, undecided as to whether to be grateful to him, for opening the door to the mystery of my birth, or annoyed. I couldn't think of anything sensible to say, and resorted to the banal. 'Hello, Grandfather,' I said. 'How are you today?'

He looked at me sadly through rheumy eyes.

'I can't think of anything to say,' he replied, before looking away. His chin resting on his chest, he stared at his hands, laying idle in his lap, until he nodded off.

Caro, a frown wrinkling her brow, took me aside.

'I'm worried about Mother, Joss. I'm going to suggest that she comes to stay for a while. Will you be alright on your own? George says he is going up to the London docks next week, to try for a place on a merchantman.'

'I'm staying with Joe at the moment. I'll be fine.'

Since the accident, I had not given any thought to George's intention to go to sea. It seemed that, in the last month, my whole life had been turned upside down. Nothing was as it had been. The cottage in Trafalgar Terrace no longer felt like home. Everyone was leaving. Caro and Mother (although I stayed stupidly angry with her, I had given up trying to think of something else to call her) would be in Isleworth, George would be goodness knows where, and Joe looked set to marry Elspet Rowlatt. Even Jonty was quieter, and I did not think it was entirely due to his father's death. I was changing, too. I began to see that I should at least have a proper talk to my real mother, to hear her side of the story. I needed to decide for myself whether she was as black as she had been painted. And I also wanted to know about my father, and my little sister, who would now be about fifteen, if she lived.

George duly left the following week. Joe was short-tempered. Jonty seemed preoccupied and disinclined for company.

The next Sunday, after church, I found the spot where my brother William lay. I sat on the grass and, pulling a few weeds away, came across the remnants of a wooden marker that had fallen over and become buried during the course of time. I could, just about, make out part of William's name carved on it.

'I promise,' I whispered to the ground, 'that one day,

William, I will come back and get you a proper headstone.'

I planned what I was beginning to think of as my escape. Mother returned to Bearshott, and I moved back into Trafalgar Terrace, where relations between us remained politely strained. I decided to keep my plans to myself – I did not want anyone trying to deter me. Nor did I tell anybody that my mother had given me her address.

One evening in late August, I crammed as many of my clothes as I could into my bag, emptied the little savings I had into my trouser pocket, stowed the paper with Bebe's address inside my jacket, bid Mother goodbye, and went across to Allnutt's Yard ready for the next morning's early start.

Breakfast was horrible, the rain was tipping down, my boots leaked, the horse played up, and no one had noticed any change in me, that I was leaving, perhaps forever. I became morose and angry all over again, though mostly with myself, for not saying farewell properly.

I noticed the look Joe gave to my bulging bag as I stowed it under the seat, though he said nothing about it. Before clambering up, he went back into the house, saying there was something he had forgotten.

As we plodded on into London, I began to be excited at the prospect of meeting my mother and, presumably, her husband. I had accompanied Joe to Clapton a few times, though I had never heard of Cricketfield Road. I was certain someone would be able to direct me when it came to it. I wondered what sort of home they might keep, whether it was anything like the neat little apartment where Sarah lived.

I helped Joe unload at Covent Garden. It was still pouring down. I turned to Joe, about to tell him that I would not be going any further with him, when he forestalled me.

'You remember where Sarah lives? If you need anything, somewhere to go, go to her. And you'd better keep that cape, you'll be soaked through, else.'

'Thank you, Joe.' I could feel my eyes prick with the tears that seemed to come so easily these days.

I hefted my bag and held out my hand. Instead of taking it, Joe pressed a fat canvas purse into it, closing his other hand over mine. I could feel the coins moving about as he squeezed. I gasped. 'Joe – I can't possibly—'

'Don't worry, lad – it's not mine. I've no idea how much there is – I never looked inside. You have just as much right to it as anyone, I reckon. I'm glad to have found a good use for it.'

'Thanks, Joe,' I said again, feeling very awkward. 'Tell them – tell them all – I will write. Soon.'

14: Hide and Seek

Cricketfield Road was lined with two-, three-, and four-storey terraced houses. Number seventy-five, at the top end of the street, was single-fronted. A short path and a flight of stone steps led up to the front door on the first floor. Two further storeys above rose to a gable-end, embellished with fretwork, whilst below, a wrought iron gate set in the railings to one side of the path opened onto a flight of steps giving access down to the basement area. The bay window, lintels and porch, painted cream, contrasted smartly with the buff brickwork.

Joss felt immeasurably cheered that Bebe was apparently a person of some means, providing one did not dwell on how those means might have been earned.

He took a turn or two up and down the street, trying to pluck up the courage to rap on the front door. The door was opened to his knock by a slight, rather mousy, servant girl.

'I've come to – I wish – to see Mrs Elizabeth Caxton.'

'No one here of that name,' the maid said, after a brief pause, beginning to close the door.

'Oh!' Joss looked at the paper in his hand, then at the number displayed on the front door. 'But – are you sure? See, this is what she wrote.' He held out the paper for the girl's inspection. She squinted at it, looked up at him searchingly, and opened her mouth. Before she could speak, a male voice came from the hall behind her.

'I'll deal with this. Get back to the kitchen, girl. You know you shouldn't be up here.' A large, liveried manservant stood framed in the doorway. 'Now, what is it you want, young man?'

Joss held out the paper Bebe had given him once more. 'I was given this address by my mother—'

The man stiffened. 'There is no one here of that name,' he said, unconsciously parroting the maid's words. 'Be off with you.'

Finding the door closed in his face, Joss had no choice but to descend the steps back to the pavement. He stood for a moment, entirely at a loss as to what to do next. The little maid darted out of the basement door. Grasping a couple of railings, and with her head only just above pavement level, she hissed up at him, 'White Lion Street!' before disappearing back into the house.

'Thank you,' said Joss to empty air.

The only White Lion public house that Joss knew of was back in Covent Garden, and he was certain that none of the streets around was named after it. He made his way back down the road, to a tavern that he remembered passing earlier. With the money Joe had given him, he could well afford to indulge in a beer and an ordinary. It would be pleasant to sit somewhere dry. Although it had stopped raining some while before, his feet were still wet, and he would be glad to take off the cumbersome cape Joe had lent him. Ordering a pint and some mutton broth, bread and cheese, Joss asked the barman if he knew where White Lion Street might be.

'Nah, mate. Not round 'ere.'

Carrying his drink to a quiet corner table, whilst he waited for his lunch to be brought, Joss dried his feet as best he might with his handkerchief, put on a clean pair of socks and his best boots, and forced the damp cape into his bulging haversack. Fishing his copy of *Cross's London Guide* out of his pocket, he spread it out on the table. Joe had marked on it the principal places where they made deliveries. Unfortunately, there was no street index included, and it took the best part of half an hour, pouring over the map, before Joss found White Lion Street. He had had enough of walking and carrying the heavy bag. He decided to spend threepence on the fare to Islington.

Omnibuses, hackney carriages, and delivery carts plied up and down the busy thoroughfare. The foetid smell of horse manure hung over the street, the sharp odour catching in Joss's nostrils. The recent heavy rainfall had washed the roads, turning the ever-present caked dung into slurry. The wheels of passing vehicles churned the muck, spraying it over unwary pedestrians. Crowds thronged the pavements.

Joss was disheartened to see how long White Lion Street was, how many premises – shops and tenements – opened onto its pavements. However was he to find Bebe amongst all this bustle? And why couldn't that stupid girl have told him the building number? His shoulder was beginning to ache from the weight of his haversack.

One thing that Joe had told him about Bebe came to mind: she frequented public houses. He would make his first enquiries at any taverns in the street. Drawing a blank at the first he came to, he next reached The Three Johns, on the corner of Barron Street. Ordering a gill of mild, he asked the barman if he knew an Elizabeth Caxton. He did not, saying he only knew the names of regular customers. Joss described Bebe to him. The barman shook his head. Despondent, Joss ordered another drink. How he wished Jonty, or George, were with him; they would have turned the search into some sort of adventure. How he wished he were home.

Huffing on a glass before giving it a good polish, the barman cocked an eyebrow at Joss. 'Your girl, is she?'

'No, no. She's my sister,' Joss replied, prevaricating. 'She gave me her address, but they told me she's moved here. They didn't know the number.'

'Funny she didn't let you know, then.'

'I daresay she did, but I've been away from home for a bit.'

'Looks like you've got a job on your hands, then. I daresay you'll be needing a bed for the night?'

'I guess,' Joss answered gloomily. 'Do you know of any lodgings nearby?'

'Well...' the barman considered the matter. 'There are some lodging houses up the top end of the street. Or,' he added, 'we have a room here that the missus sometimes lets out. I could ask her for you, if you like.'

'Would you? That would be great, thanks.'

Joss had not previously thought about where he was to stay that night. It was plain to see that his search was unlikely to be concluded that day. He would be glad to leave the heavy bag somewhere whilst he tried to trace Bebe. The barman returned.

'That's all right and tight. She says one and a tanner, including clean sheets. In advance, o' course. Dinner extra.'

The room was small and stuffy. A rather grimy window looked out onto the noisy street, but the bedlinen did indeed look clean. Joss foresaw that he would not be getting a peaceful night's sleep. Unpacking his bag, he draped the damp cape over the back of a chair to dry and hung his wet socks over the edge of the washbowl.

He decided that his next move should be to enquire in all the shops. Hopefully, the shopkeepers would know the names of the people living in the apartments above or would perhaps recognize Bebe from her description. The canvas purse full of coins was a problem. Joss did not want to leave it in the room – he had not been offered a key – and Joe had often impressed upon him how many pickpockets there were in London. Finally, he removed the laces from his old boots and, threading them through the drawstring, hung the purse about his neck. It was somewhat uncomfortable, as it swung about as he moved, and it seemed likely that the lace would cut into his neck. Rummaging in his bag once more, he took out a muffler and knotted it around his throat, to disguise the strange lump the purse made under his shirt.

Three hours spent going in and out of shops and commercial premises elicited no information. As nobody reacted to either the name or Bebe's description, Joss was pretty sure that the denials were genuine. The traders started to put up their shutters. He decided to abandon the fruitless search for the day.

It took until the middle of the following afternoon to visit all the shops, but with no success. Dispirited, Joss went into a coffee house and, as he drank his coffee and ate a bun, pondered over his options. It did not seem at all likely that he would find Bebe, however long he spent trailing up and down the busy street, unless by pure accident. A passing omnibus, bound for Clapton, caught his eye. He resolved to return to Cricketfield Road and ask the maid if she had any more information.

This time, he went down the iron steps to the area and knocked at the tradesmen's entrance. He had an imperfect knowledge of the duties of a butler, entirely based on remarks Phia had made from time to time, but the one working in this household seemed to him far too grand to be answering the kitchen door. He just hoped there was no cook, footman, parlourmaid or housekeeper who might. The little maid opened the door. She gave a start at the sight of him but did not appear displeased to see him.

'I've gone up and down White Lion Street,' Joss began, 'but I can't find anyone who knows Mrs Caxton. Do you know what building number it is?'

The girl shook her head. 'No. But it's next door to a pub.'

Relieved, Joss asked, 'The Lord Wolseley or The Three Johns?'

'The Pewter Platter,' she said, frowning. 'It's on the corner with Blossom Street.'

Joss pulled out his map. Muttering 'Blossom Street' to

himself, he scanned the area around White Lion Street. The maid peeked over his shoulder, giggled, and said, 'Not *Islington*. Spitalfields!'

Joss had only visited Spitalfields once before, when delivering, with Joe, produce to the market. Joe had warned him that, although there were several prosperous streets around about, inhabited by the well-to-do, there were also several renowned for their low-class and criminal occupants, to be avoided at all costs. Joss had no idea which category White Lion Street might fall into.

He had spent the previous night at an inn in Hackney, not wanting to arrive in Spitalfields just as the light was fading. On his way from Cricketfield Road, he had come across a fancy goods shop, where he had bought a sturdy leather purse, threaded onto a belt. In his room, he had thankfully taken off the canvas bag from around his sore neck, emptied it out onto the bed and counted the money it held. He was amazed to find that the assortment of coins added up to nearly twenty pounds. Keeping back enough to pay his shot at the inn and cover his expenses for the next day or two, he put the rest of the cash into the money belt. Even so, he was very conscious of the coins jingling in his pocket and was glad when the morning turned out to be wet, and he had an excuse to put the waterproof cape back on, protecting him from more than the rain.

Joss stood across the road from The Pewter Platter which did, indeed, stand on the corner of Blossom Street. He had been relieved to find that the houses in White Lion Street were, for the most part, well-kept. That next to the public house was a single-fronted, three-storey, end-of-terrace townhouse. Realising that he was himself beginning to attract some unwelcome attention with his bedraggled appearance, his voluminous cape, and the large bag slung over one shoulder, he strode briskly across the street and knocked smartly on the front door. He had to knock twice more before it was finally opened by a man in his thirties (Joss guessed), wearing a leather apron and holding in his hand a button boot.

'I beg your pardon for disturbing you,' Joss began, 'but I'm looking for Mrs Caxton. I understand she lives here?'

'Top floor,' the cobbler replied, adding, 'but she'll likely be in bed.' Joss's heart sank. The last thing he wanted was to find his mother 'at work'. With some trepidation he mounted the stairs to the second floor and tapped on the door at the top. A sleepy voice called out, 'Who is it?'

'Josiah.'

There was silence for a moment, then he heard hurried footsteps, and the door was flung open. Bebe stood before him, barefoot, clutching a filmy wrapper around herself.

'Josiah!' she exclaimed. 'You came! Come in, come in.' She made as though to put her arms around him, but, seeing Joss recoil slightly, she laughed and said, 'Too soon? What should I call you?'

'Josiah's fine,' Joss replied. He did not feel that she had the right, yet, to call him by his familiar name. He had no idea how he was going to address her. She waved him towards an armchair, seating herself in front of a dressing-table littered with an untidy array of make-up, scent bottles, hair ornaments, brushes, and combs. She made no move to cover her déshabille.

'Well, tell me all about yourself,' she invited. 'How clever of you to track me down! I gave you the old Clapton address, didn't I?'

Joss told her about his visit to the house in Cricketfield Road and the two days he had wasted in Islington, due to the incomplete information furnished by the servant.

'Oh, dear. Poor you!' Her mouth twitched. 'Yes, she's not the brightest, that one. Never mind, you're here now. I expect you think me a slugabed? I was out with some friends last evening, celebrating. I'm afraid I have to catch up on my beauty sleep after late nights these days.'

Joss looked at her critically. She was a handsome woman and, though not in her prime, looked to be in no need of 'beauty sleep'. If she were fishing for compliments, he was not going to gratify her. Instead, he asked, 'Celebrating?' 'Why, yes. The first night of our play. Did you not know that I am an actress?' He shook his head. 'We opened yesterday, in the theatre just around the corner. An old play, but it always goes down well with audiences. Perhaps you'd like to see it? I could get you a ticket if you like.'

Joss hesitated.

'Oh, do come! It would be such fun. I could introduce you to my pals, after, and we could have a nice supper somewhere. So, how about it?' She smiled prettily at him. He wondered just how many men she had looked at in just that way. He was determined to get answers to his questions, but perhaps socialising a little would give him a better understanding of her. He nodded.

'Excellent. I shall leave a ticket for you at the box office. Afterward, just come around to the stage door and ask for me. Now, do you have somewhere to stay?'

She gave him directions to the theatre, suggested some addresses to try for a bed for a night or two, told him she had things to do, and airily waved goodbye. Without quite knowing how, he found himself on the landing outside her apartment, with the door firmly closed. She must, he reflected bitterly, have become well-practised in so easily dismissing male visitors.

He was pleasantly surprised to find that the first address she had given him was a respectable lodging-house along the main road, not far from the theatre itself, where they were able to offer him a room, plus breakfast, for two or three nights, at what seemed to him to be a reasonable rate. Having been given a key, he was happy to unpack his haversack and put his few clothes in the cupboard provided, though he was still determined to wear the money belt. He transferred some

166

more of the coins to the canvas purse. If he were going out for supper later, he was determined to pay his own way.

Having enjoyed an excellent lunch at an eating-house recommended by his landlady, he had some hours to fill before the evening performance of *Black-Eyed Susan*. He spent the afternoon walking up and down Norton Folgate, browsing in the shops, before returning to his lodgings. He decided to dash off a couple of lines to Jonty, care of Elspet Rowlatt – Joe would have told his family where he was, and he would be back with them in a few days – but once he got started, he included a description of his travels to Clapton, Islington, back to Clapton, and finally to the east end. As he wrote, he saw the funny side of his useless search in Islington and knew that Jonty would likewise find it amusing. His letter finished, he lay down on his bed, intending to take a short nap before going along to the theatre.

Two hours later, he awoke with a start. The evening was drawing in. He hurried up the road to the City of London Theatre. Claiming his ticket, he took his seat at the back of the stalls, to the annoyance of a number of other theatre-goers. Having missed the first act entirely, the finer points of the plot escaped him, but he was surprised, and oddly pleased, to find that Bebe had the second female lead, in the character of Dolly Mayflower. He was not surprised to discover that she excelled in this admittedly somewhat undemanding role. After the performance, he went, as instructed, to wait at the stage door.

It was some time before Bebe put in an appearance. When she finally appeared, she was one of a chattering group, some of whom Joss recognised from the play. He caught a fleeting look of annoyance cross her face when she saw him. Had she forgotten she had invited him, or did she regret doing so? It occurred to him that she had not expected him to arrive at her door and had probably only given him her address in the expectation that he would cause some sort of stir by sharing it with the family. She greeted him gaily, introduced him as her son – it hardly seemed possible (she laughed) that she could be mother to such a grown-up young man! How the years had flown! – and linked an arm through his. The party made its noisy way to a nearby restaurant which, he was told, was a favourite haunt of 'theatricals'.

Joss felt somewhat out of it. The conversation turned around the missed cues and fluffed lines of the evening's performance, their plans to take the play 'on the road', plays he had never heard of, people he did not know, and places he had never visited. Unable to join in, he spent the time observing his mother, taking note of the things she said, and how she interacted with her intimates. It seemed to him that she was acting still, whether for his benefit or for some other reason.

The party finally broke up just before midnight. Bebe suggested to Joss that they should stay for a nightcap, just the two of them, since they had had no opportunity to talk during the evening. Afterward, she said, he could walk her home, like the gentleman she was sure he was. She called the waiter over and ordered their drinks. Joss pulled the canvas purse out of his pocket. As he sorted through the coins for the correct money, he felt her stiffen at his side.

'That's a strange purse for a young man. Where did you get it?' He thought she sounded nervous. There was a serious tone to her voice that he had not heard before.

'Joe gave it to me,' Joss replied, without thinking. She picked up the purse and hefted it in her hand. There were only a few coins left in it.

'Generous,' she remarked, laying it back on the table.

Joss realised, then, who the purse had once belonged to, and how the money in it had been earned. Bebe obviously recognised it. He was about to assure her that Joe was, indeed, generous, that there had been a substantial sum in it, most of which was now secreted about his person. He hesitated. He did not want to tell anybody about the money belt. He could not be sure that she would keep the information to herself.

She might even try to persuade him to part with it. Normally, he would have stuck up for Joe. He could not bear that anyone would think that he had helped himself to his wife's kitty, that he had benefitted from Harriett's behaviour, that he should be so maligned. No. He would hold his tongue. If Bebe truly thought that Joe would do such a thing, she did not know her brother at all. Such a thought was to her discredit, not Joe's.

'Well, Josiah. Tell me all about yourself. Are you working? Have you a lady friend?' Joss told her he barely knew any girls, apart from Caro and Phia.

'Phia?'

'She lives at the big house.'

'I used to know someone who lived there, but I don't remember anyone called Phia.'

'You wouldn't know her; she was born after you – er – left. Her proper name's Philadelphia.'

Shortly after, they left the restaurant, Bebe claiming that she had a headache. As they parted, Joss told her he would meet her at noon the next day, in the pub on the corner, for lunch. She could not promise to be there, she said. He would understand that she was very busy with the play; there was to be another rehearsal in the afternoon, to resolve some issues that had arisen.

Joss was not to be put off. Rather than waiting in The Pewter Platter, he once more knocked on the door of her apartment, telling her that he had come to escort her, not liking the idea of a lady walking into a public house alone.

She raised a petulant shoulder. 'Oh, well, if you must,' she said crossly.

They found themselves a quiet table in the little garden at the rear where, Joss hoped, they might have some private conversation undisturbed. The poor weather of the past few days seemed at an end. The midday sun shone cheerfully down, throwing Bebe's face into shadow under the wide brim of her hat.

At last, she said, 'I suppose there are things that you want to know.' It was a statement, not a question. 'Very well. Ask away.'

First, he asked about the man named as his father on his birth certificate. She shrugged and told Joss he had gone back to Wales. She had not heard from him for years. Joss asked if he was also William's father.

'William? Oh, *William*. He took the chincough, poor little mite. Or was it the measles? No. No, he wasn't.'

'And Elizabeth? Was he her father?'

'Little Elizabeth? No.' She drained her glass and moved as though to get up. Joss held her by the wrist, preventing her from leaving.

'Where is Elizabeth now?'

She looked sideways at him. 'Oh, she's around somewhere, working. I haven't seen her for a while.' She looked at the little watch pinned to the front of her dress. 'Well, I'm afraid I must go. Thank you for coming to see me.'

Joss realised that he had all the answers she was prepared to give. She did not want any relationship between them. There was nothing motherly about her. However much she simpered and smiled, behind her eyes she was hard and unloving. He felt no connection to her and could not like her. He stood as she left but did not offer to escort her back to her lodging. She was, after all, no lady. He sat down again, to finish his beer.

He pondered the mystery of his family. How could such a kindly, warm, generous couple as Mother and Father have such a daughter as Bebe? Or Louisa? He could appreciate the difference between the two women. The one was all for herself, her eye on the main chance. Everything the other did, however irritating, was in support of her husband and children. Sarah Jane he had met many times, at various family gatherings. Caro and she were carbon copies of their mother. The other two older girls – Catherine and Lucy – he had never met. They had left to go into service before he was born, and never came back to Bearshott. All the sons took after Father — straightforward, steady, and diligent. Something must have happened to Bebe in her youth, to make her as she was. He realised that he had not asked about 'Mr Caxton'. Just another fly-by-night, probably. If he ever existed.

He was now eager to be home. Checking out of his lodging, he made his way across to Covent Garden, where he was hopeful of meeting Joe. He knew quite a few of the porters and stallholders, and whiled away the evening and early morning hours in their company.

Joe, not one to show his feelings readily, was absurdly pleased to see him, pumping his hand, slapping him on the back, and telling him how much everyone had missed him. What a relief it was that he was safe and sound and coming home! He asked what sights had he seen, had he found lodgings alright, had he eaten properly? Anything and everything apart from the one question that was foremost in his mind.

After helping Joe with the rest of his deliveries, Joss crawled into the back of the wagon and dropped off to sleep, oblivious to the sounds of London traffic.

Back at Allnutt's Yard, they unharnessed the horse and washed the wagon down, before going to sit at Joe's kitchen table. Bella had made a sort of stew, which turned out to be surprisingly edible. Joe asked Joss if he would like to go to The Admiral with him for the evening. Joss shook his head. At last, Joe could avoid the subject no longer.

'Well, how is your mother?'

'Lovely,' replied Joss.

Joe looked at him grimly. Joss gave a mischievous grin.

'I'm going home to see her now. Coming?'

15: New Beginnings

The Admiral Nelson was heaving. It was payday, and most of the male population of Bearshott had come to spend what was left of their wages after handing over the housekeeping money to wives or mothers.

It had been a hard eighteen months for the village, slowly adjusting itself to its new reality. Upwards of forty people – mostly children – had died, either of scarlatina or in the accident at the mill. Some families had simply packed up and moved out, to start afresh somewhere else. Matthew Greening's decision to lock his gates until the pestilence passed had ensured that none of the inhabitants of The Bury had been infected, though some had families in the village who had suffered losses. He himself had had a stressful year, refinancing and rebuilding his mill. He had, begrudgingly, paid the costs of the funerals of the workers who had died and agreed to pay small pensions to their dependents. Of Philadelphia, exiled to her aunt's home in Cambridge, the Greenings thought hardly at all.

Joss and Jonty sat at one end of the bar, nursing their ale. They were both feeling restless. The occasional letters that George had written home describing his travels overseas had made them feel vaguely dissatisfied with their lives, though with no clear idea of what else they might like to do.

It had been more than half a year since Joss's trip to

London. He was happy working with Joe but was sure there must be more to life. Joe was still walking out with Elspet Rowlatt. Even if they were to marry, it seemed unlikely that they would have children. When the time came for him to retire, Joe would, in all probability, hand the business over to Joss to run, if things continued as they were. As for Jonty, although he appeared to have recovered from his dejection of the previous year, he did not relish the prospect of working at The Bury for the rest of his life. They had spoken, in a casual fashion, of following George to sea. But Joss vividly recalled the day when Edward had been brought home half-drowned, and Jonty claimed to have once been seasick on the Isleworth ferry. They were only sure that they would prefer to do something that involved travel, and they wanted to do it together.

Apart from Saturdays, when he would go there to collect his wages, Jonty never went into the main house. The new bailiff set him to work all over the estate. Matthew Greening either did not know of, or ignored, his presence. The old cottage in Crane Lane remained untenanted, and Jonty continued to lodge at the schoolhouse.

As they sat sipping their ale, Joss idly watched a noisy game of bar billiards, whilst Jonty thumbed through an old copy of *The Times* that Joe had found discarded on one of his trips.

'This news from India doesn't sound too good, does it?'

Before Joss could ask what news his friend was talking about, they were interrupted by a newcomer.

'Tickle, isn't it? Seen you about. Quigley. Feardorcha Quigley.' The Irishman held out his hand. 'Could I buy you a drink, then?'

'No, we're alright, thanks.' Realising how abrupt his reply sounded, Jonty hastily added, 'How about one for yourself?'

'Well, that's mighty sociable. Don't mind if I do.' Quigley turned to Joss. 'And who might this be?' Although he was only two or three years their senior, he was full of a self-assurance that they had yet to achieve. He explained that he had only recently arrived in the village, to work at The Bury, and found it reminded him of his own village back in Derry. Everyone he had met had been most friendly and welcoming.

It was not long before Joss was happily chatting away. Jonty was more reserved. He knew that Quigley was the nephew of the housekeeper, recently returned from America, and he did not trust Mrs McBride.

It seemed that, whenever Joss and Jonty met up after work, it would not be long before Quigley arrived to make a third. Joss thought that Quigley had latched onto them for company of more or less his own age, but Jonty was suspicious of his motives from the beginning.

'Oh, come on, Jonty!' Joss exclaimed, mildly exasperated. 'He's just being friendly. I expect he's feeling a bit lonely.' Jonty remained unconvinced.

Joss began, unconsciously, to expect Feardorcha to join them as a matter of course, even going so far as to invite him when they had something particular planned. It was almost as though the Irishman were a substitute for George, reinstating the old Three Jays. Joss was oblivious to the wedge that was slowly being driven between himself and Jonty. They rarely now spoke of any plans for the future. For Jonty, the only guaranteed relief came on Sundays. Quigley did not attend services at All Saints and was never invited to lunch at the Farley villa.

One day in the summer, as they were enjoying the late evening sunshine in the little beer garden at the back of The Admiral, Quigley said, 'What does 'being presented at Court' mean?'

Joss and Jonty looked at one another, mystified.

'Only,' Quigley continued, 'the little Greening girl's going. You used to know her quite well, didn't you?'

'We used to play together sometimes as children,' Joss said.

'More than sometimes,' Quigley grinned. 'My aunt's told me all about your adventures in the icehouse.'

'That was all a long time ago,' Joss insisted. 'We haven't

really talked to her in years.'

'Oh? That's not right, though, surely? Is it, Jonty? Didn't the pair of you used to meet up, before her folks sent her packing?'

Jonty flushed. 'Sometimes. When she was out for a walk and bumped into me.'

'Come, now, Jonty! More than sometimes, surely?' Quigley teased. 'I heard it was every day, and not just for a quick chat. Or maybe I've got that wrong?'

'Completely,' Jonty replied gruffly. Puzzled, Joss searched his friend's face, which was now white as a sheet.

'Jonty? Is that why—' Joss began. But Jonty got up and walked out of the pub, his drink unfinished.

'Bit chippy, isn't he? Shame to waste this.' Quigley poured the rest of Jonty's beer into his own glass. 'Didn't you know? Well, mates don't always tell each other everything, do they?'

Joss, predisposed though he was to think well of the Irishman, recognised this as a blatant attempt to sow dissension between himself and his best friend. Excusing himself, he hurried out of The Admiral, but Jonty was nowhere in sight.

It was not until the following Sunday that the pair met again. Jonty had avoided the pub, and whenever Joss called at the schoolhouse, Elspet Rowlatt could only tell him that Jonty was not in. That he was present on Sunday only under sufferance was obvious, declining his usual seat in Jonty's cart and choosing to walk to church.

The verger was unpinning a notice from the church gate when they arrived. Tutting, he carried it to the porch, where he laid it with some others on the bench. After the service the vicar stood, as was his custom, bidding each member of his congregation 'Godspeed' as they left the church. A gust of wind caught the pile of papers. Jonty, waiting behind as Louisa monopolised the conversation, bent to help pick them up. One took his eye. This he folded carefully and stuffed into his pocket.

He tried to avoid the usual Sunday lunch at the Farley villa, but Joss would have none of it, telling him he was expected, and it would give a very poor impression if he failed to attend. Even the youngest Forrester was now permitted to take her seat at the Farley lunch table. The resulting lively chatter took Jonty out of himself for a time, and Joss was encouraged to think that his gloomy mood would soon pass. Never having suffered the pangs of love, requited or not, Joss could only sympathise with his friend, in a somewhat vague way. To discover that Jonty cherished romantic feelings for Phia came as something of a bombshell. Quigley's insinuations he dismissed out of hand. He knew Jonty and was at last coming to know the Irishman.

The following evening they met at The Admiral, for 'a quick half'. As they parted outside afterwards, Jonty surprised Joss by giving him a brief hug.

'Thanks, Joss. Thanks for everything.'

'That's alright. What're friends for?' Joss replied, somewhat embarrassed.

The following day, Joe and Joss started out early, having deliveries to make to London and then into Bedfordshire, and not expecting to be back before Thursday afternoon. Bella was left in charge of feeding and watering the other pony, at which she had become surprisingly adept, with instructions to call on Elizabeth Broughton or Elspet Rowlatt if she needed help with anything else.

Late on Thursday, Joe drove the big rig back into Allnutt's Yard. Elspet Rowlatt came hurrying out of his house. Before they could even begin to alight, she had run across the yard and called up, not to Joe, but to Joss, 'It's Jonty. He's gone!'

'Gone?' Joss echoed, puzzled. 'Gone where?'

'I found this in his room.' She offered a folded paper up to him. Mystified, he opened it out. '*Young men of good character aged eighteen to twenty-five years*' (he read) '*are invited to join The London and Middlesex (Prudhoe's Own) Regiment of Foot. Bounty on Acceptance £3. Apply at The Drill Hall, Hounslow, Thursday and*

Friday, eleventh and twelfth of June. God save the Queen.'

'But – he can't have done. Not without saying,' Joss stammered.

That night, he tossed and turned restlessly in his bed. He had known, almost as soon as he had realised what Jonty had done, what he himself would do.

In many ways, this was the ideal solution. They would undoubtedly travel, and in one another's company, but worrying about the distress that his family would feel if he went off with no warning was causing his sleepless night. He could not afford to wait, to visit them all and say his goodbyes. If he did not get to the recruitment office the next day, but were to wait for the next enlistment drive, there was the danger that Jonty would be posted goodness knows where, and he would never catch up with him.

In the morning, he laid the poster on the table for Elizabeth to see. 'Jonty's already gone.'

'Well, then,' she said, after a brief pause, 'you'd better get a move on, hadn't you, or you'll miss him.'

It took him two hours of hurried walking to reach Hounslow, all the while fearful that, by the time he arrived, the recruiting office would be shut. As he approached, he was relieved to see the sturdy figure of Jonty, standing outside the drill hall. He called out to him. Jonty turned to him, glad to see him but on the defensive.

'Have you signed up yet?'

'Not yet, but I'm going to. Don't try to talk me out of it.'

'No such thing. You might have waited for me. We'll go in together, shall we?' Joss grinned at the ludicrous expression on his friend's face. 'You didn't think I'd let you go off on an adventure by yourself, did you?'

Hawking onto the toecap, Jonty puddled the mess around with a cloth-covered fingertip, working methodically in small circular motions. He rather liked bootblacking; there was much satisfaction to be had from a pair of highly polished boots, he had found.

Joss watched him from the next cot, hands linked behind his head, feet crossed at the ankle.

'D'you ever see them before? On your trips to London?'

'No,' Joss shook his head. 'We were never called upon to deliver anything to the palace.'

Jonty began to give the boot a brisk rub. 'What will you do?'

'Go down into the town and gawp, I expect. Watch you taking the shine out of the locals.'

'Don't you think it's odd, though? I mean, no one knowing they were coming?'

'I suppose you can be as odd as you like if you're the Queen. It's the royal whatchamacallit.' Joss yawned. 'Are you going to be much longer?'

The regiment had been in Jersey for some months, on garrison duty. This unscheduled visit by the royal family made a welcome change from the usual routine. The 15th were to provide the guard of honour and the band, and would be stationed at the pier, but the other regiments presently serving on the island were to provide men to line the route at strategic points. Jonty, tall and broad-shouldered, smart in his regimentals, was an obvious choice to be one of those representing the London and Middlesex. Joss, barely of average height, and still slightly-built, despite all the exercise he was getting, was not.

Jonty marched away immediately after breakfast. Those men not detailed to be of the party were instructed to go into the town to swell the crowds. Joss made his way down to the quayside. Across the water, he could see the royal squadron at anchor off Elizabeth Castle. from where there boomed a twenty-one-gun salute.

The band struck up, entertaining the onlookers awaiting the arrival of Victoria, Albert, and a gaggle of young princes and princesses. Joss was surprised to find himself carried away by the moment. When the royal party made its way along the red carpet to the waiting carriages, he waved his helmet and hurrahed with gusto.

'Careful!' came an indignant voice. He turned to see a young woman straightening her hat. He began to apologise, but some of the crowd nearby beginning to mutter, in Jèrriais – a language he had not a word of – he prudently moved away. He had been on the island long enough to know that not all the locals welcomed the troops stationed there.

The royals were driven on a circuitous route around the town, giving Joss ample time to go directly to where Jonty was stationed outside the college that was named in honour of the Queen herself. As the carriages approached the troops snapped to attention.

The awaiting dignitaries were thrown into some slight disorder, as the little convoy entered the college grounds by a different gateway than expected. The royals alighted and were greeted – and outnumbered – by several worthies of the State, none of whom Joss recognised, except that he had seen one or two earlier down at the pier.

The crowds in the street outside had to wait whilst their majesties were conducted around the college out of public view, but were alerted to their eventual reappearance by the cheers of the pupils in the quadrangle. The carriages drove sedately back to the harbour, followed by many of the excited crowd.

Jonty and his comrades were stood down as soon as the carriages were out of sight and, having acquitted themselves well, were given permission to spend the rest of the afternoon at leisure. Deciding that they had seen enough royalty for one day, he and Joss sauntered down into the heart of St Helier, with no plan other than to take some refreshment somewhere. Even in the town centre they could hear the cheering crowds down by the harbour, another gun salute, and the faint strains of the band playing *Rule Britannia*.

Coming upon a photographic studio, Joss suggested that they have their likenesses taken, to send home to their nearest and dearest, just in case they had forgotten what they looked like. Jonty pointed out that he had no nearest and dearest, but Joss assured him that Elizabeth and Caro, and also Elspet Rowlatt, would be glad to hear from him – even George, if they could ever catch up with him. In any case, it would be a pity if Jonty's splendid uniform were not captured for posterity. Provided, of course, that the reflection from the gleaming boots and brass did not damage the camera nor, indeed, blind the photographer. Jonty allowed himself to be persuaded.

That evening, back in barracks, Joss wrote two letters, one to Elizabeth and the other to Caro, describing the day's events, and what he could recall of the appearances of the Queen and the princesses. That to Caro was rather longer, as he also dwelt on some of the more absurd aspects of the day, such as the flap when the Queen's carriage entered the college grounds by the 'wrong' gate, and the sweaty appearance of several of the notables there to greet her – occasioned, he had no doubt, by the necessity of running up to the college ready to greet her having already been presented to her down at the harbour.

The following week, having collected their photographs, Joss enclosed one of each of them with his letters, together with a Jersey one-thirteenth-of-a-shilling coin that he thought might be of interest. Posting his letters in one of the new bronze-green pillar boxes, he remarked to Jonty that Will would have been very interested in this innovation, as he had been collecting stamps since they first came out. Joss was sure that the stamps, with their Jersey franks, would be passed on to him, which was why he had chosen not to send his letters via the army mailbag.

They wandered on toward St Aubin's Bay and, coming across a quiet café overlooking the beach, decided to stop for a pot of tea. It was an unexpected reminder of home; the tea was served in a china teapot, with creamer and sugar basin, and cups and saucers to drink from. The tea brought across to the barrack from the mess came in a large can, ready milked and sugared, and was ladled out into the soldiers' tin mugs. The young woman who brought their tea looked vaguely familiar to Joss. It seemed as though she also recognised him. It was not until he was halfway through his second cup that the penny dropped. Jonty fortuitously called her over, asking for some hot water to top up the pot.

'You're the girl with the hat,' Joss said.

'I was very nearly the girl *without* the hat.'

'Yes; I'm sorry about that.' Joss tried to think of something else to say. 'Er – what did you think of the Queen?'

'Well,' she considered, 'I couldn't see much for all the waving arms about me. I'll fetch you some more hot water.'

'I think she likes you,' Jonty said, watching her retreating back.

'How do you make that out?' Jonty just grinned.

It seemed that, whenever they were at liberty to go down into the town, their footsteps would lead them to the little café. Her name was Mireille, they learnt. She was eighteen, and had a sister, one year younger, called Delphine. She did not work on Wednesdays, and she liked to go and sit in the Parade gardens on her day off, weather permitting. She was very surprised (she said) to find that Joss and his friend enjoyed the gardens, too. It became a regular occurrence for Joss and Jonty to squire Mireille and Delphine on gentle walks about the town, sometimes challenging one another to a game of boule lyonnaise in the park. Once, they even managed a carriage ride along the coast.

The business of falling in love was a foreign country to Joss. He began to find that thoughts of Mireille intruded at singularly inappropriate moments. When he was on guard duty, perhaps, when he ought to be watching out for steamers leaving St Malo, during kit inspection, or in the middle of a game of cards. He found himself distracted, and his mind would wander in the middle of a conversation, so that he would lose the thread. Jonty watched, and smiled to himself.

16: Meanwhile...

He was nearly ninety. His villa and emporium were festooned in an ostentatious display of grief. Black crape, ribbons, feathers, and silk flowers were abundantly draped, tied, looped, wound, and poked in every conceivable place. The shutters were brought down on the shop, to remain closed until after the funeral. Louisa Forrester had been so unrestrained with her decorations it was almost like a celebration.

Benjamin Farley was transported the short distance from his home to All Saints by the most expensive equipage the undertaker possessed, drawn by four high-stepping black horses, rather than the customary pair, and preceded along the streets by the undertaker himself, resplendent in black, carrying an ebony staff which he placed before him on the roadway with a flourish and a resounding snap at every other step.

A number of similarly sombre carriages followed behind, bearing the chief mourners. Louisa would very much have liked to be in the first but was obliged to cede the place to Elizabeth, who was, after all, the next of kin. It was with some annoyance that she saw that her mother was supported, not only by Caro, but also by Joseph, who was not even Benjamin's eldest grandson.

Naturally, the parade drew morbid interest from the

people of the town. Louisa barely restrained herself from waving to the gratifyingly large crowd, contenting herself with an occasional gracious nod. The church was packed as full as it would hold. The great and the good of Isleworth, and for some miles around, were in attendance. There was even a representative from Syon House.

A marquee had been set up in the villa's garden, with carpets laid upon the grass to ensure that no guest suffered the indignity of sinking into the lawn. Louisa had not been confident in her cook – very well for family meals and small dinner parties, but not good enough for such an important event – and had hired outside caterers. In her determination not to appear cheese-paring, Louisa had over-ordered. The table groaned with such a variety of dishes, the wine poured so freely, that the funeral meats could have been mistaken for a feast.

Benjamin Farley was laid to rest in the vault wherein lay his wife and the children they had lost.

The principal mourners gathered in the drawing room at the villa, fortified with cups of tea, for the reading of the will, which had been made some dozen years before.

'In the name of God, Amen. I, Benjamin Farley, Gentleman, of Rosamund Villa, Isleworth, in the County of Middlesex,' intoned the family solicitor, *'being sound of mind and body, Praise be the Lord, do make and declare this my last Will and Testament in manner and form following that is to say, First, I bequeath my Soul unto the hands of Almighty God believing Remission of Sins and Everlasting Life by the Merits, Death and Passion of Jesus Christ My Lord and Only Saviour, and as Touching the Disposition of Such Temporal Estate as it hath pleased Almighty God to Bestow Upon Me, I give and bequeath as Followeth.'*

There came from the assembled company a sigh, a surreptitious shifting in their seats, an intentness in their gaze. The preamble to the will done, now the real business, the bones of the matter, would come. Benjamin having only one child living, it was expected that Elizabeth would be the major beneficiary. The chief interest lay in the subsequent bequests. The solicitor resumed:

'*Firstly, I will that all my Debts and Funeral Expenses shall be paid and discharged, and all Monies due me be collected, Secondly, I Give Devise and Bequeath unto my Daughter Elizabeth Broughton whom I constitute Sole Executrix, her Heirs, Assigns and Administrators the Freehold property known as Rosamund Villa in the town of Isleworth in the County of Middlesex aforesaid, Thirdly, I do give unto my said Daughter Elizabeth Broughton the Leasehold property known as Farley's Emporium in Isleworth in the County aforesaid on the understanding that her son-in-law Simon Forrester shall for all the time that she retains it manage it on her behalf,*

Fourthly, I do further give to my said Daughter Elizabeth all my Freehold property in the village of Bearshott in the County of Middlesex known as two and five Waterloo Terrace and five and six Trafalgar Terrace together with all the rents pertaining thereto on condition that she maintains said property in a reasonable state, Fifthly, I do further give and bequeath to my daughter Elizabeth Broughton all my Stocks and Shares of whatsoever nature and value of which I die possessed,

Sixthly, unto each of the children of my said daughter Elizabeth, that is to say Louisa Forrester, Sarah Jane Wilkes, Benjamin Broughton, Joseph Broughton, Catherine Broughton, Lucy Broughton, Daniel Broughton, William Broughton, Caroline Broughton and George Broughton the sum of One Hundred Pounds apiece, Seventhly, to each of the children now living of these the aforesaid children of my said Daughter Elizabeth the sum of Ten Pounds apiece, to be paid within twelve months of my decease, Eighthly, to my great-grandson Josiah Broughton I bequeath the sum of Fifty Pounds, Ninethly—' (and here came a list of minor bequests to various of Benjamin's friends and servants).

Louisa was disappointed. Simon was only to run the shop whilst Elizabeth owned it. She had hoped – no, expected – that Benjamin would have stipulated that it would, in due course, pass to herself and her husband. It was a minute or two before the other cause for dissatisfaction occurred to her; Josiah had been left five times the sum left to each of her own children.

After the reading was concluded, the solicitor arranged with Elizabeth that she should come to his office, where they could be private. Although she was the executrix, she would undoubtedly need some assistance with the formalities and legalities. The following morning, his clerk ushered her into Ezra Stanhope's office in the centre of the town. It smelled of leather, old books, and dust. There was a faint whiff of cigar. The solicitor sat behind a reassuringly large desk, on which were placed, besides the usual furniture – ink standish, pens, perpetual calendar and so on – a pile of papers and a metal deed box.

'You will be aware,' he started, rather uncomfortably, 'that when my predecessor drew up this will for your father, there was no reason to suppose its provisions could not be met in full. With your permission, I have conducted a search of Rosamund Villa to ascertain if there has been any subsequent deposition. I found no relevant paperwork at the villa. However, there was this box,' he indicated the document box, 'which was locked. The key could not be found. I have had a locksmith open it, and found it to contain a number of papers, though not a new will. I have also made enquiries of other solicitors in the district. There has not come to light any evidence of a later will, therefore I conclude that this will must stand.'

From his tone, Elizabeth sensed that there was some bad news to come, though what it was she could not imagine. As far as she knew, the shop was doing well, and the rents on the properties in Bearshott were being collected. The villa had been in the family for years.

'What I discovered in the deed box were mortgages, on Rosamund Villa and the cottages in Bearshott. I have contacted the bank which holds them. It appears that the interest has been paid, but no payments have been made against the principal. I regret to tell you that the bank will now wish to foreclose on all those properties – unless you have some means of redeeming the mortgages?'

Elizabeth asked how much was owed. When he told her the figure, she shook her head. 'But what did he want to borrow money for? Do you know?'

'I found a number of share certificates – not those he held when we drafted the will, but other, more speculative, enterprises. I am afraid he was very unwise in his purchases – most of the shares relate to failed companies. And those few that are still trading are not worth what your father paid for them. I'm sorry.'

Elizabeth bit her lip. 'What do you advise, Mr Stanhope?'

The solicitor was relieved to find that he did not have a hysterical woman on his hands.

'You will have to sell the villa and the cottages in Bearshott. There should be some funds left over after you have paid off the mortgages. Mr Farley was only renting the shop premises, and that rent is all paid up to date. I have looked at the accounts, and I am happy to be able to tell you that the business is in a healthy position. You will, if you wish, be able to retain it, or, if you decided to sell, I believe you would realise a good sum for it. Selling would see an immediate return, which might be invested to give you a steady income. Or, you could retain the shop and derive an income from its profits, although they might fluctuate.'

Elizabeth thought for a moment. 'No, I don't think I could sell the shop, Mr Stanhope. My daughter and her husband make their living from it. As it is, they will lose their home at the villa. What about the other bequests – shall I be able to honour my father's wishes?'

'The monetary bequests to your children, grandchildren, and to the servants amount to one thousand two hundred and five pounds. Paying out such a sum will leave you very short of funds for yourself. I advise against it. However, if you are determined to proceed with those, there are, just about, sufficient funds in Mr Farley's bank account to cover at least the payments to your children and the servants. The wording of the will is such that your grandchildren can be paid at the end of a year, without attracting any comment. The bequests to Mr Farley's friends all take the form of possessions – jewellery, pictures, household goods and so forth. Those could be easily complied with. I daresay you would not want it known that your father was, in effect, bankrupt?'

'No, Mr Stanhope; I would not. Would you do what you can to allay any comment, and to expedite the sale? I daresay the bank will need to be apprised of the whole situation? Would you see to everything, please?'

'Certainly, Mrs Broughton. The longer we can keep the situation to ourselves the better. Any hint of the true state of the late Mr Farley's affairs is certain to push the price down. Leave it with me. I daresay you will discuss matters with your children? Impress upon them that discretion is imperative.'

17: The Curragh

They were sitting on the rough grass at the top of the hill, watching the cavalry and artillery charging about on the vast plain below.

'Is it the same for you?'

'When do you think about her?'

'Well, now and then, when I'm just sitting with nothing to do, maybe. Or if I see someone who looks a bit like her, perhaps.'

'Only now and then? Then, no, it's not the same,' Jonty replied. 'Ever thought of trying for a transfer to the cavalry?' he asked, after a pause.

'No way. Pernickety things, horses. I'd rather rely on my own two feet. Do you think we'll ever get sent back to Jersey?'

'I heard Sergeant Barnes say he reckons we'll be off to India.'

'D'you think this wasn't such a good idea after all? The army, I mean. Not exactly thrilling, is it? All we seem to do is a bit of training and a lot of polishing. I mean, what's the point?'

'I don't think about it. We signed up for ten years and that's all there is to it. At least if we get sent to India we should see some action. Hey, up! Here comes Sarge.'

'Right, you lot, on your feet! We're now going to practice

walking up and down in nice, neat lines. And try to keep out of the way of them on horseback. We don't want any blood on those nice clean uniforms. The ladies don't like it. Four-one-six, do that button up!'

The afternoon was spent in field exercises, bayonet drill, and volley firing. Hundreds of spectators – soldiers' families, camp followers, and locals – watched the proceedings from vantage points around the ground, clapping and cheering at everything and nothing. The weather being particularly fine, there was quite a carnival atmosphere. Amongst the chattering crowd many sutlers hawked their wares, from religious tracts to saucy photographs, cheap jewellery to tins of Blanco. It was not until the end of the afternoon, when the drills were finished for the day and they were walking back to their barracks, that Joss noticed one of these men in particular. He dug Jonty in the ribs.

'See who that is?' Jonty looked. 'Should we go over and speak to him?'

'You can if you like. I shan't.'

'Well, I think I will. I'm sure he's seen us. It'll look a bit funny if we just ignore him. I'll see you back in the hut.'

Jonty watched sourly as Joss made his way over to where Quigley was selling pipe tobacco and liquor from the back of a donkey cart, shrugged his shoulders, and trudged back to their barrack room. It was some time before Joss reappeared. Jonty looked up from the book he was reading.

'You took long enough to say 'hello'. What did he have to say for himself, anyway?'

Joss looked a little conscious. 'Well, we just fell to chatting, you know how it is. He – er – he said he was sorry if what he said upset you. And he'll show us around the country, anytime we're off duty.' Jonty gave Joss a hard look and went back to his book, not trusting himself to speak.

Over the summer, Joss fell into the habit of meeting up with Quigley once or twice a week. Jonty was always invited, but never accompanied them. He took out a subscription to the Reading Room and spent much of his free time there, away from the hustle and bustle of the noisy and noisome barrack room. Whenever he had been in the affable Irishman's company, Joss was careful, on his return, not to talk much about where they had been, or what had been said, for fear of offending his closest friend. He asked Quigley, how was it he had gone to America?

'Ten or twelve years ago, there was a famine here in Ireland. It was bad, very bad,' Feardorcha replied. He looked at Joss shrewdly. 'I don't suppose you know anything about that? Probably not something you were taught about at school.'

'No,' Joss answered, feeling very ignorant.

'The potato crops were diseased, you see, so there was nothing to eat, or to sell, so we couldn't pay our rent.'

Joss was mystified. 'So why didn't you just eat something else?'

'There was nothing else,' Feardorcha growled bitterly. 'The land was poor, not much would grow. The only crop that produced enough to fill our bellies was potatoes.' He looked sideways at Joss. 'You think your meals are bad. At least you get them three times a day. We had only potatoes to eat, and only water to drink. But then a blight came and turned the potatoes black. When we dug them out of the ground, they were rotten. None fit to eat, and none fit to plant ready for the next season. So the next year, there was no crop at all. Hundreds – no, *thousands* – of people starved to death. All my brothers and sisters died.

'When we couldn't pay the rent, the land agent came with the police and forced us out of our home, such as it was. We had nothing. No money, no home, nowhere to go. The farmers around about were told that if they gave us shelter, they would be thrown out, too. So, of course, nobody helped us. We could only tramp the roads, sleep in ditches, and eat grass. It wasn't just my family – there were hundreds of us. Some of the men got together and went to the land agent's house, to beg for help. The police fired on them, and my father was killed. Murdered, for being poor and hungry.'

'I'm sorry. I had no idea—' Joss said awkwardly.

The black mood that had come upon Quigley suddenly seemed to lift. 'O'course you didn't. Not your fault, after all.' He downed his whisky. 'So, my mother went to relatives in Dublin, and I went to America. And now here we both are, with ten thousand of Her Majesty's best camped on the doorstep. You're learning how to fight by numbers and I'm selling booze and baccy.' He slapped Joss on the back. 'Drink up, lad. Your turn.'

It was not long before Quigley had taken Joss to all the places of interest that could be reached during the course of an evening. The offer of showing him around the country boiled down to a tour of the many drinking holes edging the campsite. Most were filled with soldiers from the camp, but Quigley began to take Joss to a shebeen, off the beaten track, where the customers were all fellow Irishmen. At first, they were wary of Joss, who looked out of place in his uniform, until Quigley gave him the nudge to buy a round. As he got to know them, Joss learnt that several of them had come back from America with Quigley, having formed a sort of friendship and support brotherhood. Whenever he visited the shebeen, he was greeted warmly, encouraged to talk about himself and the camp, and made to feel perfectly at home. One evening, Quigley asked Joss if there were anywhere else he might like to visit.

'I've heard a lot of the lads talk about the 'Wrens Nest',' Joss said. 'I was wondering – perhaps I might try it out, sometime.'

Quigley looked at him with amusement. 'You mean you've never—? Ah, well, prepare to be educated.'

But Joss took one look at the squalid conditions the women lived in, how ragged and dirty they all were, and changed his mind. Whereupon Quigley told him that he knew of a much better establishment, where the women were all clean and would not try to fleece a fellow out of all his pay, or rob him whilst he was at a disadvantage. Joss's first experience caused him acute embarrassment, but the Irishman insisted that all would fall into place with practice, as proved to be the case.

One afternoon, rifle practice being done for the day, and Jonty having been sent off to the far side of the plain with a message, Joss was returning alone to his barrack when Quigley appeared from around a corner and gave a start.

'Well, bless me! If it isn't just the feller,' Quigley smiled disarmingly. 'I've completely lost meself. Now, what would that grand building over there be?'

'The Reading Room,' Joss replied.

'The Reading Room, is it now? Well, I never. And what about that one?' And so the pair wandered on around the camp, with Joss pointing out all the principal buildings and responding to the Irishman's occasional questions.

Joss did not see Quigley again for two weeks. He persuaded Jonty to accompany him on one of his visits to the women who enjoyed his custom. Afterward, Jonty said that he had quite enjoyed himself, but thought he would not trouble to come another time.

Quigley did finally put in an appearance, selling his wares to the crowds enjoying the displays of horsemanship and musketry. Joss told him that he was on sentry duty at midnight, but agreed that there would just be time for a quick drink. It was unusually quiet in the little shebeen; they were virtually the only customers. Joss declined the offer of whisky, ordering ale instead. He could not risk smelling of liquor when reporting for duty later. When they had downed their drinks, Quigley begged to be excused. He had forgotten that he had promised to look in on an old friend of his father's. And, of course, Joss had to get back to camp in good time. Joss made his way back to camp alone. As he neared the first huts, he felt a sudden stabbing pain in his abdomen and staggered to the latrines. There was no way that he could carry out guard duty that night. He reported as much to Barnes, in between trips to the privy. Exasperated, the sergeant ordered Jonty to cover for him.

At half-past two the following morning, Jonty was tramping up and down near the armoury when he caught a glimpse of figures scurrying between the buildings. Bringing his musket to bear, he shouted the challenge. One figure briefly turned toward him, his face illuminated in the moonlight. Jonty had no difficulty at all in recognizing the intruder.

'Quigley!' he yelled, as the Irishman raised his arm. Jonty felt a sting in his side and fell to the ground.

The shot had alerted not only the rest of the guard but the soldiers sleeping in the nearest barracks. The sentries chased after the trespassers, whilst half-awake soldiers poured out of their huts, in various states of undress. Jonty was carried to the hospital, unconscious. The pursuers failed to catch Quigley and his accomplices but did retrieve some large canvas bags and dynamite. Some had heard Jonty shout the Irishman's name before he fell.

Joss remained unaware of the turmoil, or his friend's injury – their barrack room was on the far side of the camp, too far for sounds of the hue and cry to carry, even on a still night. It was known that he was often to be seen in Quigley's company. When Sergeant Barnes stated that Broughton had been down for guard duty that night, but had reported unfit, it was suspected that he had some involvement in, or prior knowledge of, the raid. A squad was dispatched to arrest him and take him to the guardhouse.

Quigley was fuming. The raid on the military arsenal was meant to demonstrate to the senior officers of the Brotherhood that he was capable of being more than just a foot soldier in the cause. Now, that bloody Tickle had ruined it. Not only had he raised the alarm, so that the raid had to be abandoned, but he had also identified Quigley to all and sundry. With luck, he was now lying in the camp mortuary.

For the past fortnight, Quigley and the other regulars of the shebeen had been on a quiet farm, in the heart of the countryside, being trained in the skills needed to break into the armoury and, having stolen as many weapons as they could carry, to set explosives to destroy the rest. He had returned earlier in the day to take a final look about. The meeting with Joss had seemed fortuitous. Had he not learnt that Joss was to be on sentry duty, they would have run the risk of being identified by him. Quigley had to make sure that Joss would not be at his post. If the young soldier could not be incapacitated, he would have to be eliminated. He was loath to take such a drastic course. Aside from other considerations, he had actually become quite fond of the lad, naïve and trusting though he was. If he could avoid it, he would find some way other than a knife in the ribs to ensure his absence. He was holed up with one of the prostitutes, sympathetic to the cause. She supplied him with a powder that, she told him, the women would sometimes put into the drinks of customers who were too brutal or would not pay for their services. It would cause violent pains in the belly and severe diarrhoea. Extremely unpleasant for two or three days, but with no lasting ill effects. Most importantly, it was tasteless and did not work immediately. There should be a good half an hour between taking it and the first pains. Plenty of time to get away.

Quigley dropped the powder into Joss's ale. As soon as Joss had emptied his glass, Quigley had made his excuses and left. Unseen, he had followed Joss back to the camp, knife ready in case the powder had no effect. Seeing him arch over when the first cramps came, he had been satisfied that Joss would not be on duty that night. It was the greatest bad luck that he had been replaced by Tickle.

To say that the unit commanders were displeased with him would be an understatement. Not only had he failed in his mission, but he had also probably killed a soldier, he had been identified, and the whole countryside would be scoured by the army until he was found. If he had to kill anyone, it should have been the one that could lead the army to the shebeen, and who could describe the men he met there. They wanted him as far away from themselves as possible. They could not risk him being picked up and telling what he knew. As it was, the members of the unit would have to scatter and lie low until the furore died down. All the major ports would be alerted. The only solution was to get him across the Irish Sea by small boat and into Wales. After that, he was on his own.

Any idea that Joss might be putting on his indisposition was soon discarded. He was pale, sweating and shivering, could hardly stand, and stank. He could barely take in the news that Jonty had been shot in the abortive raid. They questioned him thoroughly. How did he know Quigley? Where had he gone with him? Where did he live? Who else had he met? What had they talked about? Had they spoken about the Republican Brotherhood? He reported, as well as he could remember, the conversations he had had, none of which seemed to him to be of any great moment. No, there had been no mention of the revolutionary movement. He had met all sorts of people, none of whom seemed in the least bit suspicious. Of late, they had gone to a quiet shebeen, not frequented by other soldiers; he could take them to it. He would be able to recognise any of the men he had met there if he saw them. He had no idea where Quigley lived, but supposed it to be nearby, as he was so often to be met with in the camp. They did not ask about, and he did not mention, the guided tour of the camp that he had given Feardorcha Quigley, two days before.

The company commander was inclined to convene a court martial. He was convinced that Broughton was not only blind drunk, but was in league with the Fenians to boot. However, the camp doctor came to Joss's rescue. He had given him a thorough examination, he stated, and could categorically say that he was not at all drunk. Furthermore, in his opinion, the soldier had been given a noxious substance, so far unidentified. He had, in effect, been poisoned.

He stood looking down at his friend's body. The top sheet was stained brown with dried blood.

'You fool, Joss. You bloody, bloody fool.'

Joss screwed his head around to look up at Jonty. He was lying on his stomach in the sick bay. The stripes on his back had stopped weeping, but were still very painful.

'I know,' he said simply.

He had been given company punishment, for being absent without leave – even though he had been off-duty at the time and permission was not usually required for an hour or two out of camp. The senior officers had been determined to exact a pound of flesh somehow. He had been sentenced to two dozen lashes and the loss of a month's pay.

Joss thought that he had got off lightly. He knew in his heart that he had helped Quigley, not on purpose, but through ignorance. He had been too ready to believe in him, too gullible, too easily persuaded by the attention of the more worldly man. Not only had he unwittingly provided the Irishman and his comrades with vital information about the layout of the camp, but it had also led to his best friend being shot. It was the merest chance that Jonty was not this moment lying dead in the ground, but had only suffered a flesh wound. Although the marks of the lash would fade in time, they would always be visible. Joss was glad. They would forever serve as a reminder to be wary in the future, less trusting, to take no one at face value. They would forever serve as a reminder of how nearly all had come to grief.

18: Isleworth

Joe loaded the last of the furniture that his mother was taking with her onto the wagon. The sticks she did not have room for were now in his house. He had given Bella a couple of pieces for her room over the stable, and a large carpet, which at last stopped most of the dust from the stalls below from drifting up through the gaps in the floorboards. Elizabeth clambered up onto the seat beside him, carefully put the front door key to her old home into her reticule, ready to give to the agent, and sat stony-faced as the cart trundled around Wyck Green at the start of the journey to her new home.

Joe had suggested that she move in with him, where she would be near all her friends, and all would be familiar, but she had declined. The view of the cottage across the road, where she had enjoyed so many happy times, would be a constant reminder of her loss, too painful to bear. Even though it was five years since Edward died, it would be hard to see another family living there. Instead, she and Caro had found themselves a small house to rent in Isleworth. She would keep house for her daughter, leaving Caro free to concentrate on her business. She could supplement her income, she hoped, with dressmaking.

The Farley villa had had to be sold. Louisa, no longer the lady of the house, had been obliged to move back into the apartment over the shop where she had started her married

197

life so many years before. Elizabeth would have liked to forego any rent, but her solicitor had persuaded her otherwise. It would be foolish to sign away this source of income when her own situation was now so circumscribed. She did what her father had done before her, setting the rent at a figure much below the market rate. Stanhope shook his head at the arrangement. Elizabeth had guaranteed Simon Forrester's salary which was sufficiently generous, he thought, to have enabled him to pay more. Furthermore, only the two youngest of his children were still at school. It was high time the older ones contributed to the family pot.

It had been more straightforward to find a buyer for the cottages in Bearshott than it had been to find one for the villa. Matthew Greening had bought the former. It was rumoured that he was going to pull down the old, dilapidated cottages in Crane Lane and move his tenants into Waterloo or Trafalgar Terraces, at, it was supposed, a higher rent. What plans he had for the land in Crane Lane remained a mystery.

The villa, having been in the Farley family for many years, was in need of renovation. Its inhabitants were so accustomed to its peeling paintwork, smoky fires, discoloured ceilings and outmoded appliances, that it never crossed their minds that it was in need of redecoration or modernisation. It was the family home; it had always been so, and they had had every expectation that so it would continue. As a consequence of its poor state of repair, its value was pitched somewhat lower than anticipated, and even then prospective purchasers demurred at the asking price. Accordingly, the property was eventually offered for sale by public auction, when it fetched even less than the valuation.

After Elizabeth had removed some cherished articles, and Louisa had taken whatever she needed to furnish the apartment, the rest of the family were invited to take their pick from the furniture and household goods that were left. The remaining items were sold off, but since many were very old-fashioned, dating back to the last century and beyond, they realised only a paltry sum.

Elizabeth was steadfast in her decision to honour all the bequests her father had made to his friends and family, however straightened her own situation might be. Once all the property had been sold, and the mortgages and the other debts paid off, the legacies were passed on to the beneficiaries. In the end, she was left with little more than the sum inherited by each of her children. Stanhope invested the outstanding balance on her behalf, recommending government issued consolidated bonds, which would provide her with a steady, and safe, return. This, in addition to the rent from the apartment and the profits from the shop, should, he stated, enable her to live in some comfort.

Life for the Broughtons settled into a pattern. In Isleworth, Elizabeth appeared at ease and at peace in the home she shared with Caro. If she cried for Edward, it was only when she was alone. Caro's renown was slowly spreading. Sometimes, her commissions would take her away from home for a few days, when Elizabeth would mind the little gallery on her behalf. Louisa was particularly affected by the change in the family's circumstances. She implied to her acquaintances that the removal from the villa had been solely because it was now too large for the remaining Forresters. They had been wanting to move for some time, she disclosed, but had only stayed on to look after Grandfather Farley, determined that he should not suffer the indignity of being committed to an asylum. Quite unexpectedly, she found that, without a large house to run, and with no very young children at home to take care of, she was able to enjoy more time spent in her husband's company.

In Bearshott, Joe plodded on in his quiet way, with the now seventeen-year-old Bella keeping house for him. After Joss had left to join the army, he had found another lad to help him in his business, which, whilst it would never make his fortune for him, amply provided all that he wanted from life.

Even the skittish and ill-tempered horse had quietened down. He was still walking out with Elspet Rowlatt, though their friends were no longer in the expectation of receiving a wedding invitation.

Elizabeth could not move on from memories of her life in Bearshott. Every Sunday, she would see many of her erstwhile neighbours in church. There were no longer family lunches at the villa to look forward to afterwards. Joe, and usually Elspet, would sometimes dine with Caro and herself, less often with Louisa.

'Pardon me. Mrs Broughton?' The elegant young woman stopped in front of Elizabeth. She glanced nervously across to where her parents and cousins stood talking to the vicar. They had their backs to her, and appeared to be engrossed in conversation. 'I don't know if you would remember me – I'm Philadelphia Greening. You used to make dresses for me when I was little.'

'Yes, of course I remember you. Have you come back to The Bury to stay?'

'No, just a short visit, with my cousins.' Philadelphia bit her lip. 'Do you still live in Trafalgar Terrace?'

'No. I live with my daughter, Caro, here in Isleworth.'

'Oh. I suppose – I wondered how Joss was going along. And George.'

'George went to sea, some years ago. Joss is in the army. They're in Ireland at the moment, I believe.'

'They?' Philadelphia asked anxiously.

'Yes, he and his friend Jonty.' Elizabeth was surprised to see that Philadelphia seemed to be upset by this news. She recollected the two photographs that she carried with her, and took them from her bag. 'They had these taken in Jersey, last year.'

Philadelphia took them eagerly. After briefly looking at Joss's portrait, she turned to the other. It was obvious to Elizabeth that it was Jonty who interested her the most, though why that might be she did not know. Perhaps she had met him when he worked for her father. She could not account for how she might know Joss and George. Philadelphia offered the photographs back to Elizabeth.

'Keep them, if you like,' Elizabeth said, suppressing a sigh. She was reluctant to lose her grandson's picture, but could hardly offer the girl only the one of Jonty.

'Oh, may I? Thank you so much,' Philadelphia said, a smile lighting her face. The Greenings could be heard making their farewells. She quickly put the photos into her own bag. 'Do you think — could you tell them that I send my best wishes? Excuse me.'

George wrote occasional letters to his mother and sister. These were eagerly received, for the descriptions of the ports he had visited and the voyages he had made. The stamps were passed on to Will, for his growing collection. Joss was a diligent correspondent, frequently writing to Elizabeth and Caro and, occasionally, to Joe. They all found his accounts of life in the army somewhat unsettling. If they had but known it, he had only told them of the less disagreeable aspects. Of Quigley and the Fenian raid, and his own subsequent punishment, he wrote not a word.

Although Joss had refrained from telling his family about Quigley, Quigley had not been equally reticent. He had made his way from Wales into England, spending some weeks taking a circuitous route to London, where he intended to meet up with some allies, eventually arriving in the vicinity of Bearshottbury one Saturday afternoon. He recalled, from his brief spell working on the estate two years before, a disused shed lying near to the Isleworth road. There he had passed the night and, from this vantage point, had been able to watch the procession of churchgoers the following morning. He had been confident that his aunt would not be among them, since it was not one of the major holy days. Although she could have ridden into Isleworth with the servants attending All Saints, the service at St Bridget's usually lasted longer, and the returning carriages would not wait for her. She confined herself to worshipping only at Christmas and Easter.

Having watched the Greening party pass by, Quigley had slipped across the fields and into the kitchen yard. Flattening himself against the wall, he had listened under the passage window. He could hear muted voices as the kitchen servants made preparations for lunch. There was no sound coming from the corridor itself. He had risked a peek around the yard door. The passage had been deserted. Cautiously, he had crept into the house and made his way to the housekeeper's room at the far end, concealing himself behind the door.

'Hello, auntie.'

Startled, Laoise McBride quickly recovered her composure, closed the door and drew the bolt across.

'Feardorcha! If they should catch you here—'

'Don't worry. I made sure nobody saw me. I could do with a bite to eat.'

'It would be dangerous to have food brought now,' she said. 'The servants would remark upon it. Wait until lunchtime. I shall have mine brought here, and you can have that.' She moved across to a small sideboard, poured a glass of Madeira, and handed it to him. 'The police came looking for you. Four or five weeks ago. They believed me when I said I didn't know anything. In the end. So, what went wrong?'

Quigley told her about the botched raid and his stupidity in not disposing of Joss when he had the chance. No doubt it was he who had told his superiors about the link with The Bury.

'And you shot Tickle?' Quigley nodded. 'Dead?'

'I think so. Saw him fall. They've cut me adrift, the commanders. Got to get out of England.' He tossed off the last of the Madeira and held the glass out for more. 'Going back to America.'

'You'll need money.' She opened a drawer in her desk and removed a metal cash box. Unlocking it, she took out a bundle of notes and a bag of sovereigns. 'Here. They won't be missed for a while. Not until the tradesmen get up the nerve to come knocking, asking for their accounts to be paid. I shall be long gone by then.'

Gratefully, he stuffed the money inside his jacket. 'Where will you go?'

'To your mother, in Dublin, to start with. Then maybe we'll come and join you in America.'

'Why don't you come with me now? We can send for mam later.'

'No. I want you as far away from here as possible. Besides, I have one or two things to do before I go. Write to your mother when you have an address.'

Carrying the empty lunch tray back to the kitchen, the housekeeper locked her office door behind her, leaving her nephew there all afternoon, sleeping on her sofa, out of sight. That night, once all the household had gone to bed, she went into the kitchen, packed him up a bag of food and let him out of the back door.

Philadelphia's visit home was coming to an end. She and the cousins were to return to Cambridge, ready for the autumn season of parties, balls, and trips to the theatre. Margaretta Greening thought her daughter looked rather pale and out of spirits. She asked the housekeeper to have a bottle of Balm of Gilead sent up to Philadelphia. Laoise McBride saw her opportunity. Taking the medicine up herself, she waited as the girl took a dose.

'That's very sad news from Ireland, is it not? I was talking to the butcher, and he told me that he had heard from the carter that that lad that used to work here had died.'

'What lad?' Philadelphia whispered.

'Why, that boy whose father died in the blast at your daddy's mill. What was his name, now?'

'Jonty. His name is Jonty.'

'Ah, yes, that would be it. Shot, so they say.'

Philadelphia dropped the bottle of tonic and collapsed in a dead faint.

19: Hougoumont

We had marched from Aldershot, entrained at Guildford, and were now en route to Portsmouth. The officers were in the front carriage, leading the charge, as it were. They caught the first hot blast of dirty, acrid smoke billowing from the funnel, peppering their uniforms with black soot and embers. Their batmen would have a fine time getting them clean.

After Ireland, we had been sent to the garrison at Aldershot, followed by another spell in the Channel Islands – Alderney, this time. I did not see Mireille. To tell the truth, I had nearly forgotten about her. Then, back to Aldershot, for another interminable round of drilling, marching, fatigues, and polishing equipment. Wherever we were stationed, our quarters were invariably cramped and malodorous, the diet poor and monotonous – boiled meat and bread, mostly, with some vegetables if we cared to pay extra. There had been brief spells of furlough, when Jonty and I had managed to get back to Bearshott for a few days, but only whilst we were stationed in Surrey. Taking leave in Kildare or the Channel Islands had seemed pointless, as we had no friends or family nearby to visit. In general, life in the British army was tedious. Now, at last, there was the prospect of a long sea voyage followed, with luck, by some 'proper' soldiering. The London and Middlesex was being posted to India.

We were ferried across the harbour to the wooden sailing ship that was to take us to Calcutta, chartered especially for this voyage – unlike the navy, the army did not have its own fleet. She was only ten years old, safe and sound, unlike Nelson's old ship, which we could see riding at her moorings. She was in such a poor state that she had sprung a leak and sunk a few years before and had had to be raised. She looked very decrepit, hardly worth the expense. But the thing about our vessel that struck us most was her name: *Hougoumont*.

Jonty and I were exchanging memories of our childhood games on Hounslow Heath, and wondering how we would have got on, had we been soldiers at Waterloo, when a cheery voice came from behind.

'Ah, those were the days!'

'George!' It had been six years since I had last seen him. I pumped his fist, delighted. He was as brown as a conker, hair sun-bleached nearly white, broad-shouldered and very muscular, half a head taller than Jonty, and towering above me. We were being hustled below by the sergeants. George called out that, as soon as the ship was under way and out in the Channel reaches, the lobsters would probably be allowed up on deck, when we might catch up on all our news.

'Lobsters?'

George laughed, waved, and was gone.

Three companies of the regiment were aboard, numbering around three hundred men, including officers, and upwards of sixty wives and children. The *Hougoumont* was the last of the three vessels chartered for the journey to leave Portsmouth. The first had sailed two weeks before, with another two companies, like our division, in the charge of a major. The colonel and his headquarters staff, with the rest of the regiment, departed next, a day or two later, on board a somewhat larger vessel. Altogether, over one thousand men of all ranks, around one hundred women, and one hundred and fifty children sailed from Portsmouth, bound for Calcutta, in the autumn of 1862. The voyage was expected to take four months. There would be no port of call before we reached Madras; it would be nigh on spring before we made landfall. Jonty and I watched the first two ships as they were tugged out of the harbour, and wondered why we had not sailed in convoy.

Although we had sailed before, travelling between Ireland, Portsmouth and the Channel Islands, our journeys had not been long enough (according to the army) to require sleeping accommodation. Overnight, we had hunkered down wherever we could, although many men preferred to smoke, play cards, or sit and talk the night through.

Our quarters on the lower deck on the *Hougoumont* were even more constricted than when we were in barracks, which seemed hardly possible. Two tiers of bunks, with barely sufficient space between to allow a man access to his cot. In the centre, in the aisle made between the ends of the bunkbeds, stood a line of tables and benches, each to serve as a mess for ten men. Canvas had been hung between some of the bunks, to provide some privacy for the married men and their families. A man and wife with no children were allocated a top bunk and a bottom bunk. The stiff curtaining between them and the pairs of bunks on either side restricted the airflow. With no ventilation, the air in these cubicles would soon become stale.

All the clean air and daylight seemed to be provided by the open hatchways in the centre of the ship, which ran through the vessel from top to bottom, from deck to deck. The men quartered nearest to these vents would benefit from the fresher air. On the other hand, they would also suffer from any rain or overwash from the upper deck. It was a chilly, damp November, but, with no windows below deck, already stuffy, and promised to become just as foetid as our barrack rooms.

There was little headroom, which hardly affected me, though the taller men were obliged to stoop. Even I had to be wary of hitting my head on the hanging lanterns. Several night soil tubs were dispersed throughout. In the daytime, use was to be made of the heads – two toilets situated in the prow, an awning constructed around them but otherwise open to the elements, which had to serve everyone on board apart from those fortunate enough to have their own cabin.

Jonty and I bagged two adjacent top bunks, halfway between the hatch and the front end of the deck. George told us later that there were about three dozen men in the ship's crew. Their berths were in the forecastle, whilst the captain and first-class passengers – our officers and their families – were accommodated in cabins below the poop deck.

We were allowed up on deck as soon as we had stowed our gear away, with strict instructions not to get in the way of the crew. All was a hive of activity. Numerous crates and barrels were being hoisted aboard and lowered to the hold, provisions that were calculated to suffice for the voyage. There was some livestock, too: coops of hens, to provide eggs, a rafter of turkeys, destined not to last beyond Christmas, and two cows, for milk. The coops were lashed along the sides of the poop deck. An area of the main deck had been fenced off for the cows, with a makeshift awning for a byre. Naturally, all the livestock – particularly the cows – felt themselves obliged to make their feelings at their cavalier treatment known, adding to the cacophony. Some of the children, carried away by the excitement of the hustle and bustle, were racing around the deck, getting under the feet of the crew and generally making a nuisance of themselves. An unfortunate accident occurred, which could have had disastrous consequences. A child ran beneath one of the cows being winched aboard. The frightened animal caught the boy's head with one of her flailing hooves, knocking him to the floor. His mother rushed forward to scoop him up from the deck. The incident served as a salutary warning to all the other mothers, who added to the hubbub with their cries to their wayward chicks, like so many demented hens.

At last, all the stores and passengers were on board, and all the visitors had been rowed back to shore, there to stand and wave their tearful farewells. Time and tide were, apparently, right for departure. The sails were set, the anchor brought in, and the *Hougoumont* slowly made her way along The Solent, past Spithead, and out into the English Channel.

We had become accustomed to the gentle rolling of the ship as she rode at anchor in the shelter of the harbour. It came as something of a shock, then, as the southern coast of the Isle of Wight slid past, to find ourselves suddenly pitched about in the heavy swell of the open Channel. George cheerfully told us that 'this was nothing'. We could only look on in awe as he and the rest of the crew – most of whom were barefoot – did mysterious things with ropes and sails, seemingly oblivious to the violent swaying of the masts. (He described to me many times during the voyage what was being done, and why, but I never could get the gist of it).

As we made our way toward the Atlantic, the weather worsened. The *Hougoumont* ploughed up and down mountainous seas, gusts of wind hit from every direction, the skies grew dark, and it began to rain in torrents. All we passengers cleared the decks, heading down to the supposed safety of our quarters. Some sat at the tables, trying to play cards, but most headed straight for their bunks. It was not long before the moans of men in the throes of seasickness vied with the sound of wind whistling through the rigging.

The storm blew itself out within twenty-four hours, but the nausea persisted for most of us for two or three days. Some people suffered a great deal, one of the women, the wife of a corporal, being particularly badly affected. She was unable to eat or drink anything, and could not be got to stand on her own two feet. Her husband found her dead in her cot, a week after leaving Portsmouth. We were, by then, going across the Bay of Biscay, where more rough weather was further exacerbated by thick fog. There was no chance of burying her with any dignity until the weather improved. Her shrouded corpse was relegated to the hold, with the stores, until calmer waters were reached. It was not until we were off the Portuguese coast that the ceremony could be carried out, by which time another fatality had occurred. The young lad who had been kicked by a cow lost consciousness, and could not be roused. Although there was only a small abrasion and a slight bump on his forehead, the surgeon said that these were signs of some greater trauma to the brain.

The bodies were placed side by side on a grating, each sewn into a sailcloth shroud, with weights at the feet to ensure they would sink beneath the waves, and covered by a single Union flag. The poor mother had requested, and the grieving husband had agreed, that the two should go to their watery grave together. All hands were called to attention. Major Eastoe-Clarke read a piece from the scriptures, and led the assembly in prayers. Three members of the regiment fired a single salute, the drummers beat a roll, and the body bearers tipped the grating. The bodies slid from beneath the flag and plunged over the side. Nobody said, but everyone suspected, that this was a ceremony that was certain to be repeated several times before we reached India.

We then enjoyed several weeks of pleasant sailing, the weather getting increasingly warmer. We were going backward through the seasons, having left England in late autumn and due to round the Cape in January – southern African summertime. By the time we reached Madras, in March, the Indian summer would have begun. Our days were filled with the usual round of drill and musketry practice, and keeping our uniforms and rifles in good order. There were not so many fatigues as when in barracks. The sailors kept the ship trim, swabbing and holystoning the decks, polishing the brasswork, and generally keeping the decks tidy and cleared of obstacles – all 'shipshape and Bristol fashion', as George would say. We had only to keep our own quarters straight – taking it in turns to empty the urine tubs – whilst a handful of men who had been brought up on farms volunteered to act as poulterers and cowmen, caring for the regimental livestock.

When drilling, we were ordered to turn out in full uniform. The seamen had no uniform as such, but were more practically dressed. Most wore loose trousers that ended mid-calf and a tunic top. Many of them wore their hair in a pigtail. Where our fellows for the most part sported moustaches and side whiskers, the majority of the sailors were clean-shaven.

It was our red coats that earned us the nickname 'lobsters'. The sailors delighted in addressing us by this epithet at every opportunity, which eventually led to some ill feeling. Some of the soldiers had retaliated by loudly miscalling parts of the ship. The poop deck – where the poultry was housed – became the coop deck; the prow was referred to as the pointy end; the sails became various items of bedding. And so it continued, with more and more outrageous and inventive names being bandied about, until one of the sailors took a swing at the catcaller and a fight broke out in earnest. The soldiers were disciplined, and we were all forbidden to use the terminology again. The sailors, not being subject to military rigour, sneered. Relations were not mended until early one morning, just as the sun was coming up, when we were ordered to fall in on deck, in full uniform, with our rifles.

We had passed the Cape Verde islands in the night, and were now sailing on down the west coast of Africa toward the Gulf of Guinea. In the pale morning light, we could just make out two ships on the starboard side. The lookout up in the shrouds shouted down that the vessels were showing pirate flags. We were ordered to line the decks facing the brigands, our red jackets obvious even in the dim light. For some minutes, all was tense, until, deterred, the two ships veered away. All those on board gave an almighty cheer. As the skies grew brighter, we watched the pirates until they were mere dots on the horizon. George explained that the *Hougoumont* had no armaments aboard – a section of her hull had been painted to resemble gunports. Pirates had become wise to this ruse used by some merchantmen, and sometimes risked an attack. The sight of so many soldiers on board had, on this occasion, averted a battle. We were ordered to stand down and the seamen slapped us on our backs, with calls of 'Well, done, lobsters!'

The following week – five weeks after leaving Portsmouth – we reached the equator. There was great excitement on board as the seamen made their preparations for the 'crossing the line' ceremony, during which the half a dozen sailors who had not crossed the equator before (known as pollywigs) would be subjected to as many good-natured indignities as their crewmates could devise.

George had been selected to portray 'King Neptune'. He wore a necklace of shells and a crown of thick brown paper, was festooned with seaweed, draped in a piece of green cloth, and held a trident – apparently brought on board especially. Another seaman stood for 'Davy Jones'. Some of the children were dressed up to represent fish and raced about the deck.

The novices had been blindfolded and were dragged from the forecastle, naked, hands bound in front protecting their modesty. They were hauled before 'King Neptune' and made to kneel and bow their heads to the deck. The sight of so many bare buttocks in a row caused some consternation amongst the women, though I noticed that none actually left. The 'tadpoles' were then interrogated by 'Davy Jones', buckets of water being thrown over them at every question, and had their heads shaved, after which a rope was run through their bonds, and they were tossed overboard for a thorough dousing. Hauled back on board, eggs were cracked over their heads, and they were obliged to run around the deck between two lines of sailors who threw flour over them, enthusiastically assisted by the children. On reaching the anchor, they swore their allegiance to Neptune and were presented with certificates confirming their new status as 'shellbacks', after which they were allowed to clean themselves up and get dressed. The festivities were concluded with a double ration of 'grog' for the crew, whilst we soldiers were given a pint of beer.

That day was one of the few highlights of the tedious journey. We had set out in a mixture of trepidation and eager anticipation, but it had not been long before the rigours of travel on the high seas had been realised. Most of the time we found the confines of the ship irksome, the drills in the limited space up on deck awkward, our quarters below increasingly insanitary and uncomfortable. One dreary day followed another. One of the men, unable to endure the conditions any longer, jumped into the sea and could not be recovered. Another had an accident whilst cleaning his rifle, his unsettling sobs and screams echoing through the lower decks for the three days it took him to die.

Five days after crossing the equator, we were becalmed in the doldrums. With no breath of wind, it became stiflingly hot, adding to our discomfort. We were still drilling in full uniform, though no longer in the middle of the day. The crew, in their more practical gear, looked on in amazement and pity. The man who had shot himself was straightway put over the side. It was imperative that his body was not left to lie for long in the heat.

We had not progressed by as much as one mile by Christmas Day. The turkeys were sacrificed, extra vegetables were prepared, and each man was given a glass of wine, courtesy of the colonel. There was plum duff for pudding. We raised a cheer for the cooks, but it was a somewhat half-hearted effort. We were all far too uncomfortable to find much joy in it.

The one consolation for Jonty and I was that, with the ship going nowhere, we were able to spend time with George. He told us of the other trips he had made, the places he had visited, the people he had met. He had sailed this route several times before, on East Indiamen, gone to San Francisco in a clipper, called at all the principal ports around the Mediterranean, and had been to Australia on a convict ship. This was the first time he had crewed a troopship, he said –

it was wonderful that it happened to be the ship carrying us to India. He had signed on just for this voyage. From our experience to date, we could not understand what drew him to a life at sea. George admitted that the work was arduous, dangerous and poorly paid, but, unlike our pay, there were not all the deductions. It was also exhilarating, the foreign places – places he could never afford to visit under his own steam – interesting and varied. Jonty pointed out that, whilst that was undoubtedly true, he was only experiencing life in port, which must be much the same the world over.

At last, the wind picked up and the *Hougoumont* was able to get under way, sailing along the west coast of Africa and rounding the Cape of Good Hope into the Indian Ocean. George had warned us that the passage around the Cape could be treacherous; however, we continued without incident.

At times we had seen pods of whales and dolphins, shoals of porpoises, and schools of sharks. An albatross on its long and solitary flight had once been spotted. A soldier had raised his weapon to shoot the bird, and had been more or less wrestled to the ground by a dozen sailors, later apologising for the rough treatment but explaining that to kill an albatross was considered by seamen to be the worst of bad luck, tantamount to a death sentence.

The most upsetting incident occurred as we were passing the east coast of Madagascar. Another of the women had died, whilst giving birth. She and the infant were enclosed in the same shroud, and the usual ceremony was carried out. The grating was tipped up, the bodies dropped down into the sea, but failed to sink. As they bobbed about on the surface, two telltale dorsal fins were seen, arrowing through the blue water. The sharks seized the shroud, ripping it open between them, almost as though they were unpacking a parcel. The cries of those nearest brought the rest of the ship's company to the rails. We watched, helpless, as the animals began to rip the woman's corpse apart. Her maddened husband jumped overboard into the pink ocean. The soldiers who had fired the salute began taking potshots at the beasts, but they only had another round each. By the time they had reloaded, and the rest of us had fetched our own weapons, the sharks had taken their prey down into the depths, and there was nothing left to aim at. There was nothing more anyone could do.

The men were quiet that evening. We all lay on our bunks, lost in our own thoughts. I heard a scratching from Jonty's direction, and asked him what he was doing.

'Carving my initials,' he said. 'You never know, do you? Might be my epitaph.'

On the morning of 16th March, 1863, we reached Madras. The *Hougoumont* dropped anchor in the Madras roads, three miles out, opposite the long frontage of the old fortress. A cannon saluted our arrival. From the deck of our ship, a church spire and a huge flagstaff could be seen, rising above the ramparts, and, in the far distance, a series of grey-green hills. The two ships carrying the majority of the regiment had been and gone. After taking on supplies, they had sailed on up the coast to Calcutta, where they would be garrisoned at Fort William. The three companies aboard the *Hougoumont* were to remain in Madras.

A swarm of high-sided boats paddled out to meet us. At first, the passengers, watching their progress through the choppy water, found them unusual and interesting. These masula boats, as they were called, were very flimsy when compared to the sturdy frigate that had been our home for the past four months, as they were constructed of light mango wood planks, sewn together with coir strands, and had no ribs to strengthen them. When the women realised that they were to be our transport from ship to shore, many were the cries of alarm and consternation.

It was decided to transfer all the women and children to shore first, that they might cease their wailing the sooner. It took half a day to ferry the regiment, its equipment and remaining stores across the roaring surf to the beach, there being neither harbour nor pier, and a further three hours to finish loading the ship with fresh supplies and cargo. The chickens were disembarked, the cows were not. The *Hougoumont* was due to leave the next morning, bound for Calcutta, there to pick up troops returning to England.

Jonty and I hung back to nearly the last boat. Since the crew were not being allowed shore leave, it was our last opportunity to be with George. He told us about his previous trips to Madras, making us a list of the most interesting places to visit and another of the places to avoid. Most especially, he said, we should not think of buying spirits from the bazaars.

The *Hougoumont* would lie off Calcutta for at least a week. On her homeward journey, she would not come into Madras. Her only port of call would be Cape Town. We promised to be on the ramparts early the next morning, to wave George off.

We were not sorry to leave the frigate, our only regret was the loss of George's company. It was good to be on solid ground once more. But it was not long before we were lamenting her departure. The barrack at the fort was as miserable as any other we had occupied, with the addition of heat and flies. A foul smell permeated the air. The temperature was nearly ninety in the shade. Even at night, it hardly fell below eighty degrees. Although we had experienced increasingly high temperatures as we sailed south, whilst at sea the movement of the ship and the ocean breezes had helped alleviate the discomfort.

Fort St George was rather antiquated, having been built over two hundred years earlier. The twenty-foot high ramparts protected the many imposing buildings within: administrative blocks, officers' quarters, workshops, a hospital, a couple of churches; and the barracks, which latter were, as ever, overcrowded and insanitary. Our three London and Middlesex companies joined the troops already garrisoned in the White Town, as the area inside the fort was known – three other detachments of foot, and a brigade of Royal Artillery.

Our first afternoon had been spent sorting out our gear and making ourselves at home in our new billet. I had in my kit a pair of sheets, issued in England. The Commissariat at the fort added a quilt, a blanket, and an article called a settringee – a sort of padded cotton rug. We were also issued with lightweight white cotton clothing – jackets, shirts and trousers – to be worn when not on duty.

Sergeant Barnes called Jonty aside. When he returned to the barrack room, he was carrying a pair of single white chevrons. Sitting on the edge of his cot, he took out his sewing kit and began to stitch them onto the sleeves of his red coat. I watched him for a while, but, though Mother had taught us all to sew and darn, he was very unhandy.

'Give it here,' I said, reaching out, 'before you stab yourself.' With a rueful grin, Jonty passed his jacket and the stripes over. He told me that one of the lance corporals had been raised to corporal, replacing one of the men who had died on the voyage, leaving a vacancy. I was pleased for him. He was just the sort of man who would make sergeant one day, at the very least, if he stayed in the army long enough. As for me, the stripes on my back would be the only ones I would ever earn.

Before turning in that night, company orders were read out. Rouse would be at half past five, there would be a parade each morning before breakfast, and sometimes another in the evening, together with drills and musketry practice. During the day, from seven in the morning until five in the afternoon, we would be confined to barracks, where we would take all our meals. So much for George's list of do's and don'ts. It seemed we would rarely stir out of the fort.

As soon as the next morning's parade was over, we raced up to the ramparts, as promised, to wave George farewell, but, by the time we arrived, the ship was already under way. We scanned the receding rigging and decks for his distinctive blond hair, to no avail.

Jonty and I only took a short nap after our midday meals. We were fortunate, inasmuch as we could occupy ourselves with a book, or in writing letters. Most of our comrades could not read, nor write anything beyond their name. Those men who had slumbered through their confinement in the heat of the day, for want of anything to pass the time, now found it difficult to get off to sleep at night. Despite the best efforts of the punkah-wallahs, the barracks were stiflingly hot and airless, even at night. Most men slept on top of their bedding, in a state of undress.

There was usually time in the evening, between the end of our confinement at five, and last post at nine, to wander around the fort or to go into the city. Many of the interesting sights George had listed for us were too far away to visit with only a couple of hours at our disposal. More helpful were the notes he had made on places to avoid, in particular his strictures on the rough local liquor. He warned us that the native spirits were very potent, containing ingredients that would not be found in English spirits – chillies, for instance – which seemed to upset European stomachs.

It soon became evident how valuable this advice was. On the voyage over, we had received a rum ration every day. Whilst in barracks, we could purchase porter or spirits from the canteen, to drink with our main meal. Many of our comrades began to supplement this ration, buying cheap liquor in the bazaars. Almost every night, one or another would be drunk and quarrelsome. Our barrack room became an ever more unpleasant place to be, even the punishment meted out to habitual drunkards failing to deter the men.

A group of us would often go into the city together. Some of the troops already stationed in the fort had advised us not to go out alone. The rebellion and atrocities of 'fifty-seven were still fresh in the memory, and there were rumours aplenty about possible attacks on British soldiers and civilians. The women in particular were very nervous, even though the Madras army had remained loyal to the Crown. But during all the months we were garrisoned at Fort St George, we never heard one report of any such attack.

On the voyage out, we had looked forward to spending time in (so we were told) such an exotic country. And it was, indeed, very colourful and, from what we saw of it in a few hours in the evenings, most interesting and diverse. The evening heat was just about tolerable when we were wearing our whites, and the air carried a heady mixture of scents from the spices for sale on the market stalls and the stands selling cooked food.

Our diet at the fort was the same as when we were at home: bread, meat, and vegetables, for every meal. Rarely potatoes, though plenty of rice instead, now we were in the country where it was grown. Tentatively, we tried the local dishes. After the initial shock, we found them surprisingly to our liking, though I did not like them as spicy as Jonty did. We ate them in the way that the natives did – with our fingers – though for myself I would have preferred a spoon.

On some evenings, Jonty and I preferred to go down to the shore, where the air was fresher than in the town. An enterprising local had set up his coffee stand on the beach. We would either sit and watch the women and children of the regiment playing and splashing about in the surf, or we would wander along the strand, attempting to talk to the fishermen, even though we had no word of their language. Fortunately, some of them had learned some English, courtesy of years of occupation by we British. Gradually, we became accustomed to their sing-song pidgin, and with much good-humoured perseverance on both sides, managed to hold some meaningful conversations.

I noticed Jonty smiling several times at one of the young Indian ayahs, and began to hope that he was making a recovery. He certainly seemed less withdrawn since we left England. Whenever I received a letter from home, I shared with him any news that I thought he might find interesting.

One piece of news, however, I kept to myself. Caro's letter, mailed at about the time we sailed from Portsmouth, finally caught up with me. *At church last Sunday*, she had written, *the bans were read for Philadelphia Greening.*

We had not been told, or perhaps we had not appreciated, how the lack of basic amenities would impact our health. Nowhere was there such a thing as a drain to carry away foul and waste water, which either lay stagnant on the ground until it evaporated in the heat, leaving fly-ridden solid matter behind, seeped into the subsoil, or leached into the waterways. The Cooum River, which skirts the fort to the south, is very bad, more or less an open sewer, contaminated with all kinds of filth. The stench is overpowering, though the natives seem not to regard it. Men began to fall ill with diarrhoea and dysentery, and cholera broke out in the married quarters, quickly spreading amongst the women and children in particular.

Jonty and I stopped going into the town, keeping to the fort or to the seafront. The only refreshment we took outside our mess was supplied by the beach coffee-wallah – even then, we took our own tin cups to drink from. Whether it was through luck or our own precautions, neither of us took any of the diseases.

On the 16th October, exactly seven months after we had arrived, our companies were ordered to Peshawar. Ensign Rawlings, his wife, and three children had succumbed to the cholera, as had nine other men and six children, and one of the ayahs. Dysentery had affected our numbers even more; twenty men had died, and another from chronic drunkenness. By the time we boarded the ship taking us up the coast, we had lost over fifty of the company that had sailed from Portsmouth a year before.

20: Mailbag

iss Caroline Broughton to her nephew Pte.416 Josiah Broughton
Isleworth
December 1862

Dear Joss

I hope you had a safe journey and that you and Jonty have arrived in one piece. We are all well here. Mother seems quite contented in our little cottage, and occupies herself with some needlework, although I think she cannot see quite so well as she did. I am trying to persuade her to consult an Optician.

At church last Sunday the bans were read for Philadelphia Greening. Elspet says that her husband-to-be is a cousin, her aunt's son. I cannot think it good that such closely related persons should be married. But Elspet may be mistaken in the connection. Miss Greening nodded to Mother but did not speak. She is a little thing, very striking though rather pale in complexion.

I am thinking of moving to London. My little gallery is doing steady business, and I have so many commissions that I do not really have time to run it properly. Mother has been looking after it for me whenever I have been working on my paintings, but I think it is getting too much for her. I have seen some suitable premises – a small house and a separate commercial property, which I believe will pay for itself, with a manager installed.

Some surprising news! Benjamin tells us he is to marry! I had quite given up on the idea of any of my brothers marrying. He is to bring his intended to see us the week after next. I shall write to you further with my thoughts!

We (Mother and I) are to spend Christmas Day with Louisa and her family. It will be quite a squeeze – I imagine all her children will be there, and Joe and Elspet. She misses the villa dreadfully, I think, far more than the rest of us, even Mother.

Do you have another copy of the photograph you had taken in Jersey? Mother seems to have lost hers.

Much Love
Caro   xxx   (and one for Jonty x)

Miss Elspet Rowlatt to Mr Joseph Broughton

SS Diogenes
Gibraltar
January 1863

My Dearest Joseph

We have unexpectedly put in at Gibraltar, so I am able to send you a few lines with early tidings of my Journey.

My Cabin is small but perfectly adequate. Very clean. It is near the engine, so somewhat noisy. However, I am able to take the air on the Promenade deck during the day, and there is a comfortable saloon and dining room.

After leaving London, we next docked in Plymouth. It was most amusing, watching all the sheep and pigs being loaded. Also, many geese, ducks &c. As you can imagine, this regular farmyard let us all know that they would far rather have been left on shore. We remained at Plymouth for three days.

The weather was rather choppy around the Bay of Biscay, but we came through unscathed, apart from a broken Powder Pot. The Captain tells us that the remainder of our voyage should be 'plain sailing' – an odd term from the captain of a steam ship!

I shall write again when I reach my Destination and may judge how my Brother does. I imagine he will return to England with me. The climate seems not to be to his liking.

Thankyou once again for my Cruise Diary. I have been making entries each day. I hope you will enjoy reading it when I return Home.

I hope to see you <u>Very Soon</u>.
Your loving friend
Elsie
xx

Pte.416 Josiah Broughton to his grandmother, Mrs Elizabeth Broughton

Fort St George
Madras Presidency
May 1863

Dear Mother

We landed in India in the middle of March, after a very pleasant voyage out. You will be surprised to learn that one of the crew of our ship was George!!! He looks in excellent health and spirits, and was able to tell us many interesting and useful things about India. My company is based in Madras, but the rest of the regiment has gone north. George sailed on with our ship to Calcutta, before returning to England. He must be well on his way home by now.

We are quartered in an old East Indiaman fort. It has some very fine buildings. St Mary's church is the oldest – it was built about a hundred and fifty or two hundred years ago. We attend Divine Service there every Sunday, and sometimes during the week. The city is run from the fort, and many important people come and go, including the Governor.

They often have balls to which we are not, of course, invited. Thank goodness!!

When we first arrived, we were surprised to find ourselves rather dizzy and unsteady on our feet. We had, it seems, lost our 'land-legs'. Not so much 'mal-de-mer' as 'mal-de-terre'!! However, we soon recovered and were able to enjoy our new home on solid ground.

Our barracks are long, brick-built (no tents!) inside the fort. There is a verandah running all around the outside, to keep the rooms cool. We have iron bedsteads and plenty of good clean bedding, so we are quite comfortable at night.

Madras is full of very interesting sights. They use a lot of spices in their cooking here, and the air is full of exotic smells. There are also many beautiful flowers that we do not see in England. I shall try to obtain some seeds or cuttings before I return to you, in the hope that you will be able to persuade them to grow in your garden.

There seem to be only two seasons here. One, very hot and humid, the other, very wet and warm. The only umbrellas you see are carried by the British. It seems the natives would just as soon get wet. Grand people have painted paper sunshades – carried by a servant of course! – perhaps they stay indoors when it's raining!

We are able to go down to the beach. Many of the women and children enjoy themselves down there as well. The surf is very fierce along this shore, so we do not risk trying to bathe.

Jonty has been made lance corporal. We are both keeping well, as I hope you and all the folks at home are. I enclose a couple of copies of a photograph of the pair of us we had taken last week, in all our finery. The camel is stuffed, but the servant holding it is not.

Please thank Caro for her letter and the socks, and tell her I will write soon.

With much love
Joss xxxx

New York
September 1863

Dear Aunt L

Just a quick line to tell you that all is well. I am hopeful of returning to London shortly, to join up with some compatriots. We have some plans to put into execution, God willing we may succeed where Guy Fawkes failed. I am glad to hear you have moved – mam is not of our mind, and Dublin is not safe for you.

F x

Joseph Broughton to Miss Elspet Rowlatt [Undelivered]

Allnutt's Yard
Bearshott
January 1864

My Dearest Elsie

I hope this finds you well.

Mother and Caro have heard from Joss. The regiment has been sent to India. He is now in Madras, with Jonty, who is now a lance corporal. They seem to be having a fine time of it.

Mother is staying with Caro, but comes here very often, although I don't think she likes to see her old home. She misses father very much indeed, as you can imagine.

Bella continues to take care of me in her own special way. She still experiments with different recipes, some of which are actually quite nice. She has not succeeded in poisoning me yet! Mother takes over the kitchen when she comes, when Bella tends to flounce off to her loft in high dudgeon!

The only news I have to tell you of our Bearshott friends concerns the Greenings (not exactly friends, I know). Matthew Greening died suddenly at Christmas, in the middle of their Christmas dinner, would you believe. They were not here at the time, but were spending the festive season with Mrs G's sister in Cambridge, so we did not witness all the excitement (don't tell Charles I said that!). His eldest boy Tudor has inherited The Bury, but is hardly ever seen here. The twins have taken on the gunpowder mill. Many of the villagers are worried about any changes that they may make.

Your little school now has a new schoolmistress installed. Her name is Mrs Winifred Smith, and she is rather a tyrant. The pupils are scared stiff of her and mind their lessons most diligently! There is no sign of a Mr Smith, nor does the lady wear a wedding band, so it is thought that 'Mrs' is a courtesy title.

The business goes on much as usual. I call in on Sarah from time to time, and once saw my sister Elizabeth, of whom I told you, though not to speak to. She was with a skinny young woman who <u>might</u> have been her daughter – she had something of Elizabeth's look, though not her colouring.

I hope you find your brother Charles much improved and able to travel. Remember me to him.

Write soon, my dear

With fondest love

Joe xx

Dispatch from Commander-in-Chief Sir Hugh Rose, G.C.B., G.C.S.I., P.C. to Colonel Lionel FitzHugh, C.B., London & Middlesex Regiment of Foot, Fort William, Calcutta

Bengal Army
October 1863

Colonel FitzHugh

Please bring your regiment without delay to Peshawar, to join the Yusufzai Field Force, under the command of Brigadier General Sir Neville Bowles Chamberlain.

(Sgd.) Sir Hugh Rose

Dispatch from Colonel Lionel FitzHugh, C.B to Major Eastoe-Clarke, London & Middlesex Regiment of Foot, Fort St George, Madras

Fort William
Calcutta
October 1863

Major Eastoe-Clarke

The Regiment is ordered to join the Yusufzai Field Force. Two and five companies have already been deployed elsewhere, therefore I must require you to bring the companies under your command to Peshawar by whatever route may be devised. I depart immediately with the main contingent, leaving a depot of the women, children and the sick at Fort William. Any of your own sick should be sent to Calcutta, together with your own women and children. Any sick too ill to be moved, have them attached to another regiment in Madras.

(Sgd.) Col. Lionel FitzHugh

Pte.416 Josiah Broughton to his uncle Joseph Broughton

Fort William
October 1863

Dear Joe

We are on our way via Calcutta to join an Expeditionary Force in the North West Frontier (Punjab region). It seems that there may well be some hard fighting.

Should anything happen to me, please would you take care of my affairs in England? There is the money that Grandfather left me – I have left this to Jonty. Mother's solicitor will have all the details – I don't remember his name. If it should happen that Jonty does not return either, this money is to be divided equally between yourself, Caro and George. There will be some pay outstanding, and money from the regimental savings scheme, but the army will sort that out. It would go to my next of kin, whom I have given as Mother.

There is a properly witnessed will to all the effect above, presently held by the army, in which you are named Sole Executor.

Yours as ever, in a rush
Joss

Mr Ezra Stanhope, Solicitor, to Mrs Elizabeth Broughton
Ref: BF/ES/9/60
Isleworth
August 1864

Dear Madam

<u>Re: the Estate of the Late Mr Benjamin Farley</u>

Further to my communication of the 11th ult. I can confirm that a significant sum may be raised from the sale of the property that has recently come to our notice, viz. the house in Kensington. Although of modest size, it is delightfully situated and in a sought-after neighbourhood. I estimate that you would realise sufficient funds to enable you to purchase another property and an annuity.

The tenants have now quit the premises, and all is in order for you to sell with vacant possession.

I await your further instructions.

Your obedient servant
Ezra Stanhope

Mrs Elizabeth Broughton to Mr Ezra Stanhope, Solicitor
Ref: BF/ES/9/60
Isleworth

August 1864

Dear Mr Stanhope

Re: the Estate of the Late Mr Benjamin Farley

Thank you for your letter.

I should prefer to move into this property myself. As I believe I have mentioned to you, my daughter had the intention of moving to London, and the house in Kensington will suit us very well for our own occupation.

Kindly let me know of any further documents &c. that must be signed.

Yours sincerely
Elizabeth Broughton (Mrs)

Major Hugo Galbraith to his father, Colonel Sir Hilary Galbraith (ret'd.)

Carlisle
September 1865

Sir

As you will see from this, my Commission as Major has been obtained, unfortunately at the expense of leaving my Current Regiment. I shall henceforth be attached to the London and Middlesex (Prudhoe's Own) Regiment of Foot. I am to travel to Calcutta with a new draft to reinforce the regiment. We leave from Portsmouth on Tuesday of next week.

I shall write again with my Direction as soon as I know it.
I enclose a few lines for Mama from my Wife.

I have the honour to remain respectfully yours
Hugo

Kensington
October 1865

My Dear Joss

We have quite settled into our new home, though it is very strange not to be living amongst all our old friends in Isleworth and Bearshott. We have engaged a very personable young woman to keep house for us – Caro seems to think it would be too much for me on my own.

The house is very comfortable. It has three bedrooms, so we are able to have friends to stay. There are several rooms in the attic. We have made one of them into a very comfortable nest for Alice (our servant).

We have mounted the photograph of yourself and Jonty (and camel) in a silver frame. It looks very well on our piano. ('Piano??' I hear you cry!). It is the one the Forresters bought years ago, for the children, but none of them showed much interest in it. Now they have moved back into the apartment over the shop, Louisa says they do not have room for it, and has passed it to me. It was sadly out of tune, as was I. But we have had it looked at and now it is in fine voice. I am very out of practice but try to play for an hour or so each day and do believe I am improving, though I shall never be as proficient as I was, my fingers grow too stiff. We have unexpectedly discovered that Alice has a very pleasant voice, and some evenings we have a little concert, though not in company of course. Alice sings, I play, and Caro applauds. I do not think Louisa would approve!

Caro and I have had our portrait taken, and feel quite Modern. We could not discover any photographer with a stuffed camel – or, indeed, anything else! – so had to make do with a potted plant. We do hope you like it!

I wish I had a photograph of my dearest Edward to put beside yours. However, Caro did a very good likeness of him some years ago, and we have framed that and hung it on the wall. She says to remind you that she also has the sketch she did of yourself, George and Jonty, and is keeping it safe until your return.

She tells me that Philadelphia Greening finally wed last month. Her marriage had to be postponed when her father died. The family are now out of mourning. Her eldest brother gave her away. He is now the owner of The Bury, but does not live there. His mother remains there with the twins, who have completely taken over the running of the mill, it seems, and have renamed the business – Greening Brothers. I think it is rather disrespectful to their father, after all he made the mill a success.

There is no news of their housekeeper who is thought to have returned to Ireland. I have heard it said that the Greenings blame the death of their father on all the upset, although he was eighty years of age.

The Queen is still in deep mourning, and is hardly ever seen in public. Strange to think that you saw one of the Royal Family's last outings together. It is said that she blames Prince Edward for His Highness's death, though I don't see that Edward's misbehaviour could give his father pneumonia.

There is no sign of Elspet returning, nor has Joe had a letter from her since her first. Poor Joe does not say, but I think he feels it very much.

Benjamin is to marry next month. He has asked Will to be his groomsman. Rachel is a very pleasant and sensible young woman. She is some years younger than Benjamin, so I am hopeful of having some more grandchildren soon.

Do take care of yourself, my dear, write soon. India sounds most interesting.

Much Love
Mother xxxx

21: Qatalgarh

It seemed so insignificant. A rocky outcrop with space on the top for no more than three dozen men standing shoulder to shoulder. On the opposite, northern, side of the pass lay another, similar, position: the Eagle's Nest. It was not, as its name might have suggested, the higher of the two. Whichever force could command Crag Piquet, Chamberlain reasoned, would command the pass. Up there, he put his best snipers, his most battle-seasoned soldiers. Having lost the element of surprise, his small army, comprising Fusiliers, Highlanders, Royal Artillery, native cavalry and infantry, and Ghurkas, was on the defensive.

The Umbeyla Expeditionary Force had been assembled to take punitive action against rebel Pathans of Yusufzai tribes, led by Sayyid Mubarik Shah, and the militant Mujahidin, under Amir Maulavi Abd Allah, now hunkered down in Mulkah, a town on the Mahabun mountain. The Force had covertly marched overnight from Nowakilla to the Umbeyla Pass, reaching its mouth on the morning of the twentieth of October, intending to travel eastward through it and set up base camp on the fertile plain of the Chamla Valley. From thence, they were to push forward to Mulkah, either slaughtering the rebels there or driving them across the Indus into the arms of a second British force waiting in Hazara.

A detachment had been sent to the Durrun Pass, a route

previously used by an expedition five years before, as a feint to divert attention. However, the rough terrain had proved a major setback. The Pass was a series of hills, sloping at first from the gorge, before rising steeply. Ravines between them cut across the valley floor at right angles, carrying intersecting small streams, which fed into a larger one that meandered along the length of the Pass. With only a few elephants, and they unsuited to the ground, most of the baggage train and artillery – nineteen guns – had had to be manhandled along the boulder-strewn and uneven floor. The journey through the Pass, anticipated to have been accomplished in under one day, took forty-eight hours, leaving the vanguard exposed whilst the rest of the force was strung out for eight miles behind. Two companies were sent up into the hills flanking the Pass to north and south, ready to clear out any hostiles. As the column moved on into the Pass, further detachments were sent into the next hills, whilst the first dropped back down and rejoined the rear of the advancing column. Camp was set up on the levels at the eastern end of the steep, V-shaped, ravine, awaiting the rearguard. On the morning of the twenty-second, Chamberlain sent out a reconnaissance party, to scout the plain beyond and to identify a suitable route for the advance on Mulkah.

The hold-up had given the rebels time to arouse the neighbouring tribes to join them in the jihad against the British. As the reconnaissance – a regiment of horse – was returning to camp that evening, they were confronted by Buner tribesmen, a supposedly friendly people. A letter had been sent to them, explaining that a small force of British would be passing peaceably through their territory. For a short while, it seemed as though the Bunerwals were merely curious. But the Pathans had done their work well; they had convinced them that the British were coming to annex their land. The Bunerwals attacked. Although they were initially driven off, they continued to harry the reconnaissance, and the camp pickets, all night, with casualties on both sides.

Brigadier General Sir Neville Bowles Chamberlain had to revise his plans. His force of about six thousand men was now confronted by around fifteen thousand assorted tribesmen, with every sign that this number would increase over the coming days. What they lacked in military discipline they more than made up in ferocity and determination. They also had the advantage of familiarity with the formidable country. It was out of the question to attack an army so numerically superior. Chamberlain sent for reinforcements, and dug in.

Rifles were picketed on high points along the Pass. Those on Crag Piquet on the right flank, which was enlarged to accommodate more men, were to cover and protect the camp pitched below. The Eagle's Nest picket on the opposing northern heights – the left flank – could accommodate about ten dozen men, but was overlooked by higher vantage points on the Guru mountain, occupied by tribesmen, who were there able to shoot down into the picket. Neither the Eagle's Nest nor Crag Piquet could be seen from below, screened by overhanging rocks and jungle. Whatever the defenders needed – instructions, men or equipment – had to be requested by messenger sent to the base camp, a journey that took forty-five minutes each way from Crag Piquet, two hours altogether to and from the Eagle's Nest. A number of subsidiary pickets were posted on rocky peaks in the mountainous ranges. Each post, and the camp, had defensive breastworks thrown up around, though in many cases these proved to be inadequate. On the twenty-fifth, Crag Piquet and the other right pickets were attacked by a large force, but were repulsed.

The London and Middlesex had arrived in the middle of October. The main force under Colonel FitzHugh had marched with Chamberlain from Nowakilla, Major Eastoe-Clarke's companies arriving a week later, having travelled from Madras, via Calcutta, by steamship, train, riverboat and on foot. His detachment was put to aid the defence of the left

pickets, fifteen hundred feet above, on the northern slopes –
an arduous climb up the precipitous rockface – the first time
they had faced this kind of terrain. Having gained the Eagle's
Nest, Sergeant Barnes' section was sent on up to a stone
sungar, a position that enabled the occupiers to defend the
picket below, and also to fire at the enemy massed on the
mountain opposite.

The men sank down behind the stone wall, glad of the
respite after the tiring climb. To the right, below, could be
glimpsed the men defending the Eagle's Nest itself, taking up
position along the defensive breastwork. Below that, not able
to be seen from the sungar, were more troops stationed on
broken ground, with a mountain gun battery, placed on a
slight rise, trained on the rebels' position. Jonty pulled a
handkerchief from his trouser pocket and wiped the sweat
from his face. His hands were sweating, too, slippery on his
rifle. Grabbing a fistful of dirt from the ground, he rubbed
them together, wiping them off on his trousers. Joss risked a
peak over the wall.

'Bloody hell! Hundreds – thousands – of the buggers, all
over that mountain.'

Sergeant Barnes called along the line, 'Steady, lads. Take
your positions.'

It was to be their first experience of battle – not the
disciplined charges and musketry stands they had practised
on the vast open plains of the Curragh and Aldershot, but
vicious, untidy, hand-to-hand dirty work. Never before had
they been required to actually try to kill anybody. Crouching
behind the wall, rifle at the ready, waiting for the attack, Joss
could feel his hands shaking, as though he had a palsy. He
took a couple of deep breaths, trying to calm his nerves, and
closed his eyes for a moment.

'It'll be alright, once it starts,' Jonty said. 'We shan't have
time to think about it.'

An almighty shout was heard from the warriors on the
Guru mountain, who began to shoot down into the Eagle's

Nest. Returning fire, it was at first almost impossible to identify any particular target, the mountain men were moving so rapidly, leaping from cover to cover, swords and standards waved aloft. However, they were so tightly massed that casualties amongst them were inevitable. Joss and Jonty, protected by the strong redoubt, were able to take more time over their shots – most of the enemy's fire being concentrated on the main picket – and to pick their targets. But with the movement of the Pathans, the smoke from their guns, the volleys from the Eagle's Nest, and the whining of the balls whizzing overhead from the mountain artillery, they could not distinguish for certain if any of their own bullets had found their mark.

Between the mountain and the picket lay a small tract of open land, which the rebels had to cross if they were to overwhelm the defenders. Their riflemen set up a constant fire from the Guru mountain, endeavouring to protect those racing across this plain, who were largely only equipped with tulwars. But this land lying somewhat lower than the Eagle's Nest and the sungar, the attackers lost the advantage of height, and exposed themselves to the enfilade from the picket and the marksmen occupying the higher post.

'Mark your man!' shouted Sergeant Barnes.

Joss raised his head above the parapet, found a target, took a deep breath, and squeezed the trigger. An answering musket ball pinged off the top of the wall next to him, showering him with stone splinters and dust.

The soldiers kept up a stream of fire down into the plain. The warriors running across it were so massed together that every shot found a home. Jonty thought it was like shooting fish in a barrel. The defenders kept up a constant barrage.

After four hours the Bunerwals withdrew, leaving above three hundred dead laying where they had fallen, and numerous wounded, returning under a flag of truce to collect their bodies.

The British casualties numbered less than fifty. The dead

were buried in the Pass with as much dignity as could be afforded, whilst the wounded were treated in the hospital tent. Joss cleaned his lacerated cheek with water from one of the streams falling down the mountainside.

For the next few days, the Pathans and their allies contented themselves with sporadically taking potshots at the camp from their high vantage points in the hills and mountains, doing little damage. The men of the London and Middlesex were relieved, and thankfully made their way back down to the main camp, where they were then employed in strengthening the defensive breastworks across the ravine at either end of the camp.

By the thirtieth, the rebels had been reinforced by the Swatis and their supporters, led by the Akhund, who had put aside their religious differences to join the jihad. They attacked the encampment and the Eagle's Nest in force but were repulsed by the Fusiliers, the Highlanders and a charge by the Ghurkhas, with losses on both sides. When the attackers had withdrawn, and the bodies of the dead Ghurkas could be recovered, they were found to have been severely mutilated. It was determined that in future no quarter would be given to the enemy.

Realising that the taking of the poorly defended Crag Piquet on the other side of the Pass would enable them to fire directly down into the cantonment, in the darkness before dawn tribesmen rushed the dozen men keeping observation there, killing three and driving the others out. Two hundred and fifty rebels took up position in the post. Colonel Keyes led a detachment to retake it.

Scrabbling over the loose shale and rocks, climbing over the larger boulders, clawing their way through thick shrubs, hampered by their heavy rifles and ammunition pouches, their red coats and white helmets drawing the fire of the warring lashkars above, Jonty and Joss struggled upwards, side by side.

The man climbing ahead of them suddenly fell back, shot

through the eye. The nearly spent ball passed harmlessly between them, but his brains were spattered over Jonty's tunic, and his backpack caught Joss, who was in the act of reaching up for a handhold. The rifleman swept Joss backward with him, to land heavily at the foot of the cliff. Jonty did not have time to see what had happened to his friend; he was being pressed by those climbing up below him. In any case, the swarm of soldiers down in the Pass, and the dense vegetation, hid the casualties from view.

Joss landed on his back, the dead man on top of him, knocking the wind out of him. The man's helmet fell off, tipping blood and gore onto Joss's face. His own helmet had rolled off somewhere. He felt a pain in his shoulder and realised that he was being pressed down onto a sharp rock. Beyond what was left of the rifleman's head, he could see blue sky, birds wheeling, and a moving sea of red, like a grotesque tide washing a rocky shore. A tide of humanity. He felt dizzy, as though he were standing on a high cliff looking down, instead of lying at the base of one looking up. He felt detached, quite calm. Not a participant, an observer. There was a humming in his ears. He could see men shouting but could make no sense of their muffled words. Another body thudded down next to him, turban unravelling. He felt himself crash into the present. Spitting the gore out of his mouth, and trying not to vomit. Joss gave the rifleman's body an almighty shove. A pair of hands took him under the armpits and pulled him out from under. Rather shakily, he stood up and turned to thank his helper. He saw the blossom of blood on the man's tunic and watched him drop like a stone, onto all the other stones littering the ground. Retrieving his helmet and cramming it on his head, he picked his way through the jumble of bodies, and headed back to the base of the cliff.

Joss began the awkward ascent again. His shoulder hurt where the stone had pressed on it. Not enough to hinder him, just enough to make itself felt. He realised how fortunate it was that he had not been above twenty feet from the ground when he fell. Much higher, and he would probably have died. As it was, he was lucky not to have any broken bones. He looped his rifle over his head and shoulder, freeing both hands for the climb. It would be pointless to attempt to shoot anyone from this low down. Better that he should be able to scale the cliff and hold on, should anyone else fall onto him. He wondered where Jonty was. He could not pick him out from all the other redcoats making the hazardous ascent.

Up ahead, Jonty had reached the narrow path that led into the picket. He had no time to spare a thought for Joss. He caught glimpses of the fanatics above, armed to the teeth, their tulwars catching the morning light as they wielded them. He was in more danger now. The path was only wide enough for one man at a time – a sitting target of crawling red ants for those above. Men above and below him fell, but Jonty remained unscathed. The breastworks thrown up by the troops around the picket had proved inadequate for their defence. The rebels were easily able to fire and climb over them. Now, they worked in favour of the soldiers, as the low stone walls now afforded the tribesmen little protection in their turn. Reaching the wall, Jonty clambered over it. Spotting a big lashkar raising his sabre aloft, about to slash down on Sergeant Barnes, he unslung his rifle, and fired. It was the first time he had deliberately targeted and killed another human being. He thought that he would forever remember the man's face.

By the time Joss completed the climb, the fighting was nearly over. Most of the attackers were pulling back, leaving their dead and wounded on the ground, entangled with fallen troops. A few desultory parting shots and defiant shouts, and there came a sudden quiet, broken only by the moans of the wounded and the sound of men taking deep gasps of breath.

Chamberlain decided that his present position was untenable, and moved his camp from the ravine up into the heights to the south, withdrawing from the Eagle's Nest and other pickets to the north, and concentrating his limited forces on the posts at Crag Piquet, the Water Picket sited on another peak to the west below it, and the Conical Hill, a height on a ridge further south.

Major Eastoe-Clarke's companies had suffered heavy losses, from diseases in Madras, fatalities on the journey across to Peshawar, and now in fighting in the Pass. The remnants were stationed in Crag Piquet, with Colonel Brownlow in overall command. The post had been enlarged, and the inadequate defences strength-ened. On the twelfth of November, forward look-outs reported that a large gathering was parading on the plain near the village of Umbeyla. From the number of silk standards fluttering in the breeze, it was apparent that even more tribes had come to join the fray. Reports of thousands of fighters scaling the ridge to the east, a quarter of a mile distant, forewarned the defenders that an attack was imminent. The London and Middlesex men, together with the other troops under Brownlow, set-to to throw up earth traverses, to protect them from the expected enfilade. By dusk, all was complete. Joss and Jonty crouched behind the wall facing the ridge, several yards apart. The men were relatively safe behind the wall, provided they did not raise their heads above the parapet. Unlike the Eagle's Nest, which had been overlooked by the Guru Mountain, the ridge opposite, where the tribes were expected to launch their attack, was not markedly higher.

In the dusk, Joss watched the flickering watch-fires on the next ridge. Even had the defenders been inclined to sleep, the shouts from the tribesmen silhouetted against the flames would have kept them awake. In their own camp, all was quiet, the men on the alert. The officers moved around behind them, offering words of encouragement, and ordered their own fires to be extinguished. Some of the men were getting jittery. Brownlow, deciding to shake things up a bit and demonstrate the army's superior firepower, ordered the mountain train guns to target the watch-fires. The tribesmen scattered, retreating down the hill out of sight. An annoyed grumbling from below, peppered with loud shouts of *Allah! Allah!*, told the watchers that they were still there, readying themselves for an attack, doubtless being whipped into a frenzy by their mullahs. At nine o'clock that evening, the onslaught began.

The attackers could not be seen in the darkness until they were nearly upon them. The troops' white helmets shone in the moonlight; many of the men removed them as being too easy a target, preferring to risk a bullet in the brain. Volley after volley from the defenders scythed through the massed attackers, forcing them into a temporary retreat. Again and again, the brave warriors attempted to storm the defences, each time sustaining heavy losses. One corner of the post, weaker than the rest, was overwhelmed. The attackers pulled down the wall, hurling the stones at the defenders. Brownlow led some of his men and managed to drive the invaders out, rebuild the wall, and hold it until the tribesmen withdrew. By three in the morning, the exhausted fanatics decided they had had enough for the while, and quitted the ridge, to the relief of the troops.

Joss slumped down behind the wall, next to Jonty, thoroughly spent after six hours' fighting. Sergeant Barnes walked past, calling the roll. A voice called out nearby, seemingly asking a question. For a moment, they thought it was one of the native troops inside the picket, and took no notice. Jonty nudged Joss.

'That's coming from outside the camp,' he muttered, twisting around to rest his rifle on the parapet. Joss slewed around, readying himself for another attack, straining to see anything in the inky blackness beyond. Nothing to be seen, nor heard. They might have been alone on the ridge, instead of being surrounded by thousands of Yusufzai, armed to the teeth. Several deep voices from inside the picket began to call out in their own tongue, waving their weapons aloft. Joss and Jonty had no idea what was being said, nor did any of their comrades. Puzzled, they eyed their own Bengali soldiers, assuming insults were being tossed back and forth. A short reply was hurled back then, bizarrely, a fine baritone voice lifted in song. One or two of the native contingent took up the refrain, then all joined in. They were soon drowned out by the hundreds of voices from the men hidden in the ravine below. At the end of each song, the unseen choir cheered and applauded. The strange concert continued for the best part of half an hour.

When the Pathan finally stopped singing, someone in the picket called down to him. His reply was brief, followed by a single gunshot that thudded into the wall. He could be heard scrambling down from the opposite ridge to rejoin his fellows.

The European troops asked their Bengali comrades to explain what had passed. The Pathan, they told them, had first asked if the defenders were not tired of all the noise and gunpowder, as he was. The native troops had replied variously, to the effect that they stood ready to continue the fight. The Pathan then asked if they did not think singing better than fighting, whereupon he had begun to sing the folk songs of the mountains that were familiar to friend and foe alike. At the finish, a Bengali sergeant had called down to him that he should come and fight on the side of the English, where such a fine voice would be appreciated. He had replied that he would consider it, after the present quarrel was settled, and had fired.

Three of the London and Middlesex had lost their lives, and another seven had been injured, including Major Eastoe-Clarke, who had taken a bullet in the fleshy part of his arm. Joss and Jonty had escaped with only minor cuts and abrasions. The wounded were treated as best they might be, within the picket. No detail could be spared to carry them across to Chamberlain's new encampment. The defenders were sure that the tribesmen would make another assault on Crag Piquet, as soon as they were rested and had regrouped.

At daybreak, a detachment of the 1st Punjabi Native Infantry relieved the weary troops who had been defending the position for two days, who thankfully withdrew for some respite, taking the wounded with them. They were only halfway down the ravine on the west side of the ridge on which Crag Piquet stood when shouting and the sound of gunfire was heard from above. Turning, Major Eastoe-Clarke began to lead his men back up the treacherous slopes, but they were so tired and dispirited that their progress was slow. They were overtaken by a relief column of fresher troops, sent out from the camp. A hail of missiles was lobbed down from above. The Major, hit by a large rock and unable to save himself because of the earlier injury, fell back into the gorge.

The traverses which had helped protect the British troops were now protecting the invaders. The men who had earlier been relieved had the advantage of familiarity, but the relief column was unaccustomed to the layout. Nearing the breastwork, Joss took aim at a tribesman clambering over the wall. However, his rifle jammed. The Pathan raised his own weapon, but was cut down by one of the infantrymen. Drawing his sword, Joss scaled the stone wall. Jumping down into the picket, he set about him, slashing right and left, desperate to keep the enemy at bay, dreading a cut from a steel tulwar far more than he had ever worried about being shot.

Although the wildly enthusiastic tribesmen far outnumbered the British, the accuracy of the riflemen gradually turned the tide of battle. Eventually, the last mountain man was driven out, and Crag Piquet was once again in British hands. Bodies were strewn everywhere, redcoats jumbled with their khaki-clad comrades, turbaned fighters in bloodstained khurtas. Soldiers were detailed to lay out the army dead in one corner of the picket and to retrieve the wounded. The tribesmen were not treated so respectfully. No quarter was given to the injured, who were summarily dispatched, and all their bodies tossed over the parapet.

Joss could not see Jonty anywhere. He was not amongst the living, going about their duties, nor lying in the rows of dead, nor amongst the many wounded waiting either to be treated or to be comforted on their way to oblivion. Joss began to fear that, like the tribesmen, Jonty had gone over the side. He leaned out as far as he could over the eastern perimeter – stupid, since the sides of the defile were so steep and covered in shrub that nothing could be seen more than twenty feet down – and was rewarded by a bullet. He drew back, hand to his left ear. Blood, where the shot had nicked the lobe. He had been lucky, although he did not feel so in his anxiety for his friend.

It was some hours before Joss arrived back in camp, by now absolutely certain that Jonty must be dead or, worse, injured and at the mercy of the Pathans. The relief column had reinforced the picket, the wounded had been tended to, and the dead buried. A meat stew was being served for supper, but Joss had no appetite, and went to his section's tent. To find Jonty, sitting on his camp bed, calmly reading. Jonty closed his book.

'Nasty business, up there,' he remarked. 'You all right?'

Joss touched his ear. 'Fine,' he replied shortly. He was dismayed to find how angry he was when he ought to have been feeling relieved. How dared Jonty be sitting reading, as if he were in one of the regimental reading rooms, cool as you please, when he – Joss – had been imagining all manner of dire things? And nearly got himself shot into the bargain. And Jonty didn't even seem to have been concerned about his friend.

'You saw Eastoe fall?' Joss nodded. 'Lots of broken bones, apparently, not expected to last. Pity. He's a decent one.' Jonty looked at Joss narrowly. 'You sure you're alright? You look a bit – I dunno – odd.'

'Where did you get to?'

'Messenger. Sent back to camp. Saw you having a good go before I went.'

'They told us to finish them off. The wounded, I mean.' Joss twisted his hands. 'That's not right, is it?'

'Well, it's only what they do to us. Don't worry about it. We just have to follow orders. It's the generals and the colonels who should have the guilty consciences. Which I doubt.' He tossed his book on the bed. 'Anyway, I could eat a horse. I waited for you—'

'Waited?'

'Of course. Saw you coming back down.' Jonty stood, and clapped Joss on the back. 'Now you're here, let's go and get some grub. We haven't had a hot meal since Tuesday.'

It was not until they had left the tent and were heading to the kitchen that Joss noticed Jonty limping.

'Caught a bullet on the way back up,' his friend explained. 'Nothing much. More of a nuisance, really. No climbing mountains for me for a week or so, they tell me, that's all.'

By the third week of November, Chamberlain's new dispositions had been accomplished, despite the frontiersmen's numerous attacks on the working parties carrying out operations outside the camp. As these retreated back to the safety of camp, the pursuing enemy was observed slaying the wounded and plundering the dead. The tribesmen, seeing the soldiers abandoning the left flank, believed that a wholescale withdrawal was underway, and attacked in force, driving back the defenders of the outlying pickets and very nearly entering the camp. Crag Piquet fell for the third time, with many of the British troops being killed. The Highlanders, led by Colonel Hope, with much bravery and dash, drove the Pathans out and retook the post. Both Hope and Chamberlain, who had accompanied the troops, were severely wounded in the action.

Every day, the tribesmen renewed their attacks, their numbers increasing as they were joined by more bands from further afield. Every day, the outnumbered defenders managed to hold them at bay. Assaults and uprisings spread all along the frontier There were so many rebels assembled that, when they paraded on the plain outside Umbeyla, the sound of their shouting could be heard reverberating around the mountain crags.

Major General John Garvock arrived to assume command in the wounded Chamberlain's stead, bringing with him three regiments as reinforcements, taking the total complement to nine thousand. A ridge lying to the south of Crag Piquet, which the British had labelled the Conical Hill, was occupied by a large number of rebels. Garvock led two brigades down from heights above the camp and stormed the Hill, driving the tribesmen out toward the village of Lalu, which they then also took and burned.

Jonty, with the other walking wounded, was part of the detail protecting the camp. The rest of the company, including Joss, was sent to man an advance picket. The enemy based down in the Pass and upon the northern slopes thought to take advantage of such a large number of troops leaving the camp, and made a concerted effort to overrun it, wave after wave surging up from the foothills and down from the ridges. They were very difficult to repulse since they deemed it an honour to sacrifice themselves for their cause, and had no fear of dying. Some were even seen recklessly pressing their bodies to the cannons' mouths and slashing at the gunners with their sabres. In the face of such single-minded fanaticism, the seemingly unstoppable onslaught, the defenders were initially thrown back, preventing any incursion into the camp proper with great difficulty.

Colonel Brownlow ordered the use of mortars. The bombs sang over the heads of the army and dropped into the ravines beyond, exploding with massive force and severely impairing the enemy. Colonel Keyes led a charge down into the valley, which carried all before and scattered the tribesmen. Colonel Probyn led his cavalry down from the heights – nearly two thousand feet – and harried any rebels that showed resistance, driving them into broken ground beyond Umbeyla. Captain Griffin with his half battery of field artillery poured shell and shrapnel into the village.

About two hundred and fifty courageous Ghazees made a sortie, and succeeded for a short while in pushing the troops back, encouraging those watching in the hills above to come down and join in the attack. However, the British force soon rallied, and the Pioneers cut down the Ghazees to the last man. Dispirited, the Bunerwals surrendered, their allies fled back to their own villages and homelands, and the Expeditionary Force burned Umbeyla to the ground.

As a condition of their surrender, the Bunerwals agreed to offer no shelter to the Mujahidin, and to burn their village of Mulkah. In the event, only one, deserted, house was symbolically destroyed. The Mujahidin fled westward, set up their strongholds in Afghanistan, and continued their deprivations all along the northwest frontier.

The dead were buried in a mass grave marked only with a small wooden cross, on the perimeter of the camp. The names of those lying there were not formally recorded. With no discernible advantage gained, thousands of men had lost their lives, particularly during the three major assaults on Crag Piquet, the bloody site that was afterward named by the natives Qatalgarh: the place of slaughter.

22: Fort William

The Expeditionary Force dispersed. The London and Middlesex began the long trek back to Calcutta, reaching Fort William in the middle of February. Joss's only injury, apart from the normal bumps, bruises and abrasions everyone suffered, was the grit embedded in his cheek from the splinters of the sungar wall, which he had not properly washed away. Strings of tiny purple beads embossed his cheek, from the bridge of his nose towards his left earlobe. Jonty's leg wound had failed to heal properly, exacerbated by the rubbing of his trousers as he marched and the lack of any means of keeping it clean. The camp surgeon had removed the bullet, which had not penetrated very far, but pus persisted in oozing out from the sides of the scab that formed. This had at first been pale yellow, but by the time they arrived back at base, it had taken on a noticeably greenish tinge, and Jonty was limping badly and painfully. The hospital doctor, having examined all the more seriously wounded men, took one look, lowered his head, and sniffed.

'Hmm. Something left in there, I should say. Hop up on the couch and we'll have a dig about. This may hurt a bit,' he added cheerfully. 'Can't waste morphine on a little thing like this.'

Twenty minutes later, Jonty emerged, looking pale and sick, his thigh heavily bandaged. He opened his fist to show

Joss the fragment of material the doctor had found still in the wound.

'Said I might like this as a souvenir.' He lurched for a nearby chair, putting his head between his knees and breathing deeply. When the dizziness had passed, he looked up. 'D'you think Caro might frame it for me?' He gave a short laugh and dusted his hands together. The tiny scrap fell to the ground. 'Give us a hand.'

Joss helped his friend to his feet and lent him a shoulder to hold on to. At the hospital orderly's room, Jonty was issued with a walking-stick.

'I have to come back tomorrow for a new dressing. But now, I'd better go and get some new trousers.'

Joss looked at the pair Jonty was wearing. 'Won't they mend?' he asked doubtfully. 'They'll charge you for a new pair.'

Jonty showed Joss the great bloodstained rent. 'I don't think even your mum would be able to save them.' He still referred to Elizabeth as his friend's mother, even though he knew she was not.

It being Sunday, they were not obliged to do anything other than attend the morning's Divine Service, for which they were thankful, being worn out by the arduous journey from Peshawar, already exhausted by the battles at Umbeyla. They were too tired even to start to explore their new home, and spent the day sitting on the verandah outside their barrack, dozing in the shade.

Fort William, like Fort St George, had been built by the East India Company, and was a replacement for an earlier structure. It had a singular outline, being polygonal, or star-shaped, with bastions at the corners of the walls that commanded the ground beyond from every angle.

A dry moat, or ditch, zig-zagged around the ramparts, to be flooded at need or used as a trench. Within, wide tree-lined avenues skirted the administrative buildings and St Peter's Church. The five barracks housed upwards of fifteen hundred men, plus families, and were, as usual, poorly ventilated, dark, and overcrowded. The Hooghly River flowed to the west, its renowned tidal bore occasionally flooding the surrounding plain.

A week after their return, news came of the approach of the two companies of the London and Middlesex that had been sent off the previous September on an expedition of their own. The garrison, and the wives and children who had been left behind, turned out in force to greet them. The troops marched smartly into the fort, anxious women craned their necks, looking for their menfolk, the garrison gave three hearty cheers, and the contingent was stood down.

Joss and Jonty – who, although still limping slightly, had dispensed with the walking-stick – sauntered over to the newcomers. These were men that they had not seen since before they left England. It was the first time the whole regiment – or what was left of it – had been all together in nearly a year. Busy greeting old comrades, it was a few minutes before they realised that they were being watched by a tall, vaguely familiar, mahogany skinned private. He grinned at them, took off his helmet, and revealed a neat crop of blond hair.

'George! What the devil—?'

George explained that, when he had reached Calcutta, he had decided not to sign on for the voyage home but instead to spend some time in the city before returning to England on another vessel. Having been paid off, he had gone into the city with a couple of shipmates, and they had got roaringly drunk. When they sobered up the next day they found themselves in the fort, having, it appeared, volunteered their services to the London and Middlesex.

'There was no getting out of it, it seems, so we decided to make the best of it. Anyway, I thought we'd soon be meeting up again. Didn't realise your stay in Madras would be so long. So, they gave me a uniform, taught me how to shoot and march, then we got sent off to Simla to rescue some refugees from China and bring them back here. And here we are. At least we'll all be together – the Three Jays reunited, eh?'

'But, George,' Joss said in some consternation, 'we won't be – not for always, at any rate. We signed up in 'fifty-eight. We'll be finished in 'sixty-eight, but you'll still have another five years to do.'

'Nah. They said volunteering wasn't the same as enlisting, I can pack it in anytime.'

'I never heard that one,' Joss said doubtfully. 'Think they might be having you on, mate.'

For a moment, George looked crestfallen. Then, 'Oh, well, I'll just have to leg it, then.'

'But, George,' Joss began again, 'that's a criminal offence – if you got caught, you'd go to prison for longer than you had left to serve.'

'Well, I'll worry about that when the time comes,' replied George, dismissing the problem out of hand. 'What've you two been up to, then?'

Between them, Joss and Jonty recounted the dash to Peshawar, via Fort William, and the bloody battles at Umbeyla.

'We lost nearly two hundred men,' Jonty said, 'and more than twice as many wounded.'

'So I see.'

'This is nothing. Just a bit of a hole in my thigh. A lot of the blokes were very badly hit. How about you? Simla's not that far from where we were, I think. Who needed rescuing?'

'Some missionaries. Got themselves attacked in China, mission burnt down. They managed to make it as far as the Himalayas – God knows how. They sent us to fetch them over and ward off any more attacks. But that wasn't too bad, only a little bit of bother here and there. The worst thing was getting over those blasted mountains. We had to go quite high up before we could come back down the Kashmir side. Lost more men in accidents than we did fighting the Chinese. When we eventually reached Simla, we had some weeks rest there, so the missionaries could recover.' George grinned. 'I'd like to introduce you to a couple of them.'

He led them through the excited throng to a doolie, its curtains drawn against the heat and flies. The bearers had lowered it to the ground. A woman was leaning in, speaking to the occupant. George bent and whispered to her. She straightened up and looked around.

'Miss Rowlatt!' exclaimed Jonty joyfully, wrapping her in a bear hug.

'Mind my bonnet!' she laughed, setting it straight. She looked him up and down. 'My, my! Don't you look all grown up! Stripes, too, I see. I think we can forget the 'Miss Rowlatt', don't you? Please, call me Elspet.' She bent down and twitched the curtain aside. 'Charles! Here are some old friends.'

Elspet looked tired but otherwise in good health. The appearance of her brother, though, shocked them. He was thin, with waxy skin and brown circles around watery eyes, and prone to shaking. Elspet told them that she thought he was suffering from dengue fever, having already been infected with malaria – the reason why she had travelled out to nurse him. She now hoped that, in the care of the fort's hospital, he would recover sufficiently to travel home to England.

Over the course of the following month, Charles's health did, indeed, improve. He had been ordained since leaving Bearshott and was invited to assist at the services held in St Peter's, which Elspet thought did him far more good than the physicking he received from the doctor. The more he became involved with the church, the less time he had to spend with his sister, who kept herself busy with helping out at the women and children's hospital, and teaching some lessons at the regimental school. Neither of which quite distracted her from thoughts of Joe. She had had no reply to the letter she had sent him from Gibraltar, nor to two others she had written after her arrival at the mission in China. Determined not to play the schoolgirl, she forbore to mention the matter to Joss, when she would have found out that he had only received her first letter, and had written to her several times since. Likewise, Joss did not speak to her about Joe, assuming that she had decided to end the connection. When he next wrote to Elizabeth, he mentioned that the Rowlatts were at Fort William. At least Joe could be reassured as to her safety. Some of the wounded brought back from both Umbeyla and Simla had died of their hurts, though their Major's injuries were not so severe as first thought, and he was on the way to making a full recovery. Joss's letter to Elizabeth was carried on the ship that took the newmade widows and their families back to England, no longer part of the regimental muster, no longer the concern of the army.

The Three Jays had their portrait taken by a local photographer, Joss seated on a chair (his friends told him he was such a short chap he would unbalance the picture if he stood) with the other two standing behind. The sepia photograph, when they collected it, looked a little peculiar – George was so sunburnt that he looked more like a native. Since they were all wearing their helmets, his blond hair was not evident. Jonty and Joss had healthy tans, but nothing like George's, who had been six years before the mast in all weathers and was already as brown as a berry. Six months of Indian sun had served to deepen his already darkened complexion.

'They could use you as a spy if it weren't for the blue eyes, blond hair and the Middlesex accent,' Jonty remarked. 'You only need a turban.'

Much of their time at Fort William was spent in the familiar routine of drilling, musketry practice, and fatigues, one of which was to take turns acting as orderly at the garrison hospital. Jonty was detailed to help move some heavy equipment on the families' ward. As he pushed a bed along a corridor, he was pleased to see coming towards him the little ayah he had sometimes seen on the beach at Madras.

Smiling shyly, she told him that she was on her way to collect one of her charges who was being released from the hospital that afternoon.

They next met two days later. A cricket tournament had been arranged, with teams from the different regiments garrisoned at the fort vying for the honour of winning a somewhat insignificant trophy. Now, it was the turn of the London and Middlesex, playing against a team of Bengali soldiers. George had been selected to play. In the relative cool of the long evening, the spectators sat about on the grass, smoking, drinking, and loudly cheering – or deriding – every knock of the ball. There were a number of families present, in support of husbands and fathers taking part. A trestle table had been set up, selling fruit juices for the women and children, and beer for the men, and a tea-wallah had pitched his stand at the edge of the field. Jonty was queuing to replenish his and Joss's glasses when he stepped back to avoid being jostled by the man in front of him, and trod on the foot of the person behind. Turning around to apologise, he found himself looking down into the face of the little ayah, peering painfully up at him.

Apologising profusely, he abandoned his place in the queue and offered to fetch her a chair. She refused, horrified, sitting on the grass and rubbing her toes. He next offered to get the refreshments she had been queuing to buy. Even more horrified, she got to her feet and hobbled over to the back of the line. Jonty had much to learn about a servant's place in society.

They seemed to bump into one another more and more often over the coming weeks. He learnt that her name was Suhani, and her family came from a village on the outskirts of Madras. Her late father had been a sergeant in the Madras Regiment. What she did not tell him was that her mother had advised her to get a British soldier to marry her. Then, with luck, she would be taken to live in England. At the worst, she would receive a widow's pension from the army, as her mother did. Inevitably, Jonty's friends noticed the frequent encounters and had something to say about them.

'She's got her eye on you,' remarked George one evening as, yet again, Suhani put in an appearance. Jonty was startled.

'Don't be daft! She can't be more than fourteen or fifteen.'

'That's plenty old enough out here, chum. Wants a meal ticket, I shouldn't wonder,' Joss added. Jonty was annoyed. He was sure his friends were wrong, that Suhani was just lonely and found him easy to talk to.

'You want to be careful. They're very particular about their womenfolk. Family honour, and all that. You might have to get hitched whether you like it or not. Unless you do like it, of course?'

Thinking it over back in the barracks later that night, Jonty began to worry that there might be some truth in what they had said. Not that Suhani had deliberately befriended him, but that he might unknowingly be raising her hopes of something more. He had taken to her mainly because something in her manner reminded him of Philadelphia, and talking to her was a wistful reminder of happier times, but he truly only saw her as a child. He sighed. It was a pity, but he would have to discourage her.

The next time they met, Jonty smiled at Suhani and said 'hello', but did not stop to speak. As usual, he was with his friends, and she guessed they were on their way to some army function. However, when the same thing happened again, she became uneasy. After a week, during which he had not once stopped to talk to her, far less walked beside her, even when he was on his own, she began to realise that her quarry had slipped out of her grasp. Jonty's change of manner seemed to have come overnight.

She looked back, trying to pinpoint where she had gone wrong. She had been carefully following her mother's instructions: be visible, but not every day; always be meek and modest; always smile, but do not laugh; look interested in whatever he chooses to talk about; do not speak ill of the children in your care, or their parents who pay you; be polite to his friends. There will come a time when you can be yourself. She could not recall one occasion when she had deviated from her mother's advice. It was not long before she came to the conclusion that his friends were to blame for this change.

Captain Mantle and his wife, whose children were in her care, would have described her (if they had so thought about her at all) as being gentle, polite, self-effacing, and, most importantly, kept the children quiet. What was not evident to anyone outside her family was that her mild demeanour masked a vindictive nature. Now, she would have to find some other likely candidate. There were plenty to choose from, of course, men deprived of female company, but Jonty was big and handsome, and had not tried to take liberties. Furthermore, he had a stripe on his uniform, which showed that he was paid more than many of the other men. It would not be easy to find someone so amenable.

The time spent at Fort William was an improvement on the stay at Fort St George. The barracks were just as dark and airless, the food followed the same unvarying diet, the climate just as trying, but in Calcutta there were skittle alleys, a ball court, libraries, a gymnasium, a small golf course, and grounds where polo, cricket or football could be played in the cool of morning and evening. There was even a theatre, where some like-minded souls put on plays and the regimental bands gave concerts. It was with some regret, then, that the London and Middlesex learned that they were being sent up-country on rotation.

The regiment gathered itself up. The troops donned their thick uniforms and stuffed their possessions into kitbags. Stores were loaded onto various vehicles, children perched atop, and the women put on their most serviceable boots. The stowage of the arsenal was strictly supervised by the Ordnance Department. The garrison turned out in force to wave them off and the band commenced its repertoire of marches. The Rowlatts were remaining. Charles was intending to return to China at some time, when events there might have calmed down. He had been quite hopeful of converting a number of his parishioners. In the meantime, he would conduct Bible classes at the fort, and assist the clergy at St Peter's. Elspet had given up all hope of Joseph and, deciding there was no point in going back to Bearshott, where her little school was now in other hands, was to stay with Charles, wherever he chose to go.

On a hot, dry September morning, the regiment put its collective best foot forward and stepped smartly north along The Strand, Colonel FitzHugh at its head astride his favourite mount. To the left, the Hooghly was chock-a-block with ships at anchor and small boats plying back and forth, the sailors and dockers pausing briefly to watch the fifteen hundred or so men march past. The shopkeepers lining The Strand stood and waved, regretting the departure of so many good customers. The crowds already on the road scattered out of the way, squeezing to the sides. Litter-bearers, muttering imprecations, struggled not to overset their customers, the women clapped the band, and their children ran alongside, whooping and calling out to those perched on top of the wagons.

Three miles or so up the road, the regiment manoeuvred bodies, band, baggage and beasts across the pontoon bridge to Howrah Junction, on the other side of the river. The station master, placing his hands together and inclining his head, welcomed Colonel FitzHugh, who gave a cool nod in return. The train was standing ready, the engine gently puffing away. Small explosions of steam erupted from under its wheels, to which the Colonel's horse took predictable exception. Officers stomped back and forth, issuing sometimes contradictory orders, until finally every vestige of the London and Middlesex was aboard, ready to commence the one hundred and fifteen-mile journey to Raneegunge, and the train chuffed slowly out of the station.

The seats, the passengers found, were not conducive to comfortable travel, being of slatted wood. The troops loosened their stiff collars, undid a tunic button or two, and tried to doze. The sun blazed down and the open windows let in warm air, flies and smoke. The blinds were lowered, so that not even the view could alleviate the boredom, with nothing for the passengers to do but listen to the clackety-clack of wheels on the rails. The families had a carriage to themselves, so everyone else was spared the sound of babies crying and children quarrelling. At Burdwan, coffee-wallahs walked up and down the platform, passing hot drinks that did nothing to alleviate thirst up through the windows.

A change in the rhythm woke them. George parted the slats of the blind and peered out as the train slowed down and pulled into Raneegunge station.

'Raining,' he announced. 'In fact,' he added cheerfully, 'it's absolutely hissing down!'

Jonty yawned and stretched his long legs out in front of him, rubbing his stiff joints, and lifted up a corner of the blind to see for himself.

'We there already?' murmured Joss sleepily, sitting up. Jonty unwound the cord that held the blind down and let it rattle its way up to the top of the window. With a jolt, the train came to a halt. Through the downpour, they could make out a line of elephants and camels with their drivers, sheltering under trees, and a number of empty hackeries. The passengers spilled out onto the platform, glad to be out of the train, though not so glad to be standing in the pouring rain. Colonel FitzHugh, observing the deep puddles, conferred with his officers, mounted his horse, and set off down the road to the cantonment that stood a mile from the station, leaving his officers to supervise the loading of the stores onto the various wagons and animals.

There was not room for the whole contingent in the permanent barracks. The Colonel and his most senior officers were housed more or less comfortably, their horses were stabled, and space was made for the women and children. The men of the regiment were detailed to pitch the tents.

Joss struggled with slippery guy ropes, the canvas flapping madly and threatening to blow away. It was difficult to find ground solid enough to drive in the tent pegs, covered as it was in muddy water. George, being of a different company, was setting up tents elsewhere.

Jonty had been assigned to load the families into the hackeries provided for them. Unlike those used for baggage, they were equipped with covers made from bamboo and matting, to protect passengers from the sun and the worst of any rain.

Turning to help the next person up, he found himself holding Suhani's hand. As she looked up, he caught a glimpse of something in her expression that he could not quite identify. She smiled at him and thanked him very prettily as she climbed into the hackery beside her charges. Later, he tried to recapture the look. He had the uneasy feeling that what he had seen was venom.

They were due to break camp the following day, but the weather had worsened, and it was decided that it was too wet and the road too flooded for marching. The troops spent their time huddled in their tents, sitting on their bedrolls, listening to the thunder of rain on the canvas, and trying to avoid the necessity of going outside. Groundsheets had been laid, but could not prevent water from flowing across the floor. The weather did not let up for four days. By the time it was considered feasible to resume their journey, several people had gone down with cholera and dysentery. The drinking water had been drawn from tanks; the heavy rain had made them overflow, washing the stagnant contents onto the ground. There were no latrines. The natives generally relieved themselves in the fields and ditches, and the troops, because of the weather, did not stray far from their tents. The animals produced heaps of dung. As a result, the whole camp stood in a swamp of contaminated water. Two privates and one of Captain Mantle's children died. His wife and their little ayah were amongst the sufferers, but recovered. Shallow graves were dug at the edge of the camp. No sooner had a shovelful been dug out than the hole filled with water. The shrouded bodies were lowered into each waterlogged pit, sinking out of sight with an unseemly gurgle. It would not be long before they would make their own contribution to the unhealthy spot.

The camp was roused just after midnight. The rain had stopped, as though a tap had been suddenly turned off. The bullock drawn hackeries were laden with all the baggage and stores, the sodden rainflies spread out over the top. The women and children scrambled to get good places in the wagons, though many would have to wade through the standing water. By four o'clock, all was ready, and the regiment moved off on the first leg of the long march to Hazareebagh, guided by coolies holding aloft torches made of rags dipped in oil.

By six, day had dawned, and they had arrived at Bograh. The wet tents were pitched, with some difficulty, by the side of the road, a short distance from the village, which consisted of a straggle of native huts on either side of a single street.

The cooks and coffee-wallahs having been sent on ahead, as soon as the tents were up and such stores as would be needed before the next day had been unloaded, breakfast was served. The men spent the day under canvas, both tents and uniforms steaming gently under the increasingly hot sun, punctuated only by the midday and evening meals. Last post was sounded at seven, and the regiment settled down to sleep.

The first day's march set the pattern for those following. The rouse at midnight or thereabouts, striking camp, moving off around three, arriving at the next village by about seven, setting up camp, then resting in the heat of the day. In four days, they had covered the best part of forty-five miles, camping at Bograh, Neeamutpore, Neersa and Govindpore.

The fifth day being Sunday, they stayed put. The Colonel

read passages from the Bible, the band took out their instruments, and one and a half thousand voices lifted lustily in song, accompanied by the screeching of fleeing macaques, cross at having their peace disturbed.

By the following Sunday they had covered another sixty-five miles, overnighting at Rajapeeta, Top-chancee, Doomree, Bughodur, Utka and Burkutta. Three more children, one of the women, and a soldier had died and been buried along the way. Captain Mantle's wife succumbed to a second bout of cholera, leaving Suhani in sole charge of the remaining Mantle children.

The Commissariat was having to rations its stores, the extra days spent beleaguered at Raneegunge having eaten into the provisions. Some families were also running short, either for the same reason, or because they had relied on being able to buy supplies from the villages along the route. Many of these were poor, on the borderline of starvation themselves, with little surplus food to sell. Unable to buy provisions along the way, and with none available from the Commissariat, many families went hungry. Their menfolk shared their own rations, with the result that some were themselves so undernourished that they were unfit for the march. When one fainted, the officers banned the practice, overseeing each meal to make sure every man ate all his own portion. The only latitude was that the families of the men who had died were allocated that man's ration.

The final thirty-five miles to Hazareebagh were accomplished over three days, passing through Burhee and Soorajpoora en route. The entire journey from Fort William had covered two hundred and sixty miles, more than half spent marching, and had taken the regiment three weeks. They arrived in early October, the temperature a pleasant seventy-five degrees, and marched thankfully into the cantonment. The women were eager to visit the bazaars, once they had recovered from the journey, and the children raced around, letting off steam, happy to be out of the hackeries.

The men were just glad to get off their feet and out of their thick uniforms. The Colonel and his officers promised themselves hunting parties in the surrounding forests, where big cats abounded.

23: *Hathi*

George had had enough of army life. He couldn't understand why Joss and Jonty seemed so content with it. They were even talking about signing on for the rest of their twenty-one years. There was far more freedom at sea, even in the confines of a ship. There was always something to do, on duty or off. Drills at sea had a purpose: learn how to climb that rope, reef that sail, throw that line, stand in a gale – your life might depend upon it. Marching? What was the point of that? It only taught you to keep in step with the bloke in front and not trip over him. It was all very well being told you were doing your bit in the defence of the Empire, but what did that mean, exactly? Standing guard duty or doing fatigues, mostly. And drilling. He was glad to have learnt how to fire a rifle and had, in fact, become rather a good shot, which might very easily come in handy someday. Even his first expedition to help the Rowlatts back from China had been mostly just a scrambling affair, no proper fighting. Now, they had trekked all the way from Fort William with no other purpose than to replace troops who were being sent to Simla to replace troops who were being sent to Dum-Dum to replace troops…And so on and so forth. Where was the sense in that? He was glad to have met up with Joss and Jonty, of course, but since they were in a different company, they didn't share a barrack, or even, necessarily, a garrison. Now all their news had been exchanged, he was itching to get back to the freedom of the sea. The possibility that, as a volunteer, the notion that he could *un*volunteer might not be entirely accurate troubled him hardly at all.

Barely had the initial preparations for Colonel FitzHugh's first shooting party begun when the opportunity of going after bigger game presented itself. Reports had been received of a horrific incident. Details were sketchy. A woman working on farmland in the Damodar Valley had been killed by an elephant. The Colonel's offer to bring some of his best rifles to help dispatch the beast being accepted, plans for the tiger hunt were immediately postponed, and arrangements for the pursuit of the larger animal put in hand. Jonty, together with a handful of other crack shots, was detailed to attend, and volunteers called for amongst the rest of the garrison to make up the numbers. So many men volunteered that a ballot had to be held. George made the cut; Joss did not.

When the detachment reached the spot, the officers abandoned their horses in favour of elephants. More details of the attack emerged. The woman, with her infant strapped to her back, had been working in the fields, with others, when a bull elephant had broken through the boundary fence. The farmers were accustomed to herds sometimes breaking through at night to feed on their grain crops, and did their best to drive them out, but this attack was different.

Firstly, it had happened in broad daylight, when the elephants usually kept to the jungle. Secondly, many witnesses claimed that the animal had made no attempt to feed, but had deliberately targeted the victim, seizing her in its trunk and throwing her to the ground, before trampling her, and then running back into the bush. Since the infant had somehow been thrown clear and survived, and the elephant had one broken tusk, it was widely supposed to have been sent by the god Ganesha, and that the woman must have done something to deserve such dreadful punishment, whereas her child, being innocent, was preserved.

Native trackers had already located the animal, and several hundred men were engaged in digging a deep trench, lined with bundles of straw. An avenue of stockading was being constructed, about twelve feet high, leading to the edge of this ditch. When both trench and fence were finished, the elephant would be funnelled down the avenue and so fall into the ditch, where it could be left to starve or die of its wounds, if the pitfall had not killed it outright.

The jemadar in charge of the workers advised one of the officers that the troops on foot should remove their jackets, as elephants were known to target people wearing red. The advice being taken, the order was given for the men to go shirt-sleeved – which was something of a relief, in the humid jungle – but the officers felt themselves safe on their perches, and beneath their dignity not to be properly attired.

Once preparations were complete, the native beaters surrounded the rogue elephant at a distance, shouting, banging sticks and drums, and waving firebrands. The riflemen added to the din by firing their weapons in the air. The tusker lifted its trunk and bellowed, swinging its head from side to side. Gradually, the circle around the animal tightened, until at last it began to move toward the stockade. As soon as it was in the funnel, the fencing was pulled around behind, securing the entrance.

'Why are we doing this?' shouted George to Jonty over the racket. 'Wouldn't it be easier just to shoot the damn thing?'

Colonel FitzHugh felt much the same. He had imagined that this would be similar to a tiger hunt, with the prey eventually being brought down by some sharpshooting, something to boast about later in the officers' mess, with a trophy to be put on display. Tigers supplied rugs; elephants supplied umbrella stands. And then there was the ivory, which would fetch a good price. Driving the animal into a hole in the ground, from which there was no escape, then leaving it to die, was unsportsmanlike.

The mahouts positioned the koomkies behind the stockade, giving the officers sitting atop in their howdahs a good view of the enraged animal charging down the avenue. Suddenly, it swerved to one side and crashed through a weak spot in the barricade, directly in front of Major Eastoe-Clarke's mount. Lowering its massive head, it drove its one tusk into the tame elephant's flank. The officer, grabbing at the howdah's frame to save himself from falling, was pitched forward as the straps holding the seat broke, and the whole contraption slid sideways around the elephant's belly. The major was left hanging precariously upside down between the two elephants.

Beaters and troops raced to try to save both the officer and the mahout, who had managed to stay on the koomkie. The jemadar, with the help of half a dozen others, made valiant efforts to get chains around the bull elephant's back legs, whereby they might bring it to its knees. The soldiers fired at it but, because the two entangled animals were threshing about so much, no shot found a fatal target. Inevitably, Major Eastoe-Clarke fell to the ground.

Bravely, the beaters swarmed around until the bull elephant at last released its hold on the koomkie and was driven back into the stockade. Maddened by the numerous wounds it had received, and the scent of blood, it tried time and again to charge the screaming mob and make its escape. Gradually, it was pushed toward the pit. Coming to the lip, its back legs frantically scrabbled at the crumbling edge, before it toppled over into the trench. Now, the soldiers discovered the purpose of the bed of straw. Not, as they had supposed, to cushion the animal's fall, but so that it could be set alight. The mahout who had been driving the major's koomkie had suffered nothing worse than a broken arm. Many of the other beaters had sustained serious injuries; two had died. The rest had no qualms about burning the culprit to death and threw their torches into the pit. Despite the grisly fate of their commanding officer, most of the soldiers did not have the stomach for this operation, and fired volley after volley at the creature until it had been put out of its misery.

It was a sombre party that marched back to Hazareebagh. The mangled remains of the major had been recovered and taken back to camp, where he was buried with all due ceremony in the small cemetery. Whether he had been killed by either elephant, or by the stray bullet in his head, could not be ascertained, though everyone hoped it was the latter. Later, his commission would be sold to provide a pension for his widow.

24: *Wednesday 5th October 1864*

It started high up. The wispiest of wisps, spiralling lazily. Above, smoky grey, indigo, slate. Far below, blues and greens, slashes of brown. Azure, topaz, and cobalt; emerald, jade and olive; ochre, sienna and umber. Over the next week, it blew hither and thither, at the mercy of the vagaries of the prevailing wind, gathering speed, picking up moisture. Growing larger. Growing stronger. Spinning faster.

Off the west coast of the Andaman Islands the sky darkened. Thunder rumbled, a gusty wind whipped up the waves, and squally rain fell into the sea. A storm broke over Port Blair. Vessels in the Indian Ocean recorded heavy seas and torrential rain. Briefly, the storm abated somewhat, took a breath, veered northwest, headed for the West Bengali coast. Where it unleashed its full force.

Elspet was in the classroom, preparing for the day's lessons. She had not slept well, and her head ached. The previous evening had been very humid and uncomfortable. Occasionally, a flash of lightning lit up her room. During the night, the storm had increased in ferocity, gusts of whining wind rattling the windows. Dawn should have been at half past five, but thunderclouds obscured the sun. She gave up trying to sleep, got up, and made herself a cup of tea. She could see pinpricks of light in the barracks and married quarters. Apparently, she was not alone in having her rest disturbed. She could hear Charles snoring. Since his illness, he seemed to sleep more heavily. It would take much more than a bit of thunder and lightning to wake him up.

At seven, Charles awoke. The brother and sister breakfasted together, talked over their plans for the day, remarked on the storm that was blowing in. By eight, Charles, wrapped in his greatcoat, had left the fort, on his way to the Baptist seamen's mission moored along the river. By half past, a stream of pupils, mothers and ayahs had arrived at the school, battling against the wind to keep their feet.

A little after ten, the wind veered and approached the mouth of the Hooghly, blowing stronger and with heavier rain, uprooting shrubs and smaller trees. An hour or so later, an unusually loud clap of distant thunder was heard. Startled, Elspet and the schoolchildren stopped what they were doing and looked toward the window. All that could be seen was dark sky punctuated with lightning and driving rain, and the trees in the avenue outside the school building whipping back and forth. Some of the ayahs cried out in alarm. One decided to take her charges back to the married quarters, where she thought they would be safer. Elspet and some of the other women tried to persuade her to stay but she was too frightened. Besides, the children were crying for their mother, who was in the barracks. Taking them by the hand, she hustled them out of the classroom and was next seen, occasionally lit by lightning, leaning into the wind and tugging them down the avenue. They seemed to be making steady, if difficult, progress. Some of the other ayahs were encouraged to attempt the same journey. Despite Elspet's pleas for them to stay put, an exodus began. The more people left, the more those who remained were tempted to follow suit. Get to the barracks. Get to the mothers and the men.

The watermen of the Hooghly were accustomed to her caprices, when her tidal bore carried away, or even wrecked, the small craft of the unwary. The Bethel dragged at its moorings, buffeted by the gale. A stack of Bibles fell to the floor. Charles, finding it difficult to remain standing, grabbed a chairback. The sailors, accustomed to heavy seas, kept their footing. Outside, the heavens raged.

Elspet watched the women and children running down the avenue, the littlest struggling in the water that was now ankle-deep. Noticing one ayah struggling with three children, she went to help. In the corridor, she saw that the front door having been left wide open, rainwater was blowing in, and was now puddling across the floor. Running down the school steps, she splashed across to the woman and shouted to her that she would take one child. Her words were carried away by the wind. Elspet grabbed the hand of one boy, decided that a handhold was too slippery, and transferred her grasp, her fingers firmly circling his wrist, pulling him after her down the avenue, hampered by her wet skirts.

The cyclone made landfall before noon. A wall of water fifteen feet high barrelled up the Hooghly, picking up debris and carrying all before. The small boats moored along its banks rapidly filled with water and sank, or were tossed about and broken into smithereens. Water overspilled the banks, washing away the native huts. In the bay and along the river, nearly two hundred ships rode at anchor. Almost all would be lost or damaged by the end of the day, thrown ashore or jammed together in tangled masses. As the storm increased in ferocity, all the trees, apart from palms, were brought down, in turn destroying buildings, breaching walls, flattening railings, and breaking telegraph lines. The low-lying maidan adjacent to Fort William was flooded, as was Tank Square, near which stood the infamous 'Black Hole of Calcutta'. The storm surge flooded the railway station at Howrah and pushed on as far as Bograh and Rajshahi.

In the fort, Elspet and the boy were swept off their feet by the inrush of roiling water. A falling roof tile struck Elspet on her shoulder, causing her to release her hold. She made a grab for the child, who was being carried away from her, opened her mouth to shout, but was further battered by more debris and sank beneath the waves.

On the river, the Bethel strained wildly against her moorings. Charles, the minister, and the seamen made their way out on deck, to be met with a scene of utter devastation. On shore, only buildings of brick or stone were left standing, and they in many instances badly damaged. Charles watched as a wicker basket full of gaily coloured clothes swept past, closely followed by a naked woman's body, arms outstretched as though trying to reclaim her property. A broken door twisted in the strong current, the sailor on top clinging on for dear life. He shouted something to Charles as he was rushed along, but Charles could not make out the words, and the man was soon lost to sight. Some yards from the Bethel, two ships were entangled. Their combined efforts seemed to be withstanding the gale. Being grappled together, they formed a more stable structure.

Elspet's mouth and nostrils filled with water. She thrashed about, gasping for air. Her lungs burned. Feeling a pull on her hair, she thought it had become wrapped around some debris. Suddenly, she was lifted clear. Her eyes refused to focus; she could not make out where she was, or who she was with. Someone bent her over and started slapping her on the back. Water began to trickle from her nose, then a great gout gushed from her mouth. Her chest heaved as she gasped for air. She wished the slapping on her back would stop; she was sure that was not the correct treatment for drowning. Either because of or despite the unorthodox treatment, slowly Elspet's lungs filled with air, and she came to a proper sense of her situation. She found that she was bent over her saviour's knee, presumably in the expectation that pressure on her chest and stomach, coupled with hearty thumps on her back, would expel the water she had swallowed. She was grateful to the soldier, but rather embarrassed. The only man's knee she had been at all familiar with in the whole of her life (apart, of course, from her father's) had been Joe's.

The Bethel's front mooring suddenly broke and she swung

violently around into the pair of interlocked vessels, catching up on one of their chains. The water pushed her backwards and forwards against the chain, which began to cut through her sides. As she crashed against the wharf, those on board made a leap for some sort of safety. One of the seamen missed his footing entirely and, plunging into the torrent, was immediately submerged and lost from view. The Bethel swung like a pendulum. Each time she was cast onto the taught chain, damage was done to her sides. Eventually, the cable sawed right through her hull and holed her below the waterline. Filling with water, she half sank, her bow held up only by the chain. Her weight was too much. The two ships, which before had seemed to be riding out the storm, broke their moorings, and all three drifted out into the misty channel where they were pounded to pieces.

Charles, launching himself at the wharf, had succeeded in wrapping his arms about a bollard. He was safely out of the Bethel, but still in danger, for the wharf itself was submerged in several feet of churning water. The current threatened to drag him down into the river. Holding tightly, he looked around. The minister and some sailors had all found something to hang on to. Whether all the Bethel's congregation were accounted for, he could not tell. They could not help one another; it was doubtful that they would even be able to save themselves. If they let go of whatever it was they were clutching, they would surely be swept away. Each man had to do the best he could for himself.

Elspet, helped to her feet, found she was on one of the barrack room verandahs. Water was lapping at the steps. The air was filled with sound: the howl of the gale, the roar of water, crashing timbers, falling trees, screams and shouts and crying. The jalousies over the windows, and the ceiling punkahs, flapped noisily. The soldier helped her inside and guided her to the stairs which would take her up to the second storey, hopefully out of harm's way. Inside her ribs she was sore from her struggles to breath; she felt very weak. Slowly, she climbed up, hampered by her sodden petticoats. In the upper room, she was thankful to see the boy who had been torn from her grasp, but had no energy to walk across and see how he did. Thankfully, she sank down onto the nearest bunk.

There came an ominous cracking sound, barely discernible above the gale. A jampan was wedged between two supports, its poles snapped off, the Hooghly trying to force it through the gap. The end of the wharf suddenly gave way, tossing one of the sailors into the turbulent river. The jampan turned over and over as it was carried upstream. Charles, realising that he would have to move before the whole jetty tore itself apart, decided that he would have to try to get across to the next post, and so work his way toward what had been the river bank, but which was now under several feet of water. The water was pushing against him from the right. The bollard he was clinging to was on the downstream side of the wharf. Should he be carried away, there was the chance that he might be able to grab one of the bollards on the other side as he was swept past. He had, in his youth, been a strong swimmer, but he was now in his fifties, and the malaria he had been suffering from had sapped his strength. He doubted that he would be able to swim against the strong current. He lurched as the decking behind him splintered, pulling the bollard askew.

More tiles slid off the roof, bounced off the verandah, and catapulted into the foaming water. A hole appeared in the ceiling, letting in pouring rain; slates began to crash through. Elspet tumbled off the bed and scrabbled beneath. A kitbag stowed below was in her way. She kicked at it until she had moved it to the foot of the bed, where it made a barrier against the flying pieces of broken tile. Reaching around, she grabbed a pillow, holding it in front of her face as she cowered under the bunk, hearing the wails of the women and children, the shattering tiles, and the thumps as slates landed on the bed above her head.

The piles driven into the riverbed withstood the pounding of the waves and the battering of flotsam, but the braces and decking were not equal to the task. The front end of the pier gave way, tipping those clinging there into the hostile river. Charles took a deep breath, said a prayer, and launched himself at the next post.

The refugees from the cyclone were unable to leave the barracks until the following day, when the wind had abated somewhat, and the rain had eased. Seeing that the water covering the ground had begun to recede and was no longer turbulent, some of the men descended to what remained of the verandah. A length of rope was tied about a volunteer's waist, a firm grip taken of the ends, and the soldier tentatively stepped into the flood, and found that he could keep his feet. In other parts of the fort, people were emerging. The officers took command and began to organise food and safer accommodation. Troops were sent out into the city, to see what help could be given.

The storm surge had filled the Hooghly and spilled wildly across her banks, flooding the city and far beyond. Ships were beached higgledy-piggledy, most dismasted at the very least, trailing their canvas in the water. The river was full of rubbish, so thick that it seemed as though it could be walked upon. None of the native homes were left standing. The fine avenues and gardens of Fort William were completely destroyed, as were the ornamental parks of the city. Thousands of people had drowned. Thousands more were now without shelter, food or drinking water. It was weeks before the floodwater subsided, leaving utter devastation in its wake: mountains of jumbled debris, stagnant ponds buzzing with flies, and stinking sludge holding fast the rotting corpses of man and beast. Many thousands more were to die, of the unholy trinity of disease: malaria, cholera and typhus.

It was two days before word of the disaster reached the London and Middlesex. With the telegraph lines in Calcutta down, messengers had to make their way to Bograh and elsewhere, where the wires were undamaged. The telegram received by Colonel FitzHugh contained no detail of individual losses. The regiment was left to wonder about the fate of those friends left behind.

25: The Thunder Dragon

Her Majesty rejoices at the general tranquillity of her Indian dominions, but her Majesty regrets that long-continued outrages on the persons and property of subjects of her Majesty, and for which no redress could be had, have rendered it necessary to employ a force to obtain satisfaction for the past, and security for the future.

'Her Majesty deeply laments the calamity which has recently occasioned great loss of life and property at Calcutta and at other places in India. Prompt assistance was rendered by the officers of the Government, and generous contributions have been made in various parts of India to relieve the sufferings which have thus been occasioned.'

Queen's Speech at the Opening of Parliament
7th February 1865

'This looks familiar,' grumbled Joss.

Hot on the heels of the news of the shameful rout at Dewangiri had come the telegram ordering Colonel FitzHugh to take the London and Middlesex to Lucknow, there to await further orders. The one hundred and sixty-mile march from Hazareebagh to Mogul-ki-Serai, where they entrained for Cawnpore, had taken two and a half weeks; the march from Cawnpore to Lucknow, another four days. They had only been under canvas two nights when a second telegram arrived, ordering the regiment to join the Duar Field Force.

The trouble had been rumbling on for months. Bhootan claimed control of the Duars – alluvial plains lying between the Brahmaputra and the Himalayan foothills – a claim that was dismissed by the government. An attempt the previous year to settle the dispute had ended with the humiliation of the British envoy, who had been compelled to sign a treaty ceding the Duars to Bhootan. War had been declared on the eleventh of November and the government had ordered the formation of an expeditionary force. In December, this Field Force, divided into four columns, captured Dewangiri and several villages. The Bhooteas withdrew, the British became complacent, and the withdrawal of most of the troops was announced. In February, the Bhooteas returned, assaulting the depleted posts.

At Dewangiri, the attackers were initially repelled, but then returned, throwing up a stockade around the post – hardly more than a fortified house atop a hill – thereby cutting off lines of communication and the water supply. A relief force out of Koomrakatta could find no way through the attackers' lines and retreated. Dewangiri became indefensible.

At midnight on the fourth of February, the besieged troops began to evacuate the post, fleeing down the mountainside in some disorder. The advance guard was attacked by the enemy, whilst the main party lost its way in the darkness. The wounded and two mountain howitzers were abandoned. Both were seized by the Bhooteas.

The ignominious defeat by a supposedly inferior force could not go unpunished. It was imperative that the guns be recovered. In Calcutta, battle plans were drawn up, and arrangements were put in hand to assemble troops from across the northern territories. Pleas for the campaign to be postponed until after the rainy season, which was known to be particularly detrimental to Europeans' health, were ignored.

'This looks familiar,' grumbled Joss.

Leaving the sick, women and children at Lucknow, the

regiment had retraced its steps back to Cawnpore, overnighting at Bunthwea, Nawabgunge and Oonao. Now, they had to renegotiate the pontoon bridge across the Ganges. The boats were moored side by side, stems pointing upriver. Gingerly, Joss stepped down into the first, careful to avoid the holes in the planking bottom, and clambered over to the next. The old boats rocked alarmingly. Forming a human chain down each bank and across the pontoon, the soldiers passed equipment from one to another. On some of the ammunition boxes, Joss noticed, were stencilled the words *Greening Brothers, Bearshott, Mx*. He wondered if Jonty had seen.

'Why can't someone build a decent bridge?' he moaned, squelching up the west bank. 'I've only just got my boots dry from the last time we crossed this blasted river.'

Colonel FitzHugh divided his regiment into two, sending one wing to Sahibgunge, and from there to Cooch Behar, the other to Calcutta. At the station, Joss and Jonty bid farewell to George. The following day, they boarded their own train for the long journey back to Fort William.

As they neared Calcutta, they began to see the desolation that the cyclone of the previous October had caused. Mile after mile of poisoned farmland, with hardly a house left standing. When they at last reached Howrah junction and alighted, they became aware of an indefinable stench pervading the air, emanating from the quagmire. Shipwrecks still cluttered the Hooghly, though some progress had been made in the town, where much of the debris had at least been swept into piles and new huts were being erected.

'Wow!' breathed Joss. 'How could anyone live through this?'

'From the smell, I'm guessing a lot didn't,' growled Jonty. 'I wonder if the Rowlatts are alright?'

A great deal of the damage done in Fort William had been repaired, and the fort made tidy. The most striking evidence of the destruction was the absence of the fine avenues of trees.

As they marched in through the gates, Joss was relieved to see Elspet Rowlatt in the crowd, though of Charles there was no sign.

At noon there was a parade on the maidan outside the fort, when Sir Hugh Rose addressed the troops. It was not until after the evening meal that Joss and Jonty were able to seek out Elspet. She was, of course, delighted to see them both and to hear that George also was well. She described what had happened on the day of the cyclone. They did not tell her about the disastrous elephant hunt, which had taken place at much the same time.

'Charles will be sorry to have missed you,' she said. 'He spends most of his time helping with the rebuilding of the mission and doing what he can in the town. Sometimes he doesn't come back here for days on end. We are very short of food – the people are starving. The harbour is still so damaged that it's very difficult for boats to get in. And cholera has broken out down in the native quarters. I wish Charles would at least come back for some rest. I think he is very ill, very ill indeed.'

On the late afternoon of the fourth of March, the regiment boarded the train for Kooshtea, where the line terminated on a high bank overlooking the Padma River.

Joss looked down with disfavour at the steamer and flat-bottomed river boats moored below.

'Well, at least these look as though they can get us across without sinking,' he remarked sourly.

The land surrounding the railhead was boggy and cut up by numerous ditches. The officers repaired to the steamer for the night whilst as many of the troops as could find space were sent to bed down on the flats. Sergeant Barnes directed his squad to pitch their tent on a dry, level stretch of ground. In the early hours, they were awoken by the sound of heavy rainfall thundering on the canvas. Rainwater began to stream across the campsite, dousing the fires, and there was a scramble to raise kit off the ground. In the rush to preserve equipment from the encroaching water, one of the sentries stumbled into a flooded ditch and broke his leg, receiving little sympathy from his fellows, who now had to deal with a wounded man in addition to their waterlogged gear.

The rain easing off sufficiently for the fires to be relit, the soldiers huddled around them, trying to keep warm and get dry. The officers ordered an extra issue of rum. By the time the rain had stopped, the men were feeling warm inside, if not out, and, making the best of a bad job, whiled away the night with singing and telling tall stories until daybreak.

The next two days were spent drying equipment and loading the boats.

'What on earth—?' began Jonty. 'Surely not.'

'They are, you know.'

The bemused onlookers watched as the steamer was manoeuvred away from the bank, making room for one of the flats to pull alongside and be lashed to starboard. Another flat was moved around to the port side and equally secured. Some smaller barges, loaded with stores, were fastened to the steamer's stern. The steamer sat bobbing gently on the river, looking for all the world like a huge mechanical mother duck surrounded by her fleet of chicks. Once all was secured, the remainder of the contingent boarded, and the curious fleet set off downriver.

The officers were all on board the steamer, reserving the top deck and cabins for themselves. They sat around the upper deck, drinking tea and eating tiffin during the day, taking potshots at the somnolent alligators on the sandbanks, and broaching several bottles of wine and whisky in the evening, as though they were on a pleasure cruise, rather than off to fight a war. The sergeants and corporals were left in charge of the other ranks on the lower decks and on the flats, on which there were also a large number of natives, left to provide for themselves, who were obliged to find what space they could in the overcrowded vessels.

There was nothing to occupy the men as the strange flotilla put-puttered along on its way to Gowhatty. Joss and Jonty managed to elbow their way to the prow, where they stood, leaning on the guardrail, admiring the spectacular scenery on either bank, sometimes open and picturesque, with blue-purple hills hazy in the far distance, sometimes dense and oppressive, thickly forested to the water's edge. River, banks and sky teemed with wildlife: muggers, porpoises and turtles; geese, peacocks and pelicans; deer, elephant and buffalo.

At the confluence of the Padma with the Brahmaputra, the vessels turned northward, heading, against the current, for Gowhatty. Each night, they moored close to one of the settlements that lined the riverbanks. At Dhobree, the flats and barges were temporarily unlashed. The steamer put into the jetty to take on coal, whilst the quartermasters obtained provisions from the two ranges of sheds that held the Commissariat stores, and fresh fruit and vegetables from the many stalls. The troops were able to alleviate the boredom of the journey, disembarking for a few hours' free time.

Their wanderings around the town led Joss and Jonty up a small hill that overlooked the river, where they came across a hut, outside which sat an old man, grey beard down to his waist, an array of swords and knives laid out in front of him. One of the locals explained that he was a hermit, who long ago had been paid by a rajah to watch for his return from war in the Punjab. The rajah had died, but the hermit kept watch still. Dropping some coins into the ascetic's bowl, they left the old man to his solitary vigil.

The next day being St Patrick's, when they moored up for the night, all the Irish soldiers in the company built a huge bonfire on the riverbank and entertained everyone with their singing and dancing. Having bought some of the strong local liquor in Dhobree for the celebrations, the festivities became rowdier and rowdier, until the officers had to order the Irishmen to bed, so that everyone else could get some sleep.

The journey from Cawnpore to Gowhatty had taken the best part of a month. By the time they reached the town, many of the men were suffering from sickness and diarrhoea. Half a dozen were so ill that they were carted off to the hospital, whilst the others were isolated from the rest of the company in a couple of sick tents.

The right wing of the London and Middlesex remained under canvas at Gowhatty for five days, whilst preparations were made for the march to Dewangiri. There was little space available for the campsite, the tents being pitched very close to one another. The river ran past on one side, but between it and the encampment stood the huts of the elephant drivers, with their animals tethered nearby. Dense jungle loomed close around the rest of the perimeter. The officers remained on board the steamer, but the men were obliged to endure the insanitary conditions on shore.

'I don't feel so good,' whispered Joss. Jonty helped him to his feet and half-carried him to one of the sick bays. The tent was nearly empty, the men suffering from mild diarrhoea having mostly recovered. The doctor looked narrowly at Joss and indicated an empty pallet. No sooner had Joss lain down than his body contracted into the foetal position, and he vomited. An orderly rushed up and placed a bowl on the floor beside the bed.

'Diarrhoea?' Joss nodded. The doctor only needed a cursory examination to determine the cause. Not the stomach complaints that he had recently been dealing with, but the infinitely more serious cholera. There was little he could do to remedy matters, except to make his patient drink copious quantities of clean water.

'Third one today,' the doctor remarked to Jonty. 'I'll try him on some cholera drops. That might help. Leave him with us.'

'He will be alright, won't he? I mean, we're in the same tent, but I feel fine—'

'You feel fine *at the moment*. This can come on very

suddenly. Make sure you drink plenty of water. *Fresh* water. Don't eat any uncooked fruit or vegetables. Come back at once if you start to feel ill – the trick seems to be catching it early. Even strapping young fellows like you can catch it. As for your mate – well, he's not the stoutest chap at the best of times, is he? I can't promise anything.'

By the time the regiment broke camp, upwards of a dozen men had fallen prey to the disease. Two had died and were buried near the camp – potentially increasing the insanitary conditions for future campers. Jonty escaped contamination, but Joss remained very ill. At four o'clock in the morning of the twenty-sixth of March, the wing departed without him.

Their route arced, taking them west along the north bank of the Brahmaputra for a mile or so, before cutting off northward, then turning east, winding across open level plains and around rugged forested hills, overnighting at Kahara, Ranjiah Thanna and Tombolpore before arriving three days and thirty-five miles later at Koomrakatta. To the north loomed the vast range of the Himalayas, and Bhootan.

The repetitive slog had given Jonty time to think. He fretted about Joss. No messenger had arrived with news of the invalids, as far as he was aware. He wasn't sure that the news would be passed on, even if received. He wondered how Elspet and Charles were. Charles he only really knew as a strict schoolteacher, having only lodged with Elspet after her brother had left for China. George, he assumed, he would meet up with shortly. He remembered how kind all the Broughtons had been as he grew up, particularly Mrs Broughton. He even spared a passing thought for Louisa. He had not thought about Quigley for a long time, but the St Patrick's Day shenanigans had jogged his memory. He hoped the sly Irishman was lying dead in a ditch somewhere. Of Philadelphia, he tried to think not at all.

The camp at Koomrakatta was quite a substantial affair, consisting of a number of thatched bamboo huts, housing hospitals, the Commissariat and stores, in addition to the hundreds of tents that were home to the two and a half thousand troops that made up the Field Force, the majority of which were native regiments and police, with some British reinforcements. General Tombs and his headquarters staff were pitched in the centre of the encampment. Koomrakatta village itself was merely a collection of a few mean huts. A redoubt had been constructed before the main camp, garrisoned by some of the 43rd Native Infantry – the corps that had been driven out of Dewangiri two months before – containing several storehouses used as arsenals and protected by four guns, trained across the open plain that lay between the camp and the menacing hills to the north.

The London and Middlesex were quartered in the lines between a company of Ghurkas and men of the 55th Regiment of Foot, with whom there was some light-hearted bantering. They had not been in India as long as had Colonel FitzHugh's men, and were able to give some news of home. In the camp was a great bustle, as the General issued orders, messengers galloped back and forth to Gowhatty, and the men generally prepared their kit, and themselves, for the battle ahead.

On April Fools' Day, at two o'clock in the morning, Lieutenant Colonel Richardson led the Advance Column out of camp. Many of the remaining Field Force came out of their tents to watch them leave. All that could be heard was the tramping of feet and the jingle of harness, with the occasional quiet murmur from well-wishers. Jonty stood and watched them go. Some were new acquaintances, marksmen drawn from the 55th. The column disappeared into the night.

The second column marched out of camp that evening, bivouacking in the mouth of a pass in the foothills of the Himalayas. They were travelling light, all the equipment they could do without having been left behind in Koomrakatta: tents, hot food, even the men's bedrolls. Jonty found himself a sheltered spot under a prickly shrub, huddled into his greatcoat, and hunkered down for the night. Enough water had been heated in the morning to brew tea, but the men had to make do with dried rations for breakfast. At dawn, the fires were doused, makeshift ablutions carried out, greatcoats rolled up, rifles reclaimed, and the detachment moved off to join up with the Advance Column.

From their overnight camp, their way ran up a steep-sided gorge, through which tumbled a small river. The terrain was difficult. The path zig-zagged back and forth across the river, the men wading through water at every crossing, sometimes only ankle deep, in other places chest high. Soon, they were all wet through, their thick uniforms starting to steam in the heat as the sun rose.

Sergeant Barnes led his squad, with Jonty and the corporal at the rear. Progress was slow, each man concentrating on where he put his feet. The densely wooded sheer cliffs on either side crowded in, until there was only room on the narrow track for the men to go single file. The trees overhead interlocked, so that, despite the broad daylight, the path was in darkness. The man ahead of Jonty tripped over one of the many tree roots that criss-crossed the path, cannoning into the man in front. The track began to climb sharply, leaving the river below, and veered off to one side. Scrabbling on his hands and knees to make the ascent, Jonty was thankful not to be encumbered with all his usual kit.

A breastwork had been thrown up across the path. The column came to a halt, then, seeing no sign of any defenders, advanced once again. Suddenly, several heads appeared above the parapet and began firing down at the vanguard with some old matchlocks. Their aim was poor, and none found a target. The forward troops unslung their Enfields, loaded, and returned fire. After a volley or two, the heads above disappeared. The men at the head of the column crouched down, whilst those further down the path behind steadied themselves by clinging on to the nearest vegetation, glad of the temporary pause, despite not knowing what all the gunfire ahead meant. After some time of inactivity, scouts were sent out to reconnoitre. They reported back that the position was empty, apart from two dead bodies. The column moved on, bypassing the hurdle, continuing on the same narrow pathway through dense undergrowth until open ground was reached.

As they emerged from the track, the men thankfully sank to the ground, as they awaited the rest of the column to finish the climb. Across the clearing, they could glimpse a manned stockade on a crest, out of range of their guns. The troops and the Bhootea sentries contented themselves, for the time being, with hurling insults and gestures at one another across the divide.

When the order came to move on, Jonty's section was amongst the first to cross the grassland towards the further tree-line. A wide pathway snaking into the jungle seemed the obvious route to take, but no sooner had they gained the shelter of the first belt of trees than there came a scream from a man at the front, who fell to the floor, his face a bloody mess.

'Down!' yelled Jonty, dropping to the ground as a boulder sliced through the air above his head. For a few minutes, missiles rained upon the soldiers. Most avoided any serious injury, but some, like the first, were badly hurt. The bombardment stopped as abruptly as it had started. Faint cheering could be heard coming from the enemy stockade ahead. Gingerly, the troops regained their feet and slowly advanced. The pathway had been cleverly booby-trapped with bent withies and nets, catapulting rocks at the unsuspecting. As soon as all the traps had been sprung, the onslaught had ceased, leaving the withies with their now-empty slings gently waving back and forth. Jonty and some others were sent ahead to look for other traps, the rest of the force following carefully behind, but it seemed that the catapults were the only obstacle the Bhooteas had bothered to construct.

On the second of April, the columns converged on the

plateau overlooking Dewangiri, which stood atop a long, steep spur that jutted out from a higher hill. The fortifications consisted of eight stockades, some blockhouses and storerooms, and a number of houses and huts. The steep ridge below had been cleared of trees and other vegetation, offering neither protection nor cover for the attackers. Around the base of the hill, a series of abattis had been thrown up, but they were somewhat flimsily constructed, and the elephants made short work of pushing through.

Artillerymen set up a battery and opened fire with their howitzers, but failed to make any impression on either defenders or defences. One gun, poorly sited on uneven ground, turned over on the recoil and caught the legs of the men firing it. They were dragged away to safety and treatment at the rear, whilst their places were taken by others, who, with some difficulty, righted the piece, and resumed firing. The defenders fired down through their loopholes, inflicting some casualties. The troops were surprised at the accuracy of their aim. What damage their return fire was giving to the Bhooteas it was not possible to tell. Abandoning hope of being able to effect a breach, General Tombs ordered the force to advance and take the post by hand.

Sergeant Barnes gathered his section together and led them forward to the base of the ridge. A ditch snaking down the side of the steep hill offered some shelter from the salvos from above. They began to crawl up. Unfortunately, it soon became apparent that it had been used as a sewer, and the nearer the men got to the top, the deeper the filth that lined it. Barnes led the way, the section's corporal keeping the rear, with Jonty and the rest in between. Once committed to the ditch, there was no way they could quit it without taking fire, the land on either side being flat and open. Grimly, they pushed on, trying to ignore the muck. When they were halfway up, it began to rain. Water started to trickle down, turning the waste into slurry. The boot of the man in front of the corporal slipped on the wet mess, slamming into the corporal's face. Startled, the corporal reared up. A bullet found its mark, and he lay dead, blood and sludge pooling around his head.

Other men had been essaying the same journey, finding what cover they could where the ground was broken. The defenders kept up a fusillade from their stockades. The scarlet tunics made an inviting, and obvious, target.

A deep natural trench cut across the ridge, parallel to the stockade, and about sixty yards from it, affording deep cover for anyone who could reach it. It was with relief that Barnes realised that the drainage ditch intersected with it, and his men could crawl free of the unpleasant channel. They slithered out of the foetid gulley, leaning their backs against the trench's high side and raising their faces to the sky, that the rain might wash them clean.

Slowly but steadily, the attackers advanced up the steep spur, whilst the artillery put shell after shell over the parapet above. A group of skirmishers from the 55th and native police stole up nearly as far as the left stockade. Spotting them, the Bhooteas rushed out to confront them, thought better of it, and re-entered their fort.

A bugle sounded out for the attack. Sergeant Barnes stood up, about to leap out of the trench, but, receiving a bullet in his shoulder, fell back.

'Tickle!' he gasped. 'Take charge! Lead them on!'

Jonty, now the only able-bodied man in his section above the rank of private, yelled to his comrades to follow him, and scrambled up the steep side onto the exposed open ground that lay between the trench and the stockade. Without question, the section followed where Jonty led, a fact that was not lost on Sergeant Barnes, despite his wound and all the chaos.

All around was mayhem. The barefoot native troops had run into another of the Bhooteas' booby-traps – thin bamboo slits, about a foot long, driven into the ground, the other end viciously sharpened. Redcoats swarmed up the ridge from every direction, some falling victim to the barrage from the fort, but most making it to the foot of the walls. A heavy door barred their way in. Using their rifle butts and bayonets, the soldiers hacked away until it splintered. The Bhooteas retreated by another gateway, carelessly leaving behind their flag, which was scooped up by a sepoy, who waved the Druk aloft, to the cheers of the attackers.

In the mêlée around the gateway, Jonty cannoned into George.

'This is more like!' George exclaimed, wielding his bayonet with gusto. 'Seen Joss?'

'Cholera. Gowhatty,' Jonty panted, parrying a thrust from a sword.

For a moment, George let his concentration slip, narrowly avoiding a passing spear. 'Not – dead?'

'Dunno. Not when we left. Not heard anything since.'

The Field Force surrounded the buildings. In the face of the determined onslaught, the Bhooteas fled, attempting to escape by scattering through the jungle, followed by whooping troops, carried away by the excitement of victory. After restoring some semblance of order, the stockades were found to contain many killed and wounded, strewn all along the galleries that lined the walls. The injured were afforded some cursory first aid, whilst the dead were carried out of the stockades and piled up ready for burial, suffering the further ignominy of being stripped of anything valuable or interesting by trophy hunters. Many of the native troops clowned around in the fallen Bhooteas' steel spiked helmets. The redcoats largely contented themselves with weaponry.

George and Jonty were not part of those chasing the defeated defenders. George was assigned to burial duty. Jonty managed to return, with some of his section, to where Barnes had fallen and found him still sitting in the trench, clutching his shoulder. Together, they got the sergeant to his feet and manhandled him up the incline into the fort, a process that was very trying for the wounded man.

Tombs's force suffered around one hundred serious casualties. The Bhootea dead numbered about one hundred and thirty, with as many again wounded. However, from the traces of blood in the jungle, their losses were thought to be far greater.

The Dewangiri storehouses were found to contain a good supply of provisions: sacks of rice, tubs of ghee, bags of chillies, and sides of beef. Long bamboo tubes hung down, full of drinking water. The cooks got their fires going, and the troops looked forward to something better than field rations.

After a quiet night, a small force was left in occupation of the recaptured fortification, whilst the remainder set off to return to Gowhatty. Patrols flanked the column, wary of ambush. Progress was slow. It began to rain in earnest. The wounded had to be carried along the treacherous tracks, their numbers soon supplemented by the sick, who were succumbing to Bhootan fever. By the time they reached Gowhatty, more men had died of fever than had been killed in the battle. The force left behind at Dewangiri blew up the rajah's house, stockades and granaries, bringing all to destruction. The site was no longer habitable.

At Koomrakatta, Jonty was retrieving his belong-ings, looking forward to being able to sleep in his bedroll, rather than wrapped in his greatcoat, when Sergeant Barnes, his shoulder strapped up and his arm in a sling, entered the tent.

After thanking Jonty, again, for rescuing him from the trench, Barnes said, 'You're to report to Captain Miller. He has some news for you.'

With dread, Jonty made his way to the officer's tent. There could only be one piece of news that a senior officer would impart. Miller was seated at a small campaign table, piles of documents in front of him.

'Sergeant Barnes has been informing me of your conduct at Dewangiri,' Miller began. Jonty was thrown. He searched back, but could think of nothing he had done wrong. 'For your exemplary conduct in leading your section when both your senior officers were incapacitated, I am pleased to tell you that you are being promoted to corporal, with immediate effect.'

26: Hugo

Major Hugo Galbraith was reviewing the two companies of his new command. He walked up and down the ranks, occasionally stopping to speak to one of the parading troops, sweating in their thick uniforms. His wife was sitting in the stands, clutching a pretty lacy parasol. Sufficient shelter for the thin sun in England but offering no protection at all against the blistering heat of Lucknow, which on this day was fierce even for India. She was a sickly-looking little person who, the other ladies of the regiment had opined, would not last five minutes in this climate. They had invited her to take tea soon after her arrival. The knowledgeable amongst them had doubted her ability to carry her baby to term; even if she did (stated Molly Barnes) it was highly unlikely that she would survive the birth, being rather old for a first pregnancy.

The Major marched smartly back and forth, the watching ladies wilting stoically in the background. Pausing before Jonty, in the front rank, he asked the usual commonplace questions: How long have you been in the army? Where do you come from?

'Middlesex, sir.'

'Oh?' said Galbraith, mildly interested. 'Whereabouts?'

'Near Hounslow, sir.'

'Really? My wife is from that part of the country.' At which point, Mrs Hugo Galbraith gave a gasp and fainted clean away.

Neither Hugo nor the soldiers on parade took any notice. After all, women – and men – passing out, having been overcome by the heat, was a regular occurrence. However, when Hugo discovered that it was his wife who had been the cause of the commotion, he was exasperated. He had seen from their arrival a few weeks before that the climate was not going to suit her, but had hoped that she might become accustomed to it. It really would not do, for the company commander's wife to be making an exhibition of herself every five minutes. As soon as it could be arranged, he would ship her back to England.

He recalled when she had first come to live with his family. That had been nine – no, ten – years ago. A quiet schoolroom miss, seven years his junior, with nothing much to say for herself, but with a stubborn lift to her chin. His mother's sister's youngest, come to benefit from the company of her cousins. His aunt had married into trade. Wealthy, certainly, but several rungs down the social ladder.

His own family had a military background. His father, Sir Hilary, was a retired Colonel. His younger brother Nicholas was a sea captain, with hopes of advancement to commodore at the very least. There had been an older brother. He had died in the Crimea in 'fifty-four, leaving Hugo to inherit, eventually, his father's room. Great-grandfathers, uncles and assorted cousins were all in either the army or the navy and could be traced back as far as the first Stuarts, distinguishing themselves from La Rochelle to Sebastopol.

On the death of his brother, Sir Hilary had made it clear that it was Hugo's duty to take a wife and produce an heir. Truth be told, Hugo was not one for much petticoat company, preferring that of his fellow officers. If he had an itch, he knew where to go to have it scratched. Should he require a lady on his arm for an evening, one of his sisters' friends would usually be pleased to accompany him. But now they were all married off, and could no longer oblige. He had first asked Philadelphia to marry him on her eighteenth birthday. She had refused. He was hardly cast down. He did not care for her, except in a brotherly way, and was aware that she cared for him no more than a cousin should.

As time went by, and both remained unwed, he decided to revisit his proposal. He proposed again on her twenty-first birthday and was pleased, and somewhat surprised, to be accepted. Their feelings toward one another had not changed. It was understood, though not voiced, that it was to be a marriage of convenience. Hugo felt sure that they would rub along amicably. He would focus on his career, she on her children and whatever else women occupied themselves with.

The bans had only just been called when her father unexpectedly died, and the wedding had had to be postponed. They had finally married in the summer of eighteen sixty-five, departing for the subcontinent almost immediately.

The voyage out had not been the honeymoon it was supposed to be. Their quarters were uncomfortable and claustrophobic, and his bride had been unwell and miserable much of the time. He trusted that she would 'perk up a bit', as he put it, once they had landed and she had made the acquaintance of the other officers' wives. The child she was carrying would give them something to talk about.

The women milled around Philadelphia, hoisting her back onto her chair, and waving bottles of smelling-salts under her nose until she came out of her swoon. They noted her pale face, the two spots of livid colour on her cheeks, her over-bright eyes, and drew their conclusions. The matrons quietly assisted her to her feet, escorted her back to her bungalow, and helped her into bed. When Hugo eventually returned to their lodging, he found the regimental doctor just about to leave.

'Ah, Major. I'm afraid your wife is quite unwell. I recommend that she stays in bed for at least two weeks.'

'Two weeks? But surely it's only the sun—'

'It may well be, of course, but if she is not to lose the child, she must stay off her feet. Keep the room dark, but well ventilated. Have the punkahs going all the time. No big meals. Plenty to drink, of course. The other women will be able to help, they know what to do. Quite common out here, I'm afraid, for our delicate English ladies in the family way. Good day.'

Hugo went into the bedroom to see his wife. She was lying in the middle of the double bed, looking very feverish. Awkwardly, he took her hand and patted it.

'Well, my dear, the doctor tells me that you must rest for a few days. I shall move my things into the other room, and leave you in peace.'

Which is just what he did, contenting himself with visiting her briefly morning and evening, and otherwise getting on with his day. Inevitably, the day came when he was met on his return by one of the wives carrying away a small bloody bundle.

The camp was somewhat surprised at how quickly Mrs Galbraith recovered from this sad event. She appeared in much better spirits than they had ever seen her in before, and soon had a very becoming bloom to her cheeks.

She did not immediately enquire what had happened to her child. She assumed that her husband had seen to the burial. Hugo, learning that the infant was a girl, had shrugged off the episode, allowing his daughter to be buried anonymously amongst all the other small graves in the cemetery. Hugo also made a speedy recovery. Had the infant been his son and heir, things would have been seen differently, of course, but a daughter – well, these things happen.

Never having served in India previously, and having no acquaintance amongst his fellow officers, the Major came to rely on his second-in-command for advice. Fortuitously, their bungalows were next door to one another. During Philadelphia's illness, the pair took to sitting on one or the other's verandah, whisky glasses to hand, smoking cigars and chewing over the day's events.

Hugo was fascinated by the captain's domestic arrangements. The widower had three young children, who were cared for by an Indian nanny. Mantle confided that he was much beholden to the ayah. When his children had been struck down by an illness that the doctors could not diagnose, soon after they had arrived in Hazareebagh, she had recognised the symptoms and knew of a herbal treatment that sometimes helped. At his wits' end, he had finally let her administer her medicine, sadly too late for his youngest son, but the older children had responded to the potion and had recovered. Since then, he had deferred to her where the children were concerned, and gradually she had assumed the responsibility for running his household. The children sometimes suffered another bout of the mysterious illness but rallied after being dosed by the ayah.

Suhani was hopeful. If she could make herself indispensable, in the care of his children and the running of his home, and for his personal comfort, she was confident that she could entice, or coerce, the captain into making her his wife. The children were a constant source of annoyance, of course. She regretted the death of the toddler, which had been a mistake, but he had been a whiny little thing – even Mantle did not seem to miss him. As long as she were more careful in the future…

It was some weeks before Jonty became aware that Philadelphia was in the camp. He had no call to visit the patchery, where the officers' bungalows were, nor the officers' mess, where she sometimes accompanied her husband.

'You'll never guess who I just met,' said George one morning. 'Philadelphia Greening, as was.'

'Phil – Philadelphia?' repeated Jonty.

Before Joss could intervene, George had blundered on. 'Yeah – she's married to our Major. Looked in the pink. Recognised me, too. Couldn't speak, though – she was with the officers.'

Unlike Suhani, Jonty had no hope. He had long realised, of course, that she must be married, probably with a nursery full of babies, but whilst he did not know for sure, there was still hope in the foothills of his soul. And now, here Phia was, married to his own company commander and, apparently, very happy to be so. Jonty looked at his grimy, calloused hands. Broken dirty fingernails. Workman's hands. Then he thought of Hugo's. Clean. White. Well-manicured. Officer's hands. Of course she was happy.

More than ten years had passed since Philadelphia had left Bearshott, with not even a farewell. Joss noted the grim set of Jonty's jaw and despaired. He could not understand how absurdly steadfast Jonty had been, and was hardly surprised that Philadelphia had forgotten all about their childhood infatuation – if, indeed, she had ever felt more than friendship. It was damned unfortunate that she was here in India.

Jonty was determined not to seek Philadelphia out. In fact, to avoid like the plague anywhere she might be. When not on duty, he kept mostly to the grim safety of the barrack room. Then, in the summer, Major Galbraith detailed him to dig out a tree stump in the garden of his bungalow.

There was no sign of anyone at the bungalow. The verandahs were empty and the jalousies were lowered across the windows. No sound came from within. The stump was in the garden at the rear; Jonty entered through a side gate. To his relief, the garden was also deserted. He made his way across the parched lawn to the far end of the backyard, which was planted with shrubs and low growing trees. Beyond the back fence lay a tope of mango trees, laden with fruit. A swinging seat had been set on a small patch of open ground amongst the shrubbery, reached by a winding path, to one side of which stood the broken tree stump.

Jonty hefted his mattock and took a swing at the stump. After ten minutes, he had only succeeded in splintering the wood, the root remaining stubbornly fast. Pulling off his shirt and throwing it onto the seat, he chopped at the root.

'Jonty?'

Slowly, he turned. She was standing at the entrance to the little glade, her parasol over her shoulder, holding a glass of lemonade. Propping the mattock up against the stump, he took a step toward her, then stopped.

From the house next door, Suhani watched sourly as Jonty strode across the lawn, the pickaxe over his shoulder, and disappeared amongst the greenery, followed a little while later by the sickly memsahib, with her ridiculous sunshade. There was no denying that the strapping young man in full vigour was a far more pleasurable prospect than the middle-aged father, with his smoky whiskers and tobacco stained teeth and fingers. Whenever he came across to spend the evening with the captain, the Major, she mused, also had more than one eye on herself. Not long married, she understood, and already looking about him...Perhaps that might be turned into an advantage in the future. In the memsahib, she had no interest at all.

Until, that is, she realised just how long it had taken Jonty to empty that glass of lemonade.

Hugo Galbraith was not given to either reflection or introspection. All his talents and thoughts were centred on his career. Unlike other officers who only commanded through purchase, he was actually a good leader, who in later times could have risen through the ranks on merit alone. But even he noticed the change in his wife. She still found the climate trying, often suffering debilitating headaches, but there was a bloom in her cheeks and her eyes sparkled. Whilst he was out of the house going about his duties, Philadelphia often went to sit in the swing in the little glade at the bottom of their garden.

From the house next door, Suhani watched and waited. She noted the times when Philadelphia was most likely to appear – usually in the afternoons, when all right-minded English ladies should be indoors, out of the sun. She would always be carrying a book, and that absurd parasol. Often, a coolie followed behind, bearing a jug of lemonade and a glass on a tray. Only ever one glass, Suhani saw, but that didn't mean anything. Jonty never again appeared in the garden. But then, there was that grove of mangos at the back of the property – excellent cover for someone who did not want to be seen.

Suhani was frustrated. Although she now had bigger prey in mind, she had not forgiven Jonty, or his friends, for dashing her hopes in Fort William. If she could serve any of them an ill turn, she would, but unless she could be absolutely sure that Mrs Galbraith was meeting up with Jonty, this particular rabbit had nowhere to run. One afternoon, Major Galbraith returned to his bungalow earlier than usual. Suhani happened to be in her front room and, on impulse, dashed out to intercept him.

'Oh, Major,' she began, her expression anxious. 'Thank goodness you are come! I saw the Memsahib not an hour ago, walking down the garden, and I thought she looked most unwell. And as she hasn't returned…perhaps…?'

Galbraith, although somewhat surprised at being addressed directly by the servant, thanked her for her concern, and turned to walk into his garden.

'Would you like me to come too? Just in case the Memsahib needs help?'

His first inclination was to refuse, but, reflecting that maybe it was some sort of 'woman's trouble', accepted the girl's offer. They walked through the garden to the shrubbery at the rear, Suhani keeping two or three paces behind, to discourage conversation. If Jonty were there, she did not want the couple warned by approaching voices.

Hugo rounded the last turn in the path into the little glade, to find his wife sitting in the swing, quietly reading. She looked up, surprised.

'Hugo? You're home early today. And – Suhani, isn't it? Is there something wrong?'

'No, no, my dear. The girl saw you walking up the garden and thought you might not be feeling quite the thing. Just come to see if you're alright.'

'Oh?' puzzled Philadelphia. 'She must have very good eyesight.' A remark that immediately added Philadelphia to Suhani's ill-wish list.

Suhani was sure that Philadelphia and Jonty were secretly meeting – more because that was what she wanted, rather than through any evidence – though how such a relationship could have begun in the very regimented conditions under which they lived she could not see, nor did she care. The ploy she had used to get Hugo to check out the shrubbery would not work again. She would have to devise another scheme. In the meantime, the Mantle brats had been particularly annoying today. A day or two confined to bed would do them – and her – the world of good.

Jonty had not told Joss that he had met up with Philadelphia, though Joss suspected as much, from the change in his friend's demeanour. Jonty often went to the garrison library in the afternoons when not on duty, something he had done many times before. But when Joss went to find him one day and he was not there, he guessed where he must be. Joss was worried for his friend, for he could not see that there could possibly be any happy outcome.

The first time that Jonty and Philadelphia had met in the shrubbery had been awkward and slightly embarrassing, for neither could know whether the other still felt as they had a decade before, during which time they had had no contact at all, or whether it was just some childhood fantasy, long forgotten. Since Philadelphia was a presumably happily married woman, Jonty assumed that she had come out merely to greet an old friend. But within a short while, it was clear that their feelings for one another had abated not one jot.

The shrubbery became their special place. Philadelphia would take her book there in the afternoons, if there were not some engagement she needed to keep. When he was free, Jonty would take his own book and make his way to the rendezvous. If she were not there, he would go to the reading room and try to concentrate on his book. They never made any arrangements to meet, nor did they attempt to send one another messages. She was the wife of an officer, he a lowly corporal. The circumstances when two such might properly meet were few and far between, even though they had known one another as children – a fact that would not have recommended itself to the officers or their wives.

Between demonstrations of their affection, they found time to catch up with one another's news. Having no family of his own, Jonty could only tell Philadelphia of the Broughtons, and his time in the army. She described her life in her aunt's house, and how it was she had chosen to marry Hugo. She also told Jonty of the time when the Bury housekeeper had told her that he had been shot. Jonty's brow darkened.

'That was Quigley – her nephew,' he told her. 'He worked on your father's estate for a while, after you left. I guess you wouldn't know him. Tried to make trouble between me and Joss. Then he turned up in Ireland and started his tricks again, suckering Joss in. He led a gang in a raid on the arsenal, but we spotted them before they could do any damage and he took a shot at me. Just grazed me, luckily. They tried to find him, but he'd skipped off to America. God rot the bastard.'

'Well, she – Mrs McBride – also skipped off, with all the housekeeping money and some of the silver. Mother and father were so upset, not because of the money, really, but she'd worked for them for so many years. We think the shock of it brought on father's stroke. I don't think they ever traced her.'

'America with him, probably, or maybe back in Ireland. Don't suppose they'll ever catch up with either of them now.'

'She was often trying to cause trouble, I think. It was she who told me where to find you when you came to work at The Bury – perhaps hoping we'd be found out? I met Mrs Broughton, once. At church. She gave me a photograph of you. And one of Joss. I keep them in my jewel box.'

The conversation turned to army life. Jonty described the only two battles he had been engaged in, with some embellishments. She listened, round-eyed.

'But you might easily have been killed!' she cried fearfully.

'Well, that's soldiering,' he replied awkwardly. 'Though, out here, you're more likely to die of cholera or something.' He could not help thinking that, if Hugo should die, by either means, all their problems would be solved.

'Hugo is talking about sending me back home. He says the climate here is not suitable for me.'

'Well, I hope he does,' he said gruffly. She looked at him tearfully, a question in her eyes. 'I would rather know you were safe in England than here amongst all this disease. It's really bad for Europeans, what with the heat and the rain and flies. Even a lot of natives die of it, you know.'

'Oh, Jonty, I couldn't bear not to see you again, now.'

She asked him about Captain Mantle, and how his wife had died, telling him that the family lived next door. Jonty frowned.

'Do they have an ayah called Suhani?'

'Yes. Do you know her?'

Jonty told her how he came to befriend her, until Joss and George had warned him off.

'It never occurred to me that she thought anything more of it,' he explained. 'But – be careful of her. There's something not quite right about her.'

'Captain Mantle seems to rely on her a great deal. I suppose, left with three young children to bring up, that's only natural.' She paused. 'When Hugo first asked me to marry him, I said 'no'. I hadn't given up hope, then, of going back to Bearshott and seeing you again. But when Mrs

Broughton told me you had gone into the army, I couldn't see how we would ever meet. And then, all my cousins were married or promised, and it was made clear that I should do the same. Then Hugo asked again, and I thought it might as well be him as anybody. He's a pleasant man, quite – undemanding – if you know what I mean. So I agreed. Then, father died, and we had to put off the wedding. By the time we married, Hugo had bought his commission and was due to come out to India, and – I know it's a big place, but I couldn't help hoping... And then, at that first parade, there you were, standing in the front row, looking so smart...' Her lip quivered.

'And here we are,' Joss said heavily. 'I don't see how we're going to get out of this mess, Phia. But – I'm glad we're in it, for all that.'

The Rowlatts had arrived from Fort William, having travelled by easy stages owing to Charles's poor health. Elspet was to resume her duties in the garrison schoolroom, whilst he was to occupy himself with gentle exercise and a great deal of rest. Jonty was tempted to confide in Elspet, but decided, in the end, to keep his own counsel, for what could she say, other than they were in the wrong?

It began to be whispered amongst the officers' wives that Things were going missing. Silly, trumpery things that one would ordinarily put down as merely mislaid, or broken: a packet of buttons, a bangle from the bazaar, a notebook, a book of sewing needles, a single wine glass. But a chance remark from one led to a comment from another, and pretty soon the ladies were comparing notes. Hardly any could pinpoint the exact time of the supposed thefts, but all agreed that they must have occurred when the bungalows in the patchery were empty whilst their occupants were out for the evening. It was also noted that there were no reports of thefts from bungalows where there were children, presumably because there would always be an ayah in attendance. The ladies reported their suspicions to their husbands, who roundly pooh-poohed their conclusions. Too much tea had addled their brains. One or two officers did consider the matter more seriously, but, since the items were of little intrinsic value, merely recommended to their wives that any item of real or sentimental worth be safely locked away, out of the reach of acquisitive hands. Having delivered a metaphorical pat on the head to the ladies, the gentlemen went back to the more serious business of enjoying a convivial evening in the mess.

Captain Mantle mentioned the matter to Suhani, who, though she knew nothing of the pilfering, schemed to turn the information to good account. One Saturday evening, there was to be a reception in the mess for some visiting bigwig. Suhani brought his children out to bid Mantle goodnight, watching as he joined the Galbraiths for the stroll to the mess. She dosed her charges with her 'special medicine', which, so she claimed, guarded against all sorts of ills. It certainly ensured the children spent the night sound asleep. When she was sure they had settled down, she took a couple of glasses of the captain's brandy across to the Galbraith bungalow. The house servant was surprised to see her, but the brandy was too tempting. He let her in; they sat and talked for half an hour, after which she said she must return to check up on the children.

Carefully rinsing out the glasses, she reflected that the draught she had given the coolie had not been so strong that he would immediately fall asleep, but enough so that he would slumber deeply when he did. She waited an hour, before picking up a lantern and slipping out of the house.

The bungalows were all built to the same design. Suhani stepped up onto the rear verandah and tried the door that she knew must open into the main bedroom. As she had expected, it was locked, but a quick flick of her penknife sprung the catch. The flickering nightlight showed her enough of the room for her purpose. Quietly, she opened a few draws. The first chest she tried contained a man's belongings. This must be the major's side of the bed. She moved around to the other, furthest away from the windows. Gently pulling out the drawers in a second chest, despite the deep gloom she could tell from the light fragrances that these were the woman's things. Confident that the servant would not awake, Suhani took her time, thoroughly rifling through the garments and feeling to the backs and bottoms of each drawer for anything that might be some sort of illicit memento. A small wardrobe next drew her attention. Running her hands over the dresses, and checking all the pockets and the top shelf, she again failed to find anything. A large box on the dressing table looked promising. She carried it to the bed and tipped out its contents. An assortment of loose brooches, necklaces, earbobs and bracelets spewed over the counterpane, together with some boxes. Opening each in turn, she found only jewellery. Frustrated, she threw the casket onto the bed. There came a click and a hidden drawer, jarred loose, slid smoothly open. Inside was an envelope. Eagerly she picked it up, and saw that it contained a handful of photographs. Too dim by the light of the lantern to see them clearly, Suhani carried them across to the window, and held them up one by one to the moonlight, until finally she found what she was looking for. A picture of Jonty. Dropping the rest onto the floor, she turned the picture over. On the back, some words were scrawled in black ink. She had no idea what they said, but she knew, from cards and letters sent to the Mantle children, that the cross at the bottom represented a kiss. She slipped out onto the verandah. A sudden gust of wind caught the screen door, which slammed behind her.

When Major and Mrs Galbraith returned later that evening they were met by a worried, and rather sleepy, houseboy.

'I fear, sahib, that we have had a thief.'

'A thief?'

'Yes, sahib, most certainly. The memsahib's jewellery has

been dropped all over the bed. I have tried to gather it up.'

With a cry of distress, Philadelphia hurried into the bedroom.

'I did not know what to do with the photographs, sahib. I do not know where they are belonging.'

'Photographs?' repeated Hugo, perplexed, taking the proffered pictures. The top one, he saw, was a photograph of his aunt and uncle. 'Ah, these are the memsahib's family. Did you see who it was that broke in?'

'No, sahib. I heard a door bang, but when I arrived there was no one to see.'

Idly sifting through the photographs, Hugo made his way toward the bedroom, until he came across one that he knew was not one of his wife's family. The photographer's name and address appeared at the bottom of the pasteboard postcard. Now, what on earth was Philadelphia doing with a picture of a soldier, taken in Jersey? Carrying the picture to the light, Hugo looked more closely. There was no doubt about it – the soldier's uniform carried the insignia of the London and Middlesex. He peered at the face of the young man. It was somewhat familiar, though he could not immediately recall who it was. He sorted through the remainder of the postcards. All the rest were members of the Greening family. Tucking the other into his pocket, he walked into the bedroom.

'These were on the floor,' he said, holding them out. Philadelphia grew pale, and took the bundle from him nervously. 'I'll buy you an album, so that you can stick them in, then everyone can see them.' She glanced up at him, then away.

'Thank you. That would be nice,' she said colourlessly.

It took him some time to remember, but it came to Hugo eventually. The man in the photograph was that short-arse private, friend of the big corporal.

Now Suhani had her evidence, she pondered how to go about exposing Jonty and the major's wife without incriminating herself. She briefly toyed with the idea of handing the photograph to either the major or Captain Mantle, perhaps claiming that she had found it on the ground, but there was the risk that they would associate her with the theft, might even believe her to be responsible for all the others. Her best course of action, she decided, would be to make sure that one of the officers' wives found it. Once the message on the back had been read, the rumour mill would start, she was sure. But she could not think of any way that she might be able to leave it in such a place. She was only an ayah, and would have no business being anywhere the wives might gather. The notion of dropping the picture on the ground, hoping that somebody would pick it up, she also discarded. There was no guarantee that some galumphing great soldier would not walk all over it.

For some days, she carried Jonty's portrait around with her, hoping that an opportunity might present itself. She took the Mantle children to school, sitting herself with the other ayahs. She wished she had paid attention to the lessons. She might have been able to decipher the writing. Sitting at the back of the class, turning the pasteboard over and over in her pocket, she suddenly saw her way clear. The schoolteacher, she knew, was the sister of the sickly minister. It occurred to her that such a person would have very righteous views about the affair, and would be sure to speak of it, if only to the major. What she did not know was that Elspet and Jonty were old friends.

At first, she thought she would leave the photograph somewhere the teacher would see it, but thought better of it. Someone else – maybe one of the other ayahs, or the pupils – might see it first and pick it up. She would have to take the risk of handing it to the teacher and hope that her tale would be believed. She waited until the class had nearly emptied at the end of the day's lessons. Gathering up her charges, she shepherded them to the classroom door, out of earshot, before returning to speak to Elspet. Pulling the photograph from her pocket, she offered it to the teacher.

'Memsahib, one of the children found this. I do not know who to give it to.'

Elspet took the picture and turned it over. On the reverse was written *With kind regards, J Tickle x*. She had one just like it, sent all those years ago from Jersey, although her copy was with her belongings back in England. She frowned. Unlike Suhani, Philadelphia did know about Elspet, and in desperation had come to her the previous week with a warning for Jonty. Someone had burgled her bungalow and had taken the photographs of himself and Joss. Looking up, Elspet caught the eager gleam in the girl's eye. She thought that the ayah's story sounded unlikely, though what exactly might be the truth was unclear.

'I'll deal with this, thank you, Suhani.' She was rewarded with a beaming smile from the girl, who was convinced that Jonty and the major's wife would soon be exposed.

Elspet put the photograph in her bag for safekeeping, until she could meet Jonty and pass it to him. In the meantime, she would go to the Galbraith bungalow to reassure Philadelphia that one, at least, of her photographs had been recovered.

As the days passed, Suhani became perplexed. She had seen the frown on the teacher's face when she read the script on the reverse of the photograph, and had been confident that she would show it to the major, who would confront his errant wife and Jonty. But, nothing: no sound of argument from the next-door billet, no humiliation for the memsahib, no punishment for her lover.

Hugo, in ignorance of the existence of the other photograph, kept an eye on his wife when she was anywhere near the troops, and was rewarded one day by seeing a half-smile on her face when passing Joss standing on guard at the armoury, and receiving one in return, confirming all his suspicions. She and Jonty, also on guard, assiduously avoided looking at one another. Hugo failed to notice the peculiar way in which she was holding his arm, with her right hand threaded through the crook, her left resting on his arm, the crossed fingers of one laid on the other wrist.

Hugo vaguely recalled that the big corporal had once said something to him about Middlesex. He called his orderly to bring him all the records of the men in his company. Pawing through them, he saw that both Broughton and Tickle came from Bearshott, where the Greenings had their home. He could not imagine how the daughter of the rich industrialist might have met a village boy – maybe at some charity event or open day. So how was it that Philadelphia had a photograph of one, apparently secreting it away for some years. If there was something going on between his wife and the private, did that mean that the corporal knew about it? Hugo had no faith in the discretion of troops. Did the whole barracks know? Were they all sniggering about him behind his back?

27: Memsahibgunge

Serious trouble had flared up to the northeast of Simla. A large number of renegade sepoys, embedded in the village of Memsahibgunge, near the Nepalese border, had been making sporadic raids on British outposts for some while. Native infantry and police had been left to deal with the bandits, but, in their latest depredations, they had killed a number of European civilians, setting fire to their houses and devastating their plantations. Several settlers were reported missing. Searches had been made of the area, leading to the eventual discovery of their mutilated bodies, tumbled into a gulley. The British community in the burgeoning settlement, feeling very exposed and vulnerable, particularly those living on the outskirts, demanded that punitive action be taken.

After the Bhootan expedition, so many men of the London and Middlesex had been killed or died of fever, or invalided back to England, that the regiment's complement was much depleted, despite the fresh draft that had arrived in India with Galbraith. Colonel FitzHugh ordered the amalgamation of some of the existing sections. George found himself, for the first time, sharing a barrack with Joss and Jonty. Galbraith, leafing through the records of the soldiers newly attached to his company, came across George's. Another Broughton. From Bearshott. With the same next of kin as the first.

The Colonel himself had succumbed to fever. Too ill to go campaigning, he ordered Galbraith to take his company to join the expedition against the rebels. Troops drawn from garrisons at Cawnpore, Hazareebagh, Agra, Roy Bareilly and Lucknow converged on Chakrata. Two companies were sent from Calcutta and Dum-Dum but, due to the distance they had to travel, were to be used as a relief column. The expedition would not be delayed pending their arrival.

On the fifth of March, Major Hugo Galbraith led his men out of camp at four o'clock in the morning and, in the bright moonlight, commenced the fifty-mile march to Cawnpore. The journey took four days, in twelve-mile bursts – ground that the old hands of the London and Middlesex had now covered several times. At Cawnpore, they were obliged to wait a day for their transport to Umballa.

Many of the troops were at liberty to wander around the bazaars and sights of the town. Joss having been detailed to remain in camp to dig latrines, Jonty and George took themselves off. Fortified with coffee and local pastries, they headed for the Bibighar, the site of one of the most infamous massacres of the mutiny a decade earlier. The capped well, down which so many dismembered bodies of women and children had been thrown, was now surrounded by gardens of sweet-smelling flowers and an ornamental wall, and surmounted by a fine marble statue, entitled *The Angel of the Resurrection*. The memorial had only been completed two years before and was a moving tribute to the innocent victims of the rebellion, whose butchered remains still lay beneath. Neither the tree which had once stood nearby, on which the brains of many children had been dashed, and which had been festooned with the hair of decapitated women, blown there by the breeze, nor the gallows on which executions had afterward taken place, remained.

That evening, the train to take them on to Umballa arrived, and the kit was loaded, ready for an early start the next day. As they sat in the carriages, watching the countryside clack past, the mood was sombre. Many of the sightseeing troops had visited the well. Even though ten years had passed, thoughts of vengeance intruded. Furthermore, the rebels they were to confront were not disorganised, though undeniably brave, tribesmen, but ex-army men, who had received the same training as themselves, were schooled in army tactics and weaponry, and, above all, were desperate, as they could expect no quarter in light of the horrific murders of their captives, and would offer none in return.

The journey was somewhat stop and start. The track was single and, between one station and the next, confirmation that the line ahead was clear of oncoming traffic had to be telegraphed to the station masters. At some stations the troops were briefly allowed out of the carriages to stretch their cramped legs. Hopeful European passengers emerged from waiting rooms, eager to board. At sight of the troops packing the carriages, they made their disgruntled way back inside. But the locals who wanted a ride, barred from entering the trucks, perched precariously on top, despite the sergeants' urgings to get down. In the middle of March, the London and Middlesex arrived in Umballa.

The combined force camped on the open plain in front of the barracks, awaiting the arrival of troops from Agra and Hazareebagh, so many troops being camped together thought not to pose any significant risk of disease for the short while they were to remain in the district. The camp was situated eight miles outside the town; too far for any pleasure trips in the limited free time the troops had. However, the cantonment resembled a small town in itself and was a hive of activity. There were native infantry, cavalry, and police, sporting beards and turbans, in various adaptations of army uniform, and the colourfully-clad retinue of a visiting rajah. European ladies and their companions, ayahs pushing perambulators, jampans and palankeens carrying passengers, elephant and camel lines. And soldiers. Hundreds and hundreds of soldiers.

The barrack rooms were long, single-storey thatched huts, with plenty of open space between, through which numerous bungalows, with enclosed gardens, could be glimpsed. There were playing-fields, bathhouses, kitchens, an armoury, godowns, telegraph and post offices, and all the administrative buildings a standing army would require. Several bazaars were dotted about the area, selling all manner of goods. Souvenirs to send home, jewellery, clothing, haberdashery, coffee and tea. Little roadside cafés, from which delicious smells emanated, and fresh fruit and vegetable stalls. Saddlery for the officers' horses, sweetmeats, spices and condiments, pipes and tobacco. Leather boots and shoes, and dainty ladies' slippers, necessities for children and infants. Silverware, pierced and chased, flatware, and furniture in the English style. The streets were plentifully supplied with lamps so that shoppers could continue to make their purchases deep into the night.

There was no time for sightseeing, but many of the troops took the opportunity to take a bath and to browse the market stalls for bargains. Joss had been given sentry duty, and was confined to camp, but his friends were free to wander around the cantonment. They thought it was just hard luck that he should again miss out on the opportunity of some leisure time, an unfortunate coincidence, unaware that Galbraith had instigated both details.

Jonty and George wandered around, munching on pomegranates and preserved pumpkin, admiring, but resisting, all the trinkets that they were plied with. George bought himself a pair of stout boots, for the equivalent of one and sixpence, replacing the worn-out second-hand ones he had been issued with when he 'volunteered'. In the festive atmosphere that prevailed in the bazaars, it hardly felt like the eve of battle.

Jonty saw several items that he would have liked to have bought Philadelphia, but common sense prevailed. He had managed to see her for an hour the day before the company had left Lucknow, when he had gone to say farewell to Elspet and found her there before him. Elspet had discreetly left them alone.

'Oh, Jonty!' Philadelphia had cried, running into his arms. 'I hoped you would come to see Miss Rowlatt. I wish you weren't going.'

'Don't worry – we'll be back before you know it.' Jonty kissed her tenderly.

'You will come back! Promise! I couldn't bear it if you didn't.' She lifted her face. He looked down at her, her eyes big as saucers, brim-full of tears, lips quivering.

'I promise. Phia, I do love you so very much.'

'Show me, Jonty,' she whispered. 'Show me how much!'

By the end of the week, the contingents from Hazareebagh and Agra had arrived. The following day being Sunday, they were given one day of respite, before the convoy set off on the trek north, towards Chakrata, selected to be the site of the force's base camp. At midnight on the eighteenth of March, the heavy ox carts, laden with equipment, were sent on ahead, to make their slow progress to the next campsite at Moulanah, whilst the soldiers broke camp and loaded up the camels, elephants, and lighter carts with the remaining gear. Two hours later, they took to the road. The ground was soft and boggy, tiring and tiresome to walk on. The ox carts had carved deep furrows that had filled with water, and which were not easy to see in the dark. The fields of poppies and corn on either side, being higher than the track, leached water.

George softly swore.

'Look at my new boots!' he said, unrealistically, since it was too dark to see anything much. 'Covered in mud! And they pinch.'

'Told you to wear the old ones until you've softened them up,' Joss said unsympathetically. When they reached the Tangree, which they were obliged to wade across, George was not alone in his complaints. The uncomfortable slog from Umballa to Moulanah took the head of the column five hours. By the time the rear-guard arrived, the sun was high in the sky, blazing down on the perspiring troops as they erected tents.

The rest of the march followed much the same pattern, with no road being anything much more than a beaten track. Each day's marching took upwards of five hours. Bilaspore, Khiderabad, Kalesur, Raj-Ghat Mundee, Umbarri, Kalsi, and Siah. To the weary troops, each village was much like the one before. Only at Umbarri did they halt for twenty-four hours. After Divine Service, all they wanted to do was to snooze in their stuffy tents with their boots off.

From Siah, the road wound upwards into the foothills of the Himalayas, becoming steeper and steeper. There were tremendous bursts of scenery: waterfalls plunging down into luxuriant valleys, clear blue skies, and the snow-capped mountains of the higher peaks in the far distance. But the men were in no mood to enjoy the landscape, glad only to have finally arrived, after ten days' gruelling march, at Chakrata.

The new station had no solid buildings at all, apart from the sappers' barracks two miles away at Kaliana. A narrow ridge connected two hills, and was covered with tents, pitched, not in orderly lines, but wherever the ground was flat enough to accommodate them. In the centre stood a marquee, where the force commander, Lieutenant Colonel Marriott Shaw, had his headquarters. The residents of Simla, having vociferously made their feelings known, were to be placated with extra troops to guard them during the course of the campaign. One of Shaw's first orders to his combined force was to send the companies from Agra to protect them, thus depleting his force by several hundred men until such time as those from Calcutta and Dum-Dum arrived.

Memsahibgunge was situated high in the Himalayan foothills. It was debatable whether it were in India or Nepal.

Until the arrival of the rebellious sepoys, it had consisted of a few mean huts, scattered over a small plateau, where the inhabitants scratched a living from their crops and animals. They had few visitors. The village was remote, not on the route to anywhere, and had no shrines or special features of interest to any but themselves. So they were more than surprised when a large number of armed men arrived and took over their little community. The village elders had protested, but, as soon as they understood what the consequences of unacceptance of the new regime might be, had speedily capitulated. Indeed, in many ways, their lives improved. The sepoys were excellent foragers, and returned from their raids laden with food and other goods, passing a tithe to their hosts. Since their arrival, the villagers had not once felt the pangs of starvation, nor the lack of warm clothing and fuel to ward off the bite of a harsh winter. In return, the villagers supplied their visitors with infusions of poppy tea, brewed from the seeds of the plants they cultivated.

The sepoys had turned the village into an impregnable fortress. In the ten years since the mutiny, a sturdy wall, some four yards high, had been thrown up all around the plateau, crenellated and provided with loopholes and a shooting platform, and in which there was only one gateway. Stone godowns were erected, to store supplies and an armoury. Stables and barrack rooms had been constructed, and a treasury, which held all the valuables they had seized. There was one building that housed a brothel, where the women they had captured were incarcerated. They had, in effect, built a garrison, along the lines of those in which they had served in times past.

The escarpment surrounding the wall was cleared of jungle for a distance of one hundred yards, leaving no cover for would-be attackers in any direction. Just inside the tree-line, a series of booby-traps had been set. The only accessible route to the single gate lay through a narrow gorge, which zig-zagged up the side of the hill, flanked by virtually vertical rocks. Men posted on the clifftops could shoot down into this pass, picking off interlopers in almost perfect safety. They had only to draw back a yard or two to be out of the line of sight of the troops below – and therefore out of their line of fire.

Shaw set up his forward camp in a valley further down the mountain, having received intelligence that the companies from Calcutta and Dum-Dum would arrive at Chakrata in two days' time, where they were to wait until required. He did not envisage that the campaign to clear out the rebels would take very long. The main column and headquarters were under his direct command. The Hazareebagh and Cawnpore contingents formed the right wing. Those from Lucknow and Roy Bareilly, under Galbraith, the left. Shaw sent out his scouts. They reported back with descriptions of the fortifications, where armed men could be seen patrolling the walls, and of the deadly passage which appeared to be the only way in. Shaw summoned his commanders, to discuss tactics and formulate a plan of attack. His initial thought was that, if the gorge were the only way in, then it must also be the only way out. If necessary, they could lay siege to the village, and starve the rebels out. But that would undoubtedly mean an extended campaign, over-wintering under canvas. Besides, they had no information as to how well-provisioned the enemy might be, and how long they could hold out, which might be for months. He had heard of one such siege that had lasted over two years. Besiegement was to be considered only as a last resort. Something proactive was called for.

Captain Cunliffe, commander of the right wing, posited that there was, surely, another way out of the stronghold, for what force would only leave themselves one escape route? If there were no second gateway, there must be a tunnel. And, if there were, the sappers could be sent in to do their deadly work. Shaw agreed that this was the most likely scenario. The problem he faced was how to locate the exit to such a tunnel, which could run from any point on the compass and would finish somewhere in the jumble of rocks and crevices below the escarpment. Any diligent search was likely to be protracted, unless they were very lucky.

Fortune smiled. A small band of tribesmen were taken into custody not far from Shaw's camp. They gave plausible answers to their captors' questions, and would have been allowed to continue on their way had not a gold locket, worn around the neck of one beneath his khurta, slipped out as he bent forward. When opened, the likenesses of a European couple were revealed. The band were dragged from their horses and a thorough search made of their packs. Numerous pieces of jewellery were found, and wads of notes. Although the tribesmen were brutally interrogated, they refused to give any information about Memsahibgunge.

One of the group was a youth. He had the beginnings of a moustache on his upper lip, and looked to be about fifteen or sixteen – too young to have been involved in the uprising ten years' before. He seemed particularly close to one of the older men, constantly looking across at him when asked any question, and receiving a slight shake of the head in return. Knowing that many boys brought up in the bleak mountains of the north looked older than their years, the youth was separated from the rest, given food and drink, and assured that his companions were likewise being fed, and having their cuts and bruises attended to. If he would only tell what he knew, he was told, he and his friends would be allowed to go on their way without further harm. Away from the others, the youth soon gave in, describing the layout of the village, and the location of a tunnel. Once this last information had been verified, the tribesmen were hanged.

The initial suggestion to blow up the tunnel was dismissed. Not only would the loss of this escape route leave the rebels immured in their stronghold, where they might be able to hold out for many weeks, but the massive gate would again be the only way into the village for Shaw's force. He decided instead to send troops up through the tunnel, whilst a diversionary attack was carried out in front of the gate. The left wing would concentrate on the tunnel, whilst the centre and right would carry out the frontal assault. The first troops into the fortress via the tunnel were to be native infantry, who would endeavour to mingle with the rebels long enough to get to the gate and throw it open.

Galbraith's wing had the furthest to go. His companies were to circle the plateau to where the tunnel exited above a steep drop. A narrow path along the edge of the hill led, eventually, to a gulley. Galbraith was given twenty-four hours to get his men in place. The officers synchronised their timepieces.

Just after dawn, Galbraith led his contingent out of camp and headed west. They were only lightly armed, but even so the rugged hillside proved a challenge. Some of the men cut down stout branches, to use as walking-sticks, throwing them aside when they reached the base of the steep cliffs, where they were of no further use. The few men who were accomplished mountaineers went up first, securing belays as they went. Even so, two men slipped and fell, one badly injured, the other to his death.

Joss, reaching the top of an overhang, sat and wiped his sleeve across his face. Jonty and George shortly joined him, their height making the climb a little easier. The view across the valley below was spectacular, but no one was in the mood to admire it. A shout came from above, exhorting them to get a move on.

'Why can't we be sent to somewhere flat?' Joss groaned.

Jonty clapped him on the back. 'Such as?'

'Dunno. Bombay sounds nice,' Joss said, clambering to his feet.

The wing reached the gulley below the entrance to the tunnel in the middle of the afternoon. They were allowed neither fire nor tent and were to wait out the rest of the day as best they could. Galbraith crossed to where Barnes' section was sitting, huddled together.

'Sergeant, I want a man to take a message back to Colonel Shaw.' Galbraith looked about, then pointed to Joss, as if at random. 'You, private. Leave your pack here, and follow me.'

'But, sir—' began Barnes, Joss being obviously one of the least suited to such a task, but then stopped and held his peace. It did not do to query a senior officer's decisions, not if one wanted to get on in this man's army.

Captain Mantle frowned. He had heard the exchange, and had the same reservations. Besides, he had been at the council meeting when the plans were formulated, and knew that sending a messenger back was not part of them.

Mantle had no time for bullying and had never done it himself – not since school, at any rate. It never served. He could not think why Hugo would single Broughton out. He was such an innocuous fellow, always ready to do his duty, not given to complaining, and well-liked by the other men. There had been that business in Ireland, of course, but that was years ago, well before the major had joined the regiment. He probably didn't know anything about it. And then there were the fatigues that the major had personally given the soldier, preventing him from accompanying his friends on their excursions, fatigues that should have been left to his section sergeant to allocate.

'I want you to report to Colonel Shaw that we have arrived at the location and are ready to enter the tunnel. Dismissed.'

Mantle watched Joss make his way back along the gulley.

'Don't you think someone should go with him, Hugo?'

'No, *captain*. I do not.'

Galbraith had deliberately not given Joss the order in writing. He was hopeful that, if he made it back to camp in one piece – which seemed unlikely – it would be thought that he had deserted, and the appropriate action would be taken. He would have liked to have ordered him to go unarmed, but realised that was a step too far. He comforted himself with the thought that the rifle would be more of an encumbrance, especially as it could not be secured to his pack, and any sepoy waiting in the shadows could easily pick him off. In a better humour than he had felt for some weeks, he settled down with a tot of rum to await the morning.

'Can't we do something, sarge?' Jonty pleaded. 'I could slip away and go with him. He'll never make it on his own.'

'No, lad, you can't. You're wanted here. And that's an order, so no heroics.'

At four o'clock the next morning, the wing quietly made its precarious way along the narrow track to the mouth of the tunnel. Once inside, they lit lanterns and began to ascend in the gloom. The going was steep, the passage littered with shale on which an ankle might easily turn. One hundred yards from the entrance – about halfway across the escarpment above – they found the tunnel completely blocked. There was no way passed the blockage and the boulders were too big to move by hand, even had they the time do so.

In his final hours on earth, the boy had outwitted the British army. They had asked about a tunnel. With a show of reluctance, he had told them of one. The old one, the one that had been blocked by a rockfall. The location of the other, well-hidden in the jungle, he kept to himself. The hangman wondered why he had died with a smile on his lips.

Galbraith panicked. Had he sent a patrol ahead to reconnoitre, as he should have done, he would have discovered the obstruction, information that would be vital to Shaw, worth risking the life of more than one messenger. Instead, he had been so pleased with himself after his little ploy to send Broughton on a spurious mission that he had completely lost sight of the task at hand. The assault on the gate was due to commence at sunrise, in an hour's time, an assault which would not now be supported by men from inside the village.

Galbraith turned on his heel and began to push his way back down the tunnel, shouting 'Back! Back! Turn around!'

Apart from those at the front, the men did not know where

the problem lay, and thought armed rebels must be coming down the tunnel to meet them. Rattled, and unnerved by the sight of their wild-eyed commander charging through their ranks, they surged back. Some lost their footing, and were trampled in the crush. The men at the back of the line, still on the narrow ledge, were knocked from it by the retreating column. Upwards of fifty men were killed or seriously injured in the flight. Sergeant Barnes' section having been at the front of the column in the tunnel with the native infantry, Jonty and George were well out of the way of the chaos.

Galbraith dashed back down into the gulley where they had overnighted, intending to follow the route of the previous day back to rejoin the main force. Captain Mantle, some way behind, saw that the better way would be to go upward, to the edge of the escarpment, and cut across to Shaw along the open ground, hoping that they would be out of range of the defenders above. Yelling at the men to follow him, he scrambled up the fifty yards of rock and shrub to the lower edge of the escarpment. Those behind did so, but those already heading down into the gulley dithered. Some were for pushing on after the major, whilst others were trying to turn around to follow Mantle.

Shaw and Cunliffe's companies lay in wait inside the tree-line. A few booby-traps had been set off, but they were fairly easy to spot, if one knew what to look for, and had largely been disabled. The rays of the early morning sun began to break through the trees.

Against all expectations – not least his own – Joss made it safely to the camp, albeit with some torn clothing and grazed hands, and was directed to the commander. Crawling on his belly, he squirmed up to Shaw.

'Sir, I have a report from Major Galbraith,' he began. 'He has reached the gulley below the tunnel, and is now – was – ready and waiting to move into the tunnel.'

'Good. Excellent. Any losses?'

'I know of only three, sir: one dead, two injured.'

'Very well. Take yourself back down to camp and get a hot meal. You've earned it.'

Half an hour later, faint shouts coming from the direction of the tunnel could be heard, but no sound of gunfire. Shaw realised that something had gone wrong with the plan, that he could not rely on Galbraith's men opening the gate from the inside. He ordered his mountain guns to be trained on the massive wooden door and began the bombardment. The renegades had also been alerted by the sounds of the left wing's retreat and the walls bristled with armed men.

Bolting down his breakfast, Joss, though exhausted by the strenuous climb and descent, tagged onto the end of the stream of men still making their way up the narrow pass. Cunliffe's scouts had already dealt with the handful of guards stationed above. The gorge was steep, but free of loose rocks, having been cleared by the rebel sepoys as a safe route for their horses. By the time Joss reached the mass of soldiers firing up into the ramparts, the first men of the left wing were arriving. Mantle reported to the commander.

'Where is Galbraith?' queried Shaw. 'Fallen?'

'No, sir.' Mantle was uncomfortable. Galbraith was a friend, sort of. He did not want to drop him in it, although his actions were somewhat suspect. 'He is leading half our wing back by another route. In case we came under heavy fire on the open ground and lost a lot of men.'

'He divided his force?' Shaw looked at Mantle sceptically. 'Hmm. He may be rather late to the party, then.'

Reaching the body of men stationed along the tree-line, Joss looked about him, trying to decide where he had best stand. There was already an acrid smell of cordite hanging in the air. Puffs of white smoke from the volleys of both rebels and army drifted away on the breeze. The noise was deafening, particularly when the heavy guns were fired. The wall around the gateway was beginning to crumble. Many men were lying in unnatural poses on the ground. The wounded groaned most piteously, and the hospital orderlies were doing their best to get them away from the front line for treatment, but for most of them there was little hope. Shaw's force was shooting uphill, aiming at men who only briefly showed themselves. The rebel sepoys, trained by the army, fired down into the mass of redcoats with deadly accuracy.

Joss spotted the London and Manchester's standard, away to the left. Anxiously scanning the men grouped around it, he was relieved to see both Jonty and George, and many of his other comrades, apparently alive and well. Barnes was the first to notice him.

'Hey, up! Here's our lost sheep!'

Heads turned to watch his approach, and several men clapped and cheered. Joss threw himself down beside Jonty.

'Why aren't you inside?'

'The tunnel was blocked. No way in. So, here we are.' Jonty paused. 'Seen Galbraith?'

Joss shook his head. 'No. Just come up from breakfast.'

'Breakfast! Alright for some.' George looked about. 'It looks like hard work, here.'

Far away to the right, a great roar sounded. Men hefted their rifles uneasily, looking toward the escarpment on the other side of the pass. Suddenly, the open ground was dotted with beturbaned figures running toward them. In the momentary pause, whilst the soldiers were distracted by this new threat, the shooters on the wall managed to pick off the crew of one of the big guns. Without ceremony, a new team pulled their bodies aside and took over.

The rebels had emerged from the other tunnel, which lay more or less diametrically opposed to the first. They were fierce and desperate. Shouting *Nana Sahib!*, they rushed at Shaw's force in an attempt to overrun it. The shooters on the top of the wall had to cease firing, for fear of hitting their own comrades. The gate by now being almost completely destroyed, they drew their swords and ran out of their stronghold to join their brothers. After the horrors of

Cawnpore, the London and Manchester, at least, were keen to be up and doing. They met the rebels with gun and blade, firing, hacking, slashing and stabbing. Shouting – when they had the breath – *Remember the Bibighar!*

Joss managed to get off a couple of shots before resorting to his bayonet. He lunged at a rebel who was about to chop at George, who was himself having a fierce tussle with another. There was no time to regret the deaths of those they killed, nor to think about tactics, nor to wonder whose side was winning the field. Joss slipped on a pile of guts and was only saved from spilling his own by an upward slice, delivered by Jonty, into the belly of his assailant.

The ground in front of the ruined gateway was slathered in gore. Men were tripping over the bodies of the slain, slipping in their blood, their arms growing tired and useless after the unrelenting thrust and parry. Suddenly, a trumpet blared. The renegades raced back to the wall, facing their attackers. A new gun appeared on the parapet, muzzle trained on the besiegers. A sharp rat-tat-tat clattered.

'Where the fuck did they get that?' Jonty wondered.

The muzzle made a sweep of the ground. The attackers threw themselves to the floor as bullets pinged all around. A well-aimed shot from one of the artillery crews knocked the machine-gun sideways, killing its crew, though not before it had caused devastating injuries to a large number of men. The gun silenced, the remaining sepoys were now lined up under the wall, as though facing a firing squad. There was still some sporadic firing from the ramparts above.

The regiment's flag bearer was cut down. Joss watched helplessly as George, leaping forward to pick up the fallen standard, keeled over. Joss opened his mouth to shout a warning as Jonty dashed to George's side and reached for the flag, but, before he could give voice, he blacked out as a musket ball slammed into his shoulder.

Major Hugo Galbraith, and the few men who had followed him, arrived only at the death of the action. Lieutenant

Colonel Shaw received his report, beetle-brows drawn together. He had had high hopes of this officer beforehand. His father the colonel was held in high esteem. Obviously, the son was not of the same calibre. A sideways promotion beckoned.

Entering Memsahibgunge, the remaining rebels were rounded up and herded into one of the huts. The villagers were informed that they were now liberated. Now used to fat bellies and warm hearths, it is doubtful they shared this point of view. When some of the soldiers entered the building used as a brothel, they found two white women, and one child of about twelve, in addition to the native women. The brothel keeper, attempting to hide amongst the others, was pointed out, led outside, and shot. It was remembered that just such a woman had ordered the massacre in the Bibighar.

Shaw examined the machine-gun, a marvel of modern science. How the rebels had got hold of it was never discovered. However, it was immediately added to the army's arsenal. Its first duty was to dispatch many of the surviving sepoys. Their leaders were tied to the mouths of the mountain guns and blown to bits. Not one renegade was known to have survived the Memsahibgunge expedition. The bodies were left for the villagers to dispose of, as punishment for allowing the sepoys the use of their village. The native women in the brothel were left to go wherever they would, whilst the three Europeans were escorted back to Chakrata and an uncertain future.

The huge number of casualties could not be dealt with successfully at the base hospitals. The most severely injured, those not expected to live, remained at Chakrata. The rest of the stretcher cases were sent by steamboat to Umballa, from thence by train to Cawnpore. The walking wounded would accompany them, where there was room. The surgeon included Joss's name on the list of the latter. Galbraith deleted it, causing raised eyebrows from both the surgeon and

Captain Mantle.

Stretchers haphazardly littered the quayside, the cries of the wounded vying with the shouting of orders. Joss picked his way through the chaos, looking for his friends. He found George first. He was deathly pale, blood ominously seeping through the blanket covering him. Were it not for the fact that it was easier for the orderlies to load him onto the steamer than to thread their way through the other wounded, he should have been returned to the base hospital. Joss knelt by his side and took his hand. With his ghastly pallor and blond hair, George already looked like a ghost.

'How are you doing, old man?'

George smiled weakly. 'Been better, I think. Gosh, I'm tired.'

'Well, you're in for a nice cruise. You'll like that, George, back on the water.'

'You know, I think – once this is all over – I shall go back to sea.'

'Of course you will. And you'll write and tell us all about the places you visit.'

'Yes. Yes, I will.' George paused. 'Tell Mother – tell Mother I'll write, soon as I can.'

' 'Course. But you'll be able to tell her yourself.'

'What happened to Jonty?'

'I dunno. Haven't found him yet.'

' 'Scuse us, mate. Need to take this one.'

Joss looked up at the orderly. 'Of course.' He turned to George. 'Bye for now, Georgie. See you back in Lucknow.'

He watched sadly as his oldest friend was carried up the gangway, raising his hand in farewell.

He finally found Jonty in a queue of men waiting to board, leaning on a pair of crutches.

'Seen George?'

Joss nodded. 'Yes. He's in a bad way,' he said heavily. 'In the gut, by the look of it. He's on the boat, though. How about you?'

'Just my thigh, this time. Bullet missed the bone, luckily.' Jonty looked sideways at Joss. 'Shame about George…I suppose—?'

Joss shook his head. 'No. No chance.'

The pair were silent for a while, as the queue shuffled forward, deep in thought. They had lost many comrades over the years, from one cause or another, but this was different. This was George.

At the foot of the gangplank, Jonty said, 'You go in front of me.'

'No – I'm not on the list.'

'Oh?' Jonty frowned. There were plenty of men in the line who appeared less seriously injured than Joss. 'Well – see you in Cawnpore, I guess.' As he hobbled up the gangway, he called back over his shoulder, 'I'll find George, stay with him until—'

Joss smiled. 'That would be great. He'll be glad of that.'

Galbraith was drunk. Very, *very* drunk. What had he achieved? Broughton had come back wounded, but not badly. If he hadn't crossed his name off the list for the boat, he would be dead, now, with all the others. Worse, he had lost the respect of the officers and men. He had come out to India with such high hopes. Now, all was gone. From the expressions of barely-concealed contempt, many people thought him a coward. He well knew that his hopes of promotion were now nil, unless he were given a desk job somewhere. How on earth had it come to this? Why had he not just packed Philadelphia back off to England?

He reeled out of the mess. No one bothered to bid him goodnight. He had put a black mark next to the regiment's name.

It had been raining hard; there were puddles everywhere. He felt a slight push in the small of his back, toppled over and fell face down in a pool of water. The last thing he remembered was the touch of a pair of small hands reaching into his pockets.

28: *Indian Ocean, December 1867*

Thomas O'Malley traced the letters with his fingertips. It was too dark to read them. The light from the hatchway scarcely penetrated this far, and the lanterns suspended from the bulkheads were lower than this top bunk, deepening shadows rather than casting light. He had first noticed the carving when the man on the next top bunk had lit a cigarillo. A momentary flash, just enough to see that someone had left his mark on the planking behind his head. Maybe some other poor sod, like him, being transported to a place he had no wish to go to. Why could they not have sent him to America? He had friends there, who would have helped him escape and set up somewhere, working for the cause.

The letters were not deeply cut. It took him some while to make them out: JT 1862. Who was he? he wondered. Perhaps he might bump into him sometime, when they reached Australia. He thought he might add his own initials. He rather liked the idea of leaving some sort of memorial to himself and his fellow prisoners. Which initials should he carve? Those of the name he was known here by, had been imprisoned in Millbank under, or his real name, the one that would have got him hanged, if the authorities had realised who he really was. He took out his penknife and, somewhat awkwardly, began to carve. Like the previous occupant, he found the teak planks too hard to cut deeply. It took the best part of an hour, but eventually he was satisfied.

His initials – his *real* initials – and the date were incised below the others: FQ 1867. *Clan na Gael.*

29. Lucknow

I had not seen Philadelphia since her husband's funeral, when she was supported by Elspet and the officers' wives. It was variously rumoured that he had drowned, choked on his own vomit, or been robbed and murdered. However it came about, I hoped that it was painful.

They told me how lucky I was, that he had crossed my name off the list of wounded to be transported by hospital steamboat and train. Some sort of infection had swept through the invalids. Necrosis, the surgeon called it. Many men had died. I didn't feel lucky. I would that I had been one of them.

Contrary to all expectations, George had survived the boat trip, finally succumbing on the train, somewhere between Barrajpur and Cawnpore. I don't know if Jonty was with him. I doubt it. His own wound was infected by then, he'd have been too ill himself. He had made it as far as camp at Oonao.

I had them buried, side by side, in the cemetery at St Lawrence's. I reserved the adjacent plot for myself. I had decided to re-engage for the full twenty-one years' service. In my heart, I was sure I would never leave India. If the rebels didn't do for me, I would surely die of disease. Whenever and however my death occurred, I was content to think that I would, eventually, lay at rest beside them.

It was some months before I spoke to Philadelphia again. Recovered from my wound, I grew bitter and morose, and took more than my fair share of drink. Philadelphia grew bigger and bigger. She sent me a note, asking me to come to see her in hospital. As I sat by her bed, I was looked at askance by the nurses. She was in the ward reserved for the ladies of the officers, where it was not the done thing for one of the 'other ranks' to visit. They brought the child to her. The joy in her face when she took him in her arms was almost unbearable to watch. She cooed over the infant.

'You're going to be just like your daddy. Isn't he, Joss?'

I looked down at the child's unprepossessing features. I could see no likeness to anyone, not to Hugo nor to any of the Greening men. What he most looked like, I thought, was a roly-poly pudding.

'Will you take him for me, Joss?' I leant forward to do as she asked when she stopped me. 'No, Joss, not now. I want you to take him home for me, back to England.'

I looked at her blankly. 'But I'm not going back to England. I'm going to stay on here, in the army.'

Her eyes filled with tears. 'Oh, Joss, I don't want him brought up here. I want him to go home.'

'Well,' I said awkwardly, 'you'll be able to take him yourself.'

'No, I won't, Joss. There's something wrong with me. Inside. They don't tell me anything, but I feel it. I won't be here to look after him.' She did, indeed, look very ill, which I had assumed was because of her labours.

'But they won't let me take him, Phia. We aren't family.'

'That's the other thing I want to talk to you about.' She took a deep breath. 'I want you to marry me.'

'Marry—? No, Phia, you can't mean it! You're not thinking straight. You'll be fine—'

'No, I won't, Joss. Jonty told me so much about your family, how kind they were to him, when he was growing up. That's the sort of family I want my son to grow up in, not like the stuffy Galbraiths, or my parents, who I barely knew. You aren't promised, are you? Jonty never said you had a young lady. There's no – impediment – is there?' She looked so anxious that I hurried to reassure her.

'No, there's no impediment. But – are you sure this is what you want? What would your family say? They will want to raise your son, they won't leave him with me, even if we did marry. The Galbraiths will certainly want him. They would know that the baby isn't mine.'

'Don't tell them, Joss! Don't tell them about the baby, or anything.'

'They have a right to know, Phia. He is their grandchild.'

I left her then, promising to think carefully about what she said. Early the next morning, Elspet brought an urgent message from the hospital; Philadelphia was sinking, and was asking for me.

She looked pitiful. They had taken away most of her pillows, so that she was lying nearly flat. It made her look like a corpse. She reached for my hand.

'Well, Joss? Will you?' I nodded. I could not speak for the lump in my throat.

She went on, in hardly more than a whisper, 'You know I loved Jonty, don't you? I've loved him since I was eight years old. There's never been anyone else. Not Hugo, not anyone. I've often thought if it weren't for that – if the gap in the hedge had been further down the road – I would never have seen you from my window. Would never have met you, probably, and none of us would have come to India...'

Charles Rowlatt was hovering nearby. I learnt later that she had already spoken to him about the legality of such a marriage. He had assured her that, in the circumstances, the church would forego the calling of the bans. She had also asked him to baptise the boy, immediately after the wedding ceremony. And so, against my better judgment, I married Phia, with Charles officiating and Elspet and one of the nurses as witnesses.

'Baby's name?'

'Jonathan George Josiah, for his father,' she said, firmly

334

and clearly, then turned to me. 'The Three Jays, Joss, the Three Jays. You don't mind being last, do you?'

'Father's name and occupation.'

'Josiah Tomas Broughton,' I said. 'Soldier.'

She died two hours later. I had her buried in the little plot next to Jonty. On her headstone I had carved: *Phia Broughton, 1841-1867, Beloved.*

Colonel FitzHugh had written to Hugo's family when he died, as befitted his rank and station. (I learnt, years later, that he had told them that he had died of wounds nobly won, leading his men into battle. Some joke). Now that his widow had demeaned herself, in the eyes of the regiment, by marrying a common soldier, and apparently bearing his child, it was left to me to advise whosoever I would about Phia's passing.

A letter was sent to Tudor Greening: 'Sir. It is my sad duty to write to advise you of the passing of your sister, Philadelphia, who died in childbirth on the fourteenth of November 1867. She is interred in the churchyard of St Lawrence, Oonao. Respectfully yours, Charles Rowlatt, Minister.

I swore to myself that, as soon as he could understand, I would tell young Jonathan all about his parents. He would grow up knowing exactly who he was. I would tell him everything, from alpha to omega.

From apples to Oonao.

Author's Notes

The London and Middlesex (Prudhoe's Own) Regiment of Foot is fictional, and therefore never participated in any of the actions described in this work. However, I am particularly grateful to Sergeant-Major Thomas Henry Vickers, whose record of events during his service in India between 1863 and 1869* forms the basis of the London and Middlesex's time in that country. My great-grandfather, Jesse Goldsmith, was a sergeant in the 55th. The bones of his life inspired this work, although it is not about him.

*55th Regiment in India; or, A Record of Events during six years' service in India; 1863 to 1869. Sgt-Maj T. H. Vickers H.M. 55th Regiment (Now 2nd Battalion, Border Regiment)

Works that were particularly helpful with reference to gunpowder mills are:

The Gunpowder Industry, by Glenys Crocker, Shire Publications, 1986

Pamphlet on the Manufacture of Gunpowder, as carried on at the Government Factory, Waltham Abbey, 1857, by Maj, F. Baddeley, R.A.

A Treatise on Gunpowder, by Fredk. Drayson, 1830.

(The two latter available in the Royal Gunpowder Mills Historical Reprint series, Waltham Abbey)

Bearshott Village and The Bury

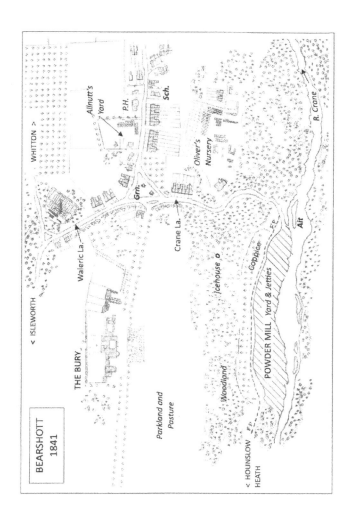

BEARSHOTT
1841

< ISLEWORTH

WHITTON >

Waleric La.

THE BURY

Parkland and
Pasture

Allnutt's
Yard

P.H.

Sch.

Grn.

Oliver's
Nursery

Crane La.

Icehouse o

Woodland

Coppice

POWDER MILL Yard & Jetties

Ait

R. Crane

< HOUNSLOW
HEATH

A big 'thank you' also to my editor, Ellie Wiseman, for her sterling work. Any remaining grammatical errors are mine.

Place Names

Victorian spellings of the names of places in India have been followed, as used in: Sergeant-Major Vickers' memoir and other records of the period. They are similar enough to modern spellings to be easily identified, with the exceptions of Bombay and Madras, now known as Mumbai and Chenai respectively.

Memsahibgunge is fictional, as is Bearshott.

Historical Figures

Brownlow, Francis CB (1836-1880) Lieutenant Colonel. Killed in action. Indian Army Officer. First Anglo-Afghan War, Ambela Campaign, Second Afghan War.

Bowles Chamberlain, Sir Neville GCB GCSI (1820-1902) Brigadier General, later Field Marshal. Indian Army officer, 1837-1881. First Anglo-Afghan War, Gwalior Campaign, Second Anglo-Sikh War, Ambela Campaign, Second Anglo-Afghan War, amongst other actions. Retired 1886.

Garvock, Sir John GCB (1817-1878) Major General, later General. Ambela Campaign.

Glossop, Henry, Reverend (1780-1869) Vicar of All Saints Isleworth 1821-1855.

Griffin, Robert Durie (1832-1908) Captain, later Colonel.

Gooch, James. Registrar, 1841 census returns. Ancestry.com

Map of Northern India

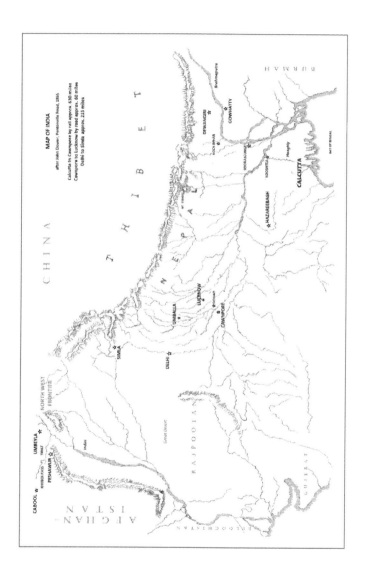

Hope, William, VC (1834-1909) Colonel. Crimean War (awarded Victoria Cross 1855).

Keyes, Charles Patton, GCB JP (1822-1896) Major, later General. Indian Army Officer. Ret'd 1891.

Probyn, Sir Dighton MacNaughten VC GCB GCSI GCVO ISO PC (1834-1924) Colonel, later General Indian Army Officer. Indian Mutiny (awarded Victoria Cross), Second Anglo-Chinese War. Ambela Campaign. 1872 appointed equerry to King Edward Vll, Privy Counsellor 1901

Rose, Sir Hugh Henry 1st Baron Strathairn GCB GCSI PC (1801-1885) Field Marshal. Retired 1870 Egyptian-Ottoman War, Crimean War, Indian Mutiny. Commander-in-Chief India 1860.

Tombs, Sir Henry VC KCB (1824 – 1874) Brigadier-General, later Major-General (1867).

Victoria Cross awards, Crag Piquet

For their heroic actions in the re-taking of Crag Piquet on 30th October, 1863, Lieutenant George Fosbery of the 4th Bengal Native Infantry and Lieutenant Henry Pitcher of the 1st Punjabi Native Infantry were each awarded the Victoria Cross.

Map of Northern India

After John Dower, Pentonville Road, 1865
Calcutta to Cawnpore by rail approx. 630 miles
Cawnpore to Lucknow by road approx. 60 miles
Delhi to Simla approx.. 215 miles

Printed in Great Britain
by Amazon

54292184R00196